AN EMPIRE ASUNDER

D1602948

ALSO BY EVAN CURRIE

Odyssey One Series

Into the Black

The Heart of Matter

Homeworld

Out of the Black

Warrior King

Odyssey One: Star Rogue Series

King of Thieves

Warrior's Wings Series

On Silver Wings

Valkyrie Rising

Valkyrie Burning

The Valhalla Call

By Other Means

De Opresso Liber

The Scourwind Legacy

Heirs of Empire

Other Works

SEAL Team 13
Steam Legion
Thermals

EVAN CURRIE

THE SCOURWIND LEGACY

AN EMPIRE ASUNDER

47NORTH

Published by 47North, Seattle

www.apub.com

Amazon, the Amazon logo, and 47North are trademarks of Amazon.com, Inc., or its affiliates.

ISBN-13: 9781503939837
ISBN-10: 1503939839

Cover design by Jason Blackburn

Illustrated by Chris McGrath

Printed in the United States of America

CHAPTER 1

Alliance Cruiser *Princess Allesia*

"Watch to port. They've sent a flanker squadron around."

The captain of the *Princess Allesia* nodded. "I see them, thank you. Helm, make your course two by nine eight five and bring our altitude to sixty thousand feet."

The *Princess* leaned into the turn a little as they hiked in the starboard sails and brought her around. In the distance, the flags of the loyalist squadron were visible, just in front of the heat haze that limited all visual scanning ranges.

The admiral, who'd given the warning, adjusted his weight so he wouldn't have to grab a railing to keep from falling over, but otherwise didn't move until the *Princess* came around to an even keel again. The atmosphere was thin and growing thinner as they climbed to the second wind layer, moving far above the tempests of the lower altitudes, but on a ship like the *Princess Allesia*, the men were used to breathing in low oxygen out on the deck.

Most lowlanders couldn't take the thinner air much above forty thousand feet without succumbing to altitude sickness. Death was a given for their sort by fifty thousand, but ship's crews were harder sorts, and the admiral had been serving on one vessel or another since childhood.

Even so, if they remained at their current elevation for much longer, even he would have to take breaths from the ship's air supply, and the cold was beginning to seep through his thermal uniform.

"Looks like three frigates, sir," Captain Blancanales said, "leading point for a cruiser or battle cruiser, I would assume."

"So long as it isn't a Bar class, captain," Admiral Rions said mildly, "then we should have no problem."

"So long as that, sir," Blancanales agreed, shivering slightly.

Rions didn't know if the reaction was from the cold or the thought of meeting an enemy Bar-class ship, but he didn't blame the man either way.

The first Bar class of battle ship had been a master work prototype built in secret, meshing together several devastating new technologies. Somehow, in the midst of the fighting over the capital, the craft had gone missing. Since then, while a lot of effort had gone into re-creating it, the Alliance production was plagued with issues that kept the lethal ships from arriving in the skies of battle in force.

That was bad, to be sure, but it was slightly offset by the fact that apparently *neither* side had control of the original vessel. Rions didn't know what had happened to the *Caleb Bar*, but the few ships that had managed to follow in her wake had proven to be pale imitations.

Unfortunately, the original was such a game changer that even a pale imitation was a deadly surprise to deal with.

The unique metal composites used in the prototype were beyond rare, so the *Caleb Bar*'s nearly invulnerable hull was not something Rions expected he, or anyone really, would have to combat even in the worst-case scenario with even the best enemy ships, but the quantum-lock drive found in Bar-class cruisers was terrifying all on its own.

Capable of ignoring the vagaries of the winds, ships with the system had relatively slow acceleration while under Quantum Drive but exhibited top speed and maneuverability well beyond the abilities of the *Princess Allesia*'s light sails.

Using a viewing lens, however, Rions had been able to determine that they were dealing with standard sky-sail frigates and nothing more.

"Run out the guns on the portside," Captain Blancanales ordered, "and stand by to fire as we bear."

His crew jumped to, as he expected them to, and soon the ship's portside blasters were cleared and ready to fire. Blancanales judged the range carefully, watching to be sure that the targets were in a diffraction zone before smiling with some satisfaction.

"They don't even see that we're ready for them," he said with a shake of his head. "Sloppy."

"The empire is hurting," Admiral Rions said quietly. "Even though they won back the seat of power, Her Majesty's forces are not what they once were."

"Of course they're not. They once were us." Blancanales grinned darkly.

"Precisely. I would suggest you not underestimate them just yet, however," Rions said, gesturing in a different direction.

The captain glanced over and grimaced as he saw a line of ships appearing out of the distant haze. "They set themselves up as bait?"

"Indeed, and now we're in a pincer, captain. Deal with the flankers as planned while I dispatch orders to the squadron."

"Yes, my lord admiral."

It was a gutsy move, Blancanales grudgingly admitted. The decoy ships were going to get mauled, no way around that, but now the captain's group was in peril of destruction themselves. That was the result of better planning—and braver men—than he'd given the Imperials credit for.

If they're willing to bleed themselves just to get us, this little war of the general's might just be a lot bloodier than he made it out to be to the governors.

That wasn't Blancanales's business, however much it was affecting his own at the moment, so he refocused his attentions on the present.

The *Allesia* completed her turn, bringing her portside guns to bear on the Imperial vessels. The sharp crack-whine of the blasters engaging and the distinct smell of burned lazite on the thin cold air announced the opening of the engagement. Smoke erupted from the Imperial unit almost in the same instant, signifying the on-target strikes, and the frigate broadsides went to steady autofire a moment later.

A glint in the distance was all that announced the return fire before lase pulses started scorching into his own ships, but Blancanales was unruffled. He'd expected *some* return fire, of course, as it was virtually impossible to take out an entire squadron without them getting in a few licks of their own, but a handful of frigates wasn't going to be taking down Blancanales's ships.

The *Allesia* shuddered slightly as a broadside took out one of her guns, setting off one of the lazite magazines, from the feel of things. Unguided and unfocused, the explosion was more a nuisance than a threat to the ship, but it was going to mean significant refit and repair once they returned to the state capital and the yards.

"One's going down!"

Sharp eyes, Blancanales thought, straining his own until he spotted the frigate dropping fast through the atmosphere.

The ship's sail anchor had apparently taken a hit, if he were to judge at a glance. The upcoming impact would probably be survivable, with the remaining sails easing the worst of the speed from the descent.

He winced reflexively as a bright flash signaled the end of another of the frigates.

That, on the other hand, won't have many survivors. Blancanales would be surprised if anyone had lived through the destruction of the reactor—which was the only thing that could flare that radiantly at such a distance.

"We'll be done with this squadron momentarily," he said, turning to the admiral and glancing over at the situation taking shape on their other flank.

"Good," Rions grunted, sending dispatch orders as he oversaw the local strategic position. "I've called for support from the Thirty-Eighth Bulls. You'll want to watch your sky space, son."

Blancanales snorted. "As you say, sir."

The Thirty-Eighth were a ground squadron, heavy support capacity, and Blancanales certainly didn't want to be sharing the sky with their munitions once they went live. The *Princess* began to shudder as hits from starboard peppered her armor; the Imperial squadron ships on that side were closing fast in the completion of their pincer.

"Hold course!" Rions cried. "Draw them in!"

"As you command, admiral," Blancanales said, turning to his crew. "Armor up the starboard flank! Close ports! We're holding course. Steady as she goes!"

The crew hurried to drop the armored hatches over the gun ports, the viewing areas exposed to the enemy forces, and any other vulnerable spots like the sail line anchor points. Blaster shots rained in from the distance. Their strikes sounded with distinctive hiss-pop noises as sections of armor were ablated away. Occasionally, there was a violent explosion when an imperfect patch of hull with an air pocket left in the ceramic substrate shattered as it superheated.

Rions and Blancanales winced as one at the number of pops heard compared with hisses, as that was a sign of a particularly shoddy construction process, but there was nothing to be done. Shipbuilding was a priority, and numbers were now more keenly valued than quality. The *Princess* would require a much heavier overhaul than either of them had calculated.

The Imperials were rapidly approaching their position, confident in the success of their maneuver, which, to be fair, *had* worked.

A perfect hit blew through the *Allesia*'s armor, sending smoke and fire through her decks. Emergency crews were already rolling, but Blancanales couldn't help but grimace as he realized that the blast had taken out one of their munitions storage lockers. The deck around it was reinforced, so the *Allesia* was in no danger, but he expected that no fewer than twenty men had been caught in the explosion. He would be surprised if any of them survived.

"Hold to the wind," the admiral ordered. "We're almost there."

It was a pointless command, for the most part. There was nothing to do but hold to the wind, as Rions had put it. Certainly, Blancanales supposed that they *could* break and run, but all that would accomplish would be to get more of them killed for no gain at all. No, they were committed now. Any windrider worth his oxygen knew that.

Of course, Rions's order did remind them of that fact, so perhaps it wasn't so inane after all. Blancanales could see several crew members within earshot stiffen their resolve, the fear they'd been feeling . . . not leaving, certainly, but becoming walled-off by a sense of duty.

The sizzle-pop sounds grew louder and more frequent. Every now and then, one shot would strike true and put a hole the armor of a ship with enough force or from a lucky-enough position to cause real damage.

Men died. Two vessels began to lose altitude as the furious exchange of fire continued apace. And then a distant rumble rolled over them all.

The chemical rockets that roared through their airspace were crude, but they packed a vicious punch as they tore into the Imperial line of battle. Unlike lase cannons, the explosives in the rockets delivered brutal force, capable of shearing massive rents in even the strongest conventional armor.

Three Imperial frigates went down immediately, with practically every other one billowing smoke and losing altitude at terrific and terrifying rates.

"Captain," Rions said stiffly from where he was standing behind Blancanales, "signal the Thirty-Eighth and deliver my compliments and thanks."

Blancanales nodded. "Yes, sir, admiral. I believe I'll add my own."

Rions smiled thinly. "Somehow, I am not surprised, captain. After that, do finish cleaning up the mess in my skies."

Blancanales nodded. The cleanup would still be dirty and costly, but the outcome was no longer in doubt.

"As you command, admiral."

Imperial Palace, Scourwind District

The Scourwind district of the Imperial capital was the center of the empire in more ways than most citizens ever knew. The palace looked like nothing else in the empire, with black metal walls angled off in seemingly random patterns. Dark, imposing, *impenetrable*.

Or so the stories claimed, and unlike many stories, these had held true for nearly the entire history of the empire—until just a very short time earlier.

The former general's coup had shaken that image of perfect invulnerability and tarnished the unstained halls of the palace, but the legend still had weight. Within the confines of the estate, the machine of the empire continued to turn as the very important people of the kingdom came and went on schedule, making deals, delivering requests, and all too often arriving with bad news.

Lydia Scourwind sat on the ebony throne, an oddly shaped mass made of the near-invulnerable metal that gave the palace its distinctive look, and closed her eyes when she saw the look on William Everett's face as he approached.

"How bad were our losses?" she asked softly, not needing to hear the gentle announcement he would no doubt have otherwise made.

"Ninth Fleet, Second Division," William told her, "total loss."

Lydia looked away for a brief moment before visibly wrenching her gaze back to her sometime friend and now full-time chief adviser. "The men?"

"Unknown," he said with a shake of his head. "Observers saw prisoners being taken, but they were too far away for a count."

"Some lived, at least," she said. "I will console myself with that."

A cold comfort, she knew, particularly since she would be sending more to the same fate in short order. Many times more, no doubt. That was what the empire—what the empress—did, after all: send men into the machine to be chewed up.

"Your Majesty, we cannot absorb losses like this."

Lydia's attention turned to the speaker, Baron Kennissy. The noble had become another of her advisers in the aftermath of retaking the palace during the countercoup.

"We are aware of that, baron," she said tiredly. "However, we have fewer options than we might wish."

"We need more Bar-class cruisers, Your Majesty," the baron insisted. "Production *must* be increased, and you should mirror the rebels' actions toward Delsol."

A hiss went up through those paying attention, which was admittedly most of the throne room by this point. Mira Delsol was a sore point among those gathered at the heart of the Imperial government.

Her actions during the former general's coup had directly been responsible for, if not victory, then the preservation of countless lives. The former Cadrewoman had also, however, spirited away the *Caleb Bar* during the confusion. Many in the room felt that the *Caleb* would have enabled the empire to end the revolt entirely in the days after the countercoup. Lydia and her military advisers didn't agree, but she had to admit that the ship would have been of great help.

"I will not put a bounty on Cadrewoman Delsol's head," she said firmly, still speaking of Delsol as though she were in active service. "This room owes her too much."

"She *betrayed* the empire, Your Majesty," Kennissy insisted passionately, pushing his agenda as best he could while those who agreed with him were present. "The woman is a traitor."

"Can you betray those who have betrayed you?" Lydia asked softly, her voice somehow carrying to every ear in the room. "Is it treason to break one's allegiance once faith has been broken with you?"

"Your Majesty didn't betray Delsol!" Kennissy objected, honestly horrified by even the suggestion.

"No," she admitted, "no, I did not. Her own squad of men, picked by my father, however, murdered a fellow knight and attempted to end her at the behest of Corian before the coup . . . and during it, a faction that warred under our flag tried to turn her over to Corian for the bounty on her head. Those were men under *our* flag, baron. Despite that, Delsol remained with us until the end of the countercoup. We will *not* put a bounty on her head."

The assembly of some of the most powerful men and women in the empire grumbled at that, but none were willing to stand against the young empress when she'd so clearly planted her feet and had no intention of budging. The issue was a minor one, frankly, since the *Caleb Bar* had not been seen since, aside from spurious and phantom sightings that were rapidly elevating the ship to the status of legend.

If the former Cadrewoman was that intent on avoiding both the empire and Corian's alliance, then there were better places to focus their efforts than arguing over what to do with her if she finally chose to appear.

"I suggest we move on to more productive topics," William said into the silence. "Your Majesty, production for the latest class of Bar-type ships has been slowed again. Alliance saboteurs destroyed several factories that were producing key components."

Lydia scowled, but nodded in understanding. "Were they totally demolished?"

"Yes, Your Majesty."

"Rebuild them closer to the capital," she declared, already holding up a single hand to forestall the inevitable arguments. "Yes, I am aware that the loss of those factories will mean devastation for the local economies. However, the fact remains . . . those factories are already gone, and the empire *needs* those components desperately. We cannot leave such priorities unprotected. Instead we'll see if we can relocate nonvital production to that area."

A few still seemed like they wanted to protest. The old duke who controlled that region appeared particularly rebellious, but the promise of something to replace the loss at least kept him from turning the meeting outright into a free-for-all.

"Objections?" William asked, looking about the room.

No one voiced any, which in itself was a minor miracle in Lydia's admittedly limited experience, and they moved on.

The meeting went as they always seemed to, with more noise happening than action, but at least a few things were determined and the gathering eventually reached its end.

Lydia sighed noiselessly as the numerous nobles and corporate representatives made their departures with varying degrees of dramatic flair. She most appreciated those who quietly arrived and quietly left, but one or two of the minor barons were amusing in their antics, not that she *dared* so much as smile.

The last thing I need now is for any of them to get wedding thoughts caught in their minds.

Lydia was rather disgustedly envious of her younger—albeit barely so—twin brother. Brennan didn't have to put up with this inanity, at least, even if his own duties had cut into his flying time considerably more than he would have preferred.

*

"Stop trying to dodge the blasts," Matani Fenn growled, shaking his head as his young student painfully picked himself up off the ground. "Even Cadre can't do the impossible."

"I've *seen* it done," Brennan Scourwind insisted as he stood shakily. "My brother and Mira—"

"Your brother and Delsol are . . . were . . . two exceptional knights," Matani cut him off, "but even they didn't do what you *thought* you saw."

Brennan had that mutinous look that Matani had come to enjoy seeing, generally because it meant he was about to get a chance to *slap* it off his Royal Highness's face. This time, however, the old Cadre trainer opted for explanation in the place of example.

Example would come later.

"A lase pistol puts out a bolt of plasma-enhanced photons," he lectured. "The lattice-linked bolt is a crude approximation of the same technology that we use for armor—"

"I know this." Brennan spat, and pink-tinged saliva hit the training room floor. "What's your point?"

"My point, my annoying little student"—Matani rolled his eyes—"is that while not true lasers, the bolts do in fact travel a very significant chunk of light speed. It is *impossible* for a human to move out of the way of one fired from any practicable tactical distance. *Impossible.* Our reaction time, even the very best of us, is a hair under a quarter of a second. In that time, a bolt from a blaster can move over thirty *thousand* miles, assuming, of course, the bolts didn't break apart after around thirty. No one and *nothing* human can dodge a blaster bolt or a gamma burster. So. *Stop. TRYING.*"

"Mira—" Brennan began again.

"If you're going to insist on comparing yourself not only to fully trained Cadremen and women but to *prodigious* ones like your brother

and Delsol, we are going to have a very long training period indeed."
Matani sighed deeply. "Delsol never dodged a blaster in her life, I assure
you, and neither did your brother. What you saw were two very well-
trained experts in body language size up a situation, determine where
the weapon was aimed, and *read* their opponents so accurately they as
good as pulled the trigger themselves. They didn't dodge the bolt, boy,
because they were out of its path before it left the weapon."

Brennan's face went slack, his objections silenced. He'd never considered their evasive maneuvers quite that way before. He'd just imagined that warriors relied on some physical trick.

"Why aren't I learning that, then?"

"Kid, crawl before you try to sprint." Matani laughed outright.
"Besides, I'm a physical trainer. You want to learn body language and
how to read tells, you do that on your own time."

The old Cadreman watched his young charge reading him just the
way he'd described and found he liked what he saw. Brennan's jaw set,
his eyes narrowing, and after a moment of tension, the boy relaxed
marginally. Matani could tell the signs of a man, young though he may
be, making a decision.

Now, he thought idly, *we'll see if you can stick to your guns when the
going gets tough.*

Honestly, Matani didn't know what Kayle Scourwind had been
smoking when he'd decided to hand his Bene over to his younger
brother. Likely he hadn't—been thinking, that was. He probably,
Matani supposed, just wanted to ensure that his Armati wasn't taken
by Corian, but the kind of mind-screw he'd put his younger sibling
through had been epic.

Kayle was the eldest brother, expected to assume the throne in due
time. He'd been trained for duty almost from the time he could walk. He
ate politics for breakfast, Cadre training for lunch, and snacked on one or
two impossible tasks before supper. His younger siblings, while certainly
not uneducated, had never had the stress put on them that Kayle had.

Perhaps they should have, Matani thought. After all, it seemed like the twins were to be the ones who would walk the path intended for Kayle. One a soldier, knight, and pilot for the empire, the other called to lead it.

Dark times. But then, sometimes in the deepest of darkness we do find the brightest of lights.

Matani had been doing this job for quite some time—more years than he cared to remember offhand—and in that time he'd seen them all come and go. Cadre was a meat grinder. For all that your average person thought the Imperial's finest to be immortal masters of war, few lived long enough to really call themselves Cadre.

Those that did, they weren't just soldiers.

Matani didn't train soldiers.

He trained legends.

And right at that moment, as he looked at the youngest remaining Scourwind, Matani could see a new legend unfolding.

Assuming the poor bastard lives long enough. Well, I suppose it's my job to make that happen. Best get to work.

"For the moment, focus on your physical training," he ordered the young royal. "This is *my* time, not yours. Do *not* waste it."

Brennan shook his head firmly. "I will not."

"Good. Again, then."

The young royal got to his feet without more protest than a mild groan as Matani prepped the light-impact blasters for the next round.

As Brennan prepared himself, he couldn't help but wonder about the woman who'd first started his training in the hold of a rather under-sized luxury yacht no small distance from the capital, and just what she was doing now. Mira Delsol had vanished from the empire's reckoning along with her own small ship and the *Caleb Bar* so many isles ago now that there were some who thought her dead.

It was a possibility, he was sure of that. Corian no doubt had assassins scouring the countryside for Mira. The general was a master of some forms of warfare, but even his allies knew him as an arrogant man. Mira had survived him twice and forced him to flee on their second meeting.

That fact more than anything else made Brennan believe she wasn't dead. Corian certainly couldn't have helped but crow about it if she were, but Brennan had a feeling that there would be a third meeting between the traitorous general of the alliance and the rogue Cadrewoman Delsol.

Troubles, portents, and events of significance happened in threes.

"Wake up, boy!" Matani snapped at him, shaking Brennan from his reverie and back to the real world and the training room. "We have an assignment for the Imperial Corps coming up, and I'd rather not have my student get himself killed in some humiliating fashion—for me, of course—the first time he's allowed out without a leash."

Brennan scowled at his mentor's choice of words but knew from painful experience that challenging the statement would only lead to worse things. Matani waited a little bit to see if his student would bite, but finally decided that the boy had been burned enough in the past to know better.

Pity. He smirked inwardly. Teaching the young royal painful lessons was one of the perks of his duties.

It can't all be fun and games, I suppose, Matani decided as he slipped into a martial stance and faced Brennan. "Time to dance."

Brennan masked a groan almost as quickly as it grew from his belly. This was *not* going to be pleasant.

Just mostly fun and games. Matani grinned.

Free Corsair *Excalibur*

The empire looked different from three hundred thousand miles above.

Mira Delsol had seen it from every possible altitude during her career, or so she'd thought. Travel past the atmosphere was an uncommon thing, but Cadre deployments sometimes required a level of stealth and speed you just didn't get inside the enveloping presence of air.

Even so, no Imperial ship had been this far above the atmosphere until *her* ship.

Her *Excalibur*.

The air wasn't thin at this altitude; it was basically nonexistent. The crew were all below, and only Mira prowled the open deck. Prowled, however, was not the right word. She drifted, like a ghost, her feet sometimes brushing the deck but never truly planting themselves there. She'd discovered that effect once the *Excalibur* had stopped accelerating away from the surface, a long time before.

Mira wasn't floating, as it seemed, but was rather undergoing an odd consequence of free fall. She, her crew, and her ship were all accelerating in the same direction at identical rates. An unusual effect similar to free fall, yet different, that she had never really understood before but now had experienced thanks to her *Excalibur*.

She moved to hang casually off the port deck, leaning way out with a foot hooked into the rail and a hand on the piton for the sail launcher, looking down on the empire. From where she was, it looked almost . . . small.

Almost.

Mira and her crew had done some surveying, something that no one had managed before simply due to the scale of things, and she knew that the empire was situated in a square . . . habitat? That might not be the right word, but Mira wasn't sure what else to call it. For now it fit, she supposed. The habitat was just under thirty *thousand* miles on a side, which was impressive in itself given that the empire didn't control quite ten percent of that, but what had really just *destroyed* her were the hundreds of thousands or more *other* habitats that existed all around them.

Beyond the Imperial habitat, the other . . . worlds? Habitats? Mira didn't like the word, honestly. She supposed they were both worlds and habitats. In either case, beyond the one she knew best, the surrounding territories were sometimes strikingly different from what she was used to.

The closest habitats to the Imperial sector were similar in many ways, but with subtle changes that she and her crew hadn't noticed until they were looking for them. Beyond those areas, however, lush greenery and expanses of deep blue water were far more common than anything the Imperial land could boast.

In the months they'd spent exploring, Mira had wondered many times what foul luck had led her ancestors to their homes. The histories were clear: they had come to the empire from somewhere else, fleeing some cataclysm, according to legend, but none of the stories explained just *how* that had happened.

Out of all the possible destinations she'd seen, Mira did wonder what it was that drew her predecessors to the dry, arid place they inhabited. There was so much more all around them.

All around everything, really.

The great sun that shone eternally down on the empire did so on countless other habitats just as large, making her realize just how insignificant her time in the Cadre had been, how little she'd really affected the state of matters in the universe. Mira supposed that no one could claim to have done much more. Even the greatest emperor of all time hadn't significantly exceeded her efforts, but that was only because there was no importance to anything any of them had ever done.

It was a humbling thought for one who'd once considered herself well on the way to being a legendary operative of the Imperial Cadre.

The final irony of it all was that it wasn't until she'd gone rogue, stung by betrayals and unwilling to put her trust in the family she had once offered her life to, that she had the scales fall from her eyes. The universe, as they had been able to expand on the imperial definition of it, was so much larger than the empire, and there were lands to explore beyond the imagining of anyone . . . anyone except her and her crew.

Yet I'm still drawn back here, Mira thought as she looked out over the dry face of the empire as it floated there below her.

"Skipper?"

"A moment, Gaston," Mira said over her comm as she adjusted her projected armor and pulled herself in. "I'm heading back in."

She drew herself along the deck back to the heavy door that led from the flying bridge to the interior of the *Excalibur*. She let herself in, sealing the door behind her, then opened the valves to equalize the air before opening the door to the rest of the ship.

Once inside, she killed her armor, making her way using the officers' access to the interior command center, her booted feet ringing on the deck with each step.

"Skipper's up!"

She didn't glance in the direction of the speaker as she made her way into the middle of the *Excalibur*'s command center.

"Gas?" She focused on the ship's second. "We have news?"

Gaston Rouche, former engineer extraordinaire for the empire and now second-in-command of the free ship *Excalibur*, looked up from whatever he was working on and nodded curtly.

"We've finally decoded those intercepts we picked up," he said, a sour look on his face. "It's not good."

"What is the illustrious general up to this time?" Mira said, sighing and taking a seat at the captain's position, a rather hilariously overdesigned throne centered on the inner command deck.

The ostentatious design of it was such that Mira couldn't take sitting in it seriously, and instead casually draped her legs over the arms and lounged under the carved symbol of the empire that rested on the high back. She really didn't know what the designers had been thinking when they'd built the *Excalibur*, though likely it was intended as a ceremonial ship in the direct command of Edvard Scourwind, then emperor.

Now the vessel was a free corsair, and considering all the betrayals done to her by those who claimed fealty to that flag, Mira couldn't help but tweak her nose at the throne every chance she got.

"It appears that Corian's alliance has begun sabotage and denial strikes against key Imperial positions," Gaston said, frowning. "Sadly, some of those include supplies that *we* had already arranged to have delivered to our own cutouts. Their loss puts us in a bit of a bind, I'm afraid, skipper."

"Send me the list," Mira said, reaching for a portable display.

The small coin-sized computer projected a tactile holograph as soon as she picked it up, and her scowl grew as she read down the list.

"I see what you mean," she said finally, slipping her legs off the arms of the throne and sitting straight for a moment. "I suppose we'll have no choice then. Corian's little alliance has stolen or destroyed property we already paid for . . ."

She looked around the command deck at all the faces staring expectantly back at her, and then slowly smiled.

"I suppose we'll just have to *take it back*," she said with a bit of a feral grin, "won't we? I'm sure Corian will be more than willing to be reasonable about all this."

The men and women around her grinned back. While none of them were exactly loyal to the empire at the moment, they weren't hostile toward it or its empress either. They'd all had time to get to know Lydia and her brother, and most considered the two kids to be good sorts. Corian, however, was a man none of them owed any allegiance to, and most had at least some small bone to pick with the man.

Plus the skipper clearly still held some small loyalty to the Scourwind family, even if she tried to deny it.

Delsol had saved every man and woman on the *Excalibur*, directly or indirectly, at one point in their lives, so if she wanted to pester the most feared man for ten thousand miles around . . . well, a fool needed company.

"Calculate a course to take us into the disputed regions between the empire and the alliance," Mira said after a moment's deliberation. "One way or another, it's time to go home."

CHAPTER 2

Airspace of Imperial Capital

The Fire Naga was skimming low, sails buried in the first wind layer just deep enough to get a respectable airspeed as the small snub-nosed fighter proceeded north from the capital. Brennan was in the hot seat, sitting above and behind his passenger as he manipulated the controls to keep them on an even keel.

"We could have requisitioned a newer ship, you realize?" Matani said from the gunner's seat, eyes lazily scanning the area around them for any signs of trouble.

He'd be shocked if he found anything this close to the capital, but it was an ingrained habit.

"This is my baby, Fenn," Brennan told him, dipping the left side so that they were suddenly hanging low and buildings were skimming by uncomfortably close. "You're not insulting her, are you?"

"You're a couple of decades early to be intimidating me, boy," Matani told him, masking a yawn. "Watch out for that transmission tower, by the way."

The Naga leveled out and winched itself up a few dozen feet to clear the spire with room to spare.

"Saw it miles back," Brennan replied and grinned. "Wondering if you were going to mention it."

"You're flying, royal," Matani reminded him. "Not my job."

Brennan was a little unenthused by his passenger, frankly. It had been a long time since he'd flown with anyone whom he couldn't at least *slightly* intimidate. His reputation as something of a thrill seeker alone normally did that job, in his experience, and if not, then a few risky maneuvers would certainly seal the deal.

Matani Fenn was a Cadreman and a long-experienced trainer of reckless youth, and thus he seemed entirely unimpressed with anything Brennan had brought to the table.

To be honest, it was starting to get on his nerves.

"If you're done showing off now," Matani said with some amusement from the front seat, "tell me what you got out of the mission brief."

Brennan took a moment to think back to the meeting in question before he answered.

"Regular forces are currently tied up holding the line against the alliance's aggression," he said as he flew, "so Cadre deployments are being used to investigate potential trouble spots in communities along the unofficial border between the empire and the Alliance of Free States."

"Correct, for all that, so why am I bringing along a barely blooded student?" Matani asked blandly.

"Other than you being a sadist?" Brennan was rather proud at managing to match his teacher's tone.

Matani actually laughed. "Other than that."

"This report seemed low profile," Brennan said. "So I assume you figure it'll be better training to put me in the field than to keep chasing me around the gym."

"More or less," Matani admitted. "I also get to see how you handle yourself in the field, which is probably more important."

"So pretty unlikely for there to be any real action then?" Brennan asked, uncertain whether he was disappointed or not.

He wasn't his brother, Kayle, who'd been the one to go looking for trouble all their lives. Brennan had normally been the one to go looking to get *in* trouble, which was a distinctly different thing and tended to drive his minders more than a little crazy. Still, he had no love for Corian or that bastard's alliance, and any shot he got to take at them was a good thing.

"Wouldn't count on it being too peaceful," Matani replied. "Trainee or not, the empire doesn't deploy Cadre on milk runs. It shouldn't be anything we can't handle, but that is a long way from being nothing at all."

Brennan nodded soberly. "Fair enough."

"How long to the lines?" Matani asked, checking the time.

"In this layer? Twelve hours," Brennan said. "If I take us up into the upper layer, I can cut that down to two, maybe three."

"We're not expected for twenty."

Brennan nodded, but something in the other man's tone made him consider the statement.

"Maybe showing up earlier than expected would be a good idea?" he suggested after a moment.

Matani smiled. "Now you're thinking like Cadre."

"All right then," Brennan said. "I'm going to hop wind layers. Hang on. This *will* be a little bumpy."

Matani didn't comment, but he did check that his straps were secure as the small fighter began climbing into the sky.

The Naga rode the jet stream that howled through the atmosphere above the surface, using sails made of photons linked in a subatomic lattice structure. Since the winds were strong and those sails were physically attached to the fighter via cables that ran from projectors, the Naga systems had to constantly adjust cable length to maintain a steady flight path.

Brennan brought the fighter up and right into the first and lowest wind layer and directly behind the massive sails of light. This increased speed but also made for a rough ride as the two men were buffeted around by the turbulence, but Brennan didn't plan on sticking around.

"Hopping layers . . . now," he said, killing power to the sail projectors and simultaneously ratcheting the cables back in as the Naga began to drop.

Their stomachs jumped as the duo entered free fall as the projectors were yanked back into their launchers, charges reloaded, and then fired back up again. The monofilament cable flew from the spools until the projectors were thousands of feet above and deep into the next wind layer, where they snapped to life.

The Naga jerked in the air, free fall a forgotten memory. The craft swept around in a tight arc as the sails caught the wind and Brennan started reeling the Naga up again. They were a little off course now, he noted, and Brennan was already figuring the tacks he would have to make before the next jump.

"We'll be holding steady for twenty minutes or so before I'm ready to hop again," he told Matani.

"Just warn me first," the Cadreman drawled as he lay his head back. "Nothing worse than waking up in free fall. Totally ruins your day."

Brennan didn't say anything, debating whether or not to prank his teacher by doing just that.

"*Your* day, boy," Matani emphasized without looking back, "not mine."

Or maybe I can wait on getting a little revenge, Brennan thought, *at least until this sadist can't order me to spar with him anymore.*

Perrin District, near the Alliance Line

"Why did we leave the Naga back in the hills?" Brennan asked as he and Matani walked toward the small township ahead of them. "They have a perfectly fine airfield here—not that I really need one, I suppose."

The local district was normally one of the quietest places in the empire, according to the files, so quiet that Brennan had never heard of it before, despite its being less than a day's travel from the capital. That had changed when the baron of the next district over from Perrin decided to side with Corian's alliance, turning the official border between the two into a combat zone in the passage of a single of the Great Islands.

Initially, the alliance had won ground quickly, taking over several smaller townships and laying siege to the single larger city in the district. But Imperial response had been swift after the countercoup, and the fighting had been stabilized just fifty miles or so from the border, though not in the alliance's favor.

Infiltration and sabotage operations were rife in the area, on both sides of the line, which was what brought Cadre interest into the area.

"No sense advertising our presence," Matani said simply, "and a skimmer out of sight and out of mind is a fallback point that the enemy can't cut us off from so easily."

Brennan thought that made sense.

"Now we're early, so we'll just wander a bit and get a feel for the place," Matani instructed. "Try not to attract attention, got me, royal?"

Brennan snorted. "I'm not the squat, scarred brute with a penchant for sadism."

"Squat, am I, boy?" The old Cadre operative eyed the young royal up and down. "Might want to remember that until I say so, you're still my trainee—and I can legally cut you down to size. See how you like being 'squat,' to say nothing of scarred."

Brennan regarded him for a brief moment, intentionally putting on as relaxed and indifferent an air as he could manage. "Chop me off at the knees and I'd still be taller than you, not to mention a lot better looking."

While that was not quite true, on the height aspect at least, Matani chuckled appreciatively and didn't seem to take any offense, so Brennan figured he'd hit the right combination of bland indifference and boasting bravado that would satisfy the Cadreman. While not Cadre trained himself, at least not until very recently, Brennan *had* grown up among them and was more comfortable with the Cadre than with most civilians, other than flyers.

"Any idea what we're looking for while wandering around?" he asked after they'd gone a little farther down the road they were following. A few scattered dwellings had already been passed, and they were about to enter a more densely populated area.

"I'll know it when I see it," Matani proclaimed. "And that's not me trying to dodge the question, either. Just too many things that could possibly be going wrong around these parts right now to give you a realistic list. If you see anything you think is odd, just let me know—not that I won't have seen it before you, of course."

"Of course. Whatever could I have been thinking?"

A glitter of sails in the sky to the north caused Brennan to hesitate for a moment before stepping a bit faster to keep pace with Matani. He frowned. "Frigate-class sails."

"Ours?" Matani asked, glancing at the far-off glimmer.

"No way to tell," Brennan admitted. "We can't see their colors from here, and they're angled parallel to the boundary line. Either way, it looks like a patrol. Ours, theirs . . . not looking for trouble, in any case."

"You can tell that from here?"

Brennan nodded. "They're running flat to the wind but dragging on their sails to run slow and low. If they were rigged for a fight, the ships would be tucked in closer to their sails."

"Ours then," Matani said.

"How do you know that?" Brennan asked, looking up at the ships again, wondering what could have possibly given that away from the distance they were at.

The Cadreman laughed. "I read the patrol schedule."

Brennan rolled his eyes. "Of course you did."

He didn't know why he expected anything different. Matani delighted in popping any sense of mystery surrounding the Cadre and himself, but only after first building it up.

"Common sense, boy," Matani told him, for possibly the thousandth time. "That will beat tricks and secrets every single time. Don't look for the impossible solution, look for the simplest one."

Brennan managed to—just—restrain himself from parroting along with the Cadreman, mostly because the last time he'd done that he'd wound up on his back, on the ground, with a big bruise forming on his forehead.

The really annoying part was that, by not mocking his most eminently mockable teacher, Brennan was well aware he was showing that he'd learned the lesson.

Common sense: keeping your smart mouth shut when you're in arm's reach of someone who could kick your ass in his sleep.

Brennan breathed deeply and shifted his focus back down to the township they were now walking through.

Keri-Perrin was a medium township for the area and relatively nondescript by Imperial standards. He was aware that it was a small manufacturing community, producing some vital piece of this or that needed for putting more ships in the sky. He didn't recognize the tech, so figured it had to be something for the new Bar-class vessels, or at least something for frigate class or larger, since his experience was mostly with personal skimmers.

As Matani liked to say, he didn't need to know what it was, just that it was important to the empire.

"Seems peaceful," Brennan commented after a few minutes.

"True enough, but there is peaceful and then there is peaceful. How many people live in Keri-Perrin?"

"Forty or fifty thousand? Something like that."

"Close enough. This feel like a township of that size to you?"

Brennan frowned, looking around. Now that it was brought up, he supposed it didn't. The streets were empty, and few people had passed them as they meandered down the roads. And while plenty of transit vehicles were moving . . . they were mostly empty too.

"No," he said after a moment, "no. It feels smaller, doesn't it?"

"It does at that," Matani said. "Read the body language of the people we do see."

Brennan focused on the closest person, trying to remember what he'd learned about body language after his last conversation with his trainer on the subject. He sized up everything he could before moving on to the next, and so on. Finally, he looked back to Matani, frustrated by the lack of information he'd been able to divine.

"They're nervous, even I can see that," he said, "but that's all I can say."

"That is patently obvious. Look to their eyes."

Brennan did, confused. Certainly he could see the vestiges of fear and nerves there, but they were close to the fighting line. He'd be surprised if they—

Wait . . .

One woman glanced toward the west and her fear seemed to grow stronger for an instant. Brennan shifted his attention to another and, after a few moments of observation, noted the same thing.

He looked west and got scared. Why?

Brennan's gaze shifted in that direction and Matani nodded in satisfaction.

"So you see it."

"The Alliance fighting line is north, so why are they afraid of the west?" Brennan wondered aloud.

"That's a good question." The Cadreman sounded completely relaxed. "Why don't we circle around that way and see if we can figure it out?"

"Yeah, sure," Brennan said, unenthused. "Why not?"

"Make sure your weapons are covered," Matani ordered. "No attracting attention."

Better and better. Brennan clipped his jacket closed after checking that the garment was over his blaster and Armati.

*

"Isn't that the sector baron's personal signet?" Brennan asked as the pair strolled past a guarded government building, neither of them appearing to so much as glance up at the banner waving gently in the wind.

"I believe it is."

"What is he doing out here?" Brennan scowled. While politics weren't his personal favorite pastime, one didn't grow up in the palace without being at least passing fair at the game of kings. "Weren't all the nobles summoned back to the palace for a meeting just a day or so before we left?"

"They were indeed."

"No way the baron beat us out here." Brennan shook his head. "There's just no way."

"I wouldn't say that," Matani said as he considered the options. "He might have requested a chemical reaction transport."

Brennan twisted his face up, mostly in irritation but also with a hint of envy.

Like most skimmer pilots, Brennan had mixed feelings about reaction craft. They were fast transport, capable of several times the speed of sound and unmatched acceleration but with extremely limited range and incredibly expensive fuel. Thus, only military pilots got a chance to command the craft, which burned that volatile fuel at incredibly wasteful rates and stank of the liquid hydrocarbons even long after passing by. But for all that, Brennan had often wished for a shot at getting his certification as a reaction pilot.

For the empire to have seconded one to a minor baron, however, seemed unusual.

"Was anything that important going on out here?" he asked, confused.

"No, not in the files," Matani said as they rounded a building's corner and slipped from the sight of the government building. "It's possible something came up after we left."

"No, even an emergency order takes time to clear," Brennan said, "and fueling a reaction craft isn't done lightly. Those chemicals are caustic. They have to be handled carefully, and just loading them into the ship means that extended maintenance will have to be scheduled. We'd still have beat them here if the order were given any time after we left."

"Well, then, it seems we have a genuine mystery here," Matani said cheerfully.

Brennan looked about for a moment, then gestured to a tower at the south end of the city. "We could tap the communications link, request information from the palace."

"If this is enemy action, that would tip them off to our presence," Matani reminded him.

"A passive tap then," Brennan pressed. "If this is official, there will be *something* in the news releases."

Matani rubbed his chin thoughtfully. "That is true. Very well. Your call; make it happen."

Brennan was surprised for a moment but recovered quickly. Linking into the empire's information network wasn't difficult, but he supposed they should get off the streets first just in case there were cause to be cautious. He looked around and nodded to an alley.

"Let's go over there."

Matani waved acceptance, following Brennan into the back road, where the young royal drew a computer link from his jacket and powered it up.

"I've got a luminal connection," he murmured, more to himself than anything. "Linked in."

The Imperial Information System was a network of light-broadcast towers that continuously fed data from one side of the empire to the other. With the correct access, a person could pull anything from daily news and weather reports to entertainment, or even classified intelligence, with the right codes.

Brennan's access wasn't actually the highest possible. That would be his sister's, but his link was nothing to scoff at either.

"I've got nothing on the baron being here," he said after a moment. "In fact, he is scheduled to be back at the sector capital tomorrow."

"That's only six hours from here," Matani offered. "He could make it."

"True," Brennan said, sounding doubtful. "But hit both places that fast in succession? That's unusual. Speaks of something important going down, and we should have been briefed in that case."

"Well, trainee, what's your call?"

Brennan considered for a long moment, knowing that he was being tested but not really sure what the test was. Probably nothing was going on, just a miscommunication or something similar, but that wouldn't excuse being sloppy.

"Caution," he said finally. "Let's observe more closely. Our meeting isn't for quite a while. We're in no rush."

"Very good." Matani swept his arms to the side. "Lead the way."

*

The old Cadreman was mildly surprised and impressed when his young trainee didn't lead them back to the local municipal building that had housed the baron's sigil. Instead they went south.

"The airfield, is it?" Matani asked idly, sounding uninterested.

"That's right."

Matani suppressed the urge to laugh outright, maintaining a bland expression. He *was* curious as to the boy's thinking, but his process wasn't that difficult to work out.

They topped a small hill that overlooked the field and came to a stop, eyes sweeping the area.

"No reaction craft," Brennan said. "No sign of one, either."

"Mmm," Matani grunted.

This *was* a good first step, he decided. Checking to see if a reaction craft was being serviced at the airfield would tell them if the baron had indeed made an emergency trip from the capital. While fast, reaction craft required a lot of fuel, and that generally stirred up activity wherever they went.

"If the baron is here, there's no way he attended the meeting at the palace," Brennan said, "so one of those two things is false."

"So it seems. What's your next move, trainee?"

There weren't many options, from what Brennan could see. "Now we check the government building and see which one is the lie."

"Lead the way."

CHAPTER 3

New Atlantia, Alliance Capital

General Arturo Corian bent over the table, examining the details projected across the surface with a fervor in his eyes that made those across from him shift nervously.

The man was a legend. No one in their right mind questioned that. Those who were closest to Corian, however, had begun to wonder about the man's . . . sanity, perhaps. The change was subtle in many ways. Corian had always been hard and unforgiving, so those who knew him only by reputation saw little in his demeanor to note any significant differences.

For some, though, the changes were more obvious.

The general had *always* been a driven man. One didn't rise to the heights he had without a near obsessive compulsion toward perfection, one reason why any Cadre operative was considered to be at least a little crazy on principle, but this was something more.

A few could be forgiven for thinking his new behavior was the result of his injuries. The loss of a leg and an eye would be enough to drive anyone over the edge, but he'd had that same look in his eye from the moment he returned from his last mission deep into the pocket kingdoms that existed beyond the empire's control.

The look that had been there since he started planning his coup against Edvard Scourwind.

The look that had no place in the eyes of a sane man . . .

"This is unacceptable," Corian growled finally, looking up from the projected reports. "The lines have stabilized, and the empire is pushing back along several fronts."

"Yes, general, while we have a slight lead in producing Bar-class warships," said Alastor Sigvun, one of the top military advisers to the alliance, "the empire still retains a powerful manufacturing base of its own. Edvard never entirely trusted private corporations to handle military production, as you know, and most of the Imperial facilities were located around the capital."

"Yes, yes, I am aware," Corian muttered, more than a little disgusted. "What's worse, they're actually running more efficiently than our own at the moment."

Alastor gritted his teeth. "A side effect of the war powers Empress Lydia now wields."

The general snarled. The fact that his enemy had actually managed to do away with one of the things he had personally detested about the empire—and largely because of him, no less—was a maddening thought, particularly as it made Lydia that much more dangerous.

He calmed himself, however, forcing his mind to approach the situation rationally.

"Even so, she is too young to properly wield such power," he said slowly, thinking it through. "She will make mistakes, so we must stand ready to capitalize on them."

He straightened up from the table, looking the projections over one last time before waving them off with a dismissive gesture.

"Continue as planned," he ordered, "for now."

"Yes, general." Alastor bowed his head, his mind awash in questions more than anything else.

For the moment, however, he knew the queries would have to wait. War with the empire was not something any of them could take lightly.

Why, though, do I have a dark feeling that this is about something else for the general? Power was never his vice, not power for its own sake at least. So why is Corian so damnably set on acquiring more now?

Alastor wished, more than anything else, that he had the answer to *that* particular question.

Outskirts of Kana Township, Alliance Sector

With her long red hair blowing in the wind, Mira Delsol made her way through the small township, eyes already on her target. She found herself fighting the urge to put a bit of a skip in her step. Significant time had passed since she'd put foot to solid ground for any length of time, and while maintaining a version of gravity while on the *Excalibur* was child's play, the sensation created wasn't really the same.

For the moment, however, discretion was key, and a tall, rather striking woman (if she did say so herself) skipping down the road would most certainly attract more attention than she wanted. The factory she'd come here for would likely have some significant security, and while she was confident that she could manage the guards, Mira would rather not deal with the ready response force out of the nearest base.

The alliance's manufacturing was diversified and decentralized, which was a smart thing by and large, but the system had its faults. Unlike the older Imperial breakdown, which largely grouped major industries with their most important subsidiaries, thus reducing the cost and time to transport materials to and from assembly points, the alliance leaned to the new school of private enterprise.

In peacetime, Mira was rather confident that the new school was superior. Competition and private management prevented, pardon the pun, empire building among administrators, but the system also introduced issues with collaboration as everyone protected their personal designs even to the detriment of the whole. This wasn't a huge problem in peacetime and, in fact, often encouraged some truly impressive out-of-the-box thinking.

The Imperial manufacturing and design were very much the opposite. A little slower to innovate, but without personal designs to protect, at least everyone was talking to each other. The specs her crew had intercepted for the Imperial Bar-class battleships were cruder than what the alliance had put forward, of that there was no doubt, but they were also far sturdier and could be repaired in-flight by far less specialized crews.

Frankly, cruder or not, she would have preferred to pick up the Imperial version of the components they needed. However, given that Gaston was in command of maintaining the *Excalibur*, she had every confidence in his ability to deal with any complications from the more sophisticated Alliance parts. More importantly, though, no one was *selling* these parts. She had to rely on every contact she still had in the Imperial bureaucracy to convince a few people to *lose* half a handful of the required pieces. With those now missing because of Alliance sabotage, there really wasn't much choice but to take what she needed.

Betrayed or otherwise, Mira was still loyal to the ideal of the empire and couldn't bring herself to target them for the parts they so desperately needed themselves.

The alliance, however, she had no such compunctions about.

Mira strolled casually past the gates of the factory, winking playfully at the visible guards as she intentionally let the breeze blow her long skirt around.

None of the avidly watching guards noticed that her teasing smile didn't reach her eyes as she located and catalogued the locations of the security personnel who *weren't* visible, then took a quick tally of all weaponry in sight.

Gamma bursters. Damn you, Corian, are you INSANE?

She'd expected the much more common lase blasters, the standard sidearm of the empire, but not for even the lowest of guards to be equipped with the much-deadlier gamma weapons. Coherent gamma energy could punch through even the Cadre armor she wore, to say nothing of the lesser armor most of her crew were equipped with.

Such zealous measures made some sense, she supposed, taking into account that most of the Cadre who'd deigned to reemerge from hiding after the coup had retained their allegiance to the empire. Still, bursters were ugly weapons that poisoned whatever they hit. Issuing them too openly and widely seemed like a bad idea to her, particularly to post guards who were likely all but untrained.

A few incidents with civilians will turn public opinion against you in a hurry, Corian. Gamma burns are an ugly way to die.

Public guards would normally be equipped with police gear rather than military issue simply for public relations reasons if nothing else. People carrying big, scary weapons didn't evoke a lot of trust, and trust was the only commodity that really mattered when dealing with civilians. So Imperial procedures called for the guards out front to carry light gear generally intended for dealing with one or two aggressive people at a time, along with a standard-issue lase pistol if they needed to step it up.

The heavy gear was kept back out of sight until needed.

For Corian to be putting gamma burst weapons right out in the front meant that he was serious about taking control of the local population. That worried her a lot more than even the coup he'd perpetrated. Everyone wanted to be emperor, but only someone who was truly lost to insanity wanted to *micromanage* the empire.

Mira put those worries aside as not being really of any direct concern to her. What the locals allowed their leadership to do to them was their problem, and she was sick of it all. The political games, the betrayals—they could all just take a flying leap off the God Walls for all she cared. And, knowing what was beyond the walls now, Mira honestly didn't even care which side they took that leap off of.

Once she was out of sight of the factory warehouse again, Mira found herself a nice quiet area and opened up a comm link back to the *Excalibur* using a secure-beam connection. Beam links were relatively short range within the atmosphere, becoming attenuated quickly as heat distortion broke them up, but within that distance they were entirely impossible to crack into, or even detect.

"Gas," she said softly. "I've scouted the site. Heavy arms evident out front, not sure what they have behind the curtains. Will proceed. Stand ready to move on my command."

"Of course, skipper," the engineer answered almost instantly. "Take care. We'd rather not lay waste to that entire place, but you know we will if they catch you."

Mira smiled. "Don't worry about me."

"I'm worried about those poor workers," Gaston told her dryly. "They've done nothing to deserve what will land on their heads if you screw this up."

She rolled her eyes, not that he could see it. Of *course* Gas would be more worried about the factory workers; he'd spent most of his life overseeing similar places. Well, that was OK by her. She had nothing against the workaday types who were putting the components together. They had no direct influence over their governing body in these circumstances.

And she didn't plan on getting caught.

Actually, no, that wasn't true. Plan A didn't involve getting caught, nor did plans B through E. She did have several contingency plans that began with the words "Oh shit," however, and getting caught played a role in several of those.

Really, though, she'd rather not initiate an OS plan if she had any other option.

Free Corsair _Excalibur_, Three Hundred Miles South of Kana Township

The _Excalibur_ was at rest a hundred and fifty feet off the ground, settled onto a quantum rail built into the substrate of reality. To the vast majority of people who might see her resting there, the great vessel appeared to be locked firmly in place in midair, never moving.

Gaston Rouche knew that impression was not only wrong, but laughable. Even as he looked over his instruments, waiting for news from Mira, the _Excalibur_ had moved hundreds, if not thousands, of miles. The universe was in motion, which meant that any stable quantum lock had to be calculated relative to the object you wanted to be at rest next to. Thankfully, that was fairly easy with the surface of the empire's habitat, which was surrounded by a massive magnetic field.

Of course, such details meant little to nothing to the majority of those on the _Excalibur_. To them, all that mattered was that the ship stayed in place, to hell with the hows and wherefores.

Gaston knew the skipper was about to open up a potential conflict with one of the two largest political bodies within their known universe. Even he wasn't immune to the single-minded fixation on what was going on three hundred miles north of their position, much to his frustration.

He continually had to recheck even the _basic_ calculations he was doing, eyes straying to the communications station as he tried to will the captain's order for their part of the mission to come through the system.

The comm link remained stubbornly silent, however, leaving him to continue his work on the inner systems of the _Excalibur_.

"Sir?"

Gaston looked up and to the side, surprised that someone had gotten so close to him without his noticing. He was clearly more distracted than even he'd realized.

"Yes, Dusk?" he asked.

Dusk was one of a pair of orphans they'd picked up along with the Scourwind twins many months earlier. He was surprised, really, that the pair had stuck with the *Excalibur*, as he was relatively certain that they'd been invited to the capital.

In either case, Dusk had proved a quick study on the *Excalibur*'s systems and had moved smoothly from junior gopher to one of his preferred assistants.

"The engine diagnostics report." She offered him a portable display. "It just came through."

"Ah, good." He accepted the device, glancing over the summary quickly.

One of the main reasons they were back in the Imperial habitat was because not every part in the *Excalibur* had been as thoroughly checked out as he might have preferred before that *butcher* Corian had taken it into battle. Since they'd . . . appropriated the ship, Gaston had realized that several key parts needed replacement if the *Excalibur*'s quantum-rail drive were to continue to operate.

So far the system was holding, so all he could do was hope that everything remained stable until they could secure the parts. If it didn't, well, unlike most ships, the *Excalibur* had alternative systems to rely on.

"Looking good for the moment," he said, handing back the display. "Thank you."

"It's no problem," Dusk answered softly.

The girl was shy, even with people she knew. Gaston knew bad things had happened to her and her brother, Mikael, during the coup, but the two didn't speak of that time. He didn't think they'd even told anyone their family's name, for that matter.

That wasn't terribly odd on the *Excalibur*, of course. Several of the crew went by single names alone, and those likely weren't their original names either. So long as they were loyal to the ship, no one cared.

He worried about Dusk, though, and about her brother as well.

Where Dusk had turned inward, or so he assumed, since the coup and her time in the refugee camp, her brother had grown angry. Mik was . . . less reliable, though he wasn't disliked among the lower decks. The boy could work, and he was clearly intelligent. Still, he couldn't be trusted with any but the simplest of tasks. Give him something utterly exhausting and straightforward and the job would be done. Anything that required thought . . . well, Mik just didn't get those jobs any longer.

Gaston was no mind healer, sadly, but he could tell one was needed—probably by every single person on the *Excalibur*, if he were honest. He knew that he had his own issues with what had happened before the coup, and the less said about the skipper's abandonment complex, the better. She hadn't taken the betrayals well, though he supposed few would.

Sadly, two orphans dealing with the loss of their parents and the shattering of their young worlds were hardly out of place on the *Excalibur*.

Kana Township

Mira vaulted the fifteen-foot wall with a running vertical jump, planting her foot as high as she could before kicking off and up, just high enough to grab the top ridge and *pull*. She flew up and over, dropping down to the other side, where she landed with a crouch and roll.

So far so good, she decided as she made her way toward the warehouse building, eyes sharp and looking for any guards who might be off their patrol schedule.

Scaling the warehouse wall to get access to the roof was simple enough, as almost all buildings in the empire captured water via exterior drains and pipes. Townships like this gathered all such water to central reservoirs, but all that mattered for Mira was the climbing purchase the pipes provided.

She'd timed her move with the passage of the Great Islands, and thus burst into motion while in deep shadow as she scaled up to the top of the warehouse and rolled over onto the rooftop. Mira was almost disappointed, really; she hadn't even needed her armor up to this point. With all the extra visible security, she had expected more on the inside.

They're trying to look stronger than they are, she realized, a little disappointed in Corian.

Visible security was a deterrent, but if someone was going to be turned away, one guard would do as well as a hundred. People who intended to get in, they didn't care. *Real* security was needed to counter determined opposition.

Mira slipped the lock on a light dome, a one-yard refractory lens that lit the interior, and popped it open to reveal the reflective conduit underneath. She glanced up at the passing Great Island, figuring out how long she had in shadow before she dropped into the conduit and pulled the dome shut behind her.

She would prefer to be inside the warehouse proper before the full light of the sun returned, as something like a body blocking the light would be noticed fairly quickly. With a couple of hours before illumination, she expected no trouble on that part.

*

It took Mira almost an hour to find an empty room lit by the conduit she'd selected, but that left plenty of time to carefully observe her chosen spot before she kicked open the interior lens and lowered herself down to the floor.

Mira had landed in some midlevel document monkey's office, from the looks of it. There was nothing to interest her other than the semisecure point to take stock of her situation, which was precisely what she was looking for.

Unsurprisingly, the halls beyond the room were empty. In the bureaucratic section of the building, the staff probably all held the same hours. In contrast, workers in the production areas would work multiple shifts to maintain a steady output; no one cared if documents were signed around the clock so long as they were signed when they were required.

She ran into her first guard as she made her way toward the production floor, hearing the soft rap of his boots on the stone in time to duck into a doorway alcove. Mira quietly checked the door behind her, but it was locked and she didn't have time to defeat a lock, so she tensed as the footsteps came closer, waiting for the last moment to act.

As the guard started to glance toward the recess, a slim arm shot out from the shadows, wrapping sinuously around his throat. Mira planted a foot behind his knee, driving the guard down to the floor while she followed along. Her arm crooked around his windpipe, the pressure focused up under his jaw to cut off the circulation of blood.

He struggled, of course, but with his vision already sparkling from lack of oxygen and a strong hand pressing his head forward while the arm blocked his carotid, consciousness fled swiftly, leaving Mira to once more be the only waking person in the quiet halls of the factory. She leaned the guard against the door behind her, then took a moment to strip the lock with a light projection from her tool kit.

The unconscious man hit the ground a little harder than she'd intended as the door popped open, leaving Mira to wince slightly at the crack his skull made on the ground.

"Sorry 'bout that," she whispered as she hefted his legs and pushed him over and into the room, clear of the door.

She paused, frowning to herself as she noted the gamma burster on his hip, and then casually pulled the weapon to slip into her own belt.

"Children shouldn't play with toys like this," Mira said, closing the door behind her and continuing down the hall. "I *really* need to speak with dear Corian about the correct handling of weaponry. He seems to have left his just floating around where anyone can get them."

＊

The production floor was as busy as she'd expected it to be, men and women working steadily on the line. She observed from above, crouched in a shaded catwalk that led off from the managers' section of the building and overlooked the floor, intent on identifying the components they were producing.

Unfortunately, unlike the Imperial sector, her intelligence on the alliance was somewhat weak. If she and her crew had better information, Mira likely wouldn't have bothered to sneak in. Hitting a transport carrying the necessary components would be more effective, but before that was feasible, she simply needed to know which transport to attack.

Looks like Gaston was right, Mira decided as she eyeballed the components being produced. *I should be getting sick of thinking that by now.*

The former top Imperial engineer was the person who would know, of course, which was why she'd trusted his advice in the first place. As one of the chief architects behind the Bar project, Gaston had unique insight as to which factories in the empire, or former empire, as the case was here, would be best suited to producing various parts.

The parts she was looked down on were the regulatory power convertors that maintained clean and unbroken energy through the quantum drive of her *Excalibur.*

What bothered her most, however, was the fact that they seemed to be building a *lot* of them.

What is going on here? Mira wondered, looking over the several *dozen* convertors in various stages of construction. *There's no way Corian can put that many ships into production this quickly, is there?*

She skirted around the production floor, quietly staying to the shadows and finally tapping her armor in order to use its unique photon capabilities to *absorb* light around her rather than openly project it. Sneaking wasn't normally her preferred method of operation, Mira had to admit, but a shoot-out seemed . . . counterproductive for the moment.

The wall on the other side of the floor had large doors that led deeper into the facility, and as her curiosity had been piqued, Mira made her way there and slunk through. No one was looking around the edges of the room, as they were far too involved in their work. She noticed light starting to stream back through the conduits overhead as she slipped away from the production floor and knew that the Great Island had nearly passed on.

Need to move fast. More people will start showing up soon for the next shift.

She wasn't worried about the guards, frankly, but rather all the nonessential civilians who'd likely soon be tripping over everything and everyone in the place.

Beyond the large doors at the back of the production floor was, predictably, the warehouse itself. Mira made her way into the aisles, moving as quickly as she could while remaining silent, and skimmed the reference numbers on each of the crates she observed.

Are these . . . all power convertors? Mira was honestly confused.

There was no possible way that the alliance could rig together as many ships as she was seeing parts for. She'd have been truly shocked if they could piece together even a fraction of such numbers, in fact, since warship production was notoriously difficult even at the best of times. But while at war with a political body like the empire, even in its currently humbled form . . . ?

Not possible.

Which meant that she was now more curious than ever.

She pulled a tracker from her pack and slipped it into a crate, then did the same thing for half a dozen other crates randomly scattered through the warehouse.

Let's see where these are going—

Of course, if they happened to pick a crate up for themselves in transit . . . well, bonus, right?

Free Corsair *Excalibur*

Gaston slumped in relief when the skipper's signal came back, calling for a pickup.

Not a bounce either; just a nice normal pickup.

The engineer felt waves of gratitude when things didn't go to hell but instead went according to plan. He stood up from his station and checked around, making sure everyone was looking his way. No worries there. They all wanted to know what the skipper had said.

"Stand ready for lift," he ordered. "The skipper is calling for a pickup thirty miles west of the target."

Smiles and soft cheers were the response. Everyone knew that meant things had gone well, and they all got to work. In a matter of moments, the *Excalibur* was humming with power and activity. The black ship absorbed all light that shone on its hull, but under power, her running lights made her less of a ghost or shadow and more a dark knight cut from the deepest nightmares of any Imperial.

Darkness.

In a land without it, the shadows are legendary.

The *Excalibur* lifted from its resting point just three minutes later, turning northwest and launching sail projectors into the upper atmosphere. Quantum drives were excellent for many things, but they really couldn't accelerate worth a damn after all.

"Sails under tension, Gas," the sailing officer, Connor Castner, informed him.

"Disengaging quantum drive," he replied as the ship broke free and began to pull into the wind and pick up speed rapidly. He accessed the ship's signals system. "*Excalibur* under sail. Secure all ports; stand down external watch. We're now instituting pressure protocols."

After that, he nodded to Castner. "Take us up."

"Yes, sir."

The dark shade of the *Excalibur* rose swiftly on its winches, climbing to the sails it had placed high in the sky above, and quickly vanished from sight.

CHAPTER 4

Perrin District

"That's the baron," Brennan said, his tone confused.

Matani glanced over at him, curious. "Are you sure?"

The younger of the two royal siblings nodded as he looked through the viewer down into the municipal building from the rooftop the pair now occupied several blocks away. The structure was one of the taller buildings in the township, thus offering a decent line of sight, but was far enough away to avoid any security cordons.

"Yeah, he's a common visitor to the palace," Brennan confirmed. "Not all that important. This is a minor sector, but it's neighboring the Imperial sector itself, so visiting is trivial. I've seen him dozens of times just since the coup, and you know how much *free time* I enjoy."

The elder Cadreman snorted at the stress the boy had placed on his words but didn't otherwise comment as he kept his attention on the facts at hand.

"I suppose he must have skipped the meeting at the palace," Matani offered, unconcerned. He was growing bored with the training exercise now that the young whelp had done fairly well. Whether some minor politico was showing up to his meetings wasn't his concern. "Our meeting is coming up shortly. Let's get going."

"Hold up," Brennan said, his voice surprisingly firm. "I saw the meeting sheet for this one, and it was a priority gathering. No one skips out on an empress's priority summons without a damn good reason, Matani."

The Cadreman still wasn't impressed.

"Not our concern, boy. Report him to your sister later if you like. We have business."

Brennan scowled but lowered the viewer reluctantly. "Yeah. All right."

The pair policed the site quickly, leaving no trace, and then withdrew from the rooftop back down to the streets below. Their own meeting in the area was with the local factory foreman, a former Imperial Navy man who had sent word about some oddity or another going on in the region.

As a navy man, their contact was waiting for them, of course, despite their being early.

"Swift," Matani greeted him as they approached.

"I suppose you're my contacts," former windman, first class, Josh Swift stated, looking them over. "Let me guess, Operations?"

"Something like that," Matani said.

"Cadre then." The older man chuckled, his tone rasping. "Kid looks familiar, though."

"Don't worry about it," Matani told him. "We're just here for your report."

Swift looked around, checking the area for a moment. Matani let him, recognizing that he was actually ordering his thoughts more than looking for anyone listening in.

Finally, Swift turned his focus back to the Cadreman. "Look, I'm not sure what it is, to be plain about it. It's just that some components have gone missing in the last few weeks . . ."

"Raids," Brennan put in. "They've been reported."

"Never saw no raid, don't know nothing about that," Swift said dismissively. "Likely must have happened in transport, I suppose. No, I'm talking about stuff going missing right out of the warehouse. I told the supervisory folks in management, but nothing happened about it, so when more things went missing I contacted an old friend who's still 'in.'"

Matani nodded, thinking about the story. The brief hadn't included anything about warehouse losses, though, of course, it probably wouldn't. That would be more to the interest of local police, perhaps Imperial Intelligence Services, but not Cadre. He could see why the navy would be interested, however, since any missing components at this point could be a critical issue.

"How much went missing?" Brennan spoke up into the silence, his tone curious.

"Hard to make an exact count. Some parts were likely shipped out," Swift admitted, "and if any of the shipments were hit in a raid, that's just going to make this whole situation a bigger mess to uncurl."

That was also true, Matani figured. Thankfully, it wouldn't be *his* job to do the uncurling.

"Still, we've lost at least a dozen crates of our best quantum-alignment systems."

Matani frowned. "What do those—"

Brennan swearing under his breath cut Matani off, and he found himself looking over at the younger man.

"Are you aware of something I'm not?" Matani asked dryly.

"Those are the core components for building the quantum drives on the new Bar-class warships," Brennan explained to Matani before turning back to Swift. "How many are in a crate?"

"Ten."

"Over a hundred alignment systems just went *missing*?"

"I'm assuming this is more serious than I'd assumed?" Matani cut in, eyes sharp despite his tone.

Whatever was going on, if a former navy man *and* someone with direct access to the empress were concerned about these missing components, he was willing to assume it was important enough for Cadre.

"Without enough of those parts, we can't produce Bar-class warships," Brennan explained. "If someone is redirecting those components somewhere, that's treason."

Matani nodded. "That's all I needed to hear, then. Treason is within our responsibilities."

He turned back to Swift. "Where is your factory?"

"On the eastern outskirts of the township. You can't miss it. It's an Imperial Redoubt design, reduced, of course."

"We'll check it out," Matani said. "Go to work, go home, whatever you should be doing. Don't worry about this anymore."

Swift nodded curtly, then turned and walked away.

Matani and Brennan left in the opposite direction.

"This puts a new spin on the baron skipping out on your sister's summons," Matani admitted as they headed south, intending to circle to the east.

"You think he might be covering up the losses?" Brennan asked.

"Or blaming them on raiders that don't exist."

Brennan whistled softly, considering that for a moment. "You think he's really with Corian, then?"

"It's possible," Matani conceded, "but he also might be an opportunist, selling out for money or power. Of course, he could be here trying to figure out the same thing we are. We won't know until we get more information."

Brennan nodded, focusing on keeping his heart rate down as it threatened to begin thudding audibly in his ears. Staying relaxed wasn't as easy as it sounded, and he could already feel the adrenaline starting to drip into his system, making him fidgety.

"Calm down," Matani chided him. "We're still a long way from fight or flight, my young friend."

"I know, it's just . . . the idea of someone selling those parts to Corian," Brennan confessed. "It makes me angry."

"Anger is to be leashed, not unleashed. Now," Matani told him, "tell me about these components."

"The quantum-alignment systems are smaller versions of what we used to lay the heavy transport lines in the upper atmosphere," Brennan answered. "They're what allows a ship like the *Caleb Bar* to lock its own quantum position relative to the ground."

"So we lost at least a dozen crates of components that can be used to build more of those monsters?"

"Yeah, that's about the height of the story," Brennan replied.

"Just fantastic." Matani swore.

"Luckily, it's not as bad as all that." Brennan took a deep breath, forcing himself to relax further. "The *Bar* is more than just its drive, though that is a big part of it. The armor was a major part of the formula. Without it, the ship would be vulnerable to counterattack before it could secure the area it flies over. Still, the situation here is bad enough."

They circled around, heading east toward the factory.

Whatever was going on, there was no question it warranted their attention.

Imperial Palace

Lydia Scourwind strode into the primary communication and control center, eyes moving to the projection that occupied the center of the room. The status map was a continually updated overview of the empire and the known regions around it, as far out as a few thousand miles into the Southern Kingdom's territory. For the moment, however, she was far more concerned with what was happening inside the Imperial borders.

"What are the Alliance movements, then?" she asked.

Major Sten looked down at the map, gesturing to several points.

"We're tracking task groups along the border at those points: mostly frigates, no Bar-class ships in sight. That is concerning, as we're sure they have at least ten skyworthy, but we've not seen any hint of them."

"We too are holding ours back," Lydia said, "waiting for the best time to field them. Is it not likely that Corian is following a similar strategy?"

"Possible. However, the reports of border raids make it something we want to keep an eye on, particularly those that lost key war materials."

"Yes. I am given to understand that my brother is on assignment?"

"Yes, Your Majesty." The major pointed to another place on the map. "He and his Cadre trainer were dispatched to investigate reports of losses of materials outside of raids. They haven't checked in yet, but that's not unusual for a Cadre operation."

Lydia nodded.

No one needed to tell her how Cadre performed. Her family had been entwined with Cadre operations for nearly their entire history since the Exodus.

That didn't make it any easier to have a family member, her *last* family member, out there somewhere unknown to her. There were times Lydia genuinely wished that she and Brennan had never come back to the capital and had simply run forever. Perhaps they could have just flown away with Mira and left the empire to Corian, as treasonous as that sounded even in her own mind. Leave Corian to deal with the puffed-up personalities of the capital, egotists with whom the general would fit right in.

A sad smile played at her lips as she considered it. She suspected that Corian would have a less-refined approach to dealing with the fools, if nothing else.

The black throne of the empire was at once the source of the greatest power known and the most insidious shackle. She'd never liked what the throne did to her father, making him hard even beyond his years, though Lydia was honest enough to admit that she hadn't really thought much about any of it before the throne was thrust upon her. Kayle should have been the one in her place, once their father had stepped aside . . . or died on the throne.

She had always been the spare, educated and trained but never with the thought that she would be really be pressed into service.

And it *was* service.

Lydia knew that many believed the throne to be a source of power and freedom, the ability to do whatever one wanted, order whatever one willed. She supposed she could do the second, but just because she ordered it didn't mean reality would bend to her will, and the simple things she wanted were now, and always, beyond her grasp. In another life, Lydia supposed that she would have been an academic, perhaps discovering some minor thing to bring note to her name. Her brother would have been a pilot, of course, and one of the best civilian pilots in the empire.

Instead . . . well, Lydia supposed it was best not to spend too much thought on what could have been.

Mira was the smart one, Lydia decided. She'd known the price that staying demanded, the sacrifice the throne would require. There was a cost to all things in the universe, and power was no exception to that rule. The price may not be in currency that most people recognized, but that made it no less dear to pay.

Perrin District

The factory was most certainly based on the Imperial Redoubts, though smaller and more true to the human form than the originals. Brennan was one of very few people in the kingdom who understood just how much the empire had discovered when they arrived from the old world after the Exodus. You couldn't live in the palace and not have it slap you in the face, after all.

The palace wasn't built for people, not people like those who now inhabited the empire at least. The doors and halls were too wide, the ceilings too low. Something unnatural appeared everywhere you turned, though not so much that the casual observer would take note. It took time and, ironically enough, familiarity to really feel how strange the palace was.

The factory ahead of them had none of that.

To someone like Brennan, acquainted as he was with the palace, the proportions of this structure were as obvious as the sun over his head. The ratios were all too . . . normal, too fit for humans.

"They're preparing a shipment," Matani noted as they walked casually by the factory, eyes flicking to the large cargo containers lined up outside the building's big doors.

Brennan nodded, having noted the containers himself. They were of the type that would fit to one of the sky trains, the original implementation of the quantum lock. A quantum tractor would pick them up, a train of dozens or more cars, and slowly accelerate the whole lot into the upper atmosphere. Tractors were sluggish but steady and immensely powerful. They could haul uncountable tons of material across the empire—more slowly over short distances than hyper trains but with the capability of carrying far more and reaching unbelievable speeds over longer ranges.

He counted fifteen containers loaded, four more at the docks.

"That's a lot of product," Brennan said. "Do we know what else they make here? That can't all be alignment systems."

Matani shook his head. "Unknown. We'll check on that too. This factory is one of the key war material producers in the empire, however, so it's all likely top-priority components."

"Our play, then?" Brennan asked.

"Right in the front door," Matani said, producing an inspector's ID for Imperial Intelligence. "You're my secretary."

"Cute."

*

Management was, unsurprisingly, not happy to host an Imperial investigator but tried very hard not to show it. Brennan and Matani were led quickly into the head foreman's office. The man behind the desk squirmed as Matani stared at him.

Not that I blame him for that, Brennan thought, amused. The old Cadreman had one damn good stare.

"What is this all about?" the foreman asked.

"We're just following up on the materials lost in the raid," Matani said. "We'd like a certified copy of the manifest, please."

Brennan blinked. Something *changed* as Matani said that. The foreman seemed relieved. That wasn't what he imagined the normal reaction to an inspector asking to see your paperwork would be. Of course, he didn't know much about factories or inspectors, really.

"Of course, inspector," the foreman said, pulling a printed sheet from the top of a pile on his desk and handing it right over. "This is everything from that shipment."

Matani accepted the sheet with a raised eyebrow. "That was quick."

"We . . . uh, had it ready. We were expecting you."

Even Brennan could read that as a lie, but he couldn't figure out what the man had to gain by having that information right at hand.

Matani didn't seem to notice, deep into examining the information on the sheet.

"That's a lot of material to lose," Matani said finally.

"Yes, a terrible blow to the empire."

"Terrible," Matani said, parroting the foreman, his tone dry. "Yes. We'll need to look over your facility, of course."

"Of . . . of course. Whatever you need."

And there's the tension flooding back, Brennan noted as the foreman rushed to his feet, sweat beading on his forehead. *This guy is terrified.*

"We'll start with the production floor," Matani went on, seemingly oblivious to the foreman's reaction.

"R-right this way."

Brennan still had no idea what was going on here, but at least he wasn't *bored* anymore.

*

"This is the floor . . ."

Matani and Brennan let the foreman drone on as they followed along behind, pretending to listen.

"What are we looking for?" Brennan whispered, his words barely audible to his *own* ear as he leaned just slightly closer to Matani.

"Whatever they don't want us to see," Matani responded in kind. "Read the man; read the situation."

Right. Of course. See what they don't want me to see. Why didn't I think of that?

Of course, that made it easier to ignore what the foreman was spouting on about. Whatever he was going to say wasn't anything they were in need of hearing, nor did Brennan have to pay much attention to the floor itself. The foreman was calming down now, clearly familiar with what he was doing and getting more into the speech with every word.

Brennan didn't know anything about factories, however, so he was having a difficult time figuring out what he was supposed to be looking for. The items here all looked the same to him—just a lot of stuff he didn't recognize, dull as sand and none looking out of place.

Most of the people were just working, going about their business, not paying any attention to either the foreman or the strangers walking around the floor. Brennan ignored them. He spotted someone shooting glances in their direction but recognized Swift and moved his attention on from the Imperial contact, not wanting to draw any attention to the man. He might be needed later, and it would be a poor reward to bring any sort of trouble down on him.

No one else caught Brennan's eye as the Cadremen walked between the workstations, having various features and components pointed out to them in turn. At the far end of the floor, large warehouse doors opened up to a massive space beyond, catching his attention as several people dressed differently from the workers appeared briefly in the space.

"What's through there?" Brennan cut in, nodding in that direction.

The foreman half turned. "Warehouse facility. Temporary storage until Imperial transport picks up our products."

"And who were they?" Matani asked as a follow-up.

"Who?"

"The men in casual dress," the Cadreman said, gesturing around. "Everyone else here seems to be in clean suits."

Brennan blinked, surprised as he took that in and realized it was true. He'd noticed, of course, that the people in the group were dressed differently but hadn't realized just how differently.

"Oh, ah . . . probably just some of the warehouse people," the foreman, said stammering a little. "They have a little more, umm, leeway in their dress."

"Ah, of course." Matani smiled. "Well, let's have a look at the warehouse next, then?"

The foreman's shifty gaze and sudden onset of nerves would have been visible to the blind and deaf, but he did try to cover up his dismay, much to his limited credit.

"I-I think they're moving heavy loads at the moment, not safe for visitors, you see . . ."

"We will have to insist," Matani said flatly, his tone no longer genial and easygoing. "Lead on. Please."

Briefly, Brennan wondered if the foreman was going to have a stroke right there in front of them.

That color red CAN'T be healthy, he mused as most of his attention stayed on the large doors and the open area beyond them.

"I . . . it's just, we shouldn't . . ." The foreman tried to object, but Brennan and Matani were already moving him in that direction even as he stammered out excuses.

Subtlety was more or less out the window. Propelling a man along the floor while he visibly objected to the direction of movement caught more than a few glances, so Brennan shifted his focus a little to see if anyone was going to make anything of it. He was surprised to find that most observers had visible looks of relief or even vindictive amusement at the foreman's situation.

Well-liked this guy is not.

Once inside the warehouse, Matani glanced around. "Where did that group go?"

Brennan nodded to the right. "Down that way."

"All right, let's find out who they are," he said, still pushing the foreman along, though the man had finally fallen silent.

As the two Cadre operatives and the foreman moved down the long stretch, Brennan glanced at the stacked materials that were mostly unrecognizable to him. There were several skimmer pieces he knew well enough from having done work on his own flyers over the years. There was nothing that would fit his Naga, sadly, but thankfully, most of the parts needed for that had long since been in the public domain.

They came to a stop as they found the people in casual dress in the process of unpacking a standard crate and shifting the parts over to a distinctly nonstandard one.

Everyone suddenly stopped, the group of eight men looking up in surprise and then anger at the foreman, who was now looking downright frightened.

"Who in the burning skies are you?" one of them demanded, stepping forward.

Matani cocked his head to one side, as if considering the question, but didn't get the chance to answer as the foreman found his voice.

"They're with the IIS!" he yelled, moving quickly to one side.

All the men went for weapons, pulling lase blasters from under their jackets and bringing them to bear on Brennan and Matani.

"Well, isn't this a fine situation we have here?" Matani said as he looked down the wrong end of eight blasters.

"I really need a new training officer," Brennan added, annoyed with the elder Cadre operative's flippant attitude.

The leader of the group sneered at them. "You two picked the wrong time to inspect this factory."

CHAPTER 5

Free Corsair *Excalibur*

"Trim the sails and let out some slack," Mira ordered from the standing con, where she was leaning slightly left to see past the rails ahead of her. She and her crew were cruising just over thirty thousand feet, running their sails bright and obvious and making no attempt to hide. So far, they'd come within visual line of sight with a half dozen or so Alliance frigates, but none of them had bothered giving the *Excalibur* a second look after a glance at her sails.

They had to keep from getting too close, however, because while at a decent range there was nothing untoward about the ship's profile, that illusion would die a hard death in short order once that range closed. If that happened, then no amount of visual trickery with their sails or signal spoofing by Gaston would hide their identity as a warship armed to the teeth.

That restriction made following the trackers she'd planted a little tricky, but thankfully, the crates she'd marked weren't going to the busiest parts of Alliance territory.

If they had been, she would have likely just raided a shipment and been done with it, but with this scenario, Mira was allowed to feed her curiosity and learn just what Corian had planned for those convertors.

"Skipper," Gaston greeted her as he stepped out of the main port that led down to the command center.

Mira turned in his direction, her red locks flowing in the wind as the cold air whipped past them. "What is it, Gas?"

"I think I know where they're taking the parts," he told her. "They haven't shifted their course in a while, and there's one of the ancients' Redoubts about eight hundred miles out that way."

Mira frowned. "I didn't know of one out this way."

"It's not used much," he admitted. "It doesn't have the same size as the palace or the desert Redoubt, but it's there: too far from anywhere important to be attractive to your average noble but not nearly far enough to be of interest for special projects."

"If these parts are going there, Corian may disagree with you," Mira said.

The crates they were following had been loaded onto a few transport skimmers, which meant that wherever they were going, it wasn't on any of the major transport hubs or they'd have used a hyper train at least, if not a quantum tractor. An out-of-the-way Redoubt made sense, she supposed, though from what Gas was telling her, this one wasn't quite as out of the way as might be ideal.

"Well," she said, "if we know where they're going, then I suppose we don't need *all* of them to arrive on schedule, do we?"

"No, no, we don't, ma'am." Gaston smiled.

"Rig us for action, Gas," Mira ordered.

"Yes, ma'am." The formerly stuffy engineer grinned as he lifted the ship's comm to his mouth. "All hands, all hands, rig for action. Skipper wants to go shopping."

She shot him a darkly amused glance for that last bit but said nothing as an alarm sounded deep in the *Excalibur* and the crew started rushing around to secure the ship to a fighting trim. The sails faded to the color of the sky, with just a hint of white haze to make them seem farther away than they really were if anyone did spot them, as the winches brought them back up tight in behind the big projected wind catchers.

The *Excalibur* jerked a little as she sped up, now starting to close the distance. Mira expected it would only take a few minutes, at their new rate of closure, to come into sight of their target.

Weapons checks were run, again, just to be sure, and Mira knew that down below the boarding crew were pulling weapons from the armory.

"I don't suppose we're going to take them out of the sky before you head over?" Gaston asked, a resigned smile on his face.

"When have I ever done things the easy way, Gas?" Mira laughed lightly.

He didn't laugh, but his smile grew a little less rueful and a little more genuine at her words.

"I wonder what life would be like without an action junkie for a captain?"

"Wouldn't want your life to be boring, now would we?"

"I could live with boring."

Mira chuckled. "You *have* lived with boring, Gas. Now look where you are."

Gaston sighed but had to give her that point at least. Even so, he wished she wouldn't keep taking the riskiest option available.

Mira took pity on him. "Relax, Gas. It's not that bad. I just don't want to risk destroying the gear we're after. Besides, this will be our way of officially announcing the *Excalibur* under its new name and management, so let's make our coming out spectacular."

Alliance Transport *Helena Night*

"Captain, spotters' report." Sam Maxwell handed off a display to the captain. "Just signaled from the rear deck."

Trase Mirren frowned, accepting it. There shouldn't be anything to report, but that was the nature of things sometimes. She glanced at the screen, then her eyes widened, and she quickly read it again before sharply snapping her hand out.

"Someone get me a viewer," she ordered as she left her station.

A viewer was slapped into her hand as she was on her way up the tight stairwell that led above deck. Outside, Trase stepped into the cold air at twenty thousand feet, ignoring the sudden chill as she put the viewer to her eyes and scanned the skies.

There it was. As the report said, the slight shimmer of a sail was following along behind the *Helena Night* and apparently gaining on them. It looked like it was just coming out of the haze, however, so they had time to figure out what they were going to do or if they even needed to do anything.

"I'm not seeing any identification yet," she said. "Still too far away. Do we have her on scopes?"

"No, ma'am," Sam told her. "Still nothing on any of our systems."

"Irritating." Trase grumbled a little, though the unidentified ship wasn't really unusual.

The ship probably wasn't Alliance or Imperial, as those normally broadcast identifiers. Of course, she rather doubted that any Imperial vessel would be doing that this deep in Alliance skies anyway.

"Probably a civilian or corporate transport," she decided.

There were a few places in the area that saw frequent-enough traffic, though the bogey had to be a fairly large ship to be visible this far out, judging from the haze on the sails.

"She's moving fast," Trase said a moment later, realizing that the dark spot of the ship under the sails had nearly doubled in size. "That skipper is running tight to the wind."

"Captain . . ." Sam's voice was suddenly sharp and filled with concern, causing Trase to lower the viewer and glance over.

"What?"

"I think she's running overtake sails."

Trase snapped the viewer back up, eyes fastening on the sails again. They were hazy, like the vessel was still coming out of the mist, and that was the tip-off she should have noticed herself. As fast as that ship was moving, the sails should have been in the clear by now.

"Damn. Sound the alarm. Have the helm pull us in as tight to the wind as we can get," Trase ordered as she lowered the viewer to crank the magnification up.

The skimmer was an odd duck, she realized. Not many were black as a nightmare, an unlucky color to most sailors. This one was bigger than she'd realized too, now that she knew the vessel's range. No matter how she looked at the situation, something felt wrong.

The *Helena*'s alarm claxon went off, and she felt the deck shift as the ship started climbing higher into the atmosphere. The air got colder and thinner in short order as the wind whipped hard over the curved deck of the transport, causing her to tighten her thermal uniform, but Trase didn't leave the position. She wanted to keep an eye on the pursuer for as long as possible, and there wasn't much she could do inside just yet.

They should be able to clear the pursuit, she told herself.

The *Helena* had big sails, and while running tight to the wind would buffet her around a bit, there were few ships that could keep up with her at a dead run.

Too bad for you, whoever you are. You almost caught us.

Free Corsair *Excalibur*

"They spotted us," Gaston announced. "They're tightening to the wind, making a run for it."

Mira nodded, accepting the information.

"They should have spotted us earlier," she said. "How long until they kill our overtake on them?"

"Ten, maybe fifteen minutes," Gaston said. "They're pulling hard, but we're already at speed."

"And how long until we catch them?"

"At current rates? Twenty minutes."

The crew around chuckled, hearing that. Catching another skimmer was difficult, and generally depended on the ratio of the sails to the ships. If the ratio wasn't on your side, you weren't going to win that race and, sadly, the *Excalibur* just didn't have sails enough to catch their quarry.

On the other hand, they were already at speed, and sails weren't the only tool in their box.

"Secure the sails, and engage tractor drive," Mira ordered.

"Tractor engaging!"

"Sails deactivated. Bringing in the cables!"

The feel of the vessel under their feet shifted then, from the slightly unsteady sensation of a ship under sail to the rock-steady stability and acceleration that came with using the tractor drive.

Though notoriously slow to accelerate, tractor drives had no known maximum velocity. Over any range anyone had been able to test them, they just kept pulling, and so the *Excalibur*, already at her best wind speed, began to speed up steadily. Though accelerating more slowly than the ship being pursued, the *Excalibur* was starting from a faster velocity, and the transport was limited by the wind. Catching up was just a matter of time.

"Fly our colors," Mira ordered, "and run out the forward guns."

"Yes, ma'am," Gaston responded, relaying the order.

The heavy clank of the forward armor plates falling open could be felt through the deck more than heard in the air, but either way, Mira knew that the *Excalibur* had been drawn.

"Signal them," she said. "Order them to put down and prepare to be boarded."

Alliance Transport *Helena Night*

Trase almost dropped her viewer as the black and white colors lit off over the stern of the pursuing ship. The crossed weapons were the stuff of stories, nothing she'd ever expected to see for herself.

The last anyone had seen those colors, to her knowledge, was just before the countercoup several months earlier. The rogue Cadre officer, Delsol, had flown them in battle many times before that, of course, but she was most infamous for blowing a loyalist encampment to the burning skies, for whatever reason.

One would have thought that would make her at least neutral in the conflict, if not unofficially on the side of the alliance, but apparently neither Delsol nor the empire had gotten the memo. Since then, the seemingly rogue Cadrewoman had simply vanished . . .

Trase blinked, a sudden jolt of terror rushing through her as she brought the viewer back up so quickly she almost blackened her eyes herself.

I don't see the sails anymore . . . Oh no.

Cadre Commander Mira Delsol had vanished the same time as the *Caleb Bar* went missing.

Trase swore a particularly vile epithet before turning and rushing back below, heading for the command deck of her ship.

"Stand ready to make for the top wind layer!" she ordered, tossing the viewer aside as she reached the deck and headed for her station. "All hands, secure every station!"

"Captain?" Sam looked over. "What's—"

"It's the *Caleb Bar*!" she snarled. "And that lunatic Delsol is in command!"

Movement on the deck came to a halt, wide eyes turning to look at the captain with shock, disbelief, and fear. Normally, Trase might have tried to be nice about things, but she wasn't in the mood.

"Did I stutter?" she snapped at them all. "Stand ready to shift wind layers! We'll never outrun the *Caleb* this low."

"Y-yes, captain," Sam stammered out, relaying the order and helping to shake everyone to their senses.

Sam kept his peace as they pulled the sails two by two, launching into the upper atmosphere as fast as they could, the *Helena* lurching under the stress of the new wind force. Once they were climbing solidly, he quietly leaned closer to Trase.

"Ma'am, we can't outrun the *Caleb*—not if they've got a jump on us," he said softly.

"I know that, but we can get into the air-defense sector around the Redoubt," she responded, "and I doubt they even know that exists yet. We just need to stay ahead of them as long as we can and call for help as soon as we're in range of the Redoubt."

Sam nodded. "Understood."

Free Corsair *Excalibur*

"They're making a run for the upper atmosphere, skipper."

"Give them a warning shot, Gas," Mira ordered. "Make them flinch."

"Yes, ma'am," Gaston said, putting the ship's comm to his mouth. "Forward guns, skipper wants them to flinch. Make it happen."

The response from the forward station was lost in the sharp whine-crack of blasters firing a brace of rounds.

"Fire away, skipper," Gaston said.

"Send them another order to put down."

Alliance Transport *Helena Night*

"Damn, that was close!"

Trase grimaced, knowing that was probably an understatement. The lase blasts hadn't actually hit the *Helena*, but they'd set off proximity alarms across every deck. Worse, as much as she liked and was proud of her ship, she knew that the *Helena* didn't have particularly great proximity scanners.

She didn't want to know just how close those blasts had come.

"They're signaling again, ordering us to put down, captain," Sam told her.

"Hold to the course," Trase responded, checking their position against the map. "We're only a few minutes from the air-defense line."

Sam nodded but didn't have the look of confidence Trase was trying to project. He kept his mouth shut, though, which pleased her. She didn't want to panic the crew—hell, she didn't want to panic herself—and she knew that a few minutes was an eternity with a ship like the *Caleb Bar* closing in on them.

She would feel a lot better if she were more confident in the ability of the air-defense systems to actually *do* something to the *Caleb Bar*. The ship was too much of a mystery for her to know exactly what it was really capable of, but the rumors were all over the place. If any of those were even *close* to the truth, she didn't have a clue what was going to happen.

It's just a ship, she told herself. *The rumors are just that. We just need to get to the air-defense line. At the very least, we'll be able to get clear while the* Caleb *is fighting.*

Free Corsair *Excalibur*

"They're holding to their course, skipper."

Mira nodded. "Gutsy. Stupid, but gutsy. What's our range now?"

"A little under a mile, continuing to close," Gaston responded. "We could target their sail pitons."

Mira considered it, though she would prefer not to resort to that, especially with the target ship climbing and gaining speed. If the *Excalibur* took out the wrong thing at the wrong time, the fleeing ship would drop out of the sky, destroying the cargo and killing a lot of people.

She'd done a lot of both of those in the past, but this time she rather needed the cargo in question and didn't want to send a few dozen people crashing to their doom for no reason.

Still, they were on a deadline, and the numbers were rapidly falling off.

"No, get us in close. Tell the boarding crew to finish suiting up and meet me on deck," Mira said, getting to her feet. "We'll go with plan A."

"For the record, skipper," Gaston said, rolling his eyes, "I *hate* plan A."

"Noted," Mira said as she headed topside while Gaston made the call as ordered.

*

The air was thinner and colder still as Mira stood at the forward rail in her armor.

The target was just off the *Excalibur*'s bow now, well under a mile away and closing fast. It was almost in her range if she wanted to jump and glide over, but with both ships crossing wind layers, that would be a rather dangerous maneuver.

Gaston and the others were bringing them in closer, however, which was what would make the whole operation something just a little less than suicidal.

"Skipper . . ." A voice caused her to look over her shoulder to where a group of a dozen were approaching.

The boarding crew were all in armor as well, not Cadre issue but instead the heavier and bulkier navy gear intended for boarding operations. Cadre armor was far more agile but not as effective against severe hits. She wasn't certain, and had no wish to test the theory, but Mira suspected that boarding armor *might* just be able to take a hit from a gamma burster.

"Ready for some action, boys?" Mira asked, grinning at them.

The men laughed, and the officer in charge, Malcom Price, waved slightly and bowed with just a hint of a mocking gesture. "With you, skipper? Any time."

"Good. Glad to hear it," Mira said, dropping the humorous tone. "I'll lead this off. When I've got the line across, you boys do what you do best."

Malcom nodded. "We'll follow in on your path, skipper. Just hold the door open for us."

Mira nodded as well, skipping the obvious joke as she focused on the job at hand. She grabbed a cable from beside her, latching it to her belt as she again looked out over the distance between the *Excalibur* and the now much closer target ship.

"The *Helena Night*," she said, reading the lettering on the side of the ship. "Good name."

She glanced back at the team. "Ready to go?"

"When you are, skipper," Malcom confirmed.

Mira planted a foot on the rail. "See you on the other side!"

Then she dove clear, bringing her armor to full flight mode. Wings of light spread out from her back.

Gaston had matched the *Helena*'s climb, keeping above the other ship even as the *Excalibur* continued to close the gap, so now as Mira dropped through the air, she could see the transport spinning below her as she fought the wind and stabilized her flight.

Here, the cable she was dragging was both a boon and a curse. It kept her steady, providing drag that would prevent gusts of wind from affecting her more seriously, but it was also that same drag that slowed her approach. Mira thus had only one chance at reaching the *Helena Night*.

She tightened up her form, arms at her sides and light wings to minimum for control, and dove in as fast as she could with the cable paying out behind her. The *Helena* spun ahead of Mira as she twisted around to align herself correctly and stabilize. The Cadrewoman then threw out her arms and abruptly spread her light wings to absorb speed.

The *Helena* rushed up at her almost as fast as she rushed down, making the final approach vector a moment of terrifying existential dread. Then Mira kicked her feet forward, shifting her body back to bring the armor wings around to cut the air rather than just catch it. Her plummeting fall turned into a steep dive, curving sharply up at the last moment just before she struck the deck of the *Helena* in a slide that sent her careening across the surface and toward the side of the ship.

Mira caught the rail to keep from being thrown clear, feeling like she'd been kicked in the ribs when she hit the deck. She managed to keep her grip, and after a moment caught her breath without any sharp pains that might indicate a broken or cracked rib. Satisfied that she wasn't out of the mission before it even started, Mira got to her feet and examined the situation.

She had to hold on to the rails as the ship banked upward, hauling in the forward cables harder than the rearward ones. The deck was clear, everyone likely belowdecks due to the growing cold and thinning air. She unclipped the cable she'd been dragging, moving it to the rail instead. Once it was clipped into place, she signaled the boarding team.

Phase one down. Get a move on, boys, before they spot us.

*

"Go! Go! Go!"

The men swung off the deck, their armor linked to the cable as they jumped out into the ether and started sliding down the line toward the other vessel. They went in rapid succession, with Malcom checking their rigging before sending each off with a slap on the shoulder.

Boarding from ship-to-ship was a highly dangerous maneuver under the best of circumstances, so he wanted this done as quickly and safely as possible. Running a line between any two objects with the sheer mass of a skimmer put anything, or anyone, on that line at the mercy of some very basic laws of physics.

Malcolm was well aware that the Imperial Navy had basically banned the procedure, which had once been used to resupply while in the air, after someone had gotten it into their head to give a disliked officer a wild ride. That ride ended with the line snapping and said officer being catapulted several thousand feet above the ships before gravity decided to serve notice again.

That incident had been between two supposedly cooperative skimmers, no less. Boarding an unwilling ship was *incredibly* dangerous.

The last man went ahead of him, and Malcolm hopped over the rail himself, pausing only to triple-check that his line was secure before he too flung himself into space after his men and his skipper.

Danger was one thing, loyalty another.

Alliance Transport *Helena Night*

Trase checked the instruments, noting that the *Caleb Bar* was still closing but keeping above them for some reason.

That didn't make a lot of sense to her as she tried to figure out what the lunatic woman over there was thinking. By approaching from above, they were giving up a significant degree of their firing arc for ship-to-ship weapons; at least she thought they were. Normal frigates and the like certainly would, but the *Caleb* might have a different design.

So why haven't they fired again?

Trase knew she was pushing her luck, not simply putting down as they had commanded, but this close to the air-defense line she couldn't help it.

Still, she'd expected to take a few shots by now and be forced into evasion. Instead they were closing steadily, but almost too steadily. Almost as if they didn't want to . . . startle her.

She grabbed Sam by the arm. "Get someone topside!"

"What?"

"Delsol is a Cadre operator, not a skimmer captain," she hissed. "Get someone up there and make sure she isn't doing anything . . . tricky."

Sam paled, but nodded jerkily and rushed off, leaving Trase to try and figure out what she was going to do about it if she were right.

Wait . . . why wait?

"New course!" she called out loudly. "Shift us away from the *Caleb*, fifteen degrees port!"

"Yes, ma'am! Fifteen degrees, ma'am!" the helmsman called back, twisting the controls. The *Helena* began to shift under their feet.

"Communications, Steir. Do we have a link to the Redoubt yet?" Trase demanded.

"Almost, ma'am. The haze is still causing interference, but we've picked up the carrier signal," Steir Alain responded.

"Start calling for help."

"Yes, ma'am."

Free Corsair *Excalibur*

Gaston swore as he saw the *Helena* start pulling off to port. "Match their course. Continue closing!"

Mitch Little, the helmsman, was sweating already; probably not a good sign, but the poor man was the best they had. He didn't respond to Gaston's order, but the *Excalibur* sure enough started turning to port, so Gas didn't bother to repeat himself.

"Someone get an eye on the boarding team!" he ordered. "I want to know when they're on the target ship!"

"On it!"

Gaston turned around, surprised by the voice. He hadn't known Mik was on the command deck; the young man normally spent his time in the lower levels.

"Take a belt and line," Gaston ordered after the receding teen, "and *use* it!"

He didn't understand the reply that wafted back through the bulkheads, but didn't have time to worry about it. Hopefully, the kid wouldn't do anything too stupid.

Just *thinking* that was probably taunting the fates.

Didn't matter. The kid was on his own for now.

"Stay with them!" Gaston ordered firmly. "I don't want any casualties we can avoid on this operation, hear me?"

*

Mikael bounded up the narrow stairwell, heading for the topside deck as quickly as he could. He wasn't really sure what he could do, but he knew most of the guys who'd gone over the side with the skipper and didn't want anything to happen to them.

He only paused briefly at the lock, grabbing a security belt off the rack and wrapping it around his waist before he wrenched the heavy door open and stepped out into the biting cold.

The wind was whistling as he closed and dogged the hatch shut, then looked around for a place to clip the safety cable. After locking the cable to a rail, Mik pulled his uniform jacket tighter and huddled up a bit as he strayed over to the edge and looked around, trying to find the guys.

He spotted the other ship first. The bogey was a lot closer than he'd expected, banking slightly as it tried to pull away from the *Excalibur*, but Mik could also feel the shift in the deck under him and knew that they were still chasing close behind.

"Oh whoa . . ." he uttered, shocked when he spotted the men.

They were halfway across, sliding along a threadlike cable with nothing else to keep them from plummeting to the ground below. Mik felt a shiver run through him that had nothing to do with the bitingly cold wind as he shifted to keep an eye on them while he reached for the hard comm to the command deck below.

"I see them," he yelled into the system, holding it to his mouth. "They're halfway across."

There was a brief pause before a response came, during which Mik watched as the line of men seemed to climb in the air slightly.

"Can you see the cable?" Gaston's voice came back over the roaring wind. "Is there slack in the cable?"

Mik looked again, squinting against the biting wind to try and make out the cable.

"It's hard to see, but I think so," he shouted into the comm. "It's tightening up, though!"

Mik was surprised to hear the normally quiet second-in-command of the *Excalibur* start swearing over the comm.

"Hold on!" Gaston said after he'd finished. "We're turning in to them!"

Normally the *Excalibur* didn't tilt while under the tractor drive but rather turned as if it were on rails . . . because, really, it was. So Mik was surprised when the deck suddenly shifted underfoot and the side of the ship dipped down.

"Oh crap!" he cried as his feet slipped on ice that had gathered, whipping out from under him and sending him sliding toward the rail.

He could see the ground now, looming in front of him as the *Excalibur* banked to port and started dropping altitude as well as shifting course. He hit the rails in a scramble, trying to grab on to something—anything—but it was all ice slick.

Mik yelled as he went over the side.

Alliance Transport *Helena Night*

Mira braced herself as the ship banked, eyes on the men who were sweeping down toward her from the *Excalibur* as she started praying. The line, while immensely strong, would never hold up to the force inherent in even minor maneuvers between two ships. Even if it *did*, the force would unquestionably snap the rails the line was secured to.

The *Excalibur* immediately turned in to the *Helena*'s course, and Mira let out a breath she hadn't known she was holding. Gaston had seen the danger at least, so they had a chance.

The first of the men was almost to the rail of the *Helena* when the sound of metal on metal caught her attention, and Mira pivoted to cover the walkway, her blaster clearing the holster in a single smooth motion.

Let's get this party started.

CHAPTER 6

Perrin District

"IIS, huh?" The lead thug pointed his blaster at them, sneering openly. "What is Imperial Intelligence doing here?"

"They're looking into the lost shipments," the foreman said from the side, letting out an annoyed breath. "I tried to keep them out of here, but . . ."

"Yeah, but," the leader snorted, "didn't do too good a job of it."

"They're IIS! What was I supposed to do? You know they have authority to check anything they like while investigating something like this!"

"Speaking of which," Matani spoke up, his voice rather casual as he kept his hands visible. "What exactly *is* this? Seems pretty high risk, stealing war materials from the empire."

The leader looked over at him and laughed. "You think I'm going to tell you anything?"

"I had hoped," Matani admitted with a half-smile.

"Right. I think we'll just eliminate you and move on," the leader said simply, hefting his weapon.

"One problem with that, I'm afraid." Matani's fingers twitched, and Brennan, reading the signal, tensed slightly.

"Oh? And that is?"

"We're not Imperial Intelligence."

The leader frowned, tensing slightly, though he looked more confused than anything. "Then what are—?"

Matani fully smiled. "We're Imperial Cadre."

Confusion turned to fear in an instant of recognition, and Matani could see the leader's finger tightening on the trigger of his blaster. The weapon went off, the bolt missing wide as Matani leaned just slightly to the left.

"Oh shit!" the leader swore. "Kill them!"

Matani and Brennan were already moving, their fists coming up to slap the Imperial emblem they wore on their jackets. Gleaming iridescent white armor erupted from the small projectors, wrapping around the two men as lase blasters spat around.

Matani stepped into the fire, bringing up his arm as a shield formed, angling it to drive the shots off to the side away from Brennan as he drew his Armati from under his armor.

It had been too long since Matani had drawn his Tor with *intent*.

The thick bar he drew narrowed and lengthened, the end spreading and forming a hammer surface with a vicious spike on the reverse side. He let the hammer face drag on the floor as he strode forward, shield in front, drawing more of the blasts from the group as they tried to stop him.

He got the moment he was waiting for when a few of them emptied their weapons, and a brief slack in the firing rhythm allowed him to sweep the field with his shield as he brought his Armati up over his head. He roared as the heavy weapon pulled at his muscles, driving it down into the ground of the warehouse.

The area shook slightly, causing a moment of silence as people registered his actions enough to look both awed and confused. Awed because the strike had actually *shaken* the ground, but confused because that was all it had done.

Matani sneered under his armor as he drew his shield arm back and choked up on the Armati so he could get in close. If any of them had been remotely intelligent, they'd have scattered. They were not, and they did not, and so when the blast erupted up out of the ground, it threw the lot of them into the air in all directions.

One flew right at him. Matani backhanded him with the Armati and sent him to the ground with broken bones. The others struck the wall behind them, the shelving of the warehouse, and crates, desks, and the ground.

Brennan was moving too, his Bene already drawn. Matani nodded, approving, for the boy wasn't just waiting for his teacher to deal with the problem. This group of thugs was nothing to a Cadreman, at least not one in armor with his Armati in hand. Still, Brennan was Cadre too, or at least Cadre potential . . . and Cadre didn't just stand around and wait for someone else to clean up a mess.

The two armed and armored Cadremen made short work of the resistance, not that there was much left by the time the men had hit the floor from where Matani's attack had thrown them. Securing them was still a hassle, since they hadn't been entirely incapacitated by the attack, but most cooperated once they saw and heard what happened to those few who didn't.

The pair then started looking over the crates the group had been repacking.

"These are . . . interesting," Brennan said, pulling some parts out of the crates. "Most of them are high-end skimmer parts."

"Most?" Matani asked, trusting the younger man's expertise when it came to flyers.

"Yeah, most. This I don't know," Brennan admitted, holding up one part while he looked over the crates with a frown.

"What is it? You're thinking something else," Matani prodded.

"Probably nothing. It's just . . . they've got almost enough gear here to build a skimmer, aside from the airframe, of course. It's what's missing that I find interesting."

"What's missing?"

"Sail projectors," Brennan said, "which makes some sense, I guess. They're grabbing components for tractor engines, so I suppose they don't need the sails . . ."

"But?"

"But even the *Caleb Bar* has sails. Probably they don't need to steal them, though. Lots of places make quality projectors. They're not regulated for sale." Brennan looked over at Matani, expression now curious. "More importantly: How the hell did you do that?"

"What?" Matani asked, unconcerned as he flipped the unknown component Brennan had pointed out in his hand.

Brennan gestured to the now secured thugs. *"That."*

"Oh . . . that." Matani chuckled. "Nothing mysterious, kid. You know about the metal under the empire, right?"

Brennan nodded. Of course he did. The entire empire, everywhere they had ever dug, had a layer of metal at a depth that varied depending on location. The Redoubts and palace were built from the same substance, which was also used in the construction of the *Caleb Bar*. Impossibly durable, which made it the most valuable commodity in the empire despite being so common. With very few exceptions, almost every source of the metal had already been smelted and worked, which could be done only once.

"I sent a force blast down through the ground, bounced it off the metal, and up into those idiots," Matani said. "It's a little tricky; you need to know your angles, but nothing too special for an Armati with Tor's capabilities."

Brennan involuntarily glanced down at his Bene.

Matani understood the look, but shook his head. "Don't get your hopes up. Yours is a blade type. They're generally a little lower on pure power, but more versatile."

"You don't know my Bene's capabilities exactly?" Brennan asked. "I thought you worked with my brother?"

"I did, but the Armati are . . . strange things, kid," Matani said simply. "None of them are identical to each other, and sometimes they change from one wielder to another. Just because your brother was able to use Bene in one way doesn't mean you will."

Brennan hadn't known that, but then few of the Cadre people he'd spoken to seemed to like talking about their Armati. He understood. It was an intensely private moment even just thinking about his Bene. He didn't know why, or how, but he couldn't escape the feeling either.

"Come on," Matani said. "We need to contact the actual IIS and get them to flood this place while we try and figure out what these fools were really up to."

Imperial Palace

"Your highness."

Lydia sighed. "We are alone, William. Call me Lydia."

William hesitated, but finally replied. "Lydia then."

The young empress smiled, grateful for the sense of normality. She'd grown up with William in the castle, one of many faces she knew better than her father's. He'd been a Cadre recruit the first time she remembered seeing him, and her father's adviser by the time she had been old enough to first notice boys.

She would never admit it to anyone, not even her twin, but William had been her first crush as a teen.

"I assume that there is news," she asked, pushing aside old memories.

"From your brother," William confirmed.

"Brennan? Is he all right?"

William nodded. "Fine. He's fine. He and his trainer, Cadreman Fenn, uncovered a theft ring or perhaps saboteurs in the Perrin District."

Lydia frowned. The district meant something to her.

"Perrin District," she murmured. "We had a shipment of components lost to a raid there, did we not?"

"Perhaps not," William said, sounding uncertain. "There are now concerns that it was thievery, with the factory foreman and perhaps management being complicit. They may have used the war and stories of raids as a cover."

Lydia sucked in a breath through clenched teeth.

"It's treason then," she said finally.

"Yes, Your Majesty." William reverted to protocol. "It *is* treason."

She cast him a weak smile at his choice to refer to her by title again.

"If it's treason, we need to know how far it has gone," she decided. "Is the baron of that sector still in the capital?"

"No, he didn't come to the meeting."

Lydia froze at that, surprised. The baron of Perrin was a minor noble, to be sure, of little power or influence, which was one reason she might have missed his absence, but he should have been at the meeting.

"Did he send a reason for his absence?" she asked.

William shook his head. That had been the first thing he'd checked once he'd realized the noble was absent.

"Then we have to assume that the issue may have gone far higher up the ranks of our government than we had hoped," Lydia said, a cold feeling of dread in her belly.

Treason against the empire.

It seemed that her nightmare, her torture, was unending. Corian had turned on them all, killed her family. Others had chosen to support him despite that, breaking her people into two. Now even those who claimed to be loyal *still* chose to betray the empire—and her.

Lydia honestly didn't know if she could continue like this, with treachery confronting her at every turn. She wasn't her father. She had never *wanted* the throne, never thought that she was intended for it. Though she had been merely born to the Scourwind legacy, Lydia didn't want her life to mark the end of her family name.

What option was there?

She was empress, and that meant she was responsible for the empire, and responsible *to* the people.

Even so, Lydia found that responsibility was akin to riding a wild beast. The only thing that terrified her more than the ride itself . . . was the idea of letting go.

"Do we know the location of the baron?" she asked, her tone chilling.

"We do, Your Majesty." William reacted to her tone. "His sigil was spotted by your brother and his trainer in the township that held the factory."

"Then we would have words with him," she said firmly. "Tell my brother to secure him for me."

"As you will it."

Keri-Perrin Township

"Remember this lesson, if no other, kid," Matani said wryly as they left the factory in the hands of the locals and Imperial Intelligence. "The reward for a job well done is another job. Usually a more difficult one."

Brennan smiled. "I'll let my sister know. I'm sure she'll be *fascinated* with your opinion of her orders."

"Ha, you're going to run and tell on me to Her Majesty?" Matani asked. "Let me tell you about the time I told your father where he could shove his suggestions about how I should run my operation."

Not walking slowly but not hurrying either, they were making their way to the municipal building where they'd spotted the baron earlier. Brennan was thankful for the time, he found, as it gave him a chance to try and bring his nerves under control.

He wasn't nervous, exactly, or he didn't think it was . . . but Brennan had felt jumpy since the fight, however brief it might have been. He had been told multiple times by Matani that this was a normal reaction, and he supposed it must be, as it wasn't the first time he'd felt like this. The jumpiness just didn't *feel* natural. It felt wrong—like he couldn't control his own body—and Brennan hated it.

"The baron will have guards." Matani spoke as they walked, either not noticing Brennan's nerves or, more likely, allowing him the sense of privacy to deal with his issues.

Either way, Brennan was grateful.

"And if he's a traitor, they'll be ready for a fight," Brennan added. "Should we really do this alone?"

"We are Cadre," Matani said. "We are the first through the breach and the last to walk off the field. We are the empress's sword and shield."

Brennan scoffed. "That may be, but nowhere in any of that does it say that the empress's lase blaster can't help out once in a while."

The old Cadreman eyed him for a long moment, then burst out laughing.

"Well said," he told Brennan, "and while we will carry out the empress's request personally, I've arranged for Imperial Intelligence to back us up after we've moved. I couldn't involve local constables, however."

"Why . . . oh, right." Brennan sighed. "We don't know their loyalty."

"Precisely."

The flat tone from the Cadreman ended their conversation as they continued toward the municipal building.

Keri-Perrin Township, Municipal Building

"My baron!"

Baron Kinder Vilhem half turned as his assistant rushed in. "What is it?"

"Imperial Intelligence has taken over the factory, my baron," Julie Sens told him. "They've locked it down entirely and are holding everyone inside."

Kinder paled as he understood just what that meant.

"How did they find out?"

"I do not know, my baron, but you must leave. If you are not here, perhaps you might be able to avoid suspicion."

He considered that, briefly, but realized such a move wouldn't work.

There were too many threads that would lead back to him, but then he'd known the risks when he agreed to this project. Now that the game was up, he just hoped that he'd done enough.

"Come, Julie," he said, "it is time to withdraw from the field."

She nodded, grabbing up what materials she could find in the office as the baron secured his things and called the guards. In moments, they were ready and moving down and out of the building to the waiting transport.

*

Brennan's eyes widened as he recognized the baron being hustled into the waiting transport outside the municipal building. He exchanged a glance with Matani, and then both of them broke into a run. But they were too far back, and by the time they got to the building the vehicle had left.

"We're too late," Brennan said, wincing. "I'm sorry. We should have hurried but—"

"But I allowed us to take our time. You have nothing to apologize for."

The experienced Cadreman looked around, then nodded off in another direction. "See that?"

"The local constables' office? So?"

"They'll have vehicles," Matani said with a grin. "Let's borrow a ride."

Evan Currie

They rushed over. While the constables were less than happy about the request, the pair were able to secure a couple of fast ground transports.

Matani mounted his rig, grinning at Brennan. "Know the plan?"

"I've got it, don't worry. I'll handle my part."

"Never doubted it, kid," Matani said as he flicked a switch and the two-wheeler began to hum. "See you on the other side."

"Don't get dead, old man." Brennan powered up his own in turn, the soft humming running through him as he leaned over and gripped the controls. "I don't feel like hauling your carcass back to the palace."

"Then leave me where I fall, boy." Matani laughed sharply as he grabbed the controls of his own ride and put power to the wheels. "Just leave me where I fall. I'll have consecrated any ground I die on with the blood of the poor damn fools who killed me, I promise you that."

The wheels squealed as he accelerated out.

Brennan watched him go for a moment, then hit the power. The acceleration pushed him back into the seat as he took another direction, heading out of town.

*

Matani knew where the baron was heading, of course. Only one spot made sense, but that same logic was what made him decide that he and Brennan had to split up. He gunned the power to the two-wheeler, skidding as he pushed it around a corner, and headed out of town in the direction the baron had taken.

Ground transports were fast, but not fast enough to evade the empire.

The baron, if he were running, as it did seem, had to be heading for the airfield.

Of course, a good pilot could land pretty much anywhere, as Brennan had earlier proven. However, an airfield was more than just a place to land and had maintenance facilities, fuel cells, and provisions. That was why most people, especially those of import who flew larger skimmers, liked to use them, just to make matters easier. If the baron were running, he would be heading for his skimmer.

Matani leaned into his two-wheeler as the road opened up outside the town, pushing the accelerator as far as it would go. The force pulled at him as dust and debris spat out from behind. The vehicle wavered a little under the Cadreman until he got it under control and turned toward the airfield.

The baron didn't have that much of a lead, so Matani figured he should be able to catch him easily enough. If he were delayed, however—well, then, it would be up to Brennan.

*

"We are being pursued, my baron," Julie informed Kinder as they neared the airport.

The baron hissed. "Have the guards stop him."

"As you order it," she told him, issuing the command to the guards, who immediately fell back and began setting up an ambush. She then tapped their driver on the shoulder, getting his attention. "Drive faster."

He nodded, tension practically radiating off him as the transport jolted ahead.

Kinder chuckled. "Don't scare the help, Julie. He has enough to worry about."

"My apologies, my baron."

*

Trouble.

Matani spotted the ambush well before it was sprung on him, of course. There wasn't enough cover in the area for a hurriedly set-up trap to be hidden. Unfortunately, that still left him with an unpalatable decision.

He could slow and reverse the ambush easily enough, but that would allow his target to get out of his reach. However, the only other option was to ride straight on into the teeth of the dragon and dare the beast to bite off more than it could chew.

Given that choice . . . well, there just wasn't a choice.

Cadre. Matani grinned fervently as the word echoed in his mind and then reached up to activate his armor projector.

With iridescent armor gleaming, he leaned in close and made certain that the accelerator was all the way open. The two-wheeler whined as its electric motors spun, driving the vehicle forward. The lase blasts opened up from a hundred yards, enough coverage to perforate any poor sucker in their path a dozen times over in the first second.

Matani wasn't any poor sucker.

Speed was his first defense. Most of the shots were off target simply because he was accelerating when they were expecting him to be either slowing or entirely oblivious and holding steady. Blast after blast flew past him, the majority never coming close.

The few that did glanced off his armor in the seconds before he was on top of the ambushers.

The attackers were firing in panic by that point, but even so, the density of blasts was dangerous. Matani leaned to one side, then lashed out with a boot that caught one shooter in the chest. A spear of pain drove up his leg, but Matani ignored it as he felt the crunch of ribs breaking under his boot and pulled his foot back as he continued through.

Lase blasts started to follow him, the shooters walking their shots along the road as he and his two-wheeler whined down the access route to the airfield. He smashed through a security fence, shattering the lightweight barrier as he powered out onto the field itself.

The baron's skimmer was just ahead; Matani recognized the sigil on the hull and the transport parked beside it. He skidded his wheeler to a stop, barely noticing that it was smoking from multiple holes that had been burned through the shroud and chassis.

His boots sank slightly into the soft earth of the field, his right hand already wrapping around his Tor as he started to approach the skimmer.

"Baron Vilhem!" he called. "Her Majesty Empress Scourwind has requested your presence!"

Matani was slightly put out when, instead of the baron, a woman appeared.

"I'm his lord baron's assistant," she said to him. "I'm afraid he has . . . another obligation."

"No obligation, short of death, excuses a man from an Imperial summons."

"Death may be arranged," she said simply, flicking a hand signal.

Men appeared from the skimmer, more than he would have guessed by its size, actually, leveling a combination of blasters and, more worrying, gamma bursters in his direction.

Matani's eyes flicked from side to side as he judged the distances and range. This group wasn't as stupid as the fools in the warehouse, unfortunately, and they'd spread out enough that he wouldn't catch them with a single attack. He mentally nudged his Tor, and the hefty weapon shifted, expanding to full size.

He stood for a moment before speaking.

"Well, then," he said coldly, "let us not disappoint Her Majesty."

CHAPTER 7

Fire Control Command, Alliance Redoubt

"Tell me you're tracking them!"

"We have them on scanners, major," the technician assured the officer of the watch. "The *Helena Night* showed up on our scans first, but we have the *Caleb Bar* now as well."

Major Irwin took a breath. "Be careful. They have a full instrumentation suite on that beast. If they spot you too soon . . ."

"We've been running extremely low power on all scanners. That's one of the reasons they got this close, major."

"Good. Stand by for orders. Do *nothing* until I give the word."

"Yes, major."

Alliance Transport *Helena Night*

Sam Maxwell led the way out onto the deck, his lase pistol in his hand as he opened the hatch and peered out.

"Looks clear, but we're not going to take any chances," he told the three men behind him.

The *Helena* didn't have a security crew per se, as it was just a light transport, so he'd gathered up a few of the rougher types who didn't have much to do until they were loading or unloading, and dragged them topside as quick as he could.

Sam didn't know what he'd have done if he were in the hot seat, but if the captain wanted to make a run for the Redoubt's air-defense sector, that was what they were going to do. If there was anyone trying to board—and that was an idea that gave him chills for two very different reasons—he supposed it was up to him and his impromptu security team to show the uninvited guests to the rails.

"Stay close. Do *not* split up," he ordered. "Anyone crazy enough to board the *Helena* in midsky is *not* someone I want to come face-to-face with alone."

The guys got a laugh out of that, which was what he was hoping for. This was bad enough business as it stood, and he didn't want jumpy idiots at his back with blasters in their hands.

He clipped his safety catch onto the rail and looked around for a moment before waving the others up. "All right, come on. Don't forget your cable either. It's a long way down."

Sam watched them all clip in before he allowed them to go any farther, then gestured forward. "With me, then."

The foursome edged forward, eyes wide as the sharp wind howled around them, biting through their thick thermal clothes and gear. The dark shadow of the *Caleb Bar* was approaching from above, but they tried not to look in the direction of the nightmarish ship.

One of the men behind him suddenly attracted Sam's attention by pointing and yelling in shock.

"Look at those crazy bastards!"

Sam twisted back and then followed the gesture out to where a line of men were seemingly flying between the two ships. He had to squint to spot the cable, and almost cried out in surprise himself. He'd heard stories about people doing things like this, but never unless both ships were in on the plan and holding steady. With the captain maneuvering to evade as she was, only a total lunatic would even *conceive* of a stunt like this.

He shook off the surprise and extended his blaster. "All right. We're not letting them get on the *Helena*. Take it easy and aim."

The men behind him nodded, getting their own guns into position.

It was a gleam in the corner of his eyes that made Sam move, starting to bring his gun around, but by then it was far too late. He felt the bones in his shoulder crunch as something jabbed him, then a feeling of weightlessness, and then it all went black.

*

Mira spun with her Armati Elan braced in the crook of her arm, using the force to throw her target over the rails and into empty space beyond the ship. His safety cable caught, swinging him back into the hull of the *Helena* with a crunch that made her wince, but she was already moving on.

She snapped out a kick that sent the next man's pistol flying out into the air on a one-way trip to the ground forty thousand feet below, then stepped in and grabbed the back of his head before he could react. Two hard smacks into the rail dropped him to the deck in a daze as she vaulted him and kicked out into the next with enough force to drive him back into the man behind him and send both of them tumbling.

They were still scrambling for their pistols when she towered over them and extended her own blaster to touch the closest man's head.

"Don't."

Her voice was colder than the wind. They both froze and looked up at her.

Standing there in gleaming armor that could only be one thing in the eyes of any Imperial—or former Imperial—citizen, they recognized instantly that they were dealing with Cadre.

Both men slowly raised their hands.

"Good move."

Mira kept the gun on the pair, but stepped back to clear a little range between them and idly kicked the man behind her who was trying to get up.

"Stay down, fool," one of the others called out, voice near panic.

Mira ignored him as she looked back to where the boarding crew were climbing over the rails.

"Everyone good?" she called to them.

One waved at her as others were helping pull their mates up. Mira nodded and turned back to the men she was holding. "You two, get up."

She gestured with the barrel of her blaster, stepping back to stay well out of their reach. Better not to give them any ideas that might get them killed. Instead she gestured to where the first guy had gone over the rails.

"Pull him up."

While they were doing that, Mira risked another glance back to see that Malcolm was the last man being pulled over the rail. The team moved up behind her, looking past her to the men on the deck pulling someone else over the rail.

"Trouble, skipper?" Malcolm asked wryly.

"Nothing I couldn't handle."

"We can see that." He laughed.

"Secure their guns, then, and leave them on the deck," she ordered. "We don't need to be worrying about them while we're belowdecks."

"Yes, ma'am."

She skipped around the prisoners, heading for the hatch, and covered it while her team secured them.

When all that was done and her boarding crew was behind her, Mira cleared the hatch and led them in. Once they were inside with the hatch closed and no one in sight, she looked her team over.

"This is just a transport," she said, "so try not to kill anyone you don't need to, but don't risk yourselves either. Be nice, but don't mistake nice for stupid. You hear me?"

They all nodded and Malcolm responded. "We hear you, skipper. No massacre, but they don't get a chance to take us down either."

"Good. Let's go," she said. "We should be able to take the command deck and own the ship from there."

They nodded and the team started down into the depths of the *Helena Night*.

*

"We're almost to the air-defense line, captain."

Trase nodded but didn't say anything. Her mind was still too distracted by the looming presence of the *Caleb Bar* sailing over her head. She was far from confident in her choice of action, but so far had been proven right. The *Bar* hadn't elected to drop them from the skies, which it was most certainly capable of doing.

Unfortunately, the fact that they hadn't done precisely that was just as worrying as the idea that they *could* have done it.

A cry of shock behind her was the first hint that something was wrong, and she was still rising to her feet and turning as a man flew across the deck and tumbled into the *Helena*'s navigation console.

"Don't move!"

Trase's heart sank into her stomach as she recognized the gleaming armor and knew that her worst fears had come true despite her efforts. She briefly considered drawing her pistol, but in the end, she knew she wasn't a soldier, so she slowly raised her hands.

"Everyone," Trase ordered, her voice clear and loud, "do as they say. We're not paid to fight."

"Indeed," the woman in the gleaming armor said as her men moved forward and started securing weapons. "Frankly, I'm surprised you held out as long as you did. Not a lot to be gained by running from us, not if you knew who we were."

"Cadrewoman Delsol," Trase said icily, "we recognized your colors, and the *Caleb Bar*."

"She's the *Excalibur* now," Delsol responded. "But that does make me wonder, what were you thinking?"

The Cadrewoman stepped into the command deck proper, eyes sweeping the deck and instrumentation consoles.

"We've got the deck weapons secure, skipper," one of the armored men said to Delsol.

"Get to the controls," she ordered him. "Bring us up into the top wind layer and tack away from the Redoubt. There's no chance she hasn't called for help, so let's not be here when it arrives, yes?"

"You got it, skipper."

Trase gritted her teeth as she had to watch the men take over her ship, but there was little she could do.

Delsol nodded to another of her men. "Take someone topside and pull those poor bastards inside before they freeze to death or suffocate."

Two nodded and headed back, making Trase feel a little better. If they were going out of their way to keep her men alive, then it wasn't likely they were going to eventually slaughter them all out of hand.

"Skipper!" One of the men yelled from the comm console he'd taken over.

"What is it?" Delsol half turned in his direction, her tone concerned even though her armor masked any expression.

"I'm seeing a call for help in their log."

"Any reply?" Delsol asked.

"Not yet, but there's something strange here . . . I think you'd better get in contact with Gas, see if the *Excalibur*'s gear is seeing anything."

"All right." Delsol bodily pushed Trase out of the way and over to the rest of the crew they had secured. "Give me a line to the *Excalibur*."

Free Corsair *Excalibur*

"Contact from the *Helena*, Gas . . . It's the skipper!"

Gaston smiled, settling down on the ostentatious throne that served as the center of the captain's command console and opening the communication line.

"Good to hear from you, skipper," Gaston said. "I assume it went well?"

"No problems, Gas," Mira's voice came back. "Not on this end at least. The captain of the *Helena* did get out a call for help, so we're getting ready to turn tail. Could you check for any sign of a response group from the Redoubt?"

"Understood," Gaston said, waving at the scanner tech, who immediately started running analyses on the data his system was reporting. "I've got Paul on it now."

"All right, we're heading for the top layer," Mira told him. "Cover us if needed."

"You got it, skipper," Gaston said as the link closed.

He got up from the command chair and walked over to the scanner station. "Anything?"

"Maybe," the technician, Paul Morvan, answered. "There are multiple carrier waves I wouldn't normally expect out this far."

"Network link at the Redoubt?" Gaston asked, before instantly answering his own question. "No, that only accounts for one."

"Exactly. I've never seen anything like this, actually," Paul admitted to him. "The signals are too low power to be military, but I can't think of any civilian application that would explain this."

"We're leaving anyway," Gaston said cautiously. "So record everything, just in case we need to come back, but I'm not going to worry about it as long as it isn't trying to bite our buttocks off."

"Right you are."

The *Helena* was still climbing on her screen, turning into the wind now as they prepared to tack. Gaston quickly ordered the *Excalibur* to follow but slowed their speed to give the *Helena* a bit more space. That would give them some maneuvering room in case they really did need to cover the captured ship.

They got just a quarter through the turn when it all went to hell.

Fire Control Command, Alliance Redoubt

"Major, something's wrong."

Irwin leaned in, looking over the technician's shoulder. "What is it?"

"The *Helena*, she's turning off from her course. She was holding true to bring the *Caleb* into the middle of our firing zone until now."

"What's her new course?"

The tech shook his head. "Not stabilized yet, but she's climbing, heading for the top wind layer."

"What are they doing?" The major hesitated, not wanting to screw up their shot at the *Caleb* by misreading the situation.

The problem with that was, quite simply, the new course change was threatening to take their target farther from the ideal fire zone. The *Caleb Bar* was, of course, altering to follow the *Helena*, which was going to force his hand.

"Signal all batteries," he said, taking a deep breath. "Fire."

Alliance Transport *Helena Night*

Mira surged forward, eyes wide as she spotted the plasma trace filling the air ahead of them on the screens. A quick check showed the same on the sides, and she swore in realization.

"They put in an air-defense network out here," she said, glancing over to where the captain of the *Helena Night* was standing with her crew. "And you led us right into it. Nicely played, captain."

Mira didn't give the transport captain a chance to respond before turning her focus back to the situation at hand. There was too much to do at the moment to indulge anyone, particularly an adversary, in even a well-deserved opportunity to gloat.

"Are we being targeted?" she demanded, leaning in to try and determine as much herself.

"Not yet, skipper," Malcolm told her. "Either they don't know we took the *Helena*, or they want to take it back."

"Get me the *Excalibur*."

Free Corsair *Excalibur*

Mikael swore under his breath as he finally managed to get his leg up over the edge of the deck after several minutes of pulling himself up by the safety strap. He rested for a moment, hooking his arm around the rail, and took a couple of breaths. Hanging by that strap, tens of thousands of feet over the ground, had been the most harrowing moment of his life.

No wonder all the guys belowdecks SWEAR that you should never, ever, volunteer for anything, he thought as his breath slowly came back.

A sudden slap of force near him almost caused him to let go and fall again, but he kept his grip as he looked around for the source.

To his horror, Mik spotted *thousands* of plasma bolts filling the air all around him, many spattering off the armor of the *Excalibur*.

In the next few seconds, Mik learned two new things.

First, a *new* most harrowing experience could appear instantaneously. And second, he *could* lift his whole body weight in under a second.

With blaster fire sizzling off the armor all around him, Mik rolled clear of the rail and scrambled for the hatch. He was in such a hurry he forgot to unclip his line and was yanked back off his feet when the tether snapped taut, landing him flat on his back.

Still gasping to refill his empty lungs, Mik unclipped the line from his belt and crawled through the hatch, sealing it behind him.

I am NEVER volunteering for anything again.

*

Alarms blared from every direction on the command deck of the *Excalibur*, all of them competing for Gaston's attention.

The low-powered "civilian" carrier waves they'd been tracking were now neither low powered nor civilian. Instead the *Excalibur* had found itself in the middle of an air-defense kill box. Plasma trace was filling the air from all sides, splashing off their armor with a near constant sizzling sound.

He wasn't too worried about the lased plasma, not against the *Excalibur*'s armor at least, but Gaston doubted the enemy would stop at just that if they had already gone to the trouble of putting a heavy air-defense network out this far.

"Secure to quarters," he ordered. "Sound combat alerts to all decks. Haeve, can you find the guns targeting us?"

"They aren't hiding, Gas," said Stan Haeve, who was standing the tactical watch.

"Show them who they're screwing with," Gaston said firmly.

"You got it!"

"Gas! Skipper on the line!"

Gaston threw himself back into the command throne, keying open the communications link.

"Skipper, kinda busy here," he said tensely.

"I can tell." Mira's voice was a hell of a lot more relaxed, which Gaston thought was rather unfair given she was the one careening about on an unarmored transport in the middle of a fight. "Seems they don't want to drop us just yet, though. How are you holding?"

"So far, no problem," he said. "We can take this light stuff all day, you know that, but I expect they're just getting our range."

"That's my read too. Make them pay for anything they get, you hear me, Gas?"

Gaston glanced up as the deck below his feet shook from the *Excalibur*'s kinetic launchers opening fire and smiled slowly.

"Hear you, skipper. No problem."

"Good," Mira said. "We're going to get up into the top wind layer and tuck in tight behind our sails. Once we're clear, get my ship out of there."

"*Your* ship?" he asked humorously. "I built her, skipper."

"And I command her, so do what I say."

"Yes, ma'am."

Alliance Transport *Helena Night*

Mira eyed the instruments as they showed the *Helena*'s altitude climbing past fifty thousand feet, well on their way up to the top wind layer. They were out of range for most ground-based air defense, but that didn't put the *Helena* out of the box just yet.

"Watch for sails," she ordered. "They'll not rely on ground guns if they have any other option."

"Yes, ma'am," Malcolm said. "What about the *Excalibur*?"

"She's armed and armored—pity anyone who messes with her," Mira said. "We're the ones who need to worry. Even a stray burst could drop this heap, with us in it. So get us tucked up right behind our sails and make all of this a bad memory."

"You've got it, skipper."

Mira was tense, far more than she had been when boarding or facing personal combat. She was used to being able to apply her own skills and force to the situation, influence things in her favor. Now it just wasn't up to her—this one was all on Gaston and the *Excalibur*'s crew.

"Clear skies, friends," she said softly.

CHAPTER 8

Perrin District, Airfield

Matani threw up his shield arm, catching a lase blast and deflecting it off to the side as he dodged a gamma burst from another shooter, closing the distance as quickly as he could. The trick was keeping all the gamma burst gunners in his sights, because while his armor couldn't *entirely* ignore blasters, a burster would ruin his day in a hurry.

This was a dance, really, albeit a complicated one that was played for the highest of stakes, but he was a *very* good dancer.

They'd made a key mistake right from the start, and that was letting him so close to his quarry before they sprang the ambush. He tightened the range before any of them managed to get off a second shot, his Tor already swinging on a vicious upstroke that caught one of the gamma burst wielders under the jaw with enough force to powder bones and teeth.

Blood and bone spattered on his armor, but lattice-linked photons don't stain, so Matani paid it no mind. He went into a spin and dropped under a series of shots that certainly killed his target if the sudden blow to the head hadn't.

He let his Tor slip in his grip as he spun until he was holding it right by the tip and then slammed the hammerhead into the knees of the next-closest man. The audible crunch of bones crushing with the force seemed to drown out the sound of blasters and bursters firing, and the man was kicked off his feet and thrown into a spin in midair.

Matani rolled forward, choking up on his Tor as he did, and came up to his feet in the middle of another group. He jabbed the head of his Armati into one man's solar plexus, driving the wind from his lungs, then snapped the weapon up into the man's face when he pitched over in pain.

A blade slid out of the haft of the hammer Matani wielded, and he drove it back into the chest of a man about to shoot him in the back with a burster, twisting the weapon once before drawing it out and letting the man drop.

A whisper of movement caught his attention, causing Matani to twist and flip his Armati Tor overhand in a power strike to the source.

Metal clashed on metal as the impact was stopped halfway through the air, a glowing curved blade holding back the force with ease in the hand of the "assistant" to the baron.

"Cadreman Matani," she said seriously, nodding curtly.

"Cadrewoman Sens," he returned, his tone matching hers as he drew back his weapons and choked up his grip so he could match the speed he knew he was about to deal with. "It's been a while."

"It has," she said as she dropped her block guard and shifted to a casual pose that didn't fool him for a second. "I had hoped most of the Cadre would have the sense to stay out of this until it was resolved."

Matani laughed, a trace of bitterness in his tone. "I'd hoped none of the Cadre would be so eager to follow Corian into infamy. It seems we're both doomed to disappointment."

Julie Sens sneered at him. "You would have followed him to the depths of the abyss once yourself."

"Everywhere," Matani said, "except into dishonor."

"Honor!" she spat. "You damn blind fool. Don't you pretend that Scourwind knew anything about 'honor.'"

"My oath was to the empire, not to any alliance, and certainly not to Corian. Was yours worded differently?"

"You have no idea what's coming!" she snarled, her blade suddenly slashing up from where it had been waiting.

He saw the attack coming well ahead of her decision to act, however, her anger exposing her intent as clearly as the sun in the sky. He batted the strike away with the flat of his hammer, sweeping the haft in a low arc to take her in the abdomen.

Unfortunately, angry or not, she was still Cadre, and Sens jumped back after her strike missed, causing him to miss in turn.

Matani leapt out of the way, clearing range as he let out his grip on the hammer to gain more power. He flipped it underhand, bringing the weapon up behind his back in an overhead arc that slammed down into the dirt hard.

Julie leapt clear just as the force of his strike rebounded off the metal barrier dozens of feet below them and exploded up, showering her with dirt and debris as she landed in a roll that brought her in past his overextended weapon.

Matani twisted as the slim blade drove in for his gut, penetrating his armor as though it didn't exist and opening a light slash in his side. He ignored the flare of pain, lashing out with a foot that caught Sens in the jaw and drove her to the ground in a rolling spin away from him as he pulled his weapon back and swung it after her.

His Tor slammed into the ground three times, each hit just missing by inches as Sens curled away from him before she finally managed to roll to her feet and get her weapon back up to defense.

"You've gotten better," Matani admitted, feeling the blood running down his leg.

"You've lost a step."

Matani shrugged, loosening up muscles he hadn't used in far too long.

"Could be," he admitted. "I was supposed to be enjoying my retirement, until you and your great leader started this mess."

"You should have stayed retired."

"Someone made a mess that needed to be cleaned up. You young fools are inconsiderate like that."

"You know what he learned," she accused. "The empire was doing *nothing*! Someone had to do something."

Matani laughed bitterly. "What was Corian's 'secret' weapon in his little coup? Oh yes, the *Caleb Bar* . . . commissioned and built at the order of the *emperor*! All to appease Corian's *paranoia*, and without even any evidence! Please, tell me again that the empire was doing nothing!"

Sens flushed. "It wasn't enough—"

"So Corian *shattered* the empire! How does *that* serve his oath? Or yours?"

"That wasn't supposed to happen!"

Matani shook his head. "The last words of the despot . . . 'It wasn't supposed to turn out this way.'"

The pair stood across from one another, as if waiting for a signal to break the standoff.

The dull thud of the baron's skimmer firing sail projectors ended the silence.

*

Brennan pumped the foot pedals, fine-tuning his sails as he dropped his Naga out of the sky over the airfield and played the tension to make the nimble flyer sit right in place as he targeted the baron's skimmer.

The loudspeaker on the Naga crackled as he powered it up.

"Baron Vilhem, stand down and retract your sail projectors in the name of Her Majesty the Empress," he ordered. "If you refuse to comply, I will engage your skimmer."

He waited until the skimmer started to move before he laid in the target and leaned his Naga forward. He could see figures on the ground, most of them scattered and not moving, while a pair was fighting in a blur below. He recognized the Cadre armor on one and knew that Matani was still kicking at least, and so Brennan decided to keep his fire well clear of them.

The gauss guns he'd taken from the old reserve depot had been retooled and loaded by the Imperial Armory in the days since the battle where he'd crashed the Naga. They'd had to dig up a few retired machinists who'd not really caught up on lase systems, but they'd forgotten more about the older gauss guns than anyone else in the palace had ever known.

So when the prince dropped his thumb on the stud, the Naga just *erupted* with fire and vengeance, shaking him to the core as Brennan worried just a bit that the guns might tear his fighter apart right under him.

They didn't, however, with the craft somehow managing to hold itself together despite the force of thousands of rounds being ejected into the lower skimmer at several times the speed of sound.

The entire front end of the baron's skimmer *disintegrated* into shards under the barrage, along with the pitons for his two forward sails. The rear sails remained intact, but as they started to drag the ship around, it was clear that they had no control.

Brennan backed his craft off so as not to get tangled in their sails, a maneuver even trickier than holding position. He kept an eye on it, but knew that the vessel was going nowhere now and so shifted most of his attention to the pair still going at it below.

Whoever Matani was battling, she or he wasn't some random thug to be discounted. The occasional flash of light on metal from both fighters told him enough. Matani was in close combat with someone who was holding their own . . . and using an Armati or something close enough to make little difference.

His thumb itched as he flexed it near the firing stud, but he was too aware that his Naga and the old gauss guns he had packed it with were *not* precision weapons.

Come on, Matani . . . Don't get dead.

*

Metal flashed on metal as the pair exchanged strikes, blocking and counterstriking in the ticks between seconds. Matani was sweating, and he could feel the blood on his leg chilling and growing sticky, the slash in his side stiffening up.

He knew he had to finish it in a hurry or the fight would finish him. Cadrewoman Sens was too good to give up any advantage too, crazy as she might be.

The sudden buzzing like the sound of a million enraged insects screaming their fury caught them both by surprise, distracting them as the entire bow of the baron's skimmer just vanished into scrap in an instant.

Julie snapped her head around, briefly spotting the Naga where it was hovering, then glaring back at him. "Brought a friend, did we?"

"Like you have anywhere to stand on that issue," Matani said hoarsely. "I told you, the empress requested the presence of the baron, remember?"

She seethed, obviously considering her options as limited as they had to be.

The skimmer behind them was dragged a short distance before it killed its rear sails, people fleeing the craft as they pointed at the angry-looking Naga still drifting slowly around the airfield.

"Julie!" a voice called. "We have to escape!"

Matani glanced to one side, recognizing the baron then as the man stumbled from the wrecked skimmer. He kept his focus on his opponent, however, not overly concerned with a civilian noble who was obviously shaken up.

Not that he *blamed* the man, mind you.

Matani knew what was loaded on that Naga, and the damn thing gave him chills.

He tensed as Julie's body language changed, indicating that she'd made an important decision. Matani readied himself for the next round of their duel, bringing his Tor up to a defending position just as she shifted her weight and her right hand dropped to her hip.

The gamma burster cleared the holster before he recognized her intent, and while he was moving Matani realized he was going to be too late.

"Apologies, my baron," Julie said simply as she leveled the burster between the man's eyes. "It seems you won't be making your next appointment."

The gamma burster fired once, the blast of energy crossing the gap instantly, burning a path through the baron's skull and cooking brain matter.

Julie continued to move, however, twisting away as Matani's hammer slammed into her shoulder. Bones cracked and she had to bite back a scream of pain, but her hand flipped her Armati over to a reverse grip. She snapped the weapon back, driving the blade into and through Matani as his attack left an opening in his defense.

They stopped for a moment, Julie holding him up as his armor failed. She looked in his eyes and smiled.

"You did say that death was the only prior engagement that took priority over the empress," she said. "Seems you were right."

Julie retracted her blade and let Matani drop to the ground as she turned and looked for a moment at the hovering Naga before the craft suddenly moved toward her. A gust of wind crossed the field, and she simply turned away from the threat, ignoring it as she walked away.

*

Brennan sucked in a shocked breath as he watched Matani's armor fail and the tough old bastard drop to the ground. He leaned the Naga forward, dropping line as fast as he could, and hit the ground in a skid that brought him within a few dozen feet of his trainer as he killed the projectors and hit the retraction winch.

Heedless of the risk, Brennan grabbed a medical kit and leapt from the Naga before the lines had cleared, and rushed to where his teacher was lying.

He slid to a stop beside Matani, who was laughing painfully, much to Brennan's confusion.

"Hold on, you old bastard," Brennan told him, popping open the kit he'd grabbed.

"Stupid, stupid, stupid," Matani repeated, sounding like he had in the training room so often in the past.

Brennan pulled a sealer from the pack and tore open Matani's jacket and shirt, plastering the thick foam over the wound, then grabbing another one as he grimaced at the sight of the wound.

"This is going to hurt," he said, pushing the Cadreman over so he could administer the other sealer on the exit wound coming from his back.

When that was done, he let Matani roll gently back, surprised that the man hadn't done more than hiss in pain during the whole move.

"That will keep you from bleeding to death," he said, "but you're going to need real medical treatment in a hurry. Can you get to the Naga?"

Matani hissed further, but grabbed Brennan's arm and started to pull himself up. Brennan helped him as best he could, trying to keep his mentor from twisting or tearing himself up any more as they made their way back to the Naga. He got the Cadreman secured in the front seat, then clambered over him to the pilot's position and dropped the canopy.

"All right, hang on. There's an Imperial mobile base not far from here," Brennan said. "I'll get you there in just a few minutes."

The projector launchers thumped, and in seconds the sails had blossomed far above them. Brennan balanced the feel, making sure that they'd caught the wind, and then, as the Naga started to drag, hit the winches and pulled the skimmer into the sky.

"What the hell was that anyway, you old bastard?" Brennan asked once they were flying true. "You just *let* people knife you now?"

"Cadrewoman Sens," Matani rasped out.

"What?"

"That was Cadrewoman Sens," the old Cadreman repeated, painfully. "And no, I don't just let people knife me now, you smart-mouthed brat."

"Looked like it to me."

Matani growled unintelligibly before he spoke again. "I screwed up, OK, boy? I screwed that one up by the numbers."

"You have *no* idea how happy hearing you say that makes me."

"Shut up," Matani said, wincing as he held his hand over his wound. "When she went to gun down the baron, I tried to stop her—figured we needed him alive."

"Not at the cost of your life," Brennan told him.

"Intelligence is often worth more than a single life, kid. Don't forget that," Matani told him grimly. "When she killed him, we lost a big chance to figure out Corian's play here."

"Corian? He is behind this?"

"Never much doubt about that," Matani said with a laugh, then groaned in pain.

"Hold on, old man," Brennan called down. "I've got a carrier wave from the base. We'll be there soon."

"Don't baby me, brat." Matani chuckled painfully. "Corian must have recruited more deeply than we ever thought. The bastard is a ruthless one, but he believes in his backup plans. Sens was never one I would have expected to be following him."

"Who is she?" Brennan asked.

"She's from your brother's generation," Matani told him. "Skilled, but a cold one as well. A viper, that one, boy."

"Sounds like Corian's type," Brennan said flatly.

"She is, in a lot of ways," Matani admitted, "but she isn't the sort who'd buy into Corian's madness. Her coldness should have kept her from being blinded by his rhetoric. Corian must have proven something to her."

"Proven something? Proven what?"

"Before the coup, Corian was trying to convince the emperor . . . your father," Matani said weakly, "of a threat from the outside . . . from beyond the walls."

"Is that even possible?" Brennan asked, working the controls on automatic as he spotted the base in the distance.

"Most figured it wasn't, but your father trusted Corian enough to make some preparations," Matani confessed.

"Such as?"

"The *Caleb Bar*," Matani said. "She was designed to investigate beyond the walls, and if need be, call down the burning skies on any threats she found."

"Instead she was used to depose my father and kill my brother," Brennan said bitterly.

"Exactly," Matani said and coughed, wiping blood away from his lips.

The Naga dropped altitude fast, flashing Imperial colors as the base signaled a challenge. Brennan was in no mood for flight lanes or listening to the controller's instructions. Instead he dropped the Naga under the base's effective targeting level and then jammed hard on the sails.

The Naga skimmed the ground at just over a dozen feet, kicking up a swirl of dust in its wake as he ran it right down between the buildings, cornering hard as he reached the hospital and then landing roughly. They scraped to a halt on the Naga's runners, stopping right in front of the hospital building as armed men charged their position.

Brennan lowered the size of the sails then popped the canopy open, slamming it back to clear access to the cockpit.

"Medical!" he yelled. "I've got an injured Cadreman here!"

The next few moments were a confused rush as some men pointed blasters at them and others fought their way through to pull Matani out of the Naga and onto a rolling bed.

"Brennan!" the old Cadreman called hoarsely.

"What is it?" Brennan shook off a guard and went to him.

"I don't know if Corian is insane, a liar, or if he really found something out there," Matani rasped as he was rolled into the building with Brennan running alongside. "But insane or real, if he believes what he said, he will stop at *nothing* to address the threat. That's why he was so good . . . what he did for your father. He doesn't know how to quit—"

"That's it," a doctor cut in. "We need this man in surgery, and you cannot follow."

Brennan was held back as Matani was wheeled away.

*

Brennan took another hour or more before he got clear of the base bureaucracy. The guardsman captain was distinctly displeased with his unusual flight path, and the base commandant seemed torn between throwing him in the detention center or bowing to him.

Brennan settled for neither, instead getting his Naga cleared back to the base airfield and checking for any problems, basic maintenance and such, while he tried to work out his next move.

Corian has infiltrated us at every level. That's the only explanation for some of what has been going on, he realized. *What did he promise the baron? It must have been big, because the risk . . .*

None of what was happening made a lot of sense to him, but Brennan was becoming used to that. He felt like, for the moment, he could trust only his Naga and a man who was currently in surgery and in no shape to help.

He made his way to the communications bunker, bullying his way in past the guards now that the fact of his identity had made its way around the base.

"I need a link to the palace," he told the watch officer. "Secure."

"Of course." The man nodded, too fast really, but Brennan was used to the reaction.

Such deference (and fear) was one reason he preferred to fly, and thus Brennan had spent a lot of his youth in the air and in competitions. No one really knew who the pilot of the skimmer was until after a match, unless he was careless at the start. Regardless, pilots mostly didn't even care who you were—they cared about what you could do in the skies.

He took a seat in the cramped room, facing the projection display as it cycled through and linked him to the palace.

"Where can I direct you?" the pleasant face and voice said from the system.

"Lydia Scourwind."

"Identity?"

"Brennan Scourwind."

"Please wait."

Brennan was aware that his voice and face were being flashed over a dozen desks, checked for authenticity by both computer systems and actual people. Seconds later, the image changed and a projection of the Scourwind emblem appeared. Lydia came on barely a minute later.

"Brennan! Are you all right?"

"I'm fine, Lyd," he said. "Ran into some problems out here. The baron was . . ."

He stopped to consider what to say, wondering if the line was properly secure or if everyone in the palace could be trusted. He just couldn't be sure.

"The baron was assassinated by a former Cadrewoman," he said. "We're assuming she was working for Corian. Matani was seriously injured attempting to stop her. He's being treated at the mobile base out this way."

"Do you know what's going on out there?" she asked, concerned.

"No, but I'm going to find out."

"Brennan, don't do anything stupid . . ."

He rolled his eyes at her. "Like be dumb enough to sit on the throne?"

"I had no choice, and you know it." She pouted at him before shaking her head. "And yes, that's the exact sort of stupid thing I'm telling you not to do. I can send more investigators out there . . ."

"Do it," he said, "but I'm still going to follow this through. Something isn't right here, Lyd."

"At least wait until I can get someone there to help you," she said. "William can—"

"No!" Brennan cut her off. "Lyd, keep William close."

The last thing he wanted was for his sister to send away one of the few other people he *knew* he could trust. If Corian had agents in the palace, William's absence would be a godsend.

"Brennan?"

"Lyd, just trust me," he said. "Keep William close. You can trust him. I'll be fine."

"I *know* I can trust William, you idiot," Lydia snapped at him. "That's why I want to send him out to help you!"

"I'll be fine," Brennan said. "Just . . . be careful, OK, Lyd?"

"Isn't that supposed to be *my* line?" she asked, confused.

"Hey, I can be overprotective once in a while." Brennan forced a laugh, not wanting to fully show his unease. "I've got to go. I'll be in touch. Get the Intelligence people to copy me their report on the factory, would you? I want to know what the hell was going on there."

"Yeah." Lydia nodded slowly. "Yeah, I can do that."

"Good. Thanks. We'll talk soon, Lyd. Bye."

"Bye."

The projection went black, leaving Brennan to sit in silence for a moment before he got up and left the communications bunker. He still wasn't entirely sure what he was going to do, but the one thing he knew was that the trail started back at the Perrin District airfield.

CHAPTER 9

Free Corsair *Excalibur*

The black ship sailed through the shooting, plasma spattering off the armor from the heavy fire below. The lase blasts were near the very edge of their range, and against the heavy armor the *Excalibur* mounted, there was little threat from that quarter.

Even so, the *Excalibur* responded in kind with heavy kinetic strikes fired back from gauss launchers. Tracking back along the carrier beams that the air-defense systems were using to follow the *Excalibur*, the kinetic munitions slammed into the tracking stations with a vengeance, silencing the carrier waves one by one.

On the command deck of the black ship, Gaston was only slightly concerned with the lase blasts, as he was aware that the plasma that made them truly dangerous lost cohesion well below the *Excalibur*'s current altitude. It didn't make the crew "safe," exactly, and he certainly wouldn't want to be flying even a lightly armored ship through this firestorm, but his concerns remained elsewhere.

"Sail blossom!"

And there it is.

"Location?" Gaston demanded.

"Launching from the Redoubt, I believe," Paul said. "It's the right vector anyway. Range is a little less certain."

"Well, they're coming, then," Gaston said. "How is the *Helena* doing?"

"Still course correcting," Paul replied. "They're tacking through the winds and it's taking a little longer, but they'll clear the outer reach of the air-defense line in a few more minutes."

"Good," Gaston said. "They're still not being targeted?"

"All clear for them. We're attracting everything still."

"Well, damn. This might actually work," Gaston said, just a little surprised.

He was too used to things spiraling out of control.

"Sail blossom!"

Of course, there was still time for that.

"Looks like cruiser size, Gas," Paul said. "Multiple sails—at least six per ship. They're pulling hard for the upper layers."

"Good for them," Gaston said. "We'll worry about them once we're clear of this kill box, or at least once the *Helena* is clear of it."

Alliance Cruiser *Victorious*

"Ascending through the first wind layer, captain," the young officer at the helm announced.

"Thank you, ensign. Scanners, do we have them on our projections?" Captain Aleks Mandr asked, eyes straying in that direction.

"Yes, captain," his scanner tech said. "She's the *Caleb* all right. Nothing else would be this hard to track. She's under tractor drive at the moment, trailing the transport *Helena Night.*"

That last bit Aleks was well aware of. The Redoubt commander had given him an earful about how vital those components were to the Alliance efforts. They wanted that ship, or at least its cargo, back in one piece.

"The *Illustrious* has launched behind us," the scanner tech said, "and they're scrambling the *Indomitable*."

"Seems like overkill," Aleks's second-in-command, Hansen Jace, said from where he was monitoring ship's systems.

"Agreed, but that is the *Caleb*," Aleks said, "so I suppose they don't want to take any chances."

"The *Bar*, certainly, but it's run by a *commando*, not a properly trained captain and crew," Hansen said disdainfully.

"Imperial Cadre are not to be underestimated, even when operating out of their depth," Aleks told him. "They have a way of destroying expectations—and adversaries."

The *Victorious* cleared the second wind layer, pulling as hard as she could for the speed of the third layer, where the ship could tuck up in behind her sails. Unfortunately, the *Victorious* wouldn't be able to get a direct pull toward the *Caleb* that way, but then she didn't really need to.

Free Corsair *Excalibur*

"That's three," Paul announced.

"All cruisers?" Gaston asked, puzzled.

"Yes, sir."

Gaston shook his head, thinking. What an odd squadron to put in the air. Normally, a cruiser would have a pair of frigates as escorts. If you saw several cruisers flying together, they were generally part of a larger force, which didn't seem to be the case here.

"Inform me when they are approaching weapon range," he ordered. "In the meantime, keep taking out ground batteries ahead of us just in case they decide to fire on the *Helena*."

"Yes, sir."

Gaston took a seat at the central throne of the command center, accessed the communications system, and hailed the *Helena Night*.

Alliance Transport *Helena Night*

"Signal from the *Excalibur*, skipper. It's Gas," Malcolm said.

"Got it," Mira said, shifting the signal to the command station where she was sitting. "Hey, Gas. What have you got?"

"Three cruisers on our backsides," Gaston answered, "but they're still a ways out. Good news is, you should be crossing the air-defense line any moment now, so you're in the clear."

"Always nice to be clear." Mira smiled. "We'll tuck in behind our sails and bolt for the border. If the cruisers get too close, take the *Excalibur* up and out of the atmosphere. We're not here to fight."

"And I'm no fighter, so you can count on that," Gaston told her. "We'll delay them enough to give you the lead you need, but watch out for ships trying to get ahead of you. They probably called for support."

Mira nodded. "Likely. We've got this one in the bag. Take care of my ship."

"Your ship, your ship. I'm the one who keeps her flying."

"Keep telling yourself that, Gas; maybe you'll come to believe it one day." Mira grinned. "*Helena* clear."

"*Excalibur* out."

Mira looked over the prize crew, who were split between manning the consoles and guarding the former crew.

"We're going to need to lock them up," she told Malcolm. "See if there's anywhere they can be secured until we can offload them."

"You got it, skipper."

She looked over to the former crew of the *Helena*. "No offense intended, of course. You did an excellent job, which is all the more reason why I can't have you running around loose. We'll drop you off as soon as we clear Alliance skies."

Free Corsair *Excalibur*

"We've eliminated the air-defense scanning stations, sir," Paul announced.

Gaston glanced at the screens and saw that the density of fire had dropped off, with the shooting becoming a lot more haphazard.

"Excellent. If we can locate any of the gun emplacements, drop kinetic rounds on them too," he ordered.

Kinetic rounds were cheap—one hell of a lot cheaper than a ship or even a gun emplacement, and any time Gaston could do Corian a bad turn, he figured it was worth it.

"Yes, sir."

Gaston's interest was mostly leveled at the now-accelerating stern of the *Helena Night*. The skipper had done what she intended, tucking the transport up behind its sails deep in the top wind layer, and was now bolting clear on a least-time course for the Empire–Alliance border.

The *Helena* wasn't the fastest hull in the empire, but with the lead she was building, the pursuing ships shouldn't be a threat to her. That just left evading Alliance intercept attempts downwind, but that would be up to the skipper.

He turned his attention to the three cruisers that were building acceleration of their own, angled a little off a direct course toward the *Excalibur* or the *Helena*, but that was because they were tacking to the wind and would come about shortly, he expected.

Gaston was unprepared for Paul's shout that started with a vile epithet. The engineer snapped around and stared at the man in honest surprise. Granted, Paul was hardly the most distinguished of gentlemen, but while he was known to swear like any navy man, he generally kept it off the command deck.

"What is it?" Gaston demanded.

"Sails just went out on all three cruisers, sir. They're running tractor drives."

Gaston felt his face pale and had to suppress the urge to swear one or two vile oaths of his own just then. The cruisers had used the sails to get up to speed, as they often did on the *Excalibur*, and then engaged their quantum-tractor drive to build from there.

"Recalculate intercept equations," Gaston ordered. "Can they catch the *Helena* before she reaches the border?"

It didn't take long to figure that out.

"You bet they can, Gas. If they accelerate like we can, they'll nail the skipper a couple hundred miles short of the Imperial border," Paul said grimly.

This time he did swear, but Gaston kept his tone down so that no one heard him. This wasn't the sort of situation he was supposed to be dealing with; this was the skipper's turf. The *Excalibur* had already built enough speed to outrun the cruisers, that was clear. The *Helena*, however, would be a fat bird for the plucking if he left them hanging out in the wind.

Abruptly Gaston realized that everyone was staring at him, waiting for a decision.

Crap.

"All right," he said. "Secure the kinetic launchers. I want all crews on our chase guns."

"Yes, sir!" Haeve answered, shifting to deliver the orders.

Gaston grabbed onto a nearby console. "This is no joke—we have to assume that those ships are armed at least as well as we are. Secure every nonessential system and tell everyone to lock down and hang on . . ." He then turned to the helm. "Mitch, bring us around."

The helmsman swallowed, but nodded.

"You got it . . . skipper."

"Only one skipper on this boat, Mitch. Call me Gas."

*

The *Excalibur* came about as tight as the ship could, running at that speed. The tractor drive allowed for extremely tight precision maneuvers at lower speeds, but multiple factors came into play as velocity increased. For one, the force of the turns could become difficult on the crew, though that could be partially compensated for by banking into a turn.

More serious was that fact that the quantum rail wasn't a perfect lock, and enough force *could* dislodge the ship from the rail. If that happened the *Excalibur* would fly free and likely be thrown into an uncontrolled spin that would prevent establishing a new rail. They'd have right up until the ship plowed into the ground to figure out how to stabilize themselves enough to solve that issue.

Gaston would prefer to avoid that situation.

So the crew came about on a wide arc, using the extra time to build more speed and arrange their intercept vector to their best advantage.

Alliance Cruiser *Victorious*

"They're splitting up, captain."

Aleks grimaced. That was their worst-case scenario. Now he had to decide between chasing down the stolen cargo or taking a shot at the *Caleb Bar*.

Unfortunately, it wasn't really a decision. The *Bar* could evade them easily since the ship had already built acceleration, and it wasn't like she was under Imperial control. Sooner or later Delsol would foul up and the alliance would nail her, and her crew, to the hull of the black ship.

"Stay on the *Helena*," he ordered, "but get a vector on the *Caleb* and put out a warning to every Alliance ship and base in that direction."

"Yes, sir." The scanner and communications stations responded almost as one.

"Hansen, what's our intercept on the *Helena*?" Aleks asked his second.

"They have a lead on us, but we're already building speed," Hansen said. "The numbers are a little uncertain because we don't know how she'll handle under their prize crew, or exactly what load they have . . . For whatever reason, that's classified intelligence . . ."

Aleks winced, as that was the sort of information that would be rather useful for them.

"Still," Hansen said, "we'll have them within a hundred, hundred and fifty miles of the border, worst case."

"Good," Aleks said, "though I could wish for a bit more room for error. We'll be moving pretty damn fast by that point, and we want that ship . . . or at least its cargo, intact."

"Not many options," Hansen admitted, "only two really."

Aleks nodded, grimacing. Neither of them were palatable options, at least not in his opinion.

They could try to board the ship, but that would be highly dangerous. For one, the Helena was running high in the top wind layer, which meant they'd be right on the edge of control the whole time. Not a stable platform to deploy men onto, to say the very least. The other option was worse, unfortunately.

"It'll have to be cables," he said as Hansen flinched.

Snagging a smaller ship with cables was possible. In fact, it was a required ship-handling maneuver required for earning a master's certificate, which Aleks had. However, doing so against a resisting ship the size of the *Helena* wouldn't even be possible without the tractor drives his squadron used.

Too bad no one had tried the maneuver yet; at least then he might know what not to do.

"Oh well, always a first time, I suppose," Aleks said lightly. "Let's make history."

"You said it, captain." Hansen laughed.

They were just starting to review the procedure when the scanner tech yelped, drawing their attention.

"What is it?" Aleks demanded.

"It's the *Caleb*, captain . . . she's not running."

Free Corsair *Excalibur*

Curving in on a smooth intercept course, the *Excalibur* was driving nose into the flanks of the three Alliance cruisers. Gaston was well aware that such a move was not considered to be a tactically advantageous position for an attacking ship to take.

His own forward guns were limited compared to the broadsides mounted on the *Excalibur*, and he was willing to bet the same was true of the opposing cruisers. That was why driving bow first into the enemy was an amateur maneuver in pretty much every strategy manual ever written.

Gaston was the man who *designed* the *Excalibur*, however, and he knew what she could take better than any man alive.

"Stand by forward guns. Don't fire until we've got range on them," he ordered, eyes on the signals that depicted the enemy ships ahead of them.

"Yes, sir. Standing by forward guns," Haeve told him. "They'll be waiting."

"Get our broadsides ready too," he ordered. "I don't care where you find the men. I want those guns prepared to fire."

"Both sides?"

Gaston nodded. "Both."

"I'll see it done," Haeve confirmed, bending to the task as he spoke through his comm link.

"Mitch, just hold us steady, don't sweat the fire," Gaston said, putting a hand on the helmsman's shoulder. "We can take a beating."

"If we can, Gas, can't they?" Mitch asked, nervous.

"Maybe, but I have my doubts. The armor on this thing took *years* to manufacture," Gaston said, "We could do it faster today, sure, but it still isn't easy. And sure as hell isn't cheap, so I doubt Corian could have gotten three fully armored Bar-class cruisers into the skies this fast."

Mitch took a deep breath. "If you say so."

Ah, such faith. He didn't want anyone to get nervous, but honestly, he didn't know *what* Corian could have managed. The man had done things that no one should have been able to, so maybe he had found a way to scrape up and then smelt enough metal to armor his cruisers.

Gaston really hoped not, though. That would be bad news all around.

＊

Mik was still trying to push the chill from his bones when a big meaty hand grabbed him by the shoulders and dragged him to his feet.

"Hey, what the—"

"No time, kid. We need all hands. Come on," the man, a guy named Claeton, told him. "You're gonna get a crash course on loading the cannons on this beast."

Mik felt his stomach twist and grimaced. "Could we not use the word 'crash,' please?"

Claeton's laughter boomed as the pair hurried through the corridors to the starboard magazines. "Sure, kid, whatever you say."

The *Excalibur* had large magazines of lasing shells, designed to be moved into the ship's cannons by autoloading mechanisms that handled most of the work. The system still needed a hand on-site, however, to ensure that rounds were aligned before they were rammed into the breech. So Mik found himself quickly instructed on how to check shell alignment before hitting the controls that rammed the lasing round in.

The task was easy enough, thankfully, though he shuddered to imagine what would happen to anyone near a magazine that took a lase strike. While lasing material didn't explode, it was quite reactive for obvious reasons. The thought was honestly terrifying.

Not as much as going back *outside*, of course, but still terrifying.

Alliance Cruiser *Victorious*

"They're charging right into our guns," Aleks said in utter shock.

He honestly couldn't believe it. There was no sane universe in which someone voluntarily charged into the guns of three cruisers while exposing only a fraction of his own guns to a reasonable firing position.

"I told you, sir, she may be hot shit on the ground, but she's no ship captain." Hansen still shook his head, surprised despite his words.

"Signal the squadron," Aleks ordered. "Once they're in range . . . light them up."

"With pleasure, sir," Hansen replied before he turned to start issuing orders.

Aleks supposed he was about to find out just how much the stories of the *Caleb Bar* compared to the truth. Ever since the general had taken the capital, and more importantly the palace, in just a few hours with the black ship, the stories of the *Caleb* had grown more and more beyond the realm of reality. In truth, however, few people aside from the general and a few of his closest advisers had any real concept of what the *Caleb Bar* could do.

Both the empire and the alliance considered the ship to be among the most secret things ever produced.

The fact that it was in the hands of a rogue Cadrewoman who'd established a name for herself as a *pirate* . . . that just made the situation all the more laughable.

"The *Bar* is in our range," Hansen told him. "All broadside armaments are ready."

"I already issued my orders on this, commander," Aleks said stonily. "Do not make me repeat them."

"Yes, sir!" Hansen responded before turning. "All guns! Open fire!"

The intermittent whine-crack of the heavy cannons lasing was a distant but distinct and recognizable sound, even in the enclosed and armored command deck.

*

The three ships of the Alliance squadron fired on the same signal, filling the thin air of the upper atmosphere with lased-plasma fire, all converging on the approaching black ship.

The *Excalibur* met the fire head-on, the angled plates of the big vessel's armor shrugging off the first rounds with contemptuous ease. But as the range dropped, the shots began to hit harder with every passing second.

Free Corsair *Excalibur*

"Hold fire," Gaston ordered. "At this range, they're just wasting munitions. Leave that to the enemy."

The tension was climbing on the command deck and, he assumed, through the entire ship. This wasn't like the air-defense network they'd dealt with earlier. Then they had been climbing *out* of the weapon's optimal range, and the underside of the *Excalibur* was pretty well armored specifically to counter that sort of threat.

Now, however, they were charging *into* the guns of three cruisers bound and determined to drop them out of the eternal sky. Everyone could hear the incoming fire increase, both in density and power, as they began to hammer the armor steadily.

"Gas." Paul frowned. "I'm seeing heat increases across our front plates. I didn't even know those gauges *worked*."

"That's because we've never been shot at," Gaston scoffed. "They're absorbing the heat from the lased plasma. If they spike into the red, then we're in trouble."

"Climbing through yellow," Paul admitted. "High yellow now."

"Haeve"—Gaston abruptly shifted his focus to the tactical station—"target the center ship, all guns."

"All guns, yes, sir," Haeve responded, making a few notations on his instruments before looking up. "We're set."

"Fire all forward cannons."

Gaston leaned back, eyes on the projections. Now was the moment of truth when he would learn just how well Corian had managed to copy Gas's masterpiece.

Alliance Cruiser *Victorious*

Aleks's eyes widened marginally as he saw the density of fire packed into the oncoming ship's forward guns.

"Burning skies, sir," Hansen mumbled. "They must have packed the guns right on top of one another. They'll overheat in seconds."

Aleks nodded absently. That was certainly the conventional wisdom on the subject, but for now there was something else that held his attention. "They're focusing on the *Illustrious*."

The lased plasma slammed into the *Illustrious*, hammering the cruiser's armor harder than he would have expected, but for the moment the shielding was holding.

"They're holding that rate of fire longer than I expected already," Aleks said and grimaced. "I don't know how long the *Illustrious*'s armor can take that punishment."

"I don't know long any of us could," Hansen hissed. "The plates on these things aren't exactly top quality."

"A problem the *Caleb* over there doesn't have to deal with, I'll bet," Aleks said, just a trace of bitterness reaching his voice.

"No bet," Hansen said.

"Pity," Aleks said before returning his attention to the situation.

The *Excalibur* was a dangerous foe, of that there was no question, but no ship was invulnerable. Aleks was certain that they could take down even as formidable a ship as this.

"Focus our fire," he ordered. "Try to burn through that armor of theirs."

"Yes, sir."

*

The three Alliance ships took a moment to synchronize their fire, focusing a stream of bursts onto the *Excalibur*'s forward plates with tighter precision as the return fire continued to hammer into the *Illustrious*. In those moments, the fight boiled down to a question of who could take a beating better than the other and, in an explosion of light and fury, the *Illustrious* lost.

A blinding flash masked the ships for an instant, and then smoke began to roil from the hole burned through the side of the cruiser.

The *Illustrious* held its course and altitude, but the big ship was clearly hurting.

While the *Excalibur* hadn't taken a similar blow yet, the scene on her command deck was far from relaxed.

Free Corsair *Excalibur*

"We've got high orange on those plates, Gas." Paul swore. "We're going to hit red in seconds at this rate!"

"We're almost through the gauntlet! Clear the deck in that area," Gaston ordered, turning afterward to Haeve. "Keep hammering the middle ship!"

"Yes, sir!" Paul and Haeve both responded quickly.

Gas wiped his forehead, moving over behind Mitch. "Try to rock our course, get those plates out of the line of fire—but whatever you do, don't rock us off the quantum rail."

The helmsman swallowed. "All right."

The *Excalibur* rolled a little starboard as the pilot started his work, making getting back across command a little harder for Gaston, as he was unused to the deck shifting underfoot. When the deck started rolling back the other way, he felt the beginnings of something down in his guts that he really didn't think he was going to enjoy.

The armor plates were now holding in high orange, however, instead of climbing into the red, so he'd deal with his personal issues and count himself lucky for as long as that held. The heat sinks that helped keep the armor from burning through from the enemy attack could dissipate energy only so quickly, and when they reached that limit, the plates would fail critically just like the inferior ones on the Alliance cruiser had.

As fast as the *Excalibur* was going, however, this engagement was going to last only *seconds*, and Gaston knew that, unlike the commanders of the Alliance cruisers. So he was willing to take a few hits if it set him up to end things the way he wanted.

Alliance Cruiser *Victorious*

Aleks swore as the *Caleb* began a rolling dance that was playing havoc with their aim, creating more difficulty in putting a hole in the onrushing ship. He could see how fast the *Caleb* was moving and knew that the *Victorious* would not get a chance, barring a miracle, to drop her on this pass. But he would like to at least see that bastard of a ship *smoke* a little.

"Signal the squadron," he ordered. "Turn in as she passes. I want to keep our side batteries on that bastard the whole pass. Don't lose track of each other. By the burning skies, you better not! If we shoot each other in this maneuver or, worse, ram one another, so help me . . ."

Nervous chuckles came from his gunners' station and the helm, but he ignored them as he considered the warning issued.

Normally they'd not be operating this close to one another; sail projectors required a certain . . . space to operate safely. The last thing one wanted to do was tangle in someone else's sails, be they friend or foe. If that happened, both ships were going down, likely as hard as possible.

The quantum-tractor drive allowed for much closer maneuvers, but with that advantage came new risks that ship handlers were only just now attempting to quantify and determine how to avoid.

"Sir, the *Illustrious* reports heavy damage," Aleks's communications officer said with a grimace. "They've lost power on their drives. The alignment systems are holding but . . ."

Aleks winced. "Tell them to drop out here. If they lose alignment and have to deploy sails this close to us . . ."

The rest really didn't need to be told. The potential for mayhem was patently obvious.

"Yes, sir," the comm officer said, turning to his console. A moment later he turned back. "*Illustrious* acknowledges. They're dropping away."

Relieved, Aleks turned his focus back to the battle at hand.

It seems that the rumors about the Caleb *were not so farfetched as I had believed. All that power, in the hands of a damned pirate.*

"Redirect all guns; adjust for that damned wobble," he ordered, picking out a spot on the onrushing ship and sending it to his gunners. "Hit here. If they have the same configuration we do, that's one of their lasing magazines."

Free Corsair *Excalibur*

"She's dropping away, sir!"

Paul's report sent a cheer through the crew who heard it, and a certain thrill of satisfaction to Gaston's bones as he saw the middle ship begin losing altitude.

The descent was clearly controlled, but it was enough. If the bogey couldn't keep altitude now, then the odds of it chasing after the *Helena* were slim to none. That meant one-third of his mission was accomplished, two-thirds left to go.

"Ah, damn it." Paul's next announcement wasn't so enthusiastic.

"What is it?"

"They're changing targets, aiming for our side plates," Paul said. "Those are heating up *fast*, sir. A lot faster than the forward plates."

"That's because they're hitting them more directly, less deflection," Gaston said, annoyed. "It's only going to get worse as we close the angle on them. Mitch, try to rock us away from that!"

"I'm trying, but they're adjusting, sir. I don't think I can."

"All right, blow through," Gaston ordered. "Stand by, broadside guns!"

"Guns standing by!" Haeve confirmed.

*

"That's good work, kid," Claeton said as they finished loading the lasing shells into the cannons and ensured the seals were solid.

"Thanks," Mik said, wiping sweat from his brow.

The work was very different from most things that went on around the *Excalibur*. Not as heavy as some but heavier than most, and the small areas they had to work in seemed to heat up quickly.

"I've got it from here, kid," Claeton said. "Go see if any of the other stations need a hand."

"All right," Mik said, stepping out.

"Don't forget to seal the hatch!"

"I got it!" Mik swung the heavy metal hatch shut and pulled the locking wheel tightly.

Alliance Cruiser *Victorious*

"Captain, they've entered range of our burster cannons."

"Focus on the plate we've been firing at," Aleks ordered, "and fire at will."

"Yes, sir!"

The gamma burster cannons required immensely more power than the lasing cannons, mostly because they tapped the *Victorious*'s reactor for power rather than being entirely self-contained like the cannons, but he was hoping that the system would be able to penetrate the *Excalibur*'s armor.

The burst of fire from the cannons actually caused the lights around him to dim as they fired, making Aleks glance around nervously for fear that the power drain would affect the tractor drive despite all the assurances he'd received on the subject. They didn't drop out of the sky, however, so apparently the experts were right.

"Hit! Hit! Look at that blow!"

Aleks looked up sharply as his gunner started screaming and saw the smoke streaming from the *Excalibur* as she continued her charge across the sky apace.

"Good!" he said. "Do it again!"

"Charging burster cannon, sir. It'll be a little while . . ."

Free Corsair *Excalibur*

Mik picked himself off the ground, vision blurring slightly from where he'd hit the wall, wondering what the hell had just happened. He stumbled around in circles for a moment, finally planting a hand on the wall and looking around him.

"What the . . . ?" he mumbled, blinking furiously.

Smoke was pouring into the corridor from the hatch he'd just sealed a moment earlier, the portal having buckled outward as if struck by some immensely powerful force.

Mik's eyes widened. "Claeton!"

He ran back, grabbed the hatch, and twisted the handle only to have his flesh sizzle and the pain force him back. He grabbed the loading gloves he'd been using from his belt, sliding them on, and tried again. The hatch gave slowly, but it gave, and he yanked it open.

A howl of wind roared passed him, sucking smoke out and through a massive hole he could see in the magazine's wall.

"Oh m-my . . . ," Mik stammered out, stunned by the destruction he was seeing.

The magazine was a smoldering mess, and at a glance, Mik figured that the only reason there weren't open flames was because the thin air had put them out. The wind was tearing through the compartment, biting cold gnawing at his exposed flesh. Mik felt his clothing buffeting around him as he looked for any sign of his friend.

"Claeton! Where are you?" he called, casting around.

The room, however, was empty of anything but destruction.

*

"What the hell was that?" Gaston demanded, pale and shaking from the shock. "Were we in the red anywhere?"

"No, sir. We were climbing fast, but nowhere near red," Paul told him.

Gaston looked around, trying to figure out the explosion, but the situation was running too quickly for him to do so at the moment.

"All right, we're about to pass right between then," he said. "I want the broadsides firing as soon as they're in our sights!"

"Yes, sir," Haeve said. "Passing in just a few seconds . . . guns firing . . . now!"

The port broadsides opened up on command with the familiar whine-crack of the rounds lasing, but Haeve paled. "Sir, starboard cannons are *not* firing!"

"Get me Fire Control on the starboard side! Now!"

*

Mik was still looking for any sign of Claeton, desperately, and losing hope with each passing second, when he heard a crackling voice through the chill air and destruction.

"Fire Control . . . starboard Fire Control . . . ," the voice repeated, growing more insistent. "Is there anyone down there?"

Mik scrambled over warped metal and debris, grabbing the comm from where it was hanging. "I'm here! We need help down here. Something blew out the magazine!"

"We'll send someone down. Listen, can you get the loader working?" The voice . . . Mik thought it was Gaston, but it was hard to tell in the thin air and howling wind.

"The loader? This place is blown to the burning skies!"

"The loader is built tough, and is mostly in the next section. Can you get it working?" The voice pressed. "We *need* the guns on that side!"

Mik cast about and found that the large heavy machinery of the loading mechanism did, in fact, look intact.

"I . . . I think so, but there's nothing here to load it with . . ." He trailed off.

"Check the next magazine after you clear the system. It should be loaded still, and we *need* those guns. Go!"

Mik went.

He was surprised to find the loader *was* still intact, but the breech had been jammed open. He reached in and yanked the half-destroyed shell clear, then cycled the system and hit the switch Claeton had told him put everything into action.

*

"Starboard guns are back!"

"Fire." Gaston leaned in. "Fire everything."

The *Excalibur* actually rocked with the force of the broadsides ejecting lased plasma into the atmosphere.

Alliance Cruiser *Victorious*

"The *Indomitable* is under heavy fire!" the scanner tech shouted. "She's going down!"

Aleks barely acknowledged the statement. He could see that. The *Caleb Bar* had opened up with her entire port broadside just as she passed between the two Alliance vessels, and the sheer density of fire was terrifying.

"She has to have three times the guns we do. How did they pack them all in?" Hansen murmured.

"I'm just happy that their port batteries seem to have been damaged by our strike," Aleks said before raising his voice. "Keep firing! How long until the burster cannon is charged?"

"Thirty seconds, sir!" The tactical officer sounded eager.

Aleks didn't blame him. That cannon was the one thing they had that was putting a real, visible hurt on the enemy in this fight. They were hammering the *Caleb* with enough lase cannon fire to put down ten other ships he could imagine, but the damn vessel just kept taking the onslaught with ease.

"Charged!"

Aleks was leaning forward as the tactical officer called out, his own order following right on the heel of the word.

"Fire!"

The gamma burster fired, dimming the power around him, but his exultation turned to shock and horror as the entire starboard broadside of the *Excalibur* erupted right back.

CHAPTER 10

Perrin District, Airfield

Damn, those gauss rounds tear things apart.

Brennan grimaced as he picked his way through the mess he'd made of the baron's skimmer. It had been a nice ship, once upon a time—a real luxury skimmer, from the looks of things. It was larger than one would expect for the crew it ran, and most of the extra space seemed dedicated to the luxury touches someone like the baron would demand.

The young Cadreman winced at the wasted space and weight dedicated to the least practical of touches. Things like a rather large hot tub at the back of what should have been the command deck just made him feel like he'd executed a mercy killing on the poor skimmer.

Those sentiments ended abruptly as he dug deeper into the lower decks and rear of the craft, which, thankfully, had been entirely undamaged in his attack.

The cargo hold was larger than he'd expected as well, making Brennan wonder just how small the crew quarters were going to be when he got around to them. But it was what he found in the cargo hold that caught him up.

There were raw ingots lining the deck, some spilled off their pallets, but most still wrapped and secure. He grabbed one up and was surprised by the weight. The metal was so heavy it really could only be one thing.

Imperanium. He looked around. *There's a fortune here. Where in the burning skies did the baron find this much raw imperanium?*

Imperanium was considered a strategic asset of the empire, and thus it was *illegal* for any private group to own any. It was one of the rarest materials in the known world and the key to building military-grade armor like that on the *Caleb Bar.*

The pallets he was looking at had to constitute high treason on the part of the baron.

"Baron, you are so lucky that bitch put a gamma burst between your eyes," he said aloud, shaking his head.

He withdrew from the cargo area and got out to where he could grab a local signal for the Imperial network. Calling in the Imperial forces to take custody of the skimmer, rather than leaving it to the local constables, was his priority.

While he was waiting in the command center, Brennan located the navigation console and yanked the logic boards.

When the Imperial skimmer landed, the Marines found Brennan sitting idly on the edge of the wrecked craft with his personal computer wired into the baron's logic boards. He was whistling to himself as he pulled course and telemetry data out of the memory of the boards, not even bothering to look up until the centurion called up to him.

"Cadreman Scourwind?"

Brennan glanced up from his work and down at the Marine centurion who was standing there with a squad behind him. "You dispatched from the base?"

"We got your call, yes. What's the emergency?" Apollon, the centurion, asked, looking over the wreck. "This should be a local cleanup job, shouldn't it?"

"This was the local baron's skimmer," Brennan said as he hopped down. "I prevented it from taking off earlier and just got a chance to look through what the baron was transporting."

"And?" the centurion asked as respectfully as he could manage despite not seeing what his squad was doing here.

"And it's carrying what looks like a year's production worth of raw imperanium," Brennan said flatly. "No chance I'm leaving that to be scavenged by the locals."

"It's carrying *what*?" The centurion's relaxed, slightly annoyed posture vanished as he stared at the wrecked skimmer.

"I think you heard me, centurion," Brennan said. "So I'm charging you with delivering this back to the capital. Do *not* let it out of your sight, do you get me, marine?"

"Sir! Yes, sir." The centurion stiffened, along with his squad.

"Good." Brennan handed him a data plaque. "Here are your orders, in my name. I don't care what ranks you have to deal with, if you show them these orders and they still try to take this from you before you deliver it to the capital . . . shoot them. Ideally somewhere nonfatal so they can be questioned, but I'll take the heat either way."

The centurion hesitated, a hand on the plaque. "Not complaining, sir, but do you really think that might be necessary?"

"The sector baron was hoarding a year's production of imperanium. The local factory was *losing* critical war materials to the other side," Brennan said, noting the Marines practically vibrating in clear outrage. "I'm not taking chances on this."

"Yes, sir . . . but, why are you trusting us?"

Brennan sighed, looking up into the sky where one of the Great Islands was approaching. Nanna's, he thought, though he wasn't sure of the time of day anymore.

"Centurion, if I can't trust the Imperial Marines . . . we've already lost this war."

The centurion saluted, accepting the orders. "You have my pledge, Cadreman."

"Thank you," Brennan said sincerely. "I'll leave you to it then."

"Where are you going, sir?"

"I still have traitors to track down," Brennan said stonily as he made his way back to his Naga.

The Marines watched the old combat skimmer launch sails and then lift into the skies, pulling hard for altitude, before they turned back to the job they'd been given.

"All right, lads," the centurion said. "Drake, you and Vaquen, you two are on guard duty. No one not in a Marine tactical uniform comes near this skimmer without my say-so."

The two young but scarred and muscled Marines nodded, taking up positions where they could keep an eye on the field.

"Pax, we're going to need secure transport," he said to another man. "Call it in; use the young royal's authority. I want our own skimmer out here, Marine pilot. See if Irons is available; I want her on this. Make sure she checks out something heavy enough to handle this crap."

"Got it, chief," Pax said, unslinging his communications pack. "I'll have it here in a jiff."

The heavyset centurion nodded absently, looking the situation over as his squad second stepped up to his side.

"This is gauss damage, isn't it, Biehn?" he said idly, eyeing the shredded metal that had once been the prow of a luxury skimmer.

"That it is, chief," Don Biehn said. "Didn't hold back much either."

"Should never have stopped using those things," the centurion said with a slow smile. "Lase blasters are fine and dandy, but if you want real kick you unload a gauss cannon on some poor sap."

Dan nodded, but didn't say anything, as he figured his boss was working up to something.

"So that was the next in line for the throne," the centurion said after a moment. "What do you think?"

Dan paused for a moment. "If his sister has half the fight he's showing, I'd say that Corian screwed up, and maybe we've got a good shot at this after all."

*

Brennan trimmed the sails of his Naga, tucking the small fighter in close behind them as he rode the middle wind layer. He'd grabbed enough navigational data from the baron's skimmer to figure out where it had been recently, but unfortunately, not where he was planning on running to when he had been intercepted.

Most of the data points were what might be expected. The Imperial capital, the barony's own capital, a few hot spots within the barony. One, however, stood out enough that Brennan wanted to have a look.

There didn't seem to be many good and innocent reasons for the baron to take his luxury skimmer out to the border lines of Alliance-controlled territory when there was nothing of interest in the region.

So Brennan was heading there now, hoping to find another clue as to what in the burning skies was going on in this district and what, exactly, it had to do with Corian.

He knew that bastard was behind this somehow, and the loss of critical military parts and the near loss of a fortune in imperanium was more than enough to motivate most people. But Brennan's take on Corian was that the man didn't move a muscle if it wasn't linked to a larger plan. The parts were critical to the empire, certainly, but their loss wouldn't cripple anything . . . The imperanium was something else, yet even that was going to be a bonus find rather than a potential loss. No one had *known* such reserves existed, so they hadn't entered into anyone's calculations.

Brennan supposed that either or both were enough . . . but he just couldn't shake the feeling that there was something more going on.

He just had to figure out what that was before Corian managed to drop another surprise on them.

Imperial Palace

William Everett found himself rather confused by his liege's actions of late.

The Lady Scourwind, empress of the Scourwind empire, had never been the sort to invite too much of a security presence. Not before she had taken the throne, and not since, despite the clear and present dangers the empire was facing.

For some reason, however, she had taken to requesting his presence in his formal duties as her head of security instead of merely as an adviser.

Such an act was an improvement to his eye, but he couldn't help but be curious as to the reason behind the change.

At the moment, the empress was going over priority reports that detailed the strategic situation between the empire and the upstart alliance Corian had managed to pull together. The fact that the general had managed to suborn enough people and resources to actually hold off the empire was a stunning achievement, though William supposed he shouldn't be as shocked as he was.

That *was* the job they gave Corian when they sent him among the kingdoms, after all.

"William . . ." Lydia Scourwind's voice was quiet, but she had her father's tone hidden in it, a tone that commanded attention if nothing else.

"Yes, Your Majesty?"

"We have a report from Brennan," she said. "It just came through."

William smiled. "And how is he handling Matani?"

"Matani Fenn has been critically injured and is being treated at a base hospital," she said darkly. "I thought you knew?"

"No, I hadn't been briefed. What happened?"

"Baron Vilhem was apparently committing treason, with the help of one . . ." Lydia frowned and reexamined the report. ". . . Julie Sens."

"Cadrewoman Sens?" William blinked, alarmed. "That is bad."

"Apparently," Lydia said dryly. "However, Brennan has elected to continue on his own. He has sent a . . . gift back, in the company of Marines."

William barked out a sharp laugh. "That must be some gift. What is it?"

"He didn't say; Brennan believes we have a security problem."

"If Julie Sens and the baron sided with Corian, I can understand that point of view," William said, frowning thoughtfully before his eyes widened. "That's why you've asked me to supervise your security more."

Lydia returned to her reports, not bothering to comment.

William let the matter go. He wasn't going to do anything that might annoy her and make her return to previous habits.

"Does he say when the Marines will be delivering this gift?"

"Not precisely. However, their journey will take some time as they will need to take a skimmer out of the district."

William nodded.

A regular transport from there would be between twelve and twenty hours, depending on the size, speed, and load the skimmer was carrying. He could guess what ships the Marines would have access to, but without knowing what they were carrying he couldn't say how long loading procedures would take.

"While we are waiting, William," Lydia said, "I want a security review done here at the palace, and through the capital."

"That . . . will take time, Your Majesty."

"Well invested, William," she told him. "If a baron of our own council has sided with Corian and not been detected until now, how many other vipers are in our nest?"

William bowed slightly. "You're right, of course. I'll issue the orders immediately."

"Excellent," she said. "Also, inform me when Brennan's . . . gift arrives."

"I'll see to that as well."

Lydia smiled. "Thank you, William. Now, I have more work to do."

She turned back to the endless reports and documents she had inherited along with the throne, looking irritated as she did. William watched silently for a moment before turning to fulfill his orders. The new information left him thinking . . .

Great. William scowled. *Now I'M curious. What did he find out there?*

Sometimes his job was a pain, and those were generally the *good* days.

Edge of Perrin District, on the Alliance Line

At twilight, Brennan landed his skimmer at the location he'd found on the baron's navigation boards. The Great Island was just starting to pass overhead, leaving the entire region covered in shadow. So Brennan pulled a spotlight from his Naga as he dropped to the ground and began a walk-through of the area.

Someone's been landing here a lot, he thought as he found nearly countless overlapping tracks from skimmer rails.

He played the spotlight along the ground as he walked, not really sure what he was looking for or what he expected to find. The site had clearly been used by some heavy skimmers, and possibly a reaction craft, if the burns he was seeing were any indication, but they hadn't left much of anything he could see beyond those tracks.

Brennan killed the light, standing out in the middle of the field and looking around, out to the surrounding haze. With the Great Island overhead, the area was dark, but the ambient twilight kept him from being enveloped by shadow. He could thus see into Alliance territory from where he was standing.

Similar to the empire's side of the line, there wasn't much on the Alliance side to interest anyone for probably hundreds of miles. Even the supposed "line" here was really more of an arbitrary number on a map drawn by the empire. The alliance certainly drew their version differently, and probably a lot farther back from where he'd come than the Imperial version.

Brennan refocused on the reason for his trip. The baron had been trading with the alliance for some time. Whether for personal profit or some other reason, Brennan just couldn't tell. That secret had probably gone with the baron into the next life.

Likely the reason he'd been killed, Brennan supposed sourly.

With no other ideas, Brennan made his way back to the Naga and put power to the intercepts system in the old machine. Thankfully, he'd made some updates to its information systems, though he'd had to beat off "helpful" offers to update the control networks.

Like I'd let anyone mess with my baby's core systems, Brennan griped. *I like this design for a reason. Why change it?*

The information suite wasn't the best in the empire, but it was certainly among the better versions available for a skimmer as small as the Naga. So he powered the suite up and started listening for signals from the Alliance side of the border. Doing long sweeps, Brennan scanned across all known frequencies while he was thinking about what to do next.

There wasn't much to find, really, just the expected civilian signals and the carrier for the Imperial . . . or rather, Alliance network. Those had simple enough ciphers on them, of course, but he didn't even need to crack them, as his Naga had the codes preloaded from Imperial Intelligence. He didn't have any use for such information, however, so he changed his focus to the few signals that stood out.

There's a lot of military traffic, Brennan noted with some concern.

Something was going down, of that there was no question. Unfortunately, the Alliance Navy used better ciphers than their civilians did, and he didn't have those codes preloaded.

The traffic was well above the peak he'd been briefed on for Alliance operations, however, and coming from multiple vectors. Something had stirred up the Alliance beehive, but the signals were too chaotic to be organized maneuvers.

What the hell is going on in there?

Irritated by the lack of solid information, Brennan swapped over to the civilian frequencies again and started listening in to the conversations between skimmers and the community of those who watched and talked about flyers. He was a fairly prominent part of said community, both as himself but also as a more nondescript Brian Vardson.

The first interesting transmission he found came from quite deep in Alliance territory, if he were to judge on signal strength and vector, but without another point to triangulate from, there was no way to know how deep.

"Just saw three cruisers run by me," a skimmer pilot reported. "Don't know what has them in a stir, but they're tearing up the sky, heading southeast."

"Oh yeah? What model? Any of the new Bar types?" another voice asked.

"No, old school. Haven't seen any Bar class yet. You?"

"Just one, a few weeks ago. It was under sail, though, so I'm not sure."

"Still a nice spot."

Brennan listened to the conversation for a moment before shifting frequencies.

He cycled through several similar conversations from a wide range of vectors before he fell upon one that caused him to stop cold.

"I swear, there's no other ship it could have been," a voice said, sounding earnest.

The second voice was skeptical. "No *way* you saw the *Caleb Bar*. What would they be doing that deep in Alliance territory?"

"I don't know, but I'm sure it was them . . . but they changed the name."

"So you didn't see the *Caleb Bar*, just one of the Bar class." The second voice laughed.

"No, it was the *Caleb*. I've seen the new ships, and they don't look anything like this. The lettering looked new, but the ship was smoking. She was in a fight, I bet."

That made the second voice interested. "Really? That's interesting. So what's the new name?"

"The *Excalibur*."

"Strange name."

"Yeah."

Brennan left the frequency on, but barely heard any of the rest of the conversation as he realized that the first voice must have, indeed, seen the *Caleb Bar*. Since he'd begun to learn how to master his brother's Armati, Brennan had also taken the time to learn the history of the weapons and the men who wielded them.

How the Armati were made was a secret lost to history, but the people who'd created them were still well-known names.

Caleb Bar was one of the original knights from before the empire, and from the lands they'd been forced to flee. He was a legend, and he was the reputed creator of one of the first five Armati to ever exist.

Excalibur.

That blade was long lost, but its name was still recorded deep in the Imperial records. So deep, in fact, that only Cadre members were likely to know it.

Mira renamed the ship but kept the tie to the original knight. What the hell is she doing in Alliance territory, though?

Knowing Mira Delsol as he did, mostly from her records but some from being with her personally, Brennan figured that answer could be damn near anything. Likely she'd taken to piracy again, for which he supposed he should be glad she wasn't targeting Imperial supplies.

Well, whatever she's up to, more power to her, but it doesn't solve my situation.

It *was* interesting information, however.

Brennan looked up, noting that the Great Island was passing. The light was growing; the blue sky was now visible up spin of the island, faded but deepening with each passing moment. He figured he'd wait it out and then walk the area again in full light.

Maybe he'd find something, anything, to give him a clue as to what direction to go in next.

CHAPTER 11

Remote Area, Just Inside Imperial Territory

"What did you do to my ship!?"

Gaston sighed, sounding much put-upon. "*Whose* ship?"

Mira glowered at him. "Why is there a hole in the side of the *Excalibur*, Gas?"

The two ships, the *Excalibur* and the *Helena Night*, were parked side by side in a large clearing with surrounding forest to provide cover. The crew of the *Excalibur* were working on the damage evident in the side of her hull and had mostly cleared out the debris left by the explosion, leaving Gaston to survey the area before repairs began.

"The three ships in pursuit weren't ordinary cruisers, skipper," Gaston said. "They all had tractor drives. They'd have caught up to you three hundred miles from the border, so there was no other option."

Mira grimaced, rubbing her forehead.

On the one hand, she wanted to tear into her second for being *boneheaded* enough to go into a fight at the wrong end of three-to-one odds, but he wasn't wrong. She knew the capabilities of the tractor drives, and while the *Helena* had the lead, the pursuing cruisers would certainly have made up the acceleration and speed differences long before the *Helena* made the border.

"Tell me that they at least look worse than this," she demanded, gesturing to the gaping hole in the starboard armor plate of the *Excalibur*.

Gaston smiled. "I don't believe that any of them will be making it to their repair depots on tractor drives, at the very least. Perhaps they'll limp in on sails, but not without some ad hoc repair beforehand."

"Well, there is that, at least," Mira snorted, rolling her eyes. "Good job."

"Thank you, skipper. So do we have the components we needed to maintain our own drive?" he asked, glancing at the *Helena*.

"More than that," Mira answered with a quirk of her lip, "and I'm starting to wonder about the humor inherent in the universe."

"Skipper?"

"Come on. I'll show you."

Gaston gestured to the damaged section. "I should begin surveying to determine what repairs are possible."

"You need to see this first," Mira said. "Trust me."

*

Gaston was wordless as he looked over the cargo.

Oh, the expected components were there, to be sure, but there was more. So much more.

"Imperanium. Raw imperanium," he whispered. "Where did they find so much?"

The raw ore, which had been smelted and worked into the final metal that existed almost everywhere in the empire, was priceless due to its scarcity. Once the ore had been worked, it was so far impossible to change it back to its raw form, and it couldn't be significantly worked further. So while anyone in the empire could find the finished product, finished imperanium was essentially useless as a material component for almost anything besides the buildings and armor it was already part of.

And now Gaston was looking at pallets of the stuff, wrapped and waiting for the smithy.

"I don't know, but this shipment is ours," Mira told him with a satisfied smile. "Think you can put it to use?"

"I'm certain I can, skipper," he said absently, "but this raises so many questions."

"I'm sure we'll figure out where they got it eventually," Mira said, surprisingly unconcerned with the mystery.

"That's not the question I was thinking of, actually," Gaston admitted, reflecting on his recent engagement with the Imperial cruisers.

"Oh?"

"The cruisers we fought, they had conventional armor," he told her. "If Corian has access to supplies of imperanium like this . . . why? Why not build a fleet of Bar-class cruisers to the same specifications as the *Excalibur*?"

Mira considered that and had to admit it was a good question.

"Perhaps he just located this supply?" she suggested.

"I hope so," Gaston admitted. "I dearly do hope so."

"Why do I suspect I'm not going to like the reason you hope that?" Mira asked.

"Well, if he just located a new source, then maybe we've disrupted it," Gaston said. "However, if this isn't a new source, and he's had access to imperanium for some time . . . then *what* is he doing with the metal?"

That brought Mira up short.

What would be more important to Corian than armoring his few Bar-class cruisers to the original's specifications? Imperanium was an ultradense metal, prized as armor for only two reasons: first, it was incredibly tough once properly smelted, and second, its properties were such that only a thin layer was required for application, so the weight issue was simple to manage.

She couldn't think of what would be a more valuable use for the metal, but then Mira would be the first to admit that she didn't think much beyond the obvious when it came to such things.

"Any ideas, then, Gas?" she asked finally.

"Not one," he said grimly. "The metal has always been in such high demand for armor shielding that no one was ever willing to sacrifice any meaningful amount of it for research. Until the Bar class it was too heavy for ships to use to the extent we do on the *Excalibur*, of course, but if Corian isn't armoring his ships with the imperanium, I have no idea what he's doing."

"Lovely." She sighed. "Well, let's be happy we intercepted this shipment, particularly as we seem to need it since *someone* put a hole in my ship—"

"Saving your backside," Gaston countered.

"—and we'll need the material for any further repairs."

Gaston wearily agreed. "Right. Well, we'll need a secure place to smelt and form the metal. I don't think this is the location for that, but I'll patch the hole with conventional materials and we'll finish it with imperanium when we get a chance."

"Excellent," Mira said. "In the meantime, you get to that job and I'll see to the disposition of the prisoners and the shifting of the cargo."

"You do that," Gaston said, taking a last look at the pallets of rare metal before retreating from the hold of the *Helena Night* and heading back to the *Excalibur*.

There was work to be done, and no small amount of it either. Treasure could wait until the sweating was over. Privately he was wondering if he might convince Mira to sacrifice some of the metal to his lab, something Edvard had always refused him flatly. He truly believed that there was so much more to be done with imperanium than just tossing it in front of oncoming attacks and hoping for the best.

The mystery of its source also bugged him, however, and not for the first time Gaston wished he still had access to all the files he'd accumulated while designing and building the *Excalibur*. There had been metallurgical analyses of every source of imperanium known to the empire in those files. But he would have to go to the palace now to retrieve that information, and he doubted that was going to happen anytime soon.

The *Excalibur*'s crew might be friendly with the empire, at an arm's length. Still, he didn't expect that there were many in the Imperial forces or government who were happy with Mira and her little band of corsair buccaneers since they sailed off with the most advanced ship the empire had ever put to the skies.

No, best to avoid the palace and capital entirely for the foreseeable future, Gaston thought, amused, as he went outside and headed for the *Excalibur*.

*

Trase Mirren looked up as the door to the secondary hold opened. Her and her crew's captor appeared framed in the open space.

"Well, good news for you lot." Mira Delsol smiled amiably at them as she stepped in.

"You're going to give us the *Helena* back and let us go?" Trase asked sarcastically.

"Halfway there, at least. Still up in the air on the fate of the *Helena*. Normally I'd sell it off, you understand, at a fraction of the value, unfortunately, because I don't have time to secure a good deal."

"Not to mention the fact that it's stolen," Trase countered sourly.

Mira wagged a finger at her, amused more than anything. "Not in Imperial territory it isn't."

Trase slumped. She had figured that they had been heading in that direction, but having their location confirmed took the wind out of her sails. Not that she had a problem with the empire, of course. She'd been a loyal citizen until politics had thrown her life into disarray and the alliance claimed her by virtue of her home field.

For most citizens, that was the extent of the choice they had in the matter. If they called a place in Alliance territory home, they were with the alliance after the coup; if not, then they were still Imperial citizens.

"The good news for you is that, as far as Empress Scourwind is concerned, you're still Imperial citizens," Mira said, drawing surprise from Trase.

"We're what?"

"You hadn't heard? Corian is better at controlling information feeds than I would have thought," Mira mused. "Well, that or the Scourwind government is still reeling and hasn't really swung their intelligence apparatus into action yet. Knowing Corian as I do, it's likely a mix of both."

She planted a boot on an overturned crate and leaned in on her knee. "You, Trase Mirren, and every other so-called citizen of the alliance, are still full citizens of the empire. Granted, your files have likely been flagged as potential infiltrators and all that, but all you need to do to clear it is walk into any IIS office and present yourself."

Trase grimaced at that.

No one just walked into the IIS willingly. Not that they were monsters or the like, but the Imperial Intelligence Services was the epitome of the empire's bureaucracy. You could vanish for days in their clutches just to get a routine security check.

And that was when they were being *nice*.

"And being Imperial citizens," Mira went on, chuckling, "I certainly can't hold you against your will now that we're in Imperial territory. Sadly, however, your ship was registered as part of the Alliance Merchant Fleet."

Trase felt a headache coming on.

"Sadly?" she asked dryly.

"Well, if it were a private vessel registered to an Imperial citizen, I probably would settle for just claiming the Alliance cargo and leave you the ship intact. So far we're not wanted in Imperial skies, you see, and I would prefer to keep it that way."

"You're *not*?" Trase asked, incredulous. "You stole one of the most lethal and advanced warships ever built. How could you not be wanted . . . *everywhere*?"

"Not quite certain, actually," Mira said honestly. "I expected the empress to put out a pro forma bounty, just for political reasons if nothing else."

Actually, the fact that hadn't happened had impressed Mira more than anything that had occurred during the coup. Whether it was the right thing for Lydia to have done was a question of debate, one that even Mira wasn't really certain of, but for the empress to have taken what was certain to be an unpopular stance . . . and then make it stick? That spoke well of the young royal's spine, if nothing else.

Her judgment, well, that was still up in the air.

"So you're free to go," Mira went on, "though you'll pardon me if I keep your weapons and have the *Helena* on lockdown. We're quite a distance from any population, I'm afraid, but you're welcome to ride with us when we take the *Helena* in to sell."

"Thanks ever so much," Trase said, a little disgusted but relieved that things were going to end markedly better than she'd been afraid they would. "Can my crew at least reclaim personal items?"

"Subject to approval?" Mira said, and then shrugged. "Certainly. None of what was in your hold qualifies, I'd like to point out. Strictly speaking, just having what you had in your possession is considered high treason against the empire."

"*What?*" Trase stiffened, exchanging confused and worried glances with the rest of her crew. "What the hell were we carrying?"

"Oh, now that's just bad form," Mira chided. "A captain should always know what she has in her holds."

"It was loaded by Alliance soldiers," Trase scowled, "and—"

Trase's voice cut off abruptly as she tensed even more, her eyes flicking to one side and alighting on a silent member of her crew. Mira's gaze shifted sharply to take in the man who was casually leaning on the deck, only his eyes betraying how interested he was in the proceedings. As he registered Mira's interest, however, he went from apparently casual and relaxed to *flying* across the hold as he produced a slim object from somewhere.

Mira's Elan was in her hand and smoothly extending to a razor-sharp curved sword just as the other man's Armati lunged in to pierce her heart. Her Elan swept the blade aside as Mira kicked out at his knee, only to have her foot knocked aside by his free hand.

His blade swept back, slashing for her throat. Mira leaned away and ducked, letting it pass overhead, then she went on the attack as she brought her Elan around her head and slashed down diagonally.

Blade met blade as he blocked. The following few seconds were nothing but a blur to anyone watching as the two Cadre exchanged blows, finally locking their blades between them as they glared at one another.

"I don't know you," Mira said, her tone questioning.

He snorted at her, maintaining the pressure on her blade so she couldn't shift without risking being caught on his edge.

"You knew only the idiots who let themselves *be* known."

"Dirty tricks squad then," she said, satisfied. "One of Corian's lackeys, assigned to the Southern Kingdoms, no doubt."

The anger in his face was actually amusing to her. Mira would have expected someone in Corian's command to be in better control of their emotions. Or perhaps she'd merely hit a particularly strong nerve.

"You're calling me a lackey? You . . ."

Mira laughed in his face, literally right in his face as he trailed off, remembering to whom he was talking.

"Yes, I'm calling you a lackey," she said, losing her humor in an instant. "Now surrender your Armati and yourself."

"Or what?" he sneered. "I kill you, and the rest of your rabble will be nothing to wipe up."

"Only one problem with that plan," Mira said, smiling thinly.

"And that is?"

Her left hand twisted, the blaster on her hip tearing free of its holster as she squeezed the trigger. The cartridge lased, burning through her target's midsection before he could react. The superheated plasma and lased photons flash-boiled flesh and blood, ejecting matter out of his body in a jet that burned back into Mira as he fell.

She grimaced at the burning pain, but took it without dropping her guard as her opponent hit the ground.

"You forgot that I wasn't in the dirty tricks group," she said through clenched teeth. "I was field ops, and we understood that sometimes you accept a hit to win the day, and you never, ever, rely on a bow with only one arrow in the quiver."

She kept the blaster leveled as she stepped forward and kicked the Armati from his grip, letting the weapon clatter to the deck in the corner. Her eyes flicked down to the wound in his gut and she winced.

"That's not looking good, friend," she said with a shake of her head.

His jaw worked, trying to launch some tirade, from what she could read, but no sound came. Mira sighed as she holstered and resnapped the straps around her blaster before allowing her Armati to slide back into itself and take its compressed form as the man died at her feet.

"Damn waste," she said as she gently checked the burns she'd just picked up.

Thankfully the plasma ejected from the man's wound was undirected, unlike the lased plasma she'd pumped into him. The burns she'd suffered were surface damage only, and would heal quickly.

Mira turned back around, eyes sweeping the room for any other sign of hostility. She hadn't noted anything during the fight, but her attention hadn't been fully on the other prisoners for obvious reasons. The *Helena*'s crew were all as far away from her as they could get.

"Did Corian stick you with any more . . . security?" she asked lightly, her tone completely at odds with the pressure that filled the room. "I ask because if he did, your best play is to give it up right now. I'm not looking to rack up a body count, but I'm not playing games either. Come at me and I'll bury you out in the field before we leave this place, right beside him."

"There's no one else," Trase said, stepping in front of her people. "The rest of them are all my crew."

Mira looked her over for a brief moment, then nodded in acceptance.

"Fair enough. I should have known that the alliance had a political officer assigned to you, considering your cargo," she said. "So no foul on this one. No more chances, though. If you're lying to me, there will be consequences."

Trase nodded shakily, eyes drifting over to the body cooling on the deck.

Mira turned away, walking over to pick up the Armati, then took a moment to search the body. Finding nothing, she looked back at Trase. "Which quarters were his?"

"He had his own room, passenger deck," Trase said. "I'll show you."

Mira nodded, straightening up. "All right. The rest of you, sorry, but you stay here. I'll send someone in to clean up the mess."

She opened the door, gesturing for the captain of the *Helena* to leave, then followed her out.

✳

"This is it."

Mira nodded, gesturing Trase aside as she opened the door and peered into the room.

Don't see anything out of place, Mira thought, though she wasn't dumb enough to assume that the room wasn't rigged to destroy evidence, at the very least.

Before the coup, Corian and his group had specialized in destabilizing the Southern Kingdoms beyond the reach of Imperial law, generally just turning them on each other and keeping them from becoming allied against the empire. Agents who did that sort of work inside enemy territory weren't exactly the trusting sort.

"Aren't you going in?"

Mira looked back at the *Helena*'s captain. "Not likely. Best case, he rigged his gear to be burned if someone messed with it."

Trase hesitated. "And worst case?"

"He had access to your reactor." Mira shook her head. "What do you think?"

From where she was standing, Mira could see at least three triggers. All of them were most likely decoys, though, because they were too sloppy, in her estimation.

"W-what are you going to do?" Trase asked, now looking around as if the entire ship had been revealed as a monster out to get her.

Which wasn't really a bad analogy, Mira supposed.

"First, we get your crew off the ship, along with my people," Mira said as she took a step back. "Then I'll worry about what's in the room. Come on, looks like you get to wait outside until we're through here."

Trase wasn't going to argue with that.

*

Gaston looked down from where he was working, noticing people clearing out of the *Helena Night* with a speed that had caught the eye of others as well.

"What do you think that's about?" Dusk asked softly from where she was taking notes for him.

"I don't know," Gaston admitted as he set his tools down, "but I'd best go find out."

He stepped off the deck, grabbing a safety line as he did, and slid down to the ground from where he'd been working on the gaping hole in the starboard magazine. Once there, he made his way over to the growing crowd that was putting distance between themselves and the *Helena*, noting that it included the captured crew, but no one seemed overly concerned about securing the prisoners.

"This can*not* be good," he said loudly enough that the crowd's leaders heard him and slowed a bit. "So talk to me."

"Hey, Gas." Malcolm grinned at him. "Turns out the alliance had a political officer on board. Former Cadre."

Gaston groaned, covering his eyes with his hand for a moment. "The skipper?"

"She's fine. He's rapidly approaching room temperature."

"Well, that's good at least. So since you're all clearing away from the *Helena*, I guess he rigged something?" Gaston sighed.

"His room at least. Skipper wants to clear it herself."

"Of course she does," Gaston grumbled, considering the situation for a moment.

Unfortunately, of the wide and diverse skill set available on the *Excalibur*, explosives disposal wasn't one in which they were well represented. They had a few hands who could play that tune in a pinch, including himself, but no real specialists.

Certainly none that he'd put up against a Cadreman's rigging, not with life on the line.

"I'll be right back," he said, walking past the group and heading for the *Helena*.

"She said to stay out, Gas!"

"I'll be fine, Malcolm," Gaston called over his shoulder. "What's she going to do? Fire me?"

Malcolm laughed at him. "Out of the cannons, maybe!"

Gaston grinned, waving his hand idly over his shoulder as he kept heading for the ship. "Not until I fix them she won't."

*

Mira didn't look up as she heard someone coming up behind her.

"I told everyone to clear off and stay clear, Gas," she said from where she was kneeling and examining the bulkhead around the door.

Gaston didn't say anything for a moment as he approached, his eyes examining the room beyond the open hatch she was kneeling at. The space looked fine to him.

"You also told me not to put any holes in your ship," he said after a moment. "I think we've established that I'm not great with the whole 'orders' part of my job."

Mira looked at him. "How did you get as far as you did in the emperor's service?"

"You mean banished to a remote Redoubt, working on a project that was so secret I wasn't allowed to speak of it to anyone the whole time? I can't imagine."

"Point," she conceded as she reached into the room and gently did something he couldn't quite see. When she withdrew her hand, there was a small item in it that she handed to him over her shoulder.

Gaston accepted the item, recognizing it as a pressure switch. He'd used thousands of them during the Bar project; they were common components onboard any skimmer or other transport, but there was no reason for one to be near the hatch to a private compartment.

"Do I want to know what this was attached to?" he asked.

"Likely not," Mira responded. "I certainly don't, not that either of our desires matter. We certainly better figure it out before we're done here. I think I've cleared the hatch. He wouldn't want anything too elaborate there. It would just slow him down and be a pain in the backside every time he came and went."

Gaston made a show of stepping back before Mira crossed the hatch, drawing a quirked smile from her before she took the step. Once inside the room, Mira looked around with sharp eyes. Gaston came over to the hatch and peered in, cautious but curious.

"What are you looking for?"

"Besides more traps? His computer, actually."

"You mean that one, on the desk?" Gaston nodded to a portable system lying there in plain sight.

"No," Mira said, "that's a decoy. At the least, he just used it for normal communications and such; at worst, he booby-trapped it."

She drew her own portable system from her clothing, rolling the coin-sized object between her fingers. "I'm looking for one of these, military issue, cipher secured."

She scowled around the room before finishing her statement. "And really easy to hide."

The only saving grace was the fact that the *Helena Night* was hardly a luxury skimmer, so there weren't all that many places one could conceal things in private quarters.

All of the hiding spots came up blank, however, with three of the more obvious ones being booby-trapped.

Starting to wish I'd left him alive, if only so I could kick his ass a couple more times. Mira sighed in irritation.

"What's that?" Gaston's voice caused her to shift and look back at him.

"What's what?"

"The wash," he said. "It looks . . . off."

Mira focused on the wash, really just a small indent in a ceramic shelf with a drain in the middle. It took her a few moments to spot what Gaston had seen from across the room, and even then she had to run her fingers lightly over the surface to feel it.

"How in the burning skies did you see that from across the room?" she asked, genuinely amazed.

"One of my first assignments after schooling was installing those blasted things," he admitted with a roll of his eyes. "Trust me, install a few thousand of anything and you get to learn what they're supposed to look like."

Mira didn't comment as she surveyed the area and quickly found the ridge that would let her open the improvised hide. She didn't, though, spotting the trap easily enough.

Too easy.

She grimaced, eyeing a line of graphite that seemed to run off unconnected to the trap. The line *could* have been an installation mark, but it could also be used to conduct a current to a second trap. Mira pulled back, then got on her back under the wash and felt around until she found another hide there. This one was trapped too, but more easily defeated, so she pulled the connections and opened the hide to show the explosives hidden within.

"Well, good news, Gas," she said idly as she worked, "the bomb isn't rigged to the reactor."

"Bad news?"

"It'll take this cabin out nice and clean," she said before pausing and frowning thoughtfully. "All right, 'clean' *may* be the wrong word."

"Then get out of there," he hissed.

"I *want* this computer," she growled stubbornly, continuing to work.

Gaston grumbled from the door. "I'd love to know how your superiors ever managed to deal with you while you were in the Cadre, skipper."

"Generally by letting me do my job," Mira countered as she found the receiver for the detonation sticks and gently pulled the power line.

When nothing happened, she let out a breath. "One down. All right, now let's deal with the rest of it."

Back up above the wash, Mira opened the hide enough to find the connections to the more obvious trap. That one was easier to deal with, and so in just a few moments she was smiling and tossing the coin-sized computer in her right hand as she walked out of the room.

"You're going to be the death of me yet," Gaston grumbled.

"Only if you keep being too dumb to run when I tell you, Gas."

"So what now?"

"Now we crack the cipher on this and maybe we figure out what in the burning skies Corian is up to," she said firmly. "So work as usual."

"Speak for yourself. Most of us didn't spend our adult lives hunting the enemies of the empire for fun and games."

"Oh, Gas," Mira said with an oddly foreboding tone, "you haven't *seen* what I consider fun and games yet."

CHAPTER 12

New Atlantia, Alliance Capital

General Corian hissed through clenched teeth as he looked over the report that had just then reached the capital.

"How did she know?" He shook a little, consciously getting his anger under control.

Somehow Mira Delsol was able to do things to him that practically no other foe he'd ever faced had managed. Of course, very few of his adversaries ever faced him more than once, and he had to admit to himself, even if to no one else, that the frustration of *failing* had to be playing a part. Normally all he needed was a single encounter to finish his enemies.

"We do not know, general." The adjutant shook his head. "It's possible it was accidental, but—"

"There are no accidents at this level of play," Corian said. "What did we lose?"

"Some components for the Bar-class ships," the adjutant said. "However, the bigger loss, other than the ships in question, would be the shipment of ore."

Corian grunted, waving the adjutant away.

A loss of a single shipment was staggering, but now they'd lost *two* in as many days. Ore, the very existence of which he had been hiding for longer than he cared to remember, just gone. Corian visibly had to restrain himself from hitting something or, more satisfyingly, someone.

"Do we have enough of the metal for the plan to work?" he asked, not looking over his shoulder to where the woman was standing.

Julie Sens stepped forward. "We should. I still contend that you were being overly conservative in your estimates."

"Better to err on the side of total obliteration when dealing with an enemy of this nature," Corian said tiredly. "However, they are not the ones that present the current problem."

"I believe that Cadrewoman Delsol has already shown you the answer to that aspect."

Corian straightened, his expression pensive as he considered the report. Finally, he smiled slowly. "I do believe that you're correct. The air-defense network was entirely worthless against her, wasn't it?"

"Even forewarned." Julie shook her head. "They had no chance against the *Caleb*."

"The *Excalibur*," Corian corrected, having found that one bit of the report rather amusing. "A fitting name. Edvard should have thought of it himself."

"Named for the weapon, rather than the warrior?" Julie was uncertain she agreed. "Perhaps. It is of little import to us, however."

"True. The fact that Delsol is back and has chosen, once more, to place herself between me and my objective," Corian said stonily, "that is of great import."

"It would be a folly to throw our forces against the *Excalibur*," Julie cautioned. "I know the specifications of that ship, Corian."

"No better than I do," he grumbled, but reluctantly acceded to her point. "You're right, of course. We could bring that ship down, but the battle would leave us deeply vulnerable to the empire at a time when we dare not invite even the slightest risk."

He paced in front of the war table, eyes occasionally flickering to the report that lay there, taunting him.

Finally he stopped. "She is a field operative."

"So?" Julie blinked.

"So Delsol has never played these games the way we have," Corian said with a tone that almost sounded like he was wondering at his statement. "A situation where we would fall back, create a new plan . . . She will attempt to drive through the opposition and finish her mission."

Julie nodded slowly. "Ambush then?"

"Yes," Corian said. "However, it will have to be something worthy of her interest, and she is good enough to spot a fake. Something that will bring her out of her *Excalibur* and into our kill zone."

"There is really only one thing that fits that criteria, general," Julie said with a crooked smile, though her tone held concern. "The risk, however—"

"I can mitigate the risk," Corian said firmly. "We need to plant a story into the network. She'll be monitoring that."

"I'll construct something believable," Julie said.

"No, it will have to be the truth," Corian said. "We don't know what she may have learned from the *Helena*'s crew . . . and our political officer."

"Gin would have held out," Julie said casually. "She'll not have learned anything from him."

"Not directly," Corian conceded. "However, if she took his computer . . . between Delsol and Rouche, there isn't an information system in the empire or alliance that would stand for long. No, it must be the truth. Plant classified details about the project, just . . . use appropriate code words. No sense in either tipping our hand here or panicking anyone before the time is right."

"As you command, general."

Palace Airfield, Imperial Capital

"Confirm, Palace Control. This is Marine flight One Nine Atalan on approach with orders from His Highness, Brennan Scourwind," Jan Irons said calmly as she brought the Marine transport skimmer down into a tight orbit of the palace strip, ignoring the instruments as they informed her that the craft was currently being targeted by what seemed like every piece of ordnance for a thousand miles.

Centurion Apollon leaned over Irons's flight seat, looking out past her to the relatively small strip they were circling.

"Can you set this down in a spot that small?" he asked flatly.

"I can set this thing down on Corian's sense of honor, centurion," Irons deadpanned, drawing a snicker from Apollon.

"You'd have to find it first, Irons," he told her, eyes still on the palace landing strip. "But as long as you're sure . . ."

"Relax," she assured him. "This is a Marine four-sail transpo, ugly as sin, but stable as the ground itself. We're good."

Apollon pulled back to stop distracting Irons as he heard a voice coming over her ear set.

Irons flipped a switch and was all business once again. "Confirm, Palace Control. One Nine Atalan proceeding as ordered."

She leaned back, turning her head to the open doorway that led to the main section of the transport. "Buckle up, boys! We're landing this sucker."

Settling the boxy transport down on the private field at the top of the palace was a bit more involved than Irons had let on to Apollon but well within her skill set just the same. An amateur would likely get themselves spread over half the palace if they tried. Balancing the wind on four sails to drop a skimmer into a landing zone was no job for dilettantes.

She brought them in to within ten feet, then popped the brakes on the lines and let the transport drop. The heavy load made the landing a bit rougher than usual, but Marines were used to getting jostled around. Once they were on the ground, she started dialing the sails back, not wanting to just kill them and drop the lines across the palace grounds before she started winching them in.

"All right, we're down!" Irons called over her shoulder to the others even as she finished winding down the transport's systems.

*

"Move your worthless hides, marines," Centurion Apollon ordered, slapping the hatch release.

The floor dropped out from under them, the front lowering to provide a ramp. The pallets of metal rocked a little as they settled in at the new angle, but he ignored them, as he knew his Marines had strapped them down tight.

Drake and Vaquen preceded the rest of the detail, the duo's weapons held to attention with the breeches open and mag wells empty. The tough twosome looked like they'd rather eat lasing rounds than present their weapons empty, but as much as Apollon sympathized with them, no one walked armed and ready for a fight into the palace.

Palace security was there to meet them, scrutinizing the Marines intently as Apollon's squad stepped down from the interior of the transport. He was surprised that they were as respectful as they were, not taking his troops' weapons while they made sure they were empty and cleared and no one was carrying any live mags.

He'd endured worse.

"We have a shipment here, direct orders from Cadreman Scourwind," Apollon said, upon refusing to hand over his personal sidearm or ammunition. "I'm to turn them over to palace authority and, I quote the Cadreman here, am ordered to *shoot* anyone else who tries to take it."

The security men exchanged glances at that but didn't say anything as their commander ignored him and stepped back to speak quietly into a comm.

Apollon was about to repeat himself when the large hangar doors on the far side of the field opened up and another group stepped onto the flight deck of the palace.

His eyes widened when he recognized one of the group, and he immediately stiffened to full attention as he snapped at the rest of his squad to do the same.

"Present!" he snarled. "Damn it, Pax, stop slouching before I kick your ass off this flight deck."

The other Marine turned around, confused for a second until he too saw who was coming and almost swallowed his tongue as he jumped to attention. Apollon grumbled at the man, but quietly and surreptitiously handed his personal weapon over to the security team without another word.

Her Majesty, Lydia Scourwind, was approaching from the head of the group while her minders clearly rushed to keep up, trying to convince her to slow down.

She came to a stop just in front of the ramp, eyes flitting over the Marines before she looked up to the rows of wrapped pallets.

"Are you in charge of this squad . . . ?" she asked as her eyes rested on Apollon.

"Centurion Apollon, Your Majesty," he told her reflexively. "And yes, ma'am."

"I understand that my brother sent something of some importance with you," she said. "I assume that is the shipment of . . . whatever?"

"Yes, Your Majesty," Apollon said, glancing around at the rather large group of people. He didn't know if this many people should be told about the shipment, but he also figured that he probably wouldn't find a group of people any *more* vetted than Her Majesty's security and advisers. "Apparently the Baron Vilhem was attempting to smuggle raw imperanium out to the alliance."

Several people, including the empress, drew in shocked breaths as they looked at the pallets with new eyes.

"I . . . see," Lydia said softly. "Well . . . I understand why he wouldn't say anything over an open channel. Had anyone known you were in possession of this, forget what the alliance would do. Every so-called free corsair for a thousand miles would have been hunting you."

"Yes, Your Majesty," Apollon agreed.

"Your orders, if you please." She extended her hand.

Apollon didn't think about it. He simply dropped the chip into her hand and waited.

Lydia opened the file, reading the contents quickly. She smiled for a moment before she handed it off to the man beside her.

"I do hope you didn't have to enforce the . . . uh . . . optional security tactics my brother authorized," she said lightly.

"No, ma'am," Apollon answered, "just had to threaten one fleet officer who thought the job was above my Marines' ability. He backed off after I threatened to make good on the order, Your Majesty."

"Angry, I suppose?" she asked.

"There were words of court-martial, Your Majesty."

"That will not happen," Lydia said firmly. "William, see to it, if you please?"

"Yes, Your Majesty." The man beside her nodded. "I'll end any talk of repercussions. They were executing legal orders, though if they had actually put a lase blast in some idiot it would have been a bit of a scandal against your brother."

Apollon had figured as much, which was why he hadn't ordered his squad to drop that idiot in the first place. Legal orders were one thing, but some things just didn't happen without repercussions. Maybe they wouldn't have fallen on his shoulders, but that didn't mean he had to make life harder for the man who'd put his trust in him.

"My brother has weathered scandals in the past, and likely as not will do so again in the future," Lydia said, again with a hint of a smile. "In fact, my own past hasn't precisely been as clean as my advisers like to pretend."

"I'm sure I have no idea what Your Majesty is speaking of," William said.

"Of course you don't," Lydia said. "All right, secure this transport here, if you please. Centurion, have your pilot lock it down. I suspect that we'll be moving the . . . material somewhere else shortly, but until then, this is as secure as we are likely to get. William, arrange to have the ship moved into the hangar."

"I'll see to it."

"As for your squad"—Lydia looked them over briefly—"my brother trusted you with this material, and he was proven right. It remains in your custody until further notice. I will endeavor to ensure that that isn't too long, centurion."

"We serve at Your Majesty's pleasure."

Perrin District, Imperial Mobile Fortress

Brennan nodded to the deck chief as he walked away from his Naga. "Have someone check the flight systems and prep a new load of canister for the guns. I'll be by later to go over the maintenance schedule myself."

"I'll see to it, Cadreman," the chief affirmed. "Anything we should check specifically?"

"I unloaded the guns on a luxury yacht," he admitted, "so check the mounts and make sure I didn't shake anything loose. Other than that, just basic maintenance that I'll handle myself, assuming your boys don't find anything more pressing."

"Understood. I'll get it on a priority list."

"Thank you," Brennan said, yawning as he made his way into the base facilities.

The Imperial Army was moving into Perrin District in force, something that hadn't been necessary until recently but was definitely well overdue by this point. Things were changing fast, had been since the coup . . . It was like the world wasn't solid any longer.

He greeted the guards at the door with a casual salute but was too tired to notice when they returned it. He'd been flying or investigating for the better part of thirty hours, maybe a bit more, and was walking dead on his feet.

As much as he loved his Naga, the craft had some clear disadvantages compared with more advanced designs and, of course, larger skimmers with more crew. Chief among those was the total lack of a reliable autopilot.

Oh, the Naga *could* fly itself, that was true enough, but no self-respecting pilot would trust that function sufficiently to take a nap.

"Cadreman Scourwind."

Brennan looked up, nodding to the young officer who was waiting for him. "That's me."

"We have your room prepared for you. I've been assigned to show you to it, if you're ready?" she asked.

"More than," Brennan admitted, barely stifling another yawn.

"This way, please."

He followed her into the depths of the mobile base, glad that they'd sent someone to show him the way. An Imperial Army mobile base was a monster of a machine, a city in all but name that crawled across the empire, moving from hot spot to hot spot and taking a small legion with it as it did. Normally they were primarily assigned to the southern border of the empire, or occasionally beyond that, putting down some brush fire in the Southern Kingdoms before peace along the border could be threatened.

Having one this deep in Imperial territory was a sign of the times, he supposed.

"Is there anything new in the reports?" he asked as they made their way down through the base. "I've been . . . focused on other things for the last few days."

"No further aggression from the alliance since the loss of Second Division," she answered. "However, there was a recent spike in Alliance Navy maneuvers . . ."

"Yes, the *Excalibur*. I was monitoring some of that as it happened. Did they track her down?"

"No, sir." The officer shook her head. "Things have calmed down a little, but the alliance is still running heavy patrols along that border."

Brennan was happy to hear that. If the alliance wasn't trumpeting their recapture, or destruction, of the *Excalibur*, then Mira was still at large. The *Excalibur* was a potentially balance-shifting piece of equipment if she entered the war on either side, but while Brennan supposed he should be in favor of hunting the vessel down for the empire . . . honestly, he was just happy that Mira, Gaston, and the crew he'd flown with were still flying free skies.

"Your room, sir." The officer stopped, nodding to the door beside her.

"Thank you," Brennan said tiredly, hitting the controls for the door and letting it slide open. "I think I'll be good from here."

That earned him a smile at least, but Brennan was too tired to try his luck with any flirting, so he offered a salute that he figured was sloppy. The officer didn't notice or take offense as she returned it.

"Enjoy your rest, Cadreman."

"I intend to," Brennan said as she left, then he let the door slide shut.

The room wasn't anything much, but it was private, which was a step above what most of the crew of a mobile base were able to indulge in. Just wide enough for a single bunk across from a wash sink and barely enough room to walk between them. He entered, shucking his flight suit and leaving it on the ground. He'd worry about getting it cleaned later; for the moment he just wanted to grab as much sleep as he could manage.

He washed up quickly and then took a seat on the bunk. Before crashing, Brennan linked his computer to the base systems and lined up a series of presets so it would grab any relevant intelligence and news reports for him to review later. That done, Brennan flopped back in the bunk and closed his eyes. Sleep wasn't going to come easily, he quickly discovered, despite how fatigued he was.

In the end, though, it did come.

CHAPTER 13

Excalibur **Landing Field, Just Inside Imperial Territory**

Gaston looked over the off-color patch that now adorned the side of the *Excalibur*, both satisfied with his work and professionally affronted by the necessarily weaker point in the armor. At least they now had enough material to manage true repairs, once he found a location where he could properly smelt the metal. Until then, conventional patch-ups would have to do.

"Good job, everyone," he said to his crew. "Looks like we're done here. Are the magazine repairs finished?"

Dusk nodded. "Yes, they finished earlier today. The autoloader has been replaced, and we've shifted enough shells over from other magazines to even out our firepower."

"All right, then we're doubly done." He chuckled. "I'll let the skipper know. In the meantime, until we're ready to leave, tell everyone to take it easy."

Dusk jotted a note down. "Yes, sir."

"Oh, and tell your brother he did good work," Gaston said. "I haven't seen him around?"

"He was working with the magazine repair crews," she told him. "Mik wanted to learn how the system was put together, I believe."

Gaston nodded, a hint of a smile on his lips. "Not too surprising."

Not surprising at all, in the engineer's opinion. Nothing like having your life, and the lives of everyone around you, resting on your knowledge of how to fix something you didn't have a clue about, to drive you to learn. Most people in that situation didn't get the chance, of course, but Gaston would be watching Mikael from this point forward. If he continued showing interest, well, there were always jobs for an engineer on a ship.

Even one with a less-than-formal education.

"Well, tell him what I said," Gaston told Dusk again, "and make sure you take some downtime yourself. Never know when we'll be under way again."

"Yes, sir," she told him, "I will."

"Good. See you later then. I'm going to go track down the skipper."

"I believe that she's on the flying deck," Dusk said, glancing up.

"Ah, yes, she would be, wouldn't she? All right, thanks."

"No problem, sir."

*

Mira was standing behind the flying deck controls of the *Excalibur*, albeit with the physical locks in place to prevent any accidental orders being sent. Gaston stopped behind her, uncertain whether he should disturb her for a moment, but of course, she already knew he was there.

"Finished, Gas?"

"Repairs are as complete as I can make them here, skipper," he confirmed. "We're a hundred percent operational again, but the armor is soft in that area. Nothing we can do about it for now."

"I understand. How's our munitions count?"

"Sixty-eight percent. Replacing those will be a bit of a challenge, I have to admit."

"Only legally. I still have a few contacts who can turn up lasing rounds in our size. Don't worry about it."

Gaston grimaced. "Just as long as they're not the same sources we were selling to during the war."

"None of those sources are still breathing," she said dryly.

Gaston didn't have a response to that, as he remembered the event well enough. Mira hadn't told any of them that she'd rigged the cargo to blow until they were well away. The fact that she'd rigged it with enough explosives to take out a quarter-mile radius was enough to make him forever nervous about what else she might try in the future.

"I suppose I'll comfort myself with that," he told her, his tone matching hers. "You will make sure we're outside of the blast radius this time, right?"

"We were outside the last time." Mira smiled.

"You and I have very different definitions of 'outside' the blast radius," he countered. "But I doubt you'll listen. What do we do now?"

"I haven't decided," Mira said, sounding unconcerned. "We have the supplies; we don't need anything else here. Probably best to pull out of the area entirely."

"Makes sense."

He didn't say anything more, letting the silence draw out. He knew that the skipper still held loyalty to the empire in her heart, and he doubted she was going to just let the threads they'd turned up lie where she'd found them.

"So what's the plan?" he asked, smiling wryly.

She gave him a look before producing her computer from a pocket. A swipe of her thumb lit the projector, displaying information. She handed it over to Gaston. "This just showed up in the Alliance military public relations feeds as well as their news sources."

Gaston checked the information, frowning. "This is . . . nonsense. What is it?"

"Code words mostly," she said, "the sort of thing you learn to read between the lines once you've been on the other side for a while. To civilians it's just normal chatter, nothing unusual. Normal maneuvers, a couple of minor trials, that sort of thing."

"And the real meaning?"

"There's an operation in play," Mira said. "Something high level—very high level."

"A maneuver against the empire?"

"Maybe, but I doubt it," Mira said. "No, this sounds more like a precursor mission. Gathering vital materials, maybe testing something new. Probably the second, judging from some of the news releases."

"I'm not following?"

"See the bit about sky stones?" She pointed to the display.

Gaston glanced at the projection, noting that it was a pretty standard notation concerning the potential of stones falling through the upper atmosphere. The disturbance didn't happen that often, but it was still a concern. Such stones would often explode in the upper atmosphere, causing minor damage from shock waves on the surface. Flights were generally advised to steer clear of them since the explosions could disrupt sail projectors, which was widely considered a very bad thing.

"What about them?" he asked.

"It's a common distraction for weapons testing," she answered. "Clears the skies out of the areas you're testing in, explains any odd flashes or sightings from the ground, and no one really questions it."

"Maybe that's what's going on then?" Gaston suggested. "They certainly have enough to test these days, from what we can tell."

"No." Mira shook her head. "What's more telling is the sectors they've emptied. Plot them out, and note the timing on the individual reports."

Gaston frowned, but did just that. He put the sectors up in the order reported, and his eyes widened as he saw what she was talking about.

"It's a direct path from the old Redoubt to the Imperial sector," he marveled. "This doesn't make sense."

"Spotted that, did you?" Mira laughed, pleased.

"Maybe it's a real sky-fire report?" he offered, confused.

"Nope. If it were, the empire would have similar reports. As it is, the warnings end at the border and, the last time I checked, sky fire doesn't care about politics."

"Then it has to be a trap," Gaston said. "You know this, right?"

"Possibly," she admitted. "Though in that case, I have to wonder . . . a trap for whom?"

"Corian and you have history."

"And a date to resolve all that, sometime in the coming future," she confirmed with a curt nod. "But if it's a trap for me, he's risking a lot. The empire is going to notice this. It's impossible that they won't."

She turned back to the controls of the *Excalibur*, laying her hands on the locked wheel and looking up at the skies above them.

"It might be a trap, Gas," she said, "but if it is, it's not *only* a trap. He's planning a real operation, and maybe using the report as bait. A risky move, certainly, but pure Corian. He enjoys eliminating multiple threats with a single thrust."

"If this is a trap, don't walk into it," Gaston blurted. "That's what he wants."

"Assuming it's a trap for me," she said, "which is a reasonable supposition at this point, but far from the only one. Besides, while Corian is admittedly something of a strategic genius, his tactical acumen has been overstated."

"The man commands an army. He doesn't have to be a tactical genius," Gaston told her. "At some point, even you will fall to sheer numbers, Mira."

"Numbers can be evaded," Mira said, a smile playing at her lips. "Besides, for now I'm just . . . curious."

Gaston rolled his eyes. "Of course. It's not like anything bad has ever happened from *that*."

He sighed, knowing by then that his warnings were pointless. He could tell when the skipper had set her mind to something.

"I'll have the *Excalibur* prepared for the mission," he said finally.

"Have it prepared, yes," Mira said, "but I'll not risk it, or you, on my curiosity. I'm going to investigate alone."

That did it.

"Have you completely taken leave of your mental faculties?" Gaston roared. "If it's a trap, the *Excalibur* is the only trump card you have to match his forces, and you know it."

"So does he," she said. "He'll have strategies in place for the *Excalibur*. I just want to see what he has planned, and I can do that better alone. We'll finish our work here, then I'm going to go have a peek at what Corian has put into motion."

"This is a bad idea, skipper."

"It won't be my first, Gas."

Gaston grumbled. "I'm more concerned about it being your *last*."

New Atlantia, Alliance Capital

"Preparations have been completed, general."

Corian looked up, nodding to Julie Sens as she approached. "Good. I've authorized the full operation, so one way or another, we'll see the end of this soon."

Cadrewoman Sens flinched. "That's a risk."

"If we miss Delsol," Corian said calmly. "Even if we don't, this could burn our plans. No, we're ready. It would be better if we had a larger stockpile, more ships . . . but we could always do with more of everything. That's in the nature of our business."

"Isn't it, though?" Julie asked. "Are we ready for this?"

"As ready as we can be," Corian confirmed, "and our trap should bait in the Imperial forces just the same as Delsol."

"You want to bring the entire Imperial Navy into a kill box?" she asked somewhat incredulously.

Julie felt her disbelief was warranted. There was such a thing as being too ambitious, after all. For a military officer, such hubris generally led to fatally bad results.

"Not the entire navy; I doubt we would ever be that lucky." Corian laughed softly at the thought, the idea amusing him. "I'll settle for a task force or two, but in any case, that will merely be a bonus."

"General, don't take this the wrong way," Julie told him, "but you and I have *very* different definitions of what constitutes a bonus."

"No, Julie, I just have a better sense of the strategic implications of the project than you do."

"In that case, why don't we drop a few more threads and draw more of them out?" Julie asked, curious.

Corian's expression grew cold. "No. As amusing as it would be, crippling the Imperial Navy would not play to our ultimate goals, Julie. Some damage will be a necessary step to solidify our control, but we want to take the empire largely intact."

"Of course."

Free Corsair *Excalibur*, Thirty Thousand Feet over Imperial Territory

"You can't be serious?" Gaston grumbled as he tucked his flight jacket in tightly to hold off the cold.

The *Excalibur* and the *Helena Night* were sailing close, a little less than a half mile between them as the two ships headed deeper into Imperial airspace. They were headed for the nearest large port city, where they could offload the crew of the *Helena* and restock a few per-ishables before the next leg of the mission Mira had decided on.

The woman in question was prepping gear as Gaston glared at her exasperatedly, not bothering to answer him since she considered the question silly. Certainly she could understand why he was less than impressed with her chosen method of locomotion for the coming opera-tion, but that didn't mean she was going to change her mind.

The gear was an Imperial military version of a thrill-seekers' kit, effectively a wearable sail projector comparable to what was mounted on a small skimmer. The contraption was the sort of nonsense that the empire forces tinkered with on occasion but generally abandoned when the project failed to deliver.

"That thing is a death trap. I don't even know why we had one on board," Gaston growled as Mira strapped the gear over her insulated, gray flight suit.

Mira smiled. "We didn't. Corian had it."

"Of course he did," Gaston deadpanned. "Too bad even he wasn't crazy enough to use the damn thing. We'd be well rid of him if he had."

She stood up, flexing her limbs to be sure she had full mobility.

"The system isn't that bad, Gas," Mira told him. "Cadre have used them successfully fairly often."

"Of course you have. Who else would be that suicidal?"

Mira shook her head, still grinning as she walked over to the edge of the deck. She kicked her right leg over the side, then straddled the rail for a moment as she did a final check.

"We'll get you a private skimmer, skipper," Gaston pleaded. "We have the money for it!"

"I'll be fine, Gas. Look after my ship," she told him, aiming her arms out with the piton launchers strapped to them.

The launcher fired with a loud report, staggering Mira briefly from recoil.

"*Your* ship?" Gaston objected as their trademark lines played out. "You have to actually command her for that to be true!"

The sail projectors snapped to life, light gray and almost invisible in the distance, and the line snapped taut. Mira glanced over her shoulder as she was plucked off the rail and pulled out into the ether.

"We'll be having words when I get back, Gas!" she yelled at him, not amused with his parting shot.

Gaston watched her go, unrepentant.

"Looking forward to it, skipper," he said as she vanished into the distance.

∗

Mira winched in the lines, pulling herself up close behind the sail as she rode the buffeting winds and headed back toward Alliance airspace.

The problems with the personal sails weren't all that hard to over-come during flight; the system had been extraordinarily successful in that phase of the project. Control was simpler than one would encoun-ter with a skimmer, though she didn't have the computer control to aid in stability either, which was a disadvantage.

Still, the problem wasn't in the flying, as most of the test pilots had determined early on.

It was in the *landing*.

Mira had a while before she had to worry about that part of her mission, however, so she just let herself enjoy the sensation of soaring, which was about as pure and unfettered as any she'd ever experienced. The feeling was rivaled only by free fall along the deck of the *Excalibur*, with nothing between her and the ether beyond, not even atmosphere.

That was a sensation that was almost hers alone, for the moment, and one she would treasure to her dying day.

Being dragged behind a giant light sail at nearly six hundred miles per hour was, however, a very close second.

CHAPTER 14

Imperial Army Mobile Base, Perrin District

"I'm up; I'm up," Brennan mumbled, rolling over in his bed and nearly falling to the floor before he caught himself and finished waking up.

Oh crap, I'm at the base, he realized, blinking away the sleep and focusing on the sound that had waked him.

His computer was chirping insistently, a familiar tone that told him it had located something on his watch list. Brennan sighed but reached over, grabbed the system, and activated it wearily. The projection lit up, making him close his eyes against the light. He blinked until he could read the display, then started wrapping his still-half-sleeping mind around the information.

An Imperial transport captain spotted the Excalibur, he noted, *and she's in Imperial territory.*

Brennan sat up, shedding his blanket, and tossed the computer aside. If Delsol was in Imperial territory, he was going to try and meet up with her.

If only to say thanks.

He cleaned up quickly, then grabbed his flight suit and grimaced as the smell of sweat hit him.

I should have cleaned it last night, damn it.

Brennan tossed the suit on anyway, brushing out the wrinkles as best he could and checking that his kit was still there. Then he was out the door and trying to retrace his steps back to the flight deck, though he made a few wrong turns in the process and had to ask directions three separate times.

On the deck, the crew chief noticed him approaching and hurried over to meet him.

"Cadreman, I didn't expect you up here for a while yet."

"New intel," Brennan said with a tired look. "Is she prepped?"

The chief nodded. "We rechecked, and retorqued, all the linkages to the guns. You were right, they were a little looser than they should be. The rest is all clear; all systems charged, and the reactor has been serviced. I thought you wanted to look it over yourself before you left?"

"I did, but I'm not going to have time," Brennan said as he reached the Naga.

Despite the rush, he started a standard preflight walk around of the craft, eyeballing with an experienced gaze everywhere it was most likely to fail.

"New mission, sir?" the chief asked, curious.

"No, actually, I want to catch up with an old friend before they pull a ghost on me," Brennan said as he finished his walk around, then paused as something else caught his eye. "What's going on here?"

Men were prepping skimmers everywhere he could see.

"Not sure yet, sir," the chief admitted. "I was kind of hoping you could tell me, to be honest. We got orders from above to shift operations, going northeast now."

"Northeast? That's the course I'm headed out on." Brennan frowned. "I think I'd better see if I can figure out what's going on."

"Good luck with that," the chief told him. "That's nosebleed territory. Every rank in there makes me dizzy just thinking about how high up they are."

Brennan laughed. "There are advantages to being me, chief."

The chief nodded as he watched the Scourwind scion march off.

"I suppose there are, kid. Good luck."

*

Two Imperial Marines were guarding the doors to the strategy room as Brennan approached. Both recognized him but still stepped between him and the doors.

"Sorry, Cadreman. No entrance."

"Call in for me," Brennan said, coming to a stop.

The Marines exchanged glances before one of them nodded and turned slightly away to speak softly into his intercom. After a few minutes of back-and-forth conversation, he looked back to Brennan and nodded.

"You're cleared, sir."

"Thank you," Brennan said, pushing open the door and walking in.

A glance around the room told him that the chief hadn't been wrong. The people in the room were practically a who's who of the Imperial military. He knew most of the faces from the halls of the palace; the few he didn't wore their uniforms a little stiffly with emblems still shiny, new, and unmarred by field time.

New promotions, filling the ranks the traitors left open, Brennan thought as a general headed his way.

"Cadreman Scourwind, I'd heard you were on base, but I was informed that you were expected to sleep for some time yet."

"General Inslaw." Brennan greeted the portly man with a polite smile. "I was wakened by my computer alerts, I'm afraid."

The general frowned, glancing around. "I thought this meeting and the reasons behind it were still secured."

"Oh, I'm certain they are." Brennan waved off the man's concerns. "My alerts were for another reason, however. When I was prepping my skimmer I heard of your alert in the most general of terms and feared that they may be linked."

"Oh? What were you monitoring?" Inslaw asked. "You're certainly cleared for what is happening here, of course, but I'm wondering what link you might have spotted?"

"Whatever is going on is happening to the northeast, as I understand it?" Brennan asked.

Inslaw grimaced but nodded in agreement. "That much has already slipped out?"

"Hard to hide when you have the base shifting course and the deck crews preparing for flight operations."

"I suppose." Inslaw sighed. "But yes."

"Perhaps it hasn't hit the general alerts yet," Brennan said, "but an Imperial transport captain reported the *Excalibur* in that region."

"*Excalibur*? I'm not familiar with that . . . ship, is it?" Inslaw said as he was clearly raking his mind for the reference.

Brennan smiled. "That would be the former *Caleb Bar*. Delsol apparently renamed her."

Inslaw stiffened, his expression growing colder. "That woman. Well, her presence might explain what we're tracking."

"And that is?"

Inslaw sighed again. "Some major Alliance ship movements, as well as what looks like some sky clearing for a significant operation right up to airspace we control."

"Well, that's not good. Damn . . . all right, well, I'm heading up that way to see if I can contact Delsol. She might know more about what's going on, but either way, I'll keep an eye out and send back any information I spot."

Inslaw nodded. "We'll be a few days behind you, but the Imperial fleet will be moving into that region soon as well."

"I'll keep an eye for them as well," Brennan promised. "Do we have any indications of what Corian is planning?"

"No specifics, I'm afraid. He's cleared a significant swath of sky from deep inside his territory right up to our border. More than enough to move a *heavy* force with no one seeing it if they stay above the cloud layers and have even a little luck on their side."

"Corian won't need luck," Brennan said. "He'll not move until he's certain he has his plans all in order."

"We'll be ready for him."

"I learned the hard way, general," Brennan said, "no one is ready for Corian."

Imperial Palace, Operations Room

Lydia watched the men and women of the operations team, the room abuzz with action as people tried to figure out the latest information they'd captured from the Alliance networks. No one seemed to know quite what to make of the intelligence, and that sent a cold chill down her back as she considered the last time Corian had had a mysterious plan.

William was standing in the middle of the commotion, directing it like a musician, but Lydia had to wonder if their actions would be enough.

"We have fleet units moving into position along the border, sir," a young woman said from her station. "Data feed is coming online from them now."

"Give it to me on the central display," William ordered.

The central display took up the area William was standing in, photons linking together in a lattice that showed the 360-degree view from the ships stationed on the border. He turned, looking into Alliance territory for a moment, but didn't see anything in particular.

"How long until the sky-fire threat is supposedly due?" he asked.

"Two more days, sir."

"All right," he replied. "Get pickets into place along the disputed border, but keep our main force back. He's playing a game here. We don't know what it is, so we're going to cover this area, but we are *not* going to forget to watch our flanks."

He turned and stepped through the imagery, disrupting the projection noticeably as his body temporarily broke the photon lattice.

"Your Majesty," he said to Lydia, bowing his head deeply. "I didn't see you come in at first."

"Do not mind me, William," Lydia said wearily. "I am more concerned with the outcome of this operation than I am with the niceties of my position."

"The niceties exist for a reason," he reminded her gently.

"Do we have any clue as to what Corian is planning?" she asked softly, not wanting her uncertainty to spread to any of those around her.

"Not yet." William shook his head slightly. "Whatever it is, he's playing it strangely. He has to know we'd tap the Alliance networks and recognize the signs of an operation in the works."

"A feint, do you suppose?"

"Possible, but we're watching for that too. We have every Bar-class ship at our command flying high patrols over the disputed territory. There's no *way* he can move a significant force without our seeing it."

"He knows that, does he not?"

"He does, unquestionably," William said. "And yes, I'm aware that this means Corian likely has some more intricate operation in the works."

"The last time he put one of his operations into the works," she reminded him quietly, "my entire family, save my brother, ended on the same day. Stop him, William."

William nodded curtly, turning on his heel, and hurried off.

Lydia watched one of the few people she had left from her youth walk off, and wondered where it was all going to end. Or even *if* it was ever going to end. Since taking control of the empire, Lydia had felt more and more like she was riding some out-of-control beast. The only thing worse than being thrown off honestly seemed to be if she hung on.

She didn't know why she was doing anything any longer, other than it was what she was born to do.

Imperial Army Mobile Base, *Sunken Muria*, Perrin District

Brennan dropped into the pilot's seat of the Naga, running last-minute flight checks on the instruments as he brought them online one by one. He was going through the list on autopilot for the most part, his mind a whir of thoughts as he tried to figure out all he'd just learned.

I wish Matani were here, Brennan thought as he signaled the ground crew outside his Naga and they waved back. *I never thought I would wish that.*

He settled back as his Naga was wheeled out to the open deck of the mobile base, turning the nose of the fighting skimmer against the prevailing wind of the first layer. He punched in the navigation data for the projector launchers as the crews untethered his Naga and moved clear.

One crew member remained, just inside his peripheral vision, standing away from his expected direction of travel, and Brennan waited for him to signal the all clear.

"Deck Control, Naga Oh One," the Cadreman said into his comm.

"Oh One, Deck Control," came the fast response. "We have you cleared for solo launch from HL-five, confirm flight check."

"All systems clear," Brennan replied. "Launch ready."

"Confirmed, Oh One. Launch when instructed by the deck chief."

"Confirm," Brennan acknowledged, glancing over to where the chief was standing.

The man cocked his helmeted head to one side, clearly listening to orders over his own comm, then bobbed as he lifted his fist high. Brennan responded in kind, then dropped his hand back to the controls as the chief dropped his own fist and thrust it forward as he tensed and got ready to jump clear if anything went wrong.

Brennan's thumbs jammed down on the controls, and the Naga's twin launchers thudded in response as the projectors were sent skyward. A few thousand feet above, they blossomed into a pair of gleaming sails that caught the wind of the first layer and started pulling the Naga along the deck toward the edge of the mobile base.

He hit the winches and dialed up the size of the sails with a single smooth motion, pulling the Naga into the skies as it began to accelerate with the wind.

"Naga Oh One, clear of deck," Brennan signaled back. "Thanks for the hospitality, Muria."

"Good hunting, Oh One."

The Naga was climbing fast, running with the wind a little away from the course he needed, so Brennan adjusted the angle of the sails and put himself on the correct vector. With the new course locked in, Brennan set the skimmer to automatic and leaned back in his seat as he turned his focus back to the information he'd learned.

His immediate thought was, of course, that the entire thing was a feint, the only conclusion that seemed to make any sense. But that was the problem. There was no way in the burning skies that the empire was going to fall for something that obvious. It just wasn't going to happen.

Sure, they'd move some forces into place just in case it wasn't a bluff, but Brennan knew that the entire line was being reinforced and reserves were being put on alert. Such an obvious operation wasn't the way to announce a new offensive, so he didn't understand Corian's plan.

"What the hell is that psycho up to this time?" Brennan murmured darkly, as the Naga sped onward through the skies over the empire.

He felt like he had a puzzle with missing pieces in his brain, the pieces trying to fall into place but him not quite able to make what he had fit.

Did the components and imperanium stores factor into all of this? And, if so, then *how*?

*

The Naga's computer chirped to warn him as he entered the region the *Excalibur* had been spotted in, turning Brennan's attention away from his thoughts as he stopped staring out of the cockpit and began *looking*.

Like most of the empire and surrounding environs, the immediate area was arid, with limited foliage and almost no water to be seen. What little of the precious liquid there was flowed below the surface, visible mostly in occasional patches of rich flora. Unlike some parts of the world, there were few places in the empire where people wanted for water. Even so, waste of the precious resource was not tolerated lightly.

The terrain consisted of rolling hills, covered in scrub brush for the most part, but visibility was good enough to see for miles in every direction until the encroaching mists finally obscured things in the distance. Brennan was looking for a rather specific ship, however, a ship that should be easily recognizable if he could just lay eyes on it.

There were flyers in the skies, but not as many as there would be normally since the region was so close to disputed territory.

The *Excalibur* was nowhere in sight, of course, nor on his instruments as he entered the region. That didn't surprise him much, though technically it wasn't legal for her to be flying without proper transponder identification. In practice, the law was rarely enforced since you had to get caught first, and for that the local authorities had to have a reason to think you were running dark. Generally, if they had a reason, then running dark was probably the least of your crimes.

Brennan linked into the local communications traffic boards, falling back on his old ident-sign rather than the sparkling new military-approved one.

"Skyhawk calling all flyers in the region," he put out over the local area. "I'm looking for a black skimmer, likely dark; prow lettering reads *Excalibur*."

"You're a little out of your territory, Hawk," a voice came back.

"Who's this?"

"Marrow Wind."

Brennan laughed. "Haven't heard from you in a while. Last time was at the Imperial flight competition in the capital, I think?"

"So it was, Hawk. Good to hear from you again," Wind told him. "Was wondering if you bought it in the nastiness a while back."

"Came close a couple of times, but I squeaked through."

"Glad to hear it. Afraid I don't have your skimmer in sight, though. Anyone out there know different?"

A few other voices popped in and out, mostly just chatting, none of them having much information, though everyone seemed to know someone who'd seen the black skimmer. Almost twenty minutes later, a more serious voice entered the conversation.

"So, Skyhawk, why are you looking for the *Excalibur*?"

Brennan frowned, not recognizing the voice either from memory or recent conversation, but something about it hit him as familiar. "Who am I speaking with?"

"Call me Caleb."

Brennan almost laughed. "Gas, is that you?"

The voice came back, sharper this time. "Who is this?"

"Put me on with the skipper, she'll remember," Brennan said, chuckling. "Tell her Elan vouches for me."

"Skipper's not available, but we can have a chat if you like," the voice, which Brennan was now nearly certain belonged to Gaston, replied a few moments later.

"Just tell me where to go," Brennan said.

"Don't worry about it; we have that covered."

Brennan felt a chill pass over him just before a shadow *actually* passed over him, and he twisted in his seat to look up and behind him as the sun was blotted out by the smoothly flowing bulk of a black skimmer settling in right over his position.

"How in the burning . . ." Brennan swore before he remembered he was still live and cut the signal to the local boards.

His instruments were still saying that there was no skimmer for miles around him, which told him volumes about the quality of the *Excalibur's* stealth capabilities. His Naga wasn't top-of-the-line as far as such things went, but there wasn't anything in the air that should have been able to get that close to him all the same. About then was when his computer chose to suddenly start screaming that active scanners had targeted him.

"Oh, *now* you wake up!" Brennan scowled at the instrument cluster of the Naga before swapping over to a private signal to the ship above him. "*Excalibur*, is this channel secure?"

"It is."

"Well then, Gas, this is Brennan Scourwind," he said. "I want to speak with Mira."

There was a long pause before Gaston came back.

"We'll bring you onboard. Stand by to kill your sails."

Brennan sighed as the *Excalibur* maneuvered tighter in over him, getting close enough to pluck his cables out of the sky.

"I hate this part," he groaned, but he killed his sails as the big ship began reeling him into the hold that had opened up in her belly, hanging on as his fighter jerked and bucked in the control of the big cruiser.

Free Corsair *Excalibur*

Gaston rose up from the command throne as the young prince was shown onto the bridge.

"Your Majesty." He nodded simply.

Brennan scoffed openly at him. "Call me Bren, Gas. We may not be old pals, but we've shared too much of the same sky for that nonsense."

He wasn't exaggerating, either. Gas and Mira had saved Brennan and his sister, and they'd flown through some bloody skies together. In Brennan's ledger, that was enough to allow anyone the use of his name, ranks be damned.

Gaston smiled. "Welcome aboard the *Excalibur*, Bren."

"Glad to be here," Brennan said, looking around. He whistled softly. "Damn. This looks like the operations room at the palace."

"I expect that was the idea," Gaston said. "The *Caleb* was specifically designed to allow the emperor to command his forces from closer to the front."

Brennan frowned. "Dad wanted that? *Why?* There are no enemies that would have required that. We spend most of our time just putting down brush fires along the Southern Kingdoms, or we did."

"I don't know His Majesty's thoughts on the matter. I merely designed her to his specifications," Gaston admitted with an uncertain gesture.

"Well, whatever he was thinking, it's clear his ego was as big as I remember." Brennan chuckled as he looked at the black throne, clearly reminiscent of the one in the palace. "Where's Mira? I'd like a word."

"If she were here, you could even have two. However, she left a short while ago."

"Left for where?"

Gaston didn't answer, looking over to the myriad displays around him as if checking the status of the ship.

"Gas, come on," Brennan said. "I'm not here to arrest her, or any of you."

Gaston grimaced slightly before he said, "The skipper is investigating an oddity in the Alliance network."

Brennan froze. "The sky-fire reports?"

"You saw them." Gaston looked up at him sharply.

"Half the Imperial military has seen them by now, and the only reason the other half hasn't is because you can't fit that many people in conference rooms at one time," Brennan said. "Does she have any idea what Corian is playing at?"

"If she did, I'd like to think she'd have just told me rather than run off to investigate."

"It's got to have something to do with the component theft and imperanium," Brennan said, rubbing his head.

"What?" Gaston snapped around to look intently at him.

Brennan held up a hand. "Just forget I said that. Less hassle for you that way. I was out with my trainer looking into something before I heard about this mess."

"You said imperanium," Gaston said, pausing for a moment before coming to a decision. "Come with me."

Brennan was confused but followed as the engineer pushed past him and headed off the command deck.

*

"Holy winds," Brennan swore softly as he looked down at the stacks of raw imperanium ore loaded into the hold of the *Excalibur* that Gaston had led him to. "Do you know how many years you'd all get in a stockade for even *having* this?"

"Better us than Corian," Gaston told him.

"No argument there," Brennan said, still not quite believing what he was seeing. "This is more than we recovered from the baron. Where did Corian *find* this much imperanium?"

"More to the point, if he had this much on one ship," Gaston said, "and you found a similar shipment in another sector . . . how much does Corian *have?*"

"I need to contact my sister," Brennan said after a horrified moment.

Gaston examined him for a moment, then nodded. "Do you have the codes?"

"I do."

"Then we have the secure comm."

CHAPTER 15

Silpheth Sector, Deep in Alliance-Controlled Territory

Jockeying a personal sail in for a landing was more of an art than something that could be repeated reliably, the most dangerous part unsurprisingly being when one got close to the ground. Mira had always laughed a little at how much the trainers had stressed that, but there was logic to the emphasis. Within a few hundred feet of the ground, you had less of an opportunity to abort the landing attempt if something went wrong, which most people tended not to think about much as the solid mass came rushing up at them.

The trick was to feather the approach and not try to make a perfect landing, instead focusing on making it as soft as possible no matter where you were putting down.

That was what your average thrill seeker had to worry about, at least. Cadremen were used to making insane landings using little more than their armor and wits to ensure survival. Mira unbuckled from the personal sails and let herself drop clear fifty feet above a flat strip of loose dirt and sparse vegetation.

She fell for only a second before the light wings of her armor blossomed, guiding the energy of her descent more horizontally and turning her path into an arc. A dozen feet or so off the surface, she was moving near a hundred miles an hour parallel to the ground thanks to the redirection of her momentum, but it still was *not* a survivable situation for touchdown.

The dozen-foot vertical distance was fine; the horizontal speed was now the issue.

Luckily, bleeding that off was considerably easier to calculate than the initial arc. Mira spread her armor's wings out to their fullest, turning them flat to the wind, and braked as hard as she could. Speed bled off amazingly fast but, along with it, so did her altitude.

She hit the ground in a twenty-mile-per-hour tumble that turned into a foot-first skid ending several dozen feet from where she had first touched dirt, and then she just lay there for a moment.

Why do people do this for fun?

She laughed there, on her back and looking up in the sky, because she knew the answer to that. Before she'd joined the Cadre, she'd done some of the craziest things possible herself. The reason was easy: You did it to feel *alive*. Cadre operations had filled that quotient for her a long time past, in Cadre time at least. Even a couple of years of operations could age you.

Cadre operations tended to leave a person dealing with some of the worst sorts. Nice people didn't generally attract the attention of operations. For many, including Mira, that side of things wore on your soul whether you were engaged for the best reasons or not. Cadre didn't quit, however. Such an act wasn't in their mind-set.

Not without extreme provocation.

Mira shook off those thoughts and climbed to her feet, checking herself for injuries she might not have noticed while riding on an adrenaline rush. Nothing broken, which was the only real risk her armor couldn't fully cover her against, so aside from a few acceleration bruises she was in fit shape to move.

She'd picked her landing site carefully, aiming to put herself on the ground as close to Corian's projected site of operation as possible, and now figured she had only a few hours' hike to close the rest of the distance. Personal sail projectors were much smaller than anything a ship needed, for obvious reasons, which was the only way she'd been able to make it in this close. A ship would have been spotted, its thousand-foot sails gleaming in the skies from as far away as one could physically see before the mists swallowed even light. A personal sail was only a few dozen feet across and, tuned to a darker spectrum of light or into the nonvisible, could be all but impossible to see more than a dozen miles away even to sophisticated scanning systems.

Mira took a moment to get her bearings before she started out, the sun's heat beating down on her head and shoulders as she began to hike.

∗

She knelt just under the peak of a hill to keep her profile from being contrasted against the sky behind her and examined the Redoubt in the distance.

The structure's design was familiar, similar to schematics used by the *Excalibur* and Imperial palace. The dark burnished metal reflected little of the sun's rays, but she knew from experience that it would be cool to the touch nonetheless. Unlike almost everything else in the habitat occupied by the empire, the eternal sun didn't seem to touch imperanium.

There's a lot of movement there for what was supposed to be a largely useless Redoubt.

There were a few such Redoubts scattered around the habitat, she knew. Some, like the palace, were situated in strategically advantageous locations. With access to water reserves and easy trade routes, the Imperial palace had been a natural location to settle in. Other Redoubts were so far removed from anything of value that their isolation became valuable in itself, like the Imperial Redoubt where the *Excalibur* had been built and where high-profile prisoners were quietly secured until interest in them died down.

And then we have places like this, Mira thought as she looked over the small Redoubt and the small army that was milling around it.

This locale was too far from anything useful to be strategic, but too close to be isolated. With no significant military value under the Pax Imperia, such places had been left to gather dust and be buried by the drifting sands. Occasionally they were turned into bases by criminal groups or those who wanted to disconnect from the empire. The latter generally got tired and gave up in short order, while the former often had to be dug out with military force. But for the most part, they were simply empty.

However, now that the Pax had been shattered, Corian obviously saw value in the old fortress.

Well, not going to learn anything from out here, Mira decided, sliding down the hill and setting her sights on the path ahead.

Sneaking in through that security was going to be fun, Mira decided with a smile curling her lips. She just hoped that whatever she found was worth all the effort she was putting in; otherwise she was going to be rather put out with Corian.

Imperial Palace, Operations Room

Lydia strode into the space, conscious of how many eyes were on her every step. The feeling of being watched was nothing new, to be certain, but there was a certain added intensity since she'd taken the throne.

Or perhaps that's just my imagination, she thought.

Imagination or not, the feeling was real and beginning to generate an all-too-real strain.

"Your Majesty." William was already there, prompting her to wonder if the man ever slept.

"I understand my brother wants to speak with me," she said softly.

William bowed slightly. "He's waiting for your return signal."

"Send it, if you please."

William gestured to a technician, who bent to the task without a word. A few moments later, the main projector flickered to life and a familiar face looked out at them with an oddly familiar backdrop behind him.

"Hey, sis," Brennan said and grinned. "Like the new place?"

Lydia raised an eyebrow as she found herself looking behind her brother at what *seemed* to be the throne just a few rooms away right there in the palace.

"A little presumptuous, I believe I would say," William said with a slight twitch to his lips. "I see you located Cadrewoman Delsol."

"No, as a matter of fact." Brennan leaned forward from what Lydia now realized had to be the command deck of the *Caleb Bar*, or rather, the *Excalibur*.

Father had issues, she thought as she barely kept from rolling her eyes at the realization that he'd put a throne on what was to have been his personal flagship.

"That *is* the *Caleb*, is it not?" William asked.

"The *Excalibur*, yes, it is. However, Delsol isn't on board for the moment," Brennan said. "Are you secure over there?"

"Of course."

Brennan glanced to one side, but looked troubled as he turned his focus back. "Lydia, you remember the delivery I had made to you a short while ago?"

"Yes, certainly." Lydia looked confused, and noted from the corner of her eye that William didn't seem much better. "The—"

"Delivery, yes." Brennan cut her off. "Delsol located another such shipment."

Lydia and William stared at one another in open shock for a moment before William recovered his composure and refocused on the projection.

"The same amount?" he asked tersely.

"No," Brennan said, drawing some measure of relaxation from William before he went on. "Twice as much."

William staggered back a step, slumping into a chair.

"That's not possible," he said, face ashen.

"Well, unless it's somehow counterfeit," Brennan returned, "I believe that reality has insisted that it *is*."

"Where is he getting it all?" William muttered, eyes cast down at the ground as he considered the implications, then looked up sharply. "Where is Delsol?"

"Not here," Brennan said flatly. "More than that I'm not saying. Secure or not, something very strange is going on out here, William."

"We are aware of that, Bren," Lydia cut in. "Corian is planning some sort of operation—"

"I know," Brennan said. "Whatever he has in the works, I think we can all agree that it would be best if we were to prevent it from happening, yes?"

"That would be a good assumption, Bren," Lydia said.

"I'm going to keep looking into things on this side," Brennan said, "but I wanted you to know what they found out here. I don't know how it's all connected, but there are too many common factors turning up the more we dig into things."

"Agreed," William added. "Try to stay in touch."

"I will," Brennan said, looking over to William for a moment. "Is there any word on Matani?"

"Cadreman Fenn will survive, but he's out of action for a good long while," William told him. "You got him to the medics fast enough."

"Good, thank you," Brennan said. "They weren't able to tell me much before I headed back to the skimmer I shot up."

"You did what you had to do, and so did Fenn," William assured him. "I wish you'd stand still long enough for us to get another senior Cadreman out to your position, though. This is likely to get dangerous, Brennan."

"It'd take too long and you know it," Brennan said with a shake of his head. "Whatever Corian is up to, the clock is ticking."

"Agreed."

"Be careful, Bren," Lydia said, her face concerned.

"I'll watch my back, sis," Brennan said and smiled as reassuringly as he could. "You better do the same. Remember his last operation."

Lydia stared at her twin. "I will."

Brennan's image blanked out, leaving William and Lydia looking at one another with matching expressions of worry.

"Where did Corian locate that much imperanium?" Lydia asked softly, eyes roving the room to ensure no one was close enough to overhear.

"I have no idea, Your Majesty," William answered candidly. "That's more than should even *exist*, to my knowledge. The raw material has long been one of the greatest bottlenecks in Imperial technical development. There is no possible way that Corian just happened to discover this amount of resources out of the blue sky."

"I agree," Lydia said. "He located these resources before he began his plan."

"Somewhere," William said, "not here. Not in the empire. It's just not possible that we missed this much for so long."

"Right, so he found it on assignment for the Cadre then," Lydia hypothesized, considering the possibilities from what she knew of Corian's record. "Likely to the south. He had to have used his resources to secure the material and then ship it back to the empire."

"But he stored it near the capital," William guessed, realizing how much that would explain. "He didn't expect to lose the palace, and now he's scrambling to get his caches back under his control."

"We need to start searching every skimmer that approaches within a hundred miles of the Alliance line," Lydia said firmly. "Perhaps we're already too late, but . . ."

"I'll issue the order."

Free Corsair *Excalibur*, Second Wind Layer, over the Empire–Alliance Border

Brennan settled back for a moment, forgetting where he was as he considered the situation.

"I need to get to Mira," he said finally, looking up to find Gaston smirking at him. "What?"

"You look comfortable there," the engineer told him, causing Brennan to look down and realize he was still sitting in the throne that was central to the command deck of the *Excalibur*.

He got up quickly, shaking his head. "My father had serious issues."

Gaston laughed openly, as did several of the others from their posts. "That seems to be the general consensus, yes. In fairness to him, however, the *Caleb Bar* was designed as a field command warship. It was intended to be his palace in battles far from the empire."

"Why he felt the need for such a thing is what's worrying me," Brennan said. "We haven't fought a real war since the founding of the empire—not of the sort that would require this kind of mobile command base."

"I just designed the ship systems, kid," Gaston said. "They didn't even bother sending me the specifications on the interior. Someone else handled the aesthetics."

"Right. Well, I suppose it doesn't matter right now," Brennan said, wishing he really believed that for a moment. "Where was Mira heading?"

Gaston looked over to the central projection system on the command deck. "Put it up."

"You got it, Gas," Dusk said.

The system lit up, showing a map that Brennan recognized of the disputed territory.

"That's where the sky-fire alert ends," he said. "Last I heard, there was a division of Imperial Army and Navy forces converging there."

"That's right," Gaston said, flicking his hand in a casual gesture that sent the map on the screen scrolling. "Skipper went to check out the other end of the alert."

Brennan whistled. "That's deep in Alliance territory."

"Can you think of another reason she'd go herself?" Gaston asked dryly. "The skipper is not someone to operate from behind the lines."

"There's being at the front, and then there's taking on Corian's entire army singlehandedly, damn it!" Brennan blurted, unable to quite believe what he was hearing, though the idea became more and more believable by the second. "She's out of her mind."

"Cadremen are often addicted to the action," Gaston said wearily. "Many think they're adrenaline addicts, but it's more than that. They thrive on the conflict, on besting their opponents, and nothing else matches up to the satisfaction that brings. She may have cut ties with the empire, Brennan, but Mira is Cadre to the core."

"Cadre has access to backup," Brennan grumbled, "supplies, support. This isn't being Cadre, Gas, this is being suicidal. I'm going after her."

Gaston just barely managed to keep from laughing in the young royal's face.

"You really don't see the irony in that statement, do you?" he asked after he got control of his reaction.

Brennan's death glare answered that question, much the way Gaston had expected it to be answered.

There was a world of difference between seeing the irony and giving a damn.

Alliance Redoubt, Silpheth Sector

Armor in stealth configuration, Mira slipped past another guard on her way into the Redoubt. She would have been disgusted with the ease by which she had made it so far, except the scent of trap that had been lingering in the air ever since she arrived had been increasing steadily. So now she was more disgusted with Corian for laying out the trap so obviously.

It was, frankly, insulting.

Of course, there was the off chance that his machinations were aimed at someone else, but really, who other than a Cadre member would even try for something this dangerous?

She slipped into the Redoubt while stowed away in a supply delivery, mostly water and foodstuffs from what she could tell in the time she was buried in the back of the transport. Any force the size Corian had gathered would work, travel, and fight on their stomachs, and that meant a near continuous line of supplies rolling right in through security.

No matter how tight you normally were when it came to security, the weakest point would always be anywhere you had routine. Corian knew that, no question, and Mira could see that he'd taken obvious precautions. The shift looked fresh, which meant he was probably rotating people in more often than normal, but for all that, they only gave a cursory look into the transport. Given the darker interior, and their eyes not being adjusted to shadow, her armor's stealth abilities were almost ideally suited to handling their inspection.

More concerning were the various electronic scanners the supplies were passing through, but Mira didn't see anything she didn't recognize, so she was confident of being able to skirt those as well.

Once they were inside, however, the danger really started.

She dropped quietly to the ground beside the transport after it had been stopped a few moments. She didn't want to give anyone time to get it into their heads to go unload the vehicle, as unlikely as that probably was given the normal procrastination she had come to expect from the Imperial military. Corian might have managed to rid his forces of the habit, but Mira expected that it would be easier to convince people to stop breathing.

The dimmer light inside the Redoubt was again to her advantage—less direct luminescence to degrade her camouflage. So Mira took full advantage of that and quickly made her way out of the common areas.

The Redoubt was laid out similarly to the palace as well as every other known Redoubt that existed. Whoever had built the things had been working from a common set of plans, which made Mira's task that much easier. There were only so many places one could install the needed power and communications lines into a Redoubt, as the composition of the structure made running lines too difficult.

Internal security was even worse than that outside, something Mira supposed could be attributed to overconfidence on Corian's part as well as too much trust in the relative isolation of the Redoubt.

More likely he's luring me in, she thought.

For most people she supposed the idea of walking into an obvious trap was a good sign of insanity, but for her it was just another challenge. She knew that she and Corian were too much alike in that manner. Neither could turn down a chance to prove themselves, particularly against someone by whom they'd previously been bested.

In their earlier encounters, Mira knew that they'd effectively matched one another, though she was galled to admit such a thing. They'd been unable to prevent the other from accomplishing immediate goals but had thoroughly trashed each other's long-term plans. Both had survived the very best attempts of the other to end their lives.

For people with egos like those of Corian and herself, Mira knew damn well that there was only one ultimate outcome. Eventually, one of them would mark up a decisive win . . . and the other would be cooling on the ground.

The universe alone help the survivor if the other died by another hand in the meantime. Mira couldn't speak for certain about Corian, but she knew that the open wound of not finishing this herself would eat at her for as long as she lived.

Such things were the curse of the very mind-set that made her good at what she did. Few Cadremen or women were what most of society would describe as mentally stable and balanced individuals. Cadre had different standards; the sort of people capable of serving at that level of the Imperial forces were often poorly adapted to doing much else.

The Redoubt was only in partial use, she found as she moved from section to section as stealthily as she could. Most of the structure was empty and had been long enough to gather a thick cover of dust and even sand in some areas where it hadn't been sealed well enough against the elements.

The areas in use, however, were a hive of action.

*

"Be wary with that," Alastor Sigvun ordered as he oversaw the final preparations. "Those systems are delicate outside their casing."

The men working nodded as they lowered the tracking and drive systems into the large dull-colored blocks of metal they were working on. Sigvun's eagle eyes observed every detail in the preparation sequence, his expression positively *daring* someone to screw up.

They knew their jobs, however, and the casing was closed up and welded shut before the block was moved across the large hall in the

Redoubt to where a stack of dozens, if not hundreds, more were sitting in wait.

Sigvun stepped aside as another block was slid into place and the whole process began again, his attention shifting as a commotion caught his eye across the hall.

"General," he said as he recognized Corian approaching.

"Admiral," Corian returned the greeting, eyes sweeping the hall. "Are we on schedule?"

"We are, though it is close," Sigvun admitted. "When you pushed forward the timetable it made things difficult . . ."

"A necessary move," Corian said, still looking around with wary eyes, "I assure you."

"As you say," Sigvun allowed. "We will be ready on time."

"Excellent; proceed then. Do not allow me to slow the process."

Sigvun nodded, turning back to his supervisory tasks.

*

What are those things?

Mira was crouched in a third-floor alcove, looking over the former great hall of the Redoubt. Hundreds of people all worked feverishly on some project she didn't understand. They had blocks of what appeared to be imperanium—though if it was, then she had *vastly* underestimated Corian's stores of the material—that they were fitting some sort of instrument package into.

There were stacks of the blocks right under her alcove, piled ten high and ten deep for row after row. Whatever they were, Corian wanted—and had—a lot of them.

It looked like a drive system, she rather thought, but that made little sense. No drive system she knew of would require that much solid mass to shield it.

I need a closer look at one of those, Mira decided.

She was about to move when a slight flurry caught her eye and she was startled to see Corian himself on the floor. The man strode through the throngs of people like he owned the place, which she supposed he did for all practical purposes.

Mira watched as her nemesis stopped to speak with a man who seemed to be the one in charge. He didn't seem unhappy with the conversation, but they were too far away to read their lips, so all she got of the conversation were the emotions the two expressed via body language.

Corian was satisfied, and eager, though he was trying to conceal the latter. The other man was tense but didn't seem deeply concerned about what they were discussing. Whatever they talked about, Corian was happier as a result, and both seemed confident. That didn't bode well for the empire.

She didn't move for as long as Corian was there. The man was clearly on guard, and he would see through her stealth abilities and systems if anyone could. Once he had turned away, heading for the other side of the hall, she moved, dropping out of the alcove and down onto the closest stack. She knelt down, staying low and out of sight, even with her armor matching the colors around her, and examined the material.

Definitely imperanium, she thought as she ran a hand over the exterior of one of the objects.

The weld seams kept her from opening the casing to see what was inside, but she could recognize some of the components from where workers were still installing them across the hall. *Drive components for the quantum-tractor drives.* She knew the items mostly from having recovered so many on the *Helena Night* along with the imperanium ingots.

As she examined the blocks more closely, Mira became certain that they were nearly solid imperanium. That was completely baffling, though she supposed it explained the quantum-drive components.

There was no other method of getting that much mass into the air without adding a lot more systems to support the likes of a sail projector.

Why the hell does he want these to fly?

After checking the welds again, confirming that they were indeed permanently shut, Mira considered what was next. This was clearly not some minor operation. The level of investment she was seeing around her was more than Corian had put into the coup, by every account she'd been able to ascertain.

That meant he was moving on a significant offensive, at the very least, but she just didn't see what he was going to do with the tractor drives in a block of imperanium. They weren't much use as ships—far too small—and the slow acceleration of the tractor drive meant that they wouldn't be of much use as kinetic weapons.

Imperial forces might not be at their peak, but they'd be able to hammer these things long before they became a real threat.

I've got to be missing something, Mira thought as she retreated from her position, ducking back out of the hall and heading into the darkened corridors of the Redoubt. She needed to find a records room or, failing that, someone who would have the answers she needed and wouldn't be missed for a while.

She was flexible. Either would serve just fine.

CHAPTER 16

Imperial Sky Vessel *Bier's Firewind*, on Patrol at the Alliance Line

"There's another one inbound from sector ninety, skipper."

Maximillian Gowan glanced toward the identified sector and grunted slightly before telling his communications officer to flag them.

"Yes, sir."

This was the eighth skimmer they'd halted since the order had come down from the Imperial governor in command of the sector. There was a surprising level of activity along the line, though perhaps he shouldn't have been so surprised. The artificial border of the Alliance line had done little to change the habits of the people living along it. They still went about their business, as they always had, and if that meant crossing some political boundary, well . . . so be it.

Stopping and searching ships was a hassle for both the empire and the poor bastards being flagged, but he supposed there was a reason for the actions.

Smuggling supplies or some such, I suppose, Max figured.

So far they'd found nothing worth the time of his ship and crew. Some illegal substances, generally used recreationally, were discovered along with a lot of supplies for hard-up communities put in a pinch by the hostilities.

He'd let them all pass after a search, cargo intact.

Collecting taxes and enforcing civil laws wasn't his job, and he wasn't wasting the time of his crew to do someone else's work.

"Skipper!"

The sharp yell brought Max back around. "What is it?"

"They're running, sir!"

"Damn it. All right, people! Pursuit course! Pull us into the wind!"

The *Firewind*'s crew instantly went to work as the ship's action station alarm went off. Her winches buzzed into immediate motion as the ship keeled over just slightly, bringing them up and tight to the sails in the wind layer above them. The relaxed motions they'd been going through fell by the wayside as the gentle breeze turned bitter and sharp.

"Clear the chase guns," Max ordered. "Stand ready to fire a warning."

"You got it, skipper," the gunner chief replied instantly, sending on the order.

"She's getting tight to the wind, captain," Allyson Mier, his second-in-command, said as she made her way over. "They're going to—"

They both winced as the smaller ship winched itself right into the wind layer, riding dangerously rough in the buffeting winds.

"I don't think they're running minor pharmacopoeia, skipper," Allyson said through her grimace.

"If they are," Max said, "their captain is an idiot."

"He's an idiot anyway," she countered, shaking her head. "No chance that ship holds together. We'd have to put in for refit after a maneuver like that. They're sure to . . . yeah, there they go."

The ship had been caught in a rhythmic undulation that had pitched it over and thrown it clear of the wind layer. The sails were keeping it in the air, but Max wouldn't have given much for the chances of any crew that hadn't been strapped tightly down after a ride like that.

"They're drifting loose now," Allyson said. "If someone doesn't get control of her, they'll plow in before we catch up."

"Not my worry for now," Max said. "Get a few Marines ready to check the wreck. I want to know what was so important that they'd do something that dumb to escape us."

"You got it, skipper."

Alliance Redoubt, Silpheth Sector

Anderson Tan stifled a yawn as he made his way back from the supply rooms, heading for the assembly hall. The pace on the builds had been fast before, but in the last day or so the pressure to push production ahead of schedule had been intensified beyond all recognition. He didn't know what the guys up top were thinking, but if the squeeze didn't let up soon, people would start making errors in assembly.

Given what they were building, a few errors were probably not going to be that big a problem, but only in that the damn things wouldn't be aimed anywhere near *his* family.

Anderson was crossing a dark alcove in the old Redoubt, just a few dozen feet from the assembly hall, when a shadow moved in his peripheral vision. He half turned toward it, intent on identifying the source of the motion, but before he could an arm snaked around his throat. He was yanked clear off his feet and into the darkness.

Anderson struggled, but the grip around his throat was like imperanium itself. His breathing started to come more and more raggedly, pressure on either side of his throat tightening even as his efforts slowed, until a darkness deeper than that of the alcove claimed him.

*

Mira let her arm relax from around the man's throat, lowering the limp body to the floor as she checked to be sure her actions hadn't drawn notice. Luckily, the Redoubt was immense, swallowing sound like the mists swallowed light, and the immediate area's motion and activity drowned out what little noise might have been heard.

With no shortage of empty areas to retreat to with her prey, Mira dragged the unconscious man into one of the spaces she'd found earlier. She propped him up against the wall, kneeling beside him to check his pulse.

He was breathing steadily, and his pulse was fast but strong.

Satisfied, Mira settled back to wait.

He woke up, groggily rolling his head from side to side a few minutes later. Mira let him waken just a bit before her hand snapped out and grabbed him around the throat.

This time she wasn't cutting off blood flow, but the pressure she put on his trachea made drawing air a chore. His eyes widened, his arms coming up reflexively as his hands clawed at her armor. Mira ignored the struggles as she leaned in, looking him in the eyes, knowing that this moment was crucial.

"Would you like to breathe again, unaided?" she said softly in his ear. "I can arrange things either way."

"W-what do you want?" he gasped out as she relaxed her grip just slightly.

Mira knew that the moment rode on a fulcrum. Give the man enough time and, if he were determined and smart enough to think, she'd never get anything useful out of him. Real interrogations took *time*. Not hours, not even days, but weeks or longer. Sometimes, really important ones could take *years*.

She had seconds.

Mira had to hit him hard and fast, giving him no time to think of anything *but* the truth.

"What are you building here?" she asked in a hiss, putting the pressure on while she spoke, making him gasp as his eyes bulged. "Tell me. Now!"

"K-kinetic . . . torpedoes," he gasped out as she relaxed again.

Mira blinked, shaking her head as she pushed hard on his throat again.

"Try that again. Those things can't possibly accelerate fast enough to take out a ship."

"Not . . . for ships," he gasped as she let up again. "They're designed to accelerate up, out of the atmosphere, then turn around and come back down . . . keep speeding up until they strike the target."

Mira shifted back, relaxing her grip almost entirely as she thought about that with some degree of shock.

That's the plan. That much mass, accelerated continually by a quantum drive . . .

Her thoughts trailed off as she tried to work the math. Mira didn't know the total mass, but as heavy as imperanium was, she didn't have to know the exact specifications to know what the end result would be. If the tractor drives could get the torpedoes up to a critical velocity, they would strike with enough force to destroy *cities*.

She turned, eyes filled with cold fury, back to the man before her, his breathing only now beginning to return to normal. She again leaned in, cutting off his breath with her hand.

"Here's what you're going to tell me now . . ."

Imperial Palace

"Something going on?" William asked as he walked toward a murmuring of voices.

"Yes, sir," one of the young aides said. "The *Bier's Firewind* reported a blockade runner just went down. They're dispatching Marines to investigate the ship."

"Did they shoot it down?"

"No, sir. The ship tried to run, got too close to the wind, and was bounced around until it lost altitude and went down."

William winced. "Ouch. Any survivors?"

"The Marines haven't reported back yet, but it went down pretty hard."

Probably not then, William decided. "All right, keep me posted."

"Yes, sir."

A ship trying to run the Alliance line was no big concern. Most of them were small-time smugglers, either running supplies to hurting populations on the other side of the border . . . or sometimes the Imperial side, William had to admit, or looking to exploit the sudden shift in markets to turn a profit. Oftentimes both at once, if one were to be honest, but either way, such matters weren't really a concern for the empire at this time, if they ever would be.

He cared little for people looking to make their way in a rough world, so long as they didn't get too cocky and rub the empire's public face in their success.

A ship that wrecked itself trying to run from an Imperial frigate, however, that was of some significant interest.

Either the captain was an imbecile or he was running something over which he knew the empire wouldn't look the other way. That meant either war supplies to the alliance or perhaps something nastier. Given the times, however, William had a good idea what the Marines would find when they cracked that ship open.

His eyes fell on the map of the explored territories, drifting south along the downward spin of the Great Islands. *It has to be there, somewhere in those old Cadre assignments I wiped from the Imperial servers. Corian located a treasure trove. Imperanium enough to power the next* revolution of Imperial industry, in the right hands. In the wrong ones, the burning skies alone could exceed the damage potential.

Right now, unfortunately, William had no doubt . . . those resources were most emphatically in the wrong hands.

Near the Alliance Line

"Smoldering flesh," the lead Marine swore, stepping over a broken and unmoving body as he led with his blaster carbine to sweep the room of the downed vessel.

He needn't have bothered. There was nothing moving.

Nothing except the blood that was still running down the bulkheads.

"This was one hard ride, centurion," another man said, looking a little green as he examined the next section of the ship. "Same thing over here."

"All right," Centurion Gav Hirat said, waving his men on in. "Spread out by pairs. Check the ship section by section; clear *every* deck body by body. I want them all checked, no matter how mangled they look. No one gets killed by the dead on my watch, understood?"

"We've got it, centurion." The squad leader nodded. "We'll check them all."

He gave his men a hard glance, getting only nods in return.

"All right, Pall, you're with me." The centurion clapped the closest man on the shoulder. "We're going for the cargo."

"Right with you, centurion."

Imperial Sky Vessel *Bier's Firewind*

Max looked over the wreck from the flying bridge of the *Firewind*, shaking his head.

"That dumb bastard should never have been allowed to captain a personal skimmer, let alone a cargo vessel," he growled, his sense of professional discipline affronted by the sheer stupidity of the crash.

"Cargo captains aren't trained to handle the streams," First Officer Sara Conn said calmly. "Speed isn't worth that risk."

"Whatever he was carrying wasn't worth it either," Max said. "Lost his ship, lost his crew . . . and we still get to find out exactly what he was carrying. Stupid."

"He wasn't thinking, Max. He was running scared."

"Doesn't excuse it," Max growled. "I just hate the waste. Men and gear are too valuable to be trusted to fools."

"Right. Now I just want to know what he was transporting."

*

"Bulkheads are twisted, centurion," Pall said as he wrenched at the hatch, unable to budge the metal blockage at all. "Hatch is jammed."

"Well, crap," Gav grumbled, looking around as he considered the layout of the ship class they were on. "We can drop back two sections, then go up to come down. With me."

"Yes, sir."

Navigating the wreckage was difficult. The sky ship had come down heavy on one side and rolled before it came to a stop. That meant they were walking on the walls as much as on the deck, and crawling across ladders more than climbing, but the centurion had investigated worse wrecks in his career.

They reached the top deck, then moved over to the next section and found the bulkhead there had burst open.

They lowered themselves down, controlling their slide into the hold by using the ladder grips, until they were balanced on the edge of the deck and wall in the middle of the ship's main hold.

"Light it up," Gav ordered.

Pall nodded, breaking out a set of omnidirectional ball lights and flicking them on. He tossed them up and away, letting them clatter into the debris, where they cast a glow around the whole of the compartment.

"What is this stuff, centurion?" Pall asked, looking around.

Gav frowned, climbing over a broken box and bracing himself so he could examine some of the strewn cargo closer.

"Targeting blades," he said quietly. "Haven't seen these in . . . well, I was wetter than you the last time."

"They important?" Pall asked, confused.

Gav grabbed one. "Depends on what's coded on them. They were used for ballistic missile guidance, before those were all scrapped. Too costly to maintain. Reaction chemicals eat through most storage tanks over time. Ugly stuff."

"Why get yourself killed for this?" Pall asked, confused.

"Like I said," Gav told him seriously, "depends on what's on them. Come on, let's go topside. I need a link back to the *Firewind*."

Imperial Sky Vessel *Bier's Firewind*

"Targeting blades? You mean for reaction missiles?" Max asked, puzzled. "I thought those things were all decommissioned before I signed up."

"The missiles were. The blades were surplused and stored in Imperial warehouses in case anyone figured out a use for them," Sara told him. "We're running the codes the Marines sent us now, seeing if that gives us anything."

"Why the hell would they run from us over obsolete equipment that the empire probably forgot existed? None of this makes sense."

"That just means that we're missing an important piece of information, cap."

"Don't I know it, Sara."

"Captain . . ." A young officer spoke up, attracting their attention. "We have information on the data coded onto the blades."

"I'm assuming they're targeted at the Southern Kingdoms," Max said, walking over. "That's where they were coded for before being decommissioned."

"That would have made sense, yes, sir," the officer told him, shaking her head, "but those are not the coordinates we're reading."

"Where are they aimed for then?"

"The capital, sir. The coordinates are hard coded for the capital," she told him.

Max frowned. "Why would any of those damn things have been coded for that?"

"None of them were," she told him. "They had to have been recoded, sir."

"Burning skies . . ."

Imperial Palace

William scowled openly, his mood not improved by his complete lack of understanding of what he was looking at.

"I don't understand," he said. "The *Firewind* found crates of these things?"

"Yes, sir. We're still checking numbers, but so far they've all been recoded to target the palace directly," the analyst Hiland Peers told him seriously.

"Why would Corian, or anyone, need these?" he asked. "We have better targeting systems today, I'm sure."

"Nothing intended for this purpose, however, sir," Peers said. "We never continued developing this technology once we discontinued the extra-atmospheric reaction technology. It's possible that Corian has renewed one of those old programs, I suppose."

"How dangerous would this be?" William asked.

"Our defenses should be able to handle inbound ballistic warheads, or even ones under reaction thrust."

"Well, that's good at least," William said.

"Yes, sir, but we have another problem."

"Of course we do." He sighed. "What is it?"

"The technology to recode those blades is rather bulky," Peers said, "and it was maintained only in one place. Here in the capital."

William swore, half turning. "Security!"

A palace guard rushed over. "Sir!"

"Get a team," he ordered. "Take Peers with you to plan."

He looked back at Peers. "I want any, and all, facilities that can encode those blades to be raided, secured, and *scoured* for any evidence. Then do the same for the warehouses those things were stored in."

"Yes, sir." The guard nodded, gesturing to allow Peers to pass him. "After you, Mr. Peers."

The young analyst suddenly looked nervous but nodded as he joined the guard and left the control room.

William was left to glower at the tactical and strategic displays as he tried to figure out just what in the burning skies Corian was up to.

Alliance Redoubt, Silpheth Sector

He's not planning an attack, Mira thought as she looked over the facility again. *Corian is planning an atrocity. This isn't war any longer; it's madness.*

The stacks of metal blocks had more significance in her eyes now that she knew just what they represented. Each one was probably enough to annihilate a city. Their destructive power would depend on just how long they could be accelerated, but outside the atmosphere, without any forces acting to slow them, she expected that the maximum velocity they could achieve would be . . . substantial.

Gaston would know the exact numbers, but I know enough, Mira decided.

Corian had to be stopped, and this time for good. Unleashing this nightmare on the empire was beyond the burning skies. Mira didn't want to see what would happen if others tried to copy—or, far worse, top—this insanity.

Her source for the information she'd just picked up would be out for a while longer, and she couldn't be sure exactly when someone would notice him. She had limited time to decide just what she was going to do, get it done, and then get her backside out of the Redoubt.

She would prefer to destroy everything in sight, but the weapons were made from bloody *imperanium,* of all things. Even if she'd brought every piece of demolition kit she had on the *Excalibur,* there was no chance she could have put a dent in the depot supply she was seeing here.

It'll have to be a sky strike, she concluded finally.

That meant it was time to leave.

A full Imperial sky strike would have to punch through the Alliance line, fight its way through to the depot, and then bombard the area with enough munitions to drive a crater right down to the bedmetal.

First, however, the empire had to know just what Corian was up to.

Mira shook herself from her thoughts and began the process of extricating herself from the Redoubt.

Getting out would be marginally easier than getting in, Mira expected. The security she'd seen had been arrayed outward, intending to keep people from investigating the Redoubt. It wasn't a prison, which made things simpler.

She navigated the halls, retracing her original path as she considered whether to try sneaking out within an empty transport or simply walking. Most likely she'd have to walk, Mira figured, as she hadn't seen a lot of transports leaving during her reconnaissance.

Mira dropped from an alcove into a deserted section just outside the walls of the Redoubt, making ready to extract through the few remaining security lines, when the scraping of boot metal against grit caused her to freeze. Her blaster cleared the holster in the next instant as men poured from the alcoves on either side and brought their carbines to bear on her.

She was still processing the sudden change of fortune when a steady staccato beat of something heavier than a footstep drew her attention, and Corian himself walked through the line, his artificial foot thumping hard with every step.

"Welcome to my territory, Cadrewoman Delsol."

"Traitor," Mira said, eyes flicking to check her armor's status.

She had been using it in stealth mode for some time, which was a draw on the power reserves. Not so bad as combat would have been, of course, but bad enough. If she chose to turn this confrontation into a showdown, Mira estimated that her armor would fail within the first few minutes.

Should be enough. If I'm not clear in three minutes, I'm dead anyway.

"Lower the blaster, Delsol," Corian said, not blinking at being called traitor. "You know you have no chance of escaping as well as I do."

"Perhaps I'm willing to go down fighting," she suggested, her left hand unwavering as she held the weapon on Corian, her right dropping to the Armati riding on her right.

"Of that I have little doubt," he conceded, "but do you really think it'll do anyone any good? I know you, Delsol, I know your type. Suicide

isn't in your makeup, and while you'd sacrifice your life for a cause without hesitating . . . you would need to see a *reason* to do so."

"I know what you're planning here, Corian. Insanity," she said,
head turning just slightly as she swept across the faces of each guard
pointing weapons at her.

They were stone faced, no hint of anything beyond the normal
prefight nerves, and little enough of that. Mira figured them for Corian's
personal guard, likely cold-blooded killers each and every one. With
fifteen to twenty guns on her, she started running the numbers in her
head, looking for a way out.

They all had gamma carbines, of course, which meant her armor
wouldn't do much more than prolong her inevitable death in a straight-
up fight.

A few more dead among Corian's guards, sure, but her body would
be cooling on the ground beside them.

Escape was out.

Mira shifted her attention to Corian now, a new question forming
in the front of her mind.

Can I take him down with me?

Corian's grin widened as he watched Delsol shift her stance.

It didn't take a mind reader, nor even as accomplished a reader of
body language as himself, to tell what the woman in front of him was
thinking. Of course, he would probably be gauging the same possibilities in her place.

"Please, Delsol," he chided. "Do you truly think I'd place myself
this close to you if I believed there was even the slightest chance of you
killing me?"

She scoffed audibly. "You didn't believe there was the slightest
chance of us retaking the palace and capital either, now did you,
traitor?"

All right, that took the smile from his face.

"You're trying my patience, Delsol. Surrender now, or die. I honestly no longer care which," Corian said in clipped tones.

He slowly and deliberately drew his own Armati, extending the wide blade with a thought to punctuate his statement properly. He let a silence linger between them for a moment before nodding curtly, accepting that as her response.

"Very well, Cadrewoman," Corian said coldly, "this is where your journey ends. Fire!"

CHAPTER 17

High Above Imperial–Alliance Line

The Naga bucked around him as Brennan worked the controls of both sails with feverish intensity. He was running far closer to the wind than he would normally dare, the old fighter actually up inside the jet stream behind the sails, tossing him around like a rag in a tornado. He was flying that close for two reasons: First, gaining as much speed as he could was vital to minimizing the drag of the fighter. Second, flying close to the wind allowed him to reduce sail size and cut his Naga's profile significantly.

Given that he was flying right into Alliance territory without any real backup, Brennan wasn't going to underestimate the value of remaining hidden.

The young royal didn't know what the hell Mira had been thinking, but then again he supposed that was being a little hypocritical.

Lydia is going to kill me when she finds out I decided to go after Mira on my own, he thought ruefully as he worked the controls.

Waiting wasn't an option, though, not with Mira gunning for Corian and looking to beard the lion in his den.

Particularly not given the apparent operations that Corian was mounting.

A small alarm went off, grabbing Brennan's attention and derailing his line of thought as he glanced down at the threat board set just above his right hand.

Contacts coming out of the mist, he noted, wondering if they'd seen him or not.

The mist was simply the name for the limit at which light eventually became diffracted as it passed through the atmosphere. The actual range could vary wildly, depending on more factors than Brennan could count, but generally on a clear, dry, day you got less than fifty-odd miles before every form of visual identification was rendered worthless.

Some long-range scanners bought you a bit more distance, but even those tended to degrade heavily in the mist.

Light patrol skimmers. Brennan read the tonnage numbers off his threat board.

The skimmers weren't any serious threat to his Naga, he knew, but they could give him a hell of a lot of trouble if they spotted him and signaled on ahead. That was pretty much exactly what that class of skimmer was intended for, of course. He tuned his sails down a few more notches, tucking even more dangerously up behind them, and kept a close eye on the board.

The closing rate was prodigious, the miles dropping by the second, and he had altitude way over the skimmers as they sailed slowly on their path with no signs that they'd spotted him.

Brennan silently thumbed the safety off his gauss cannons, resting his finger just beside the garish red button. If they twitched, he'd have to drop them in the dirt as fast as he could, which wouldn't be good for anyone on the two patrol skimmers. But leaving them to signal back would be considerably less good for him and the empire.

The Naga was buffeted in all directions as it blasted over top of the two skimmers, neither so much as shifting their course by a single arc second while he watched. As they began to recede behind him, Brennan let out a low breath and flicked the safety back over his guns.

Live to fight another day, friends, he thought.

Alliance Redoubt, Silpheth Sector

"Fire!"

She saw the order coming before Corian's men did, so when he started to shout, Mira fully extended the blade of her Armati Elan and swept it across in time to intercept the first burst from a carbine.

The deflected blast was thrown back into the face of a different trooper, dropping the man in his tracks before he could even blink, and she jumped as several others began firing. Gamma bursts tore into the wall behind her as she angled her jump back and landed in the alcove she'd exited from, bursts splashing off surrounding metal.

Corian was snarling orders, and he didn't sound happy in the slightest. She supposed that he'd expected her to make a suicide rush on his position. Truthfully, she *had* considered it, but only briefly. Death was one thing, but dying without ensuring that her target went down *too* . . . well, that just wasn't acceptable.

With that many troops, Corian was right. She wouldn't have been able to eliminate him before they got her and put her down for good.

A scrambling sound behind her told Mira that at least one of the troops was getting more ballsy than she'd prefer, so she glanced back just as a head appeared in the gap, and she casually put a lase blast through it.

The head vanished from sight instantly, a few different voices cursing loudly. Mira didn't wait around to see what they intended to try next, instead opting to retreat into the interior of the Redoubt. Out in the open, Corian's troops had all the cards. No matter how well trained she was, she could predict and intercept shots from only so many at a time.

Inside the Redoubt, however, with tight corridors and places she could mount ambushes, Mira figured she could cost Corian dearly before he had the satisfaction of seeing her fall. Unfortunately, there wasn't much chance of any other outcome that she could see. If Corian had orchestrated the trap as she would have, there was no chance she could get far enough to clear the Redoubt and make her escape. The terrain was too open, with no cover to speak of, so Corian could easily have his men plaster all angles with enough firepower to see her dead.

That was a problem.

She wasn't ready to die yet.

Imperial Palace

"William."

"Your Majesty." William nodded solemnly as Lydia approached him in the center of the operations room.

"I have observed the . . . activity," she said quietly. "Explain, please."

"Patrols near the line brought down a transport," he said. "They were running targeting blades."

"Blades?" she asked, confused. "I'm unfamiliar with those."

"Not surprising, Your Majesty," he told her. "They were rendered obsolete before you were born when we discontinued use of the technology they functioned with. However, it seems Corian has a use for them, and he had them recoded to target the palace and the capital."

"What sort of weapons?" she asked.

"Ballistic missiles," William said. "I was unaware of any remaining in Imperial stocks. However, it seems Corian managed to locate some."

"That man has a tendency to do the impossible," Lydia said. "Do you think this ties in with the predicted operation?"

"I don't know," William admitted. "I can't see how, but this *is* Corian, of course. All I can assure you of, Your Majesty, is that our defenses are perfectly able to handle ballistic targets."

Lydia nodded at that, but didn't appear moved.

"The palace defenses were perfectly able to handle any assault imaginable the day before Corian made his last move, William," she told him firmly. "Find the man. Figure out what he is planning. Until we know, we are *not* safe."

Alliance Redoubt, Silpheth Sector

Mira ran through the corridors, the sounds of boots on metal and men shouting assaulting her from every direction.

She was heading up, looking for Corian's communications center. If she were to die here, she intended for her death to mean something. What she knew about Corian's plans *had* to get out.

Two men appeared in front of her, coming from one of the side corridors and looking almost as surprised to see her barreling down on them as she was by their sudden entrance. Mira didn't bother going for her blaster—she was already within twenty feet of them and running at a dead sprint. The distance closed in an instant as their carbines leveled on her. She could feel time slowing as the first man tightened his finger on the trigger.

The carbine wasn't even aimed at her yet when it went off. Mira ignored it.

The second had a better sense of timing, however, and she swept her Elan into position to intercept the burst as the weapon discharged.

The gamma burst burned against the metal wall, and at the same instant, Mira was among her attackers.

She grabbed the first man's carbine, twisting it up until she had it jammed against his arm, then jerked hard while twisting farther. A crackle of bone was barely audible above his screams as she lashed a kick into the next man's knee, driving him to the ground.

She dropped her Elan, opting to stay in close as she grabbed the first man's head with that hand and proceeded to slam his face repeatedly into his own weapon until he finally lost his grip, toppling back with blood spraying from his nose and cheeks. Mira let him fall, shifting her focus to the second man as he struggled to get his carbine aimed in the tight quarters.

Her ridge hand blow chopped across his throat as she brought her knee up to block the barrel of the weapon from swinging toward her. The man's eyes bulged as he gasped for breath, but she gave him little time for that before snapping her lifted leg out into a kick that sent him slamming back into the wall and his weapon clattering to the ground.

Mira took only a moment to ensure they were both incapable of engaging her further before hooking her foot under her dropped weapon and kicking her Elan casually into the air, where she caught it.

Communications should be this way, she thought as she stepped over the fallen men and continued running down the corridors.

I hope.

*

I wish I could say I was surprised by how much trouble one woman could give us, Corian thought as he gritted his teeth, *but at this point I'm beginning to wonder why I really expected anything different.*

Certainly he *hadn't* expected her to retreat. He could admit that freely.

He supposed that he should have, but he could see little value in the action. Fleeing would simply prolong the inevitable end that she would certainly meet, the trap having been sprung. He would have made the attempt at eliminating his primary target or, failing that, surrendered with an eye to escaping at a later time.

Withdrawing into the Redoubt was all the more of a surprise given that he hadn't read that in her body language at all.

This is going to be a pain.

Digging a trained operative out of a defensible network of corridors was the very definition of a pain in every sensitive body part one might imagine. However, he was quite certain that just inflicting a little more damage wasn't her objective. Killing peons was beneath a Cadreman of Delsol's caliber.

What is she up to? Why give up a clear shot at me in order to run around making a minor annoyance of herself?

"General, we have two men down in the third-floor corridor heading toward the interior," a guard said, running up.

"Dead?"

"Badly injured, but nothing life threatening."

Corian grunted. "So she's either playing nice with them, or is too focused on her goal to bother killing them."

"Her goal, general?" the guard asked, confused. "What goal?"

"If I knew that, then I would not be standing here with you."

*

Mira delivered an elbow strike to the side of a man's head before he even knew she was there, sending him careening into the wall with a distinct ringing sound before he crumpled to the ground at her feet. She kicked his carbine away, sending it clattering down the corridor, her eyes scanning the ceiling as she looked for cable runs.

Corian would want the communications center to be protected, she knew, but no signals would penetrate the metal that the Redoubt was composed of, so he'd have to have cables run down from the antennas mounted outside. She was working her way upward and inward, figuring that the most likely cable run would link a central room to an antenna array mounted on the Redoubt's roof.

Since most of the search for her was still focused below and seemingly toward the outer rim of the Redoubt, that left her with plenty of room to move. Such search procedures wouldn't last much longer, unfortunately, before Corian or someone figured out that she wasn't looking to escape. Once they fully accepted that, there were only so many objectives she could be aiming for, and only one that would make sense to someone like Corian.

She found a ramp heading up and sprinted, knowing that time was on the enemy's side and not hers. She was now on the eighth floor, with probably another three or four levels between her and the roof.

I'm lucky it's just a small Redoubt, Mira thought. *If it were the Imperial palace, I would likely need a rest break before I got anywhere near the roof.*

Of course, if they were in the palace, she would better know her way around.

Win some, lose some.

She heard a shout and threw herself back just as a barrage of gamma bursts slammed into the wall behind her, raising radiation alerts in her armor that she ignored as she shifted her blaster to her right hand and risked a glance around the corner she was sheltering behind.

There were four of them, arrayed across the corridor stupidly, only two having any decent cover. Mira pulled back as another flurry of bursts splashed off the metal walls and raised the radiation level again. She kept their positions in her mind as she brought her blaster up and waited for a pause in the firing before she twisted out and squeezed off two quick blasts.

The lased rounds caught the same man in the chest and throat, vaporizing armor, flesh, and bone. The ejection of the resulting plasma from his body threw him back to the ground, but she knew he was dead without looking again.

One down. Three to go.

The sudden death of their compatriot had delivered a sharp education in tactics to the remaining three, however, and they had scrambled for cover by the time she risked another glance.

Damn it. Would be nice if the enemy were always craven and stupid. Mira silently bemoaned the trouble of intelligent foes, echoing the thoughts of nearly every soldier in a very long history of war.

Her lase blaster dropped comfortably back into her left hand as she drew her Armati with her right and extended the blade to its full size with a thought. Mira took a breath before she burst from cover and charged down the hall, blaster lasing rounds as fast as she could fire.

*

"General, there's report of a lase fight on the eighth floor."

Corian stopped in his tracks, turning around and looking past the aide who'd run up to him, his eyes climbing up to stare as if through the metal that surrounded them. "Where on the eighth?"

"Um . . . sector three, at junction . . . uh . . . nineteen."

"What is she doing *there?*" Corian blustered, stomping now in the opposite direction from which he had been heading. "There's nothing up there. Not even Delsol would survive jumping *off* this blasted Redoubt . . . well, she would if her armor isn't discharged yet. But that still puts her inside our perimeter. There is no escape."

"General?"

Corian ignored the aide as he waved his troops to follow and headed for the nearest ramp going up, still grumbling to himself.

"She seems to be working her way toward the interior, which makes *no* sense unless she . . ." Corian stopped dead, causing several troops behind him to almost slam into him as a result.

"General?" one of them ventured hesitantly, wondering what was going on.

"Burning skies . . . ," Corian mumbled. "How much time did she have inside the Redoubt? Could she have figured out . . . ?"

He nodded slowly. "Yes, she could. I could. She knows the plan, or part of it at least." He turned around. "To the comm center! Secure it as tightly as possible."

"General, what's going on?" the closest trooper asked.

"Just do as I command," he ordered, "now!"

Deep in Alliance Airspace

It didn't take an experienced flyer to recognize trouble of the magnitude Brennan was looking at, but having as many flight hours as he did certainly lent a distinct level of panic to the situation.

He was several hours inside Alliance territory now. The target Redoubt should only be a short while from appearing from the mists, but he had hits on his threat board from every side, and the only thing he could figure is that none of them thought anyone would be *stupid* enough to be doing what he was doing, and that was the only reason they hadn't taken notice of him yet.

To foster that belief, he'd dropped out of the stream enough to stabilize his flight, because any observer officer who saw him bouncing around like a lunatic would know something was up. Even priority couriers didn't take those sorts of risks.

Sweet gentle rain, Brennan thought, with a hint of an appeal to any higher power that might be watching. *The alliance has at least two full task forces out here. They have to be planning a full-on invasion.*

That was insane, but he didn't see any other explanation for the sheer number of ships he was seeing. Transports, cruisers, scouts—basically the works. He was fairly sure that there were several Bar-class ships in the mix, though it was hard to tell since he didn't want to get close enough to lay eyeballs on the cruisers and risk getting spotted in return.

Whatever Corian was up to, he wasn't planning on pulling any punches.

Alliance Redoubt, Silpheth Sector

Smoke was still curling off the walls where lase blasts and gamma bursts had splashed harmlessly from the exchange of fire. Mira ignored it as she stepped over the bodies on the ground, favoring her left leg slightly as she stood in the juncture of several corridors and looked up at the tight bundle of fiber secured to the ceiling above her.

The line went to the left and up, and in the other direction, right and down. Mira nodded and turned right, breaking into a limping jog as she did. Her leg had burns, she didn't know how bad, and her armor was almost depleted, but at least she finally knew where she was going.

Under the flickering helm of her projected armor, Mira smiled darkly as she moved.

She'd often considered just how she wanted to end her career in the Cadre, and while she'd never once considered "as a pirate" to be one of the possible answers, running into certain death with the intent to finish her objective at any cost . . . *that* had been rather high on her preferred list.

Come, Corian, she thought through the pain in her leg as she jogged, following the fiber lines, *we have a dance to finish.*

CHAPTER 18

Alliance Redoubt, Silpheth Sector

Men ran into position, arraying around the communications room as they'd been ordered to just moments earlier. Few of them seemed to know exactly what was going on, but that wasn't a general requisite for the life of a trooper. They were told to secure the communications center, so that was what they proceeded to do.

Most had already figured out what was going on, more or less, as there was only one real threat known in the area. The empire was hundreds of miles away, so unless the alliance had decided to turn on the general, Cadrewoman Delsol was the only danger anywhere nearby.

For many of them, that was a comfort.

After all, she was only one person. They had several full squads taking cover in the alcoves of the Redoubt, and every approach was covered by enough burster carbines to hold off an army.

For a few of them, however, the tension slowly began to ratchet higher as more and more men got into position.

"Would you calm down," one told the man at his side. "We have enough troops here to hold off an army."

"If we were facing an army, that *might* be reassuring," his clearly nervous compadre said bluntly. "Delsol isn't an army."

"She's one woman. Just relax a little."

"Would you relax if it were the general we were about to face?"

That question brought the first man up short, and he managed to pale just a little as he forcefully kept his attention down the corridor they were guarding.

"She can't be that bad," he said after a long silence.

"She likely isn't, but she survived the general's attempt to kill her . . . twice so far. There's a reason he's wearing prosthetics."

"Delsol?" The question was whispered, panic hinting in the voice.

"I was there that day in the great desert," the man answered with a curt nod. "A half century of men at arms on the train, another full century in ambush. She saw it coming and disabled the safeties on the general's compartment. It was a miracle he lived through it. When he ordered us to kill her, dozens of carbines should have turned her body to black paste on the sand."

"What happened?" Another man, who'd been listening in from across the corridor, asked.

"I don't know," the man answered. "There was a flash, we all blinked . . . and she was gone."

"Great," the first grumbled. "A ghost."

Silence descended among them as the soldiers refocused again, settling in to wait for something to happen. All coped with mounting dread, whispers eating at them moment by moment while they looked over the sights of their weapons down the empty corridor.

The explosion was almost a relief.

*

Mira dropped her right hand, fingers tingling from the tension of the projected light string that she had just loosed to launch the bolt into the midst of the gathered defenders. She shook out the recurve of her Armati idly as she moved, bolting into the corridor as her Elan snapped out into staff form.

The chaos of her first strike was filling the corridor with confused cries, random shots blazing in nearly every direction. Mira wasn't even noticed before she closed the distance to within arm's reach of the nearest standing guards. The first man went down as she snapped the tip of her Elan in a vicious arc that connected with his temple and drove him to the ground in a pile of limbs.

She let the weapon spin in her hand, curving the arc around the back of her head as she shifted it to her left side and snapped the staff into a swing that broke fingers as a second man tried to aim his weapon at her. Mira didn't stop moving, pressing forward without bothering to ensure that her targets were down.

Her mode of attack wasn't the smartest. In fact, it was downright stupid under most circumstances. The odds of being shot in the back went up sharply when you left an enemy behind who could still work a trigger.

For this objective, however, survival was *not* mission critical.

Getting to the communications center *was*.

So Mira didn't slow her charge as she took only the time she absolutely needed to put down the men who were actually in her way.

She counted on the chaos to cover her from those who weren't a direct threat at the moment she passed, knowing that if she took the time to properly end all threats, then she would most certainly fall to the coordinated defense. That could still happen, but she only needed to stay breathing just long enough to make one call.

*

A burning demon was among them.

That was the only thing most of the men could have equated the terror to, had they any time to really think, as the shimmering, flickering figure drove through them. Nothing human could have survived the sheer density of the fire the defenders could lay down, but they didn't have a chance to lay down that fire as planned.

A blinding explosion tore through a group of three, bodies flying out across the corridor like rag dolls, and then the demon was in their midst.

Her flickering armor seemed to be failing, but nothing they did was able to touch her, so what did that matter? The staff in her hand could reach all the way across the corridor from either side, but as she was striding right down the middle, again . . . what did that matter?

Those few who kept their cool and managed to return fire would *swear* that they'd struck her with gamma bursts, but she would *not* go down, not even when her armor finally failed entirely and the slim woman was revealed fully to them.

The burning intensity in her eyes made some of them wish they were still facing the impersonal intimidation of the projection armor instead of the fiery-eyed demon before them.

*

Mira had taken at least three hits from gamma bursters, one after her armor had failed entirely. She knew it, intellectually, but for the moment she was riding on a cocktail of adrenaline and other chemicals that prevented her from feeling pain.

In fact, as she strode through the ever-increasing chaos and destruction, Mira felt herself start to smile and then laugh. She couldn't hear it. Her mind had begun to edit out any sound she made in its efforts to let her lock on to the myriad threats assaulting her from every side.

She could hear tendons crackle as one man started to tighten his finger on the trigger of a carbine, and automatically responded by willing her weapon to blade form and swiping it across his throat on her way past. She heard the whispered prayer of another, who dropped his weapon in pure panic, and ignored him on her way past his position.

She could not, however, hear the lightly amused laughter that rolled from her own throat to slowly be heard over the sounds of the fight, to slowly penetrate the already terror-filled minds of those who heard it.

The demon among them was laughing gleefully as they fell, and that was the last straw.

The defenders broke and ran for their lives and for their eternal souls.

Mira didn't even notice them leave.

The comm center doors were closed, but not sealed. She jammed the edge of her blade in the crack between them and the wall and then put her weight into the weapon, using it as a lever. No Armati had ever broken, to her knowledge, not in combat or otherwise, and her Elan was no different. Between the impenetrable doors of the ancient Redoubt and the strength of her Elan, it was no contest.

The doors screamed in protest, but the black metal gave way as she forced her way in.

Mira paused only briefly once inside, her blade flashing out to knife into the side of a guard who was trying to blindside her. His body fell to the ground as she started forward again, her steps slowing with each passing moment as she blinked and focused on the equipment around her.

She adjusted the frequency, picking out an Imperial Navy line that she knew would be monitored, and opened the channel.

"Cadrewoman Delsol to any Imperial vessels hearing this," she said. "I have a priority message for the empress."

She waited a moment, then repeated the message.

Mira slumped a little, leaning over the console as she waited for a response. Seconds ticked by, feeling like days and weeks.

"This is Cadrewoman Delsol to *any* Imperial vessels. Please respond," Mira rasped out before coughing and spitting blood that spattered across the console in front of her.

Her blood was black.

After a minute, or maybe an hour—Mira couldn't seem to tell time right then—still nothing had come back. She felt herself waver, her balance almost nonexistent, but planted her feet and stayed upright by a sheer act of will.

Answer me, damn it, she thought desperately. *Answer me!*

*

"Is it done?" Corian demanded as he gathered his remaining guard force.

Those few who weren't still *running*, at least. Corian didn't bother hiding his contempt for the men who'd fled battle with a single opponent, but for the moment he needed them. No one was sure just whether Delsol was injured or not. If she wasn't—hell, even if she was—he would prefer not to face someone who had no intention of surviving the fight. Not alone, at least.

"Yes, general, we killed long-range transmissions," his aide said. "The antenna has been disabled. No signal will reach the empire."

"Good. Then we do this by the numbers," he ordered. "I want the assault team in place, now."

*

Mira slumped over the console, no longer able to stay on her feet. She just kept signaling out, over and over again.

"This is Cadrewoman Delsol for any Imperial vessel. I have priority information for the empress. Please respond."

There was still nothing, just dead air as she waited.

So this is how it ends? Mira laughed, blood staining her teeth black as she grinned darkly. *In death, destruction . . . and failure.*

She'd come to expect, and even secretly almost hope, for the first two . . . but the third, that . . . that was a disappointment.

She almost missed the crackle of response over the radio.

"Delsol? Mira?" A voice vaguely penetrated her foggy mind. "Mira!"

She blinked, looking up and focusing hard on the console for a moment, reading an open channel and a clean connection.

"Delsol here, who is this?"

"Mira, it's Brennan! Where are you?"

Brennan? The Scourwind?

Was she delusional? Mira didn't know. It didn't matter.

"Brennan," she said. "Listen to me very carefully—"

"Mira, where are you?"

"That doesn't *matter*," she hissed, a second rush of adrenaline, serotonin, and dopamine flooding her system. "Just *listen*. Corian has a new weapon. It's a kinetic torpedo designed with tractor drives."

"Mira, that's crazy . . . Those are too slow. Where are you? I'm in the area. I'll come find you."

"Listen to me! The design is intended to accelerate up and out of the atmosphere and keep speeding up as it turns around and comes back. They'll take days to hit their target, but they'll strike with a force unlike anything we've ever seen. You have to warn your sister, Brennan."

Silence passed for a few seconds, and Mira was afraid for a moment that Brennan had indeed been a delusion and the moment had faded.

His voice came back just before she could start to lose hope again.

"All right, I'll do it. Now where are you? Are you at the Redoubt? Get to the roof. I'll pick you up."

"No!" she snapped, shaking her head. "No. Don't worry about me. I'll be fine. Just go."

"Mira, you don't sound fine. Put on a visual."

"You don't have time for this," she growled. "Just go!"

"Put on the damn visual!"

Mira sighed, but reached an unsteady hand forward and entered a command. In a moment, Brennan was staring out at her from the screen, his eyes widening as he took in her shape.

"Mira . . ."

She smiled, ignoring how he flinched at the sight. "I'm not getting out. Go, warn your sister."

"I can come get you, Mira," he said. "I'm Cadre too. Don't tell me to abandon you."

"Be a Cadreman, then. Do your duty to your empire and your empress," she told him, head turning as she heard a sound beyond the door. "They're outside. I don't have any time. Go!"

Brennan hesitated again, but closed his eyes and turned away. She could see him tilt in the image as his skimmer banked hard, and nodded in satisfaction.

"Brennan?" Mira rasped out quietly.

"Yeah?" He opened his eyes again and forced himself to look at her.

"My crew," she said, "they deserved better than me. Look after them, will you?"

He nodded. "My word."

"Good enough for me," she said as she forced herself to her feet, plucking up her Armati in her right hand as she drew her blaster in the left. "Good journey, Scourwind."

"Good journey, Delsol," Brennan managed to get out without outright sobbing.

The door blew open then, the concussion throwing her back against the wall as she opened fire with the blaster. The first two through the door went down. The third did too, but only after he scored a hit to her shoulder with his burster.

As she slid down the wall, more men rushed into the room with their carbines ready.

She levered herself off the wall, leaning on her Armati staff, and lifted the blaster again only to have three more blasts to strike her and drive her to the ground. Her blaster clattered off to the side. Sitting with her back to the wall, Mira saw Corian walk through the surrounding men. She shifted her Armati to blade form with a thought.

Before she could even weakly swing it at him, Corian drove the broad blade of his own Armati through her right shoulder and pinned her to the wall. He smiled at her, shaking his head as he planted a boot on her right arm and leaned down to relieve her of her Elan.

"You are the most stubborn fool of a woman I have ever known," he said, "but this time, you lose."

Mira just smiled as the darkness claimed her.

*

Corian did *not* like that smile on the be-damned woman's face.

That wasn't a smile of humor, or pity . . . it was a smile of victory. He yanked his Armati from her shoulder and turned around, leaning over the console she had been using.

There was an open channel, and it was still connected.

"How . . ." He breathed out, looking around wildly. "Who?"

He checked quickly, confirming that the channel was, indeed, a short-range one. That meant someone was listening even then, someone *close* to the Redoubt. Corian silently signaled the men, waving at them to get the technical staff back into the room.

While he was waiting, he checked the channel and noted that the visual was open, but a glance at the screen showed it to be blacked out.

"I don't know who you are," he said, hoping to rattle the listener, "but I will find you. I've spent a very long, very distinguished, career doing just that. I am *very* good at it. Make it easy on yourself and come in willingly. I will guarantee your safety and well-being."

There was, of course, no response. He hadn't really been expecting one.

Technicians entered the room, and he signaled to them to get to work as he continued to speak.

"If you make me chase you, you will regret it. Delsol is dead. If you're one of her little pirate crew, why not join the winning side?" Corian offered. "I assure you, I can pay you far better than she could."

The technicians were working feverishly as he spoke, but in a few more seconds, Corian felt his frustrations rise as the channel began to break up and finally disconnected entirely.

"Did we get *anything* from that?" Corian demanded as he straightened up.

"Just basic vectors, general. The connection on the other end was a skimmer, high altitude, moving fast for the Imperial line."

Corian closed his eyes briefly, the rage building inside him.

When it broke out, he just screamed inarticulately as everyone fell back from him. He ignored them all as he calmed himself and reached out to the console, switching the line over to a secured Alliance channel.

"All Alliance vessels, there is an Imperial skimmer running for Imperial airspace from my position. Their last known speed and vector follows . . . ," he said, waving to the tech, who quickly sent the information before Corian continued. "Intercept and destroy at all costs. Do *not* allow this skimmer to reach Imperial-controlled airspace. That is all."

He slammed his hand down, closing the connection in frustration.

Sighing deeply, he changed the channel to a local one in the Redoubt.

"This is General Corian," he said. "Authorization, Atalan Lemur Iram. Launch Operation Godstrike."

Alarms sounded almost instantly as Corian planted his fists on the console and just leaned there for a moment.

One woman. One DAMNED woman.

"General?"

He glanced over to the source, a man who was leaning over the woman in question's body.

"What?"

"She's still breathing."

Corian snarled angrily. "So *fix* that."

The man nodded and rose to his feet, stepping back to bring his carbine up.

"Wait," Corian growled, sounding incredibly annoyed at himself for stopping the man.

"General?"

"If she lives, she has information I want," he said. "Just get her out of my sight."

"Yes, general," the man said, slinging his carbine and gingerly grabbing one of the demon woman's legs before he dragged her out.

Corian would have laughed outright at how quickly the men cleared room for the limp body, but he really had no humor in him right then. He looked down at the Armati he'd put on the console a few moments earlier and picked it up, turning the slim and compact weapon over in his hand for a moment.

"Elan," he said quietly. "I believe I have better use for you than your last owner."

He mentally commanded the weapon to extend to its full length, only to frown when nothing happened.

Did she really blood lock her weapon? he wondered.

He had thought that to be a bluff back when she'd told him that so long ago, honestly. He'd never really known any Cadremen who'd condemn their weapons to death when they themselves fell. Even he had never been that spiteful, and Corian was well aware that he was more than capable of legendary spite.

He flipped the Armati over, checking, but found no blood lock.

Another command to the weapon yielded no results, angering him more. With no blood lock on the weapon, it should have responded. Frustrated, he tossed Mira's Elan aside.

I have other things to do.

CHAPTER 19

Above the Top Wind Layer, Alliance Airspace

Brennan had the Naga just over the wind stream, sails as wide as the projectors could manage. His flight profile was barely stable, moving so fast that even in the thin air of the upper atmosphere the rough aerodynamics of the Naga were good enough to lift the skimmer *over* its own sails. He was working hard to keep her there, with a focus to help quell the screaming inside.

I left her behind. I left Mira. We owed her. How could I leave her . . . ?

No choice.

That was all he could keep telling himself, and he even believed it on some levels.

Whether he would ever believe it fully, that was something Brennan couldn't say just then. He had to focus on the mission—Mira's last mission. That could *not* fail.

What she'd told him was hard to believe, though he did understand the potential at least. No one had thought to use tractor drives as the impetus for a weapons strike before, at least not to his knowledge. But since the drives continued to accelerate almost endlessly, they could certainly propel an impressive kinetic strike.

The potential effectiveness of such an attack depended on the mass they were pushing, of course, but the tractor drive could push a *lot* of mass.

His threat board chirped at him, drawing Brennan's attention as he methodically went through his checklists.

The contacts detected were more Alliance ships, new ones almost directly behind him. Brennan frowned, briefly wondering if someone was trying to pursue him, but the contacts were on a very different vector. They seemed to be climbing vertically, slow enough that they were either tractor drives or very skilled scout skimmer pilots.

With a dread forming deep in his gut, Brennan fought the resistance of the air around him and caused his Naga to rotate slightly so he could lay eyes behind him even as the ship was pulled along its same course by the sails.

At first he saw nothing, but then Brennan saw one black speck that became two, and then a dozen, and finally he couldn't count anymore as they continued to rise into the skies above the receding Redoubt.

Brennan twisted the Naga back head-on and dropped the old fighter right into the jet stream without hesitation. As it began rocking roughly around him, he fought the turbulence with grim determination and watched the locator numbers roll by.

Alliance Cruiser *Baran Knight*

"Contact along the course we've been ordered to secure, captain."

Captain Jode Leif nodded. "I see it. Fast mover. Can we hang with it?"

"No chance, sir," the scanner tech told him firmly. "Our tractor drive doesn't have that kind of acceleration, and with our mass, we can't match the contact under sail either."

Unsurprised, Leif nodded. "Well, then we only get one shot at this, so let's not screw it up."

He stepped forward to the center of the command deck and took a moment to observe the converging vectors before issuing his orders.

"Bring us to combat stations," he said, ignoring the alarm that sounded in response. "Let's put this one in the dirt as he passes. Clear all starboard guns. Put us on vector Nine Ninety-Three South. Secure all sails. Engage tractor drive."

"Starboard guns cleared. All gunners report ready for operations." The tactical officer responded first, then quickly went over the orders with his belowdecks counterpart.

"The *Knight* is coming around to vector Nine Ninety-Three South, captain. Tractor drive initiating, will switch from sails in a few seconds."

Leif nodded, happy with the response of his ship. The *Knight* was a Bar-class cruiser, and frankly, it was overkill sending her against the contact they were tracking, but he wasn't going to question orders. Whatever it was, the contact had clearly pissed the general off.

More's the pity for them, I suppose, Leif thought.

"We're getting a profile on the skimmer, sir," his scanner officer said.

"What are we looking at?" Leif asked, mildly curious.

The officer looked a little confused. "I'm honestly not sure, skipper. It's a bit bigger than a scout skimmer, but not by a lot. I would almost place it as a Seps, but it doesn't mass quite enough."

Leif frowned, leaning in to take a closer look. His officer was right, of course, he saw immediately. Whatever it was, it most resembled a Seps fighter–skimmer but was noticeably smaller. He didn't think the empire ran anything in that weight class.

Must be nonstandard, he supposed.

Nothing that size would pose a threat to the *Knight*. They might not have the armor of the *Caleb Bar*, but they could stand up to a slugging match with anything up to twice their size and give as good as they got, blaster to blaster.

"Probably a fast scout," he said. "Maybe some kind of classified spy skimmer. Doesn't matter. Just lock it in."

"Locked already, sir."

"ETA to contact?" Leif asked.

"Five minutes, twenty-two seconds, if it holds current speed and vector," the scanner officer answered calmly.

Top Wind Layer over Alliance Airspace

"I see them," Brennan growled, punching the threat board to silence the insistent alarm telling him that he'd been targeted.

Ships were bearing down on his vector from all sides.

His immediate problem wasn't the majority of the Alliance ships, however. Brennan could outfly practically all of them, and at the speed he was moving . . . he didn't even need to outfly most of them. One, however, was already in position to take him as he passed, and the ship had gone so far as to lock him up.

Brennan would be in blaster range in just a few more minutes, so he had to make a decision in a hurry. He could try to evade, and probably even succeed, but he knew that if he did, he would have to divert the Naga away from a least-time course to Imperial airspace. Worse, he'd have to leave the jet stream to do so, which would vastly lower his skimmer's speed. And evading one ship could very easily put him right in the gunsights of several more.

No, I don't believe I'll be doing that.

So that left one option. Thankfully, it was an option Brennan *lived* for. He was going to have to outfly the bastards, in close if need be.

The smile on his face had nothing to do with humor or happiness, as it would be some time before Brennan felt either of those emotions. Instead it was all about *anticipation*. As he fought the turbulence of the

257

jet stream, Brennan watched the numbers slowly drop as he licked his lips and set himself to test his skills against a foe that would no doubt be expecting to splatter him and his Naga all over the Alliance landscape.

Let's see who wins this one, he thought to himself. *Too bad for whoever you are, though . . . I'm not in any mood to lose.*

Alliance Cruiser *Baran Knight*

"Intercept in thirty seconds, captain."

Leif nodded, not bothering to say anything. He'd already given his orders, and his people knew what to do. All he could do from this point forward was either let them do their jobs or get in their way. He opted to let them do their jobs.

The numbers on the projections were dropping quickly as the small skimmer closed on their position at very nearly world record speeds. Under most circumstances, Leif knew that he would be impressed with the piloting ability the flyer was showing, but as things currently stood, he would have to settle for dropping said flyer from the sky and scattering him all over the terrain below.

"Starboard broadsides locked onto target, firing in three . . . two . . . one . . ."

A shudder went through the *Knight*, a distant pulsing whine just barely reaching the command deck.

"Fire out," the tactical officer continued calmly from his countdown. "Impact in—"

"Target change!" the scanner officer cut him off. "He's dropped out of the wind layer, captain! Sails . . . he's killed his sails. He's in free fall!"

"Track him!" Leif ordered, surging to his feet. "Get visual scanners on him, now!"

"Tracking; he's maneuvering . . . OK, I've got him," the scanner officer rambled, sending the results of his work to the main projection display.

All eyes fell to the display as a green blob in the middle of the blue sky appeared, shifting around a bit randomly as the system tried to zoom in and focus at the same time.

"What the hell is that?" Leif asked, frowning as the image cleared up a little. The craft sure as hell didn't look like any design he was familiar with.

"That's . . . an Imperial Marines Naga, captain," his tactical officer said, sounding surprised. "They were decommed before I was born. Flyers still use stripped-down versions today, usually for high-speed, high-altitude runs."

"Looks like a flying brick," Leif muttered. "Track and take him *out*."

"Working on it, captain."

The *Knight's* guns fired again, staggered this time instead of the whole broadside, sending out a stream of lased plasma like water from a hose. Red-orange trace filled the sky and drew a line to the oncoming Naga, only to continue missing as the free-gliding craft maneuvered unpredictably.

Leif gritted his teeth, irritated by the lack of results, something that apparently drew some notice.

"Sorry, captain, our guns just aren't designed to track something that small and maneuverable," the tactical officer admitted. "He'll be inside point defense range soon, however."

"Make sure they're ready for him," Leif ordered.

"Already done, captain."

Fire Naga

Red-orange plasma trace stitched the sky around him as Brennan twisted his Naga into a tight roll, never taking his eyes off the cruiser growing in the distance. In a few moments, the ship would have him inside their defensive perimeter and things would get really hot, but for now it was child's play to stay clear of the heavy fire.

He'd started with more speed and a *huge* altitude advantage over his foe, both of which he intended to play for all they were worth. Killing his sails had, of course, neutralized his propulsion, but now Brennan ruthlessly traded altitude for speed as he charged into the teeth of the enemy's maw.

Almost unnoticed, the airspeed indicator briefly peaked a few dozen feet per second over the world record. Brennan, at any other time, would have been whooping and celebrating like a madman. Now, however, he merely thumbed the safety off his guns and settled on his attack run.

He crossed into the cruiser's defensive perimeter and a virtual *wall* of lased plasma erupted from the smaller, faster tracking guns that peppered its outer hull. Brennan waited until the last second, then rolled the Naga over and completed an inverted drop as hard as he could in order to keep from passing out from a blood rush to his head.

Plasma trace followed him down, but he ignored the attack. Either he would outmaneuver the defensive fire or he would die; second-guessing it now would just lead to the latter.

With only a few hundred feet over the cruiser, Brennan rolled the Naga back over and yanked hard on the air surfaces to suddenly trade speed for altitude. He began to grunt and gasp under the hard acceleration that was threatening to make him black out. His vision tunneled, and all he could see was the deck of the cruiser as it twisted ahead of him, rushing up as Brennan dropped both thumbs down hard on the Naga's firing studs.

Amid the plasma trace and the high-stress maneuvers, it suddenly felt like his Naga had decided to shake itself to pieces as the gauss cannons erupted in a moment of incredible violence.

He tried not to think about what it would be like to anyone on the *other* end of the equation.

Alliance Cruiser *Baran Knight*

Leif couldn't get a word out through his shock as the fighter they were tracking practically seemed to *explode* of its own accord, despite not taking a single strike that he could see. His attempt to ask what just happened died in his throat as a sound he didn't recognize started in the distance through the armor of his ship, but then grew closer and louder with terrifying speed.

Alarms started to sound just an instant before his command deck itself was suddenly torn to *shreds* before his very eyes. Metal shards, smoke, and debris filled the air as his officers were flung around by an invisible force. Somehow the destruction seemed to pass him by, showering him with shrapnel that drew blood and left him the worse for wear but breathing and mostly intact.

The main display was dead and, as he stood there dumbly, Leif just kept wondering . . . *What happened?* over and over in his brain.

Then the instant passed and the alarms suddenly rushed back to his mind, leaving him shaking but moving as he struggled to move his bloody and limp communications officer from her console.

"Emergency medical team to the command deck," he ordered. "Get a team up here now!"

Leif barely heard the confirmation as he twisted to see his tactical officer groaning and getting up.

"What hit us?" he demanded.

The young officer just shook his head. "I . . . I don't know."

"Those were gauss cannons," an older Marine said, appearing on the bridge with a medical team at his back. "Very distinctive, aren't they?"

Leif stared at him. "What are they, and why aren't *we* using them?"

"Magnetically accelerated metal slugs," the Marine answered as the medical team rushed about him, "and lase blasters replaced them entirely before you even signed up, I would expect. They're expensive; not much metal around to waste on disposable things."

"Someone still uses them," Leif mumbled, shaking his head as he looked over to where his tactical officer was being treated. "Where's the Naga?"

"He just whipped past us, sir. We can try to turn and give pursuit, but . . ." The man trailed off.

Leif groaned. The attack had badly disrupted their systems; time was needed to get everyone working in the same direction again. Once the fighter moved back into the streams, the *Knight* would be unable to catch up to a fast-moving fighter in the range they had to the Imperial line.

"Damn it, comm . . ." Leif's voice died, his eyes on the body seated at the communications station.

Right. Damn. He walked over, moving the bloody flesh out of the way so he could open a channel.

"All ships, *Baran Knight*. Enemy skimmer has passed our position. We are unable to give pursuit. Skimmer is *armed*—and the pilot is a maniac. Be careful."

He straightened, looking around. "How bad is our damage?"

One of the medical officers glanced up. "Casualties on every deck, aside from the lower two."

"Damage control teams are responding to alarms in practically every deck as well, captain," the Marine offered. "He tuned us up nicely."

Leif shook his head.

"Unbelievable."

Fire Naga

With the cruiser half a mile to his rear, Brennan finally deployed his sails again and started winching the Naga up to a higher altitude while he had the opportunity. He had hours remaining before he would reach the line, and there was little doubt that every Alliance ship for three sectors would be converging on him now.

Crippling the cruiser had been a successful tactic, but a significant portion of his ammunition had been expended.

He just hoped he had enough firepower for when he had to fight, and enough speed not to have to do so all that often.

I could try changing course, but that would leave me in Alliance airspace for more time, he thought grimly, trying to weigh his options.

Any extra time in Alliance airspace was likely to far outweigh any gains he made by changing course. The Alliance ships would converge on his location no matter what, and any course he might take that offered realistic evasion possibilities would add . . . far too much time, given what Mira had imparted to him.

In fact, he just didn't know if he had any time at all.

Corian had already launched, as best he could tell from the climbing specs he'd spotted in the distance, and since Brennan had no way to know just how long those weapons would have to accelerate to become truly destructive. He might have days, or mere hours.

That meant he was taking the least-time course to the line, damn the alliance and anyone else standing in his way. He knew well enough that the odds were stacked solidly against him. His little fighter was a lot of things, but it had its limitations, as did he. With enough ships, the alliance would drag him out of the sky by numbers, if nothing else, and the chances were very good that they had more than enough ships. Brennan was starting to think that this was possibly his last mission, which rather hurt since it was technically his *first*.

Of course, he didn't need to reach the empire to win.

Mira had taught him that.

One lesson that Brennan swore he wouldn't forget. Not now, not ever.

The Cadreman had to force himself to stay focused on the task at hand. He didn't know if he was close enough to the border yet, but he shunted power over to the transmission system before opening a channel on Imperial frequencies. He briefly considered encrypting the message, but decided not to. Even a merchantman could get the information to his sister; he would take whatever he could get.

He hesitated, considering what to say, then made his decision. He already had all the attention the alliance could muster; it was time to get some from the empire.

"Fire Naga Zero One Zero, Cadreman Scourwind commanding," he said. "Any Imperial vessels, please respond. Fire Naga Zero One Zero . . ."

Alliance Sky Frigate *Perra Atal*

"Captain, we're picking something up on an Imperial frequency," said Kandler Bask, communications officer of the *Atal*. "It's in the open."

"Put it up," Captain Ila Jahn ordered.

"Any Imperial vessels, please respond. Fire Naga Zero One Zero . . . Cadreman Scourwind commanding. Any Imperial vessels, please respond."

Ila swore under his breath. "The Scourwind prince. This is either a nightmare or a dream, but I have no idea which. Can you get a directional fix on that signal?"

"He's not even trying to obscure it, captain . . . probably because we're already converging on him," Bask answered. "Every Alliance ship in the sector is."

"Calling for help, or maybe trying to get intelligence out then," Jahn decided. "Jam him."

"As you command," Bask said. "However, I'm not sure if we'll be able to contain him entirely. He's running high and broadcasting with a powerful system."

"Do your best," Jahn said. "Every bit you can degrade his signal is that much longer we have to pull that fighter out of the sky, one way or another. Signal the other ships in the sector. Tell them to do the same."

"That will degrade our own signals, sir," Bask warned. "We'll lose a fair degree of coordination between ships."

"Better than him getting a signal out. Do it."

"As you command."

Fire Naga

Brennan swore under his breath as intense jamming was picked up almost immediately after he started to transmit, but it wasn't anything he hadn't been expecting. He looped the signal and set it to automatic, leaving the computer to let him know if anyone responded.

The converging ships were now showing up cleanly on his threat board, their jamming signals announcing their position more blatantly than if they'd sent up flares.

Well, I gave up on subtlety. I suppose it's fair game if they do the same.

On the downside, he now saw more clearly than ever that the alliance had more than enough ships in the area to drag him down if they caught him, and he had his doubts if even his skill would be enough to outfly this many pursuers.

Still, with the jamming signals being plotted by his Naga's combat systems, Brennan could clearly see the converging ships from significantly farther off. That was going to allow him to plot a course that might just buy him a slim chance.

He was limited to some degree by his need to stay close to the jet stream with which he was hitching a ride, but different winds were moving at different altitudes, and some were almost fast enough to match his current pace.

Brennan started running the numbers in his head, based off his personal experience, even as the combat system crunched them based off the latest wind reports and what its own scanners could detect. By the time the combat system had spat out the precise optimal course to follow, Brennan was already leaning the Naga in the right direction.

He wasn't as accurate as the system on his skimmer, not by any means, but like any good pilot, he'd long ago learned the trick of being in the right general area of the answer before the computer. That was what separated a competent pilot from a gifted one, in Brennan's experience.

Alliance Sky Frigate *Perra Atal*

"He's changing course, sir."

Jahn nodded. "Delaying tactic. He's going to make us work for this."

"Yes, sir," Bask answered. "Without coordination, catching him is going to be . . . a pain, captain."

"Nothing to be done about it. Trust our fellows to know their jobs," Jahn said before shifting his attention to the board again and making some rough calculations. "Stand by to shift course!"

An alarm sounded, letting anyone not strapped down know that the small frigate was about to undergo some more serious maneuvers than normal. Jahn let the alarm run for a few seconds while he finished setting the new course.

"Conn, command," he ordered. "New course to your board. Engage."

"As you command," the conn officer said instantly. "Course engaged."

The *Atal* keeled over a bit as the sails were angled to port, bringing her nose around to intercept the racing fighter they were tracking. Jahn let his eyes flick to his threat board, noting that most of his allies were also responding in similar fashion.

Their action wouldn't be as pretty as if they had real-time coordination, but it would do the job, he decided after a moment's analysis. They had enough ships to run the fleeing fighter down and drag it out of the sky, no matter who was flying the craft or what sort of weapons it had.

It was all over now, except for the screaming.

Fire Naga

They were well trained, Brennan would give the Alliance crews that.

Of course, they should be. Graduates of the Imperial Academy to the man, he thought grimly to himself.

There was something really irritating about fighting people he would have been flying beside just a little over a cycle earlier. Horrifying, really, but Brennan wouldn't let himself dig any deeper than irritation. Otherwise, he didn't know if he could do what he had to.

Brennan stole a glance at the recording he still had running on the open Imperial channel. No response.

Need to get closer. A lot closer.

The line was approaching, fast, but Imperial territory was still hours out from his current position. His transmitters were powerful enough to reach that far, but with the jamming degrading the signal, Brennan knew the range would be drastically shortened.

Looks like we've got us a race.

Tucked in close behind his sails, the Fire Naga was riding a little rough, though not nearly so bad as if Brennan were in the stream as he had been earlier. Bouncing around enough to make running calculations on his board difficult, Brennan continued looking for his best route through the onslaught of Alliance ships coming his way.

No matter how he worked the numbers, even fudging them to account for his superior skills, there was just no way through. He glanced over at his transmitter and tapped it idly with one finger, as though that might help get him a response, but with predictable results.

Come on . . . someone hear me, he willed silently as the ships on the threat board closed in.

Barreling through the skies at hundreds of miles per hour, Brennan felt like he and his Naga had crawled to a stop while the rest of the world just kept speeding up.

Alliance Sky Frigate *Perra Atal*

"Intercept point in three minutes, captain."

"Clear all guns," Jahn ordered. "Lock on the target with active measures and begin weapons tracking."

"As you command, sir," the tactical officer replied, issuing the orders.

The *Atal* was a small ship, only forty meters across, but it was a fighting frigate and had a surplus of guns for its size. The plates protecting the lase ports from foreign debris damage banged open audibly through the small command deck, and the background whine of the tracking gimbals activating could be heard as they powered on.

"Target is maneuvering," Bask announced.

"Opening the range?" Jahn asked, having expected as much.

"No, sir, he's turning in to us."

Jahn winced.

That *was* the best move the Scourwind could make, *if* he believed he could take the *Atal* one-on-one. Any other move would give him a little longer before intercept but also open him to being caught by multiple ships at once.

"New time to intercept?" Jahn asked.

"Two minutes, eight seconds."

"Signal all decks. Stand by to swing to port," Jahn ordered. "We'll show him our broadside just as he comes into range."

The maneuvering alarm softly rang in the distance, being muted in the command deck as Jahn and the officers of the watch made ready for the coming fight. He glared at the threat board for a moment, considering what was coming. Though a good deal harder to hit, the *Atal* didn't have the armor of the *Baran Knight*, so coming out of a conflict with the fighter would leave Jahn's ship in particularly bad shape.

He'd been in the service long enough to have seen gauss cannons in use, though never in actual combat. The hard-hitting, rapid-firing weapons were a nightmare. That much Jahn remembered from the impressions he'd gathered during test maneuvers a long time ago. However, the cannons expended their load far faster than lase blasters and inflicted less damage overall when you factored weight for weight.

That wasn't going to do his *Atal* a whole lot of good.

If he and his crew could force the Scourwind to expend his munitions in this fight, however, they might just be able to give another ship a clean shot at him. Jahn shook his head, forcing those thoughts aside. That assumed that they didn't end this right here and now, and the firepower in this encounter ultimately rested on their side of the equation.

The *Atal* was on a converging course with the Naga, with the Scourwind actually on the overtake path. He would have to come up on them, entering into the *Atal*'s range, and then overtake and pass them on the starboard side if they were able to outmaneuver him. That would leave him exposed to the *Atal*'s broadside while largely keeping the vessel out of his firing arc.

If only it were that simple.

Jahn doubted if the Scourwind would cooperate.

CHAPTER 20

Imperial Palace

William rushed into the operations room just two steps behind Lydia herself, the alarm having been sent up just a couple of hours after he'd retired for the night. Apparently, the empress was a night owl.

"Situation!" he called out, still adjusting his uniform and glowering at everyone around him aside from Lydia herself.

"Heavy jamming all along the Alliance line, focused at the area of interest we've been watching," the duty officer said, snapping to attention.

"As you were, colonel," Lydia said, looking past him. "I am more concerned with your duty now than I am with appearances. Do we know what is going on along the line?"

"Not precisely, Your Majesty," the light colonel, Liem Mach, answered. "There was transmission chatter that . . ."

He glanced aside, looking at William for a moment.

"Colonel, speak to me," Lydia told him firmly.

"Yes, Your Majesty, I apologize," he said, taking a deep breath. "We picked up a signal initially that was weak but came from deep inside

Imperial territory. We identified the voice as being your brother's, Your Majesty."

Lydia's eyes and nostrils widened as she sucked in a deep breath.

"I see" was all she said.

"Did we get any particulars from the prince's transmission?" William asked softly.

"Not much, sir," the light colonel answered. "Message content is a simple priority request for contact, as best we can tell. It was weak, barely picked up by a cruiser on border patrol. They had to turn in to Alliance territory to clean up the signal, and by the time they did, the jamming lit the whole area up."

William nodded, slightly impressed. Turning a cruiser in to disputed territory was taking a hell of a risk in the current climate, and many captains wouldn't go for that. He liked those who were willing to take a chance from time to time, particularly given that the move had apparently worked.

"We got directional information on the transmission, but it's not good," Liem said with an apologetic glance toward the empress. "His signal came from deep inside Alliance territory. The compression of the transmission waves indicates he's running hell-bent for the line, but there's a small army between your brother and any Imperial forces."

"Can we send help?" Lydia addressed the question to William, but he just looked at Liem before shaking his head.

"No, Your Majesty," William admitted. "It would take hours to assemble a task force that had any chance of success, and by then it will be over."

The silence that dropped between the three of them felt oppressive in its totality. William could feel the tension as a physical force while he waited for her response.

"I see," Lydia said simply, turning away.

William let out a low breath of relief as the tension lessened. It did *not* go away. They still had a Cadreman and one of the royal line deep behind enemy lines. Tension was entirely nonnegotiable, but at least they weren't about to throw lives and resources away on an impossible task.

He looked at Liem. "Move more forces to the line. I want every eye we have looking into the Alliance sectors . . . If they see the prince's fighter and think they can get to him, make sure they're authorized to move."

"Yes, sir."

He waved the light colonel away, moving over to where Lydia was standing.

"This is the hardest part of command, whether you are in charge of a squad or an empire," he said quietly, "knowing when there really isn't anything you can do except watch and wait."

"He is my brother, William," she said softly. "If he dies . . ." She took a breath, visibly containing her emotions. "If he dies, William," she said finally, "there will be more than enough blood to go around. There is no reason to begin spilling it early."

With those words she walked away from him, leaving William with a cold chill running down his spine.

Thorin's Blade, Imperial Airspace on the Line

"Orders from the palace, admiral."

Sky Admiral Deava Orin nodded absently, reaching out to snag the order plate from her assistant. She was honestly more interested in the jamming pattern they were monitoring. Someone inside the Alliance sectors was desperate to keep the prince from getting a signal out.

A quick glance told her about what was expected from the orders, so she dropped them casually to the console in front of her and glanced over at the messenger.

"My compliments to the captain, if you will," Deava said. "Inform him the palace has officially confirmed my previous orders. Hold position until and unless we believe we can successfully reach and extract the prince, as then we are officially authorized to act."

"As you command, admiral," the aide said before hurrying off.

The admiralty deck of the *Blade* was a small room, crammed with projection displays and independently powered transmitters intended to connect Deava with every ship in her squadron. The setup left little enough room for her, to say nothing of any staff, but that was in the nature of commanding from a sky ship, even a cruiser.

So she stood in the center of a wraparound projection, staring at more information than any single person could hope to completely absorb, and found herself wishing to know just *one* thing.

What in the burning skies is the Scourwind prince doing deep in Alliance-controlled territory?

That was the question everyone was asking, and no one seemed to know the answer.

His presence had to have something to do with the events that had brought so much attention to this sector, but she just couldn't put it all together.

She looked over the projection; icons lit up showing where her squadron was as they slowly orbited the area. No fewer than three cruisers and support craft were within ten miles of the line at any given time, her own *Blade* holding back in reserve along with its escorts.

The army was moving its mobile air base into the sector, which would give Imperial forces access to strike fighters in the case they had to make a move within a hundred miles of the line, not to mention the support and medical facilities well beyond what any sky ship could carry.

That meant that this sector would shortly be the heaviest-defended internal sector of the empire in recorded history.

Unfortunately, she couldn't quite shake the feeling that it just wasn't going to be enough.

Alliance Cruiser *Grand Muria*

"General on deck!"

Corian looked over the officers of the watch, nodding to them as a whole before looking to the captain. "As you were."

"Yes, general," Captain Lister Gonn replied. "We're lifting in three, general. Orders?"

"We are to reconnect with the main Bar task force and make our way along the operation line toward the Imperial sector," Corian said. "In three days, we cross the line, take the Imperial capital, and so end this farce of a war."

Lister nodded, only slightly hesitant. "Of course, general. The fighting will be intense at the line. The empire has been strengthening their forces there."

"The empire's forces will not be a problem."

"Y-yes sir, general," Lister stammered out. "As you command."

Corian nodded absently, his eyes straying to the projection displays that were even then lit up with information fed from various ships of the alliance.

"Indeed," he said. "Lift when ready, captain. I am . . . eager to be under way."

Alliance Redoubt Airfield

The ships of the Alliance's Bar task force lifted in unison from the airfield that had been rapidly built to serve the Redoubt Corian had made his temporary base. Fifteen Bar-class cruisers riding on their tractor drives rose up vertically, turning their prows south, and then accelerated cleanly away.

The squadron passed the Redoubt a few minutes later, thundering low over the black metal fort on rails made of quantum particles.

Below the ships, the Redoubt itself was a hive of activity as the facilities were packed up, having served their purpose. Workers loaded equipment and supplies, some things being abandoned in place, everything else being loaded with rigid discipline and care.

Among the unfolding action, a small team pushed a sealed white crate onto a medical transport, which quietly left the area on its own course.

Few, if any, paid it the slightest attention.

Alliance Cruiser *Grand Muria*

In the general's quarters, after his yeoman had settled everything into place, a rattling came from inside one of the cases brought aboard for him.

The sound continued to grow rapidly for a time until a bright silver light seemed to bloom inside the case, leaking out through every tiny seam.

There was a flash, and then the light was gone and the rattling ceased entirely, leaving only the distant hum of the tractor drive as the *Muria* powered onward to the south.

Alliance Hospital Ship *Merciful Queen*

The room was empty save for the machines linked to the motionless body shackled to a bed. Outside, guards stood watch with an indifferent air that was nevertheless tinged with an undercurrent of fear. They never looked into the room for more than a second before their eyes darted away from the still form, the hint of fear replaced by vicious glee.

A flash of light caught their attention, causing them to twist and look back into the room until they saw that the body had not moved.

"What was that?" one of the guards asked, nervously looking around.

"I don't know, one of the lights must have surged," the other said after a long, and tense, moment. "I'll have maintenance go over the systems."

"Right. Sure."

The two looked away again, shivering despite the area's warmth.

Behind them, in the solitary room, a silver glow gleamed near the right hand of the motionless woman before fading away as though it had never been.

One of the machines monitoring her dutifully noted a slight increase in the neurological output of Mira Delsol, but found no cause to alert anyone.

The *Merciful Queen* sailed on its way, deeper into the alliance and away from the looming battlefront.

Fire Naga, Alliance Airspace

Brennan read the maneuver well before the frigate ahead of him turned away from his course, exposing their broadsides to him if he wanted to pass them and continue on toward Imperial space. Once he entered that firing arc, there was no question that they would pace him as long as they could, and while his Naga was faster by a significant margin, a frigate was hardly a lumbering beast, so the engagement time would be significantly long.

Worse, if he were to enter into that battle, his own guns would be pointed cleanly *away* from the frigate since the Naga's primary armaments were entirely forward locked.

Yeah, Brennan thought dryly, *let's not be doing that.*

He timed his own maneuver to the frigate's, however, so they wouldn't be able to react effectively as the two closed. Just as the frigate turned to bring their broadsides to bear on his Naga, Brennan twisted his own course to intersect with the frigate's and bring his guns to bear as he crossed her beam diagonally.

Lased blasts exploded from the frigate, and he had to skirt the edge of her firing arc to pull off his maneuver, but Brennan managed to stay just clear of the shooting as his own guns locked on.

The Naga vibrated violently as the gauss cannons roared into action, raking the top and side of the frigate in a vicious pass and tearing her starboard sail pitons apart. He watched the ship fall as he passed, momentarily extending his sympathy to the crew. It was no fun having a ship go down under you and just praying that you had left enough sail to make the landing survivable.

That moment of sympathy nearly cost Brennan his life.

Alliance Sky Frigate *Pac Mare*

"The *Atal* is going down!"

"Worry about them later," Captain Oran snarled, not even bothering to check and see who'd spoken. "Signal the others to close and engage at will!"

The *Mare* and two other frigates had, on Captain Oran's command and volition, *not* engaged jamming when they had previously been ordered to. Instead they went quiet and converged as quickly as they could on the fleeing fighter–skimmer. The way the pilot had taken down a cruiser told Oran that he wasn't to be taken lightly and, while he agreed with the order to jam all transmissions, he knew there were problems with that approach.

So he had ordered his small squadron to go silent instead, killing all transmissions, including their transponders.

The ploy had apparently worked.

The *Mare* opened fire as the Naga tore past the *Atal*, lase blasts painting the sky a red-orange as her sister ships quickly joined in.

Caught in the sudden crossfire of lased plasma, the Naga took several strikes before it was suddenly yanked hard vertically by its winches and pulled over the line of fire.

"Hard over to port!" Oran ordered over the initial cheers from those who'd seen the shots land clean on the enemy fighter. "Get our guns back on target! Watch those sail lines; don't tangle with the *Mac*!"

The *Birn Macenny*, one of their squad sisters, had also gone hard to port, and the two were coming closer than protocol advised for frigates, but Oran wasn't overly worried. There was plenty of room for error in protocol. That was practically what it was designed for, after all.

The third frigate in their little group, the *Tempus Vici*, had turned to starboard and was angling for a better firing arc in the midterm rather than immediately tracking. Oran gripped his console as the *Mare* keeled over steeply, a few unsecured items breaking loose and clattering across the deck.

He'd have to talk to everyone about proper item securement when this was over. If they were to go down hard with loose items around, those things might turn an otherwise survivable landing into a lethal impact.

For the moment, however, he just kicked away a computer that had gotten underfoot and focused on the job at hand.

Fire Naga

Brennan was swearing up a firestorm as he was slammed back into his seat by the twin powerful winches of the Naga pulling hard for the sky. The trio of frigates had come in low, using cloud cover to hide. The first frigate, keeping Brennan's attention focused away from its sister ships, caught him dead to rights in crossfire.

Only the fact that the old Naga was one of the heaviest armored ships of its size ever built had saved his life. The cockpit shell and sail pitons as well as the winches were bracketed by the same imperanium that protected the *Excalibur* on a much grander scale.

Most of the rest of the fighter wasn't nearly so durable, however. He was pretty sure he'd lost his right wing, along with the gauss cannon mounted under it and any chance of gliding or exhibiting any sort of control in free fall. Smoke and alarms were filling the cockpit, blurring his eyes and filling his lungs and ears with irritants of differing types.

He manually killed the alarms, then vented the smoke by depressurizing the cabin as he snapped an air mask over his face.

Where the hell are they? Brennan thought as he leaned forward and to the sides, looking out and down as best he could.

The frigates were below him now, but there was plenty of lased plasma filling the sky around him, so he figured that the ships were still tracking him.

"Well, this is a bit more than I'd bargained for," he muttered, hitting his emergency transponder more out of reflex than anything else.

His tattered fighter was staying just ahead of the fire from below, pulling hard for the upper wind layer.

If I can make the jet stream, I'll just try and make a straight-line run, he decided. Brennan didn't think the plan would work or he'd have tried it from the start, but he was out of options. He figured all he had to do was reach a position where he could push through a transmission to the empire.

Brennan opened his recorder and started dictating a message as he kept twisting around, looking for plasma trace.

"To any Imperial ship," he said as he flew, "relay this message to the Imperial palace, to Her Majesty Lydia Scourwind, Cadreman William Everett, or any authority of Her Majesty's forces. General Corian has weaponized the quantum-traction drive. By equipping a heavy mass of imperianium with a drive and accelerating it out of the atmosphere until it reaches a critical velocity and then turning it back, he intends to bombard Imperial locations with mass kinetic strikes. I believe he *has* launched a strike. I do not know the target but I *strongly* advise evacuating the capital and moving all key figures to secure locations *immediately*. Please tell my sister I . . . I did my best. Brennan Scourwind . . . clear."

Brennan cycled the signal to replace his old transmission and started running it on a loop.

With that done, Brennan set his mind and focused fully on his flying.

With plasma trace scorching his rear, he continued to climb into the upper reaches of the clear sky, a chill setting in around him now as the air was sucked out of the cockpit. He ignored the cold, focusing on his work as he began to shift the large light projection sails around to begin twisting his Naga in as unpredictable a path as he could manage.

Alliance Sky Frigate *Pac Mare*

"He's good, captain . . ."

"Don't tell me how good he is, Erin, just nail that prick," Oran ordered, holding on tight as the *Mare* swung in a tightly ascending circle, trying to track and shoot down the evading fighter.

He had never quite realized just how tough they must have built those old Fire Nagas until this very moment. He was certain that they'd blown enough parts off it to shave a full 10 percent or more of its mass, and all that seemed to do was make it climb and maneuver that much faster!

He briefly wondered if the newer Marine-issued Seps fighters were in the same league, or whether it really was a case of not building them like they used to any longer. Those were idle thoughts, however, and he didn't really have the time for them.

His squadron was locked in a tight spiral climb, possibly one of the most dangerous bits of formation flying he had ever attempted under combat conditions, each of them seeking to get a lock on the evading fighter. The final outcome was inevitable, barring some horrendous accident like a pair of his ships tangling sails and going down in the nightmare of any flyer who'd served more than a few weeks in a sky ship.

Part of him wanted nothing more than to start telling his helmsman how to do his job, but at the moment, doing that would be worse than anything the poor helmsman could screw up, short of actually tangling lines, of course. So, instead, he focused on telling his poor gunner what to do.

"Almost . . . ," the gunner gritted out. "I've got his arc calculated. I'll nail 'im this pass . . ."

"Don't tell me about it; just do it," Oran said, holding on tight against the banking of the ship and the centrifugal force of the spiral.

"Come on . . . just a little more . . . got you!"

The cannons of the *Mare* opened fire, spitting lased plasma with a staccato pulsing whine as they continued to spiral upward, firing as they went. Oran followed the trajectories, doing the math in his head as he watched the Naga swing around and the lased-plasma trace across the sky, and he knew that his gunner was right.

They had him.

The plasma trace and the fighter were locked on converging paths, and he could tell that the fighter had no way to evade this time.

He leaned in as the lines converged . . .

And was almost blinded as a brilliant blast of light made them all flinch away before looking out to the portside.

"What the hell?" Oran managed to get out.

"The *Macenny*! She's gone!"

Oran snapped around. "What? How?"

Before anyone could answer, a line of heavy lased-plasma blasts tore through the *Vici*, sending scraps of her drifting down through the skies below them.

"Straighten up! Full scanners! Find out what did that!" Oran ordered as the *Mare* evened her keel and began to run.

He didn't even care what direction they were running just then, as long as it wasn't on their previous course.

"Captain! Portside!"

Oran twisted just in time to see a black cruiser dropping out of the clouds, front chase guns blazing. The lased plasma tore through the *Mare* a few instants later, and he had a moment of weightlessness before the universe went black.

Fire Naga

Brennan was sweating despite the cold, having barely evaded the last line of lased plasma and not really knowing how he'd done it. He was still climbing and trying to run when a signal broke through the jamming.

"Brennan, it's Gas. You're clear." Gaston's voice was one of the most beautiful sounds Brennan had ever heard (not that he was ever going to admit that out loud). "We're coming up, portside aft approach."

"Gas," he said, feeling like he'd suddenly turned to jelly in his cockpit. "I owe you guys a big one for the save."

"No charge," Gaston said, and he could hear the grin. "Did you find the skipper?"

Brennan closed his eyes. "I . . . yeah. Gas, we'll talk. Pick me up, OK?"

There was a long silence, and when Gaston came back the grin in his voice was gone.

"All right. Stand by."

Brennan closed the channel, taking a moment to pull the combat system's recording of his earlier contact with Mira. Gaston would want to see it; he knew that.

CHAPTER 21

Free Corsair *Excalibur*

Brennan stumbled onto the bridge of the *Excalibur*, flight suit scorched and smoky, with ice still clinging where it had formed on his hair and around the garment's cuffs and collars. He looked like he'd been through a war, mostly because he had been, he supposed, but there was no time to get cleaned up and look presentable.

"Brennan," Gaston said, standing as he entered.

The engineer took in his expression with a wince, noting also the traces of blood from small scratches around the young royal's cheeks and the backs of his hands. But really only one thing was on Gaston's mind at the moment.

"Mira?" he asked.

Brennan shook his head slowly. "I'm sorry."

Gaston closed his eyes, his head dropping as he grabbed the back of the throne to steady himself. He thought that everyone around him had gone quiet but really couldn't be sure because all he could hear was the pounding of blood in his ears.

Finally, he looked up and managed to rasp out another single word. "How?"

"Accomplishing her objective," Brennan said, handing over a chip.

Gaston accepted it, a little puzzled.

"I need a line to the Imperial palace as soon as possible," Brennan said, hesitating, "and I need your help."

Gaston paused a moment, then nodded.

"Skipper's last mission isn't done," he said, "is it?"

"No," Brennan answered. "No, it's not."

"The *Excalibur* is at your service," Gaston said, making his decision and looking around for any dissenters. He got none from the crew on the command deck. "What's going on?"

Brennan told him what Mira had learned and what he'd seen. As he'd expected, Gaston caught on to the situation a lot faster than he had.

"He's insane," Gas whispered, spinning around. "Helm! Take us up!"

"How high?" Mitch asked instantly.

"All the way," Gaston answered. "I'll tell you when to stop. Paul, get on the scanners. Full power. Find those torpedoes."

"You got it, boss."

He looked back to Brennan. "We're on it. The skipper's last mission won't fail. You'd better call your sister."

"Can you punch through the jamming?" Brennan asked.

"A few more minutes and we'll be well above their range. Don't worry about that."

"Thank you, Gas."

Imperial Palace

"Sir, signal on secure channels," an aide said as she approached William from the technical pit. "Codes and authentication all confirm it as being from Brennan Scourwind."

William snapped his head around, quickly nodding and heading for the closest projection display. "Put him through here."

He would wait until he was sure before alerting Her Highness, but she wasn't the only one worried about her brother.

"Yes, sir."

He had to wait a moment, then the display flashed to life with Brennan sitting in the same position as he'd been in the last time William had spoken to him. The elder Cadreman slumped a little, relieved. "Your Highness."

"None of that, William," Brennan scolded him, more serious than was normal for the troublemaking Scourwind twin. "We have a problem."

"I'm listening." William instantly reverted to his Cadre persona, recognizing the younger man's tone well enough.

"I believe Corian has launched an attack," Brennan said, quickly explaining what Mira had delivered to him before going on. "I don't know where the strike is aimed, but—"

William was pale. "Here."

"What?"

"We intercepted targeting blades for old ballistic missiles," he explained. "They were coded for the capital. We know, for certain, that we did not get all the blades that are missing from our storehouses. The attack is most likely aimed here."

"Get my sister out of there," Brennan snapped, "and signal a full evacuation, William."

"Our defenses—"

"There's not a gun system in the empire that can take out a block of imperanium moving that fast; you know that as well as I do," Brennan said, cutting him off. "Signal an evacuation. Clear the palace and all surrounding areas, at the very least. The city as well is my advice, but take that for what you will."

"What are you going to do?"

Brennan looked up and past William, beyond the system he was speaking into. "The crew of the *Excalibur* and I will try and stop the attack. Mira's last mission was to deliver this information to you in time for it to do some good. We've done that. Now we're going for bonus points."

"I . . . all right." William nodded. "Your sister will want to talk with you."

"No time. We're going to be out of range shortly," Brennan said. "Tell her I'll contact her as soon as I'm back in the atmosphere. Just get her out of the palace."

"It will be done."

"Scourwind clear," Brennan said before the channel went dead, leaving William staring for a few seconds before he got to his feet.

He walked over to the central console and hesitated before opening a system-wide channel to the operations room personnel.

"Everyone, this is William Everett. Cadre Authorization, Luvian Spectre One Niner Niner Two. This is an evacuation order."

Stunned faces turned to look at him, trying to see if he were—for some bizarre reason—joking. One brave person spoke up.

"We're evacuating the palace?"

The tone was incredulous, and William didn't blame him. That had never happened, not since the first Scourwind had settled his forces inside the black metal walls.

The invulnerability of the palace was, or had been before Corian, one of the foundational elements of the Scourwind empire. Evacuating it would be an inestimable blow to the Scourwind name and the empire's credibility.

Not evacuating would likely end both, for good.

"We're evacuating the entire capital," William countered. "Send up the signal."

He then turned and walked out, ignoring the alarms that started in his wake and the sudden rush of motion behind him. He had other matters to attend to.

Free Corsair *Excalibur*

"No trace of any torpedoes yet, sir."

Gaston nodded as he too looked over the scanner data that was pouring back through their system. "Brennan, do you know how long ago they launched?"

Brennan hesitated. "Check the time on my exchange with Mira. It will have been just shortly after that."

Gaston nodded, quickly putting the chip back in and immediately reading the time listed.

"I wish I had the specifications on those things," he grumbled. "There's going to be a big margin for error on any calculations I make."

"No time to be precise, Gas," Brennan said. "I'll take your best guess."

"Based on the acceleration potential of a traction drive under heavy load . . ." Gaston was wavering back and forth. "To reach critical velocity they'll have to accelerate for at least twelve hours, adjusting for lack of friction resistance out of the atmosphere . . . since they've been in flight for over six now, we have to assume that they've turned and are now heading for . . ."

He hesitated. "How sure are we of their target?"

"It's all we have," Brennan answered.

"Right, OK. Helm, I'm sending you a new course," Gaston said.

Mitch nodded. "Got it. We're on track already."

The black ship had long since left the few constraints of the atmosphere behind and was now accelerating at her best speed under tractor drive. Ahead of the *Excalibur* was nothing but empty space as far as any human eye could see, but somewhere out there the command crew knew a swarm of death was on the move.

Imperial Palace

Centurion Apollon looked up as the Cadre commander stalked into the room. The alarm had just sounded, and he was getting his team together so they could receive their orders.

"Where are the rest?" William asked grimly, looking around.

"Palace ready squad has been light since they were sent out on raid teams," Apollon said. "The rest bolted when the alarms went up."

William grimaced but looked the Marines over seriously before he realized where he knew them from.

"You're the squad Brennan sent in with the imperanium, right?"

Apollon nodded. "That's us."

"Gather your team. You're with me," William ordered before he turned and walked out.

The Marine centurion barely had time to process that before he was barking orders. "You heard the man! Move!"

They moved.

*

William led the Marines through the palace, right into the royal wing, where he stopped in front of Her Majesty's personal guard.

"Inform Her Majesty that I'm here."

"Yes, sir," the guard said, disappearing for only a moment before reappearing with Lydia right behind him.

The empress was dressed in tight-fitting tactical wear rather than the ornate clothes normally recommended for someone of her position. William was pleased to note that she had included a blaster on her hip.

"William." Lydia nodded, gesturing to the alarm that was still wailing. "I assume that you know what all this is about?"

"Evacuation order, Your Highness."

"On your authority?" she asked, deceptively lightly.

"Mine and your brother's."

Lydia's eyes widened as she straightened and drew in a deep breath. "Brennan lives?"

"He does."

"I will speak with him," she said firmly.

"Later," William said, his tone matching hers. "He and the *Excalibur* are out of contact again, trying to deal with . . . a situation."

Lydia huffed but nodded. "I assume it has to do with the noise?"

"Yes, Your Majesty."

Her eyes flickered to the Marines. "My escort?"

"They are," William said simply. "I've ordered the city evacuated, Lydia. You need to go with these Marines. They'll escort you to a command cruiser that will remain mobile until the threat is ended."

"The city?" Lydia paled. "It's that serious?"

William just nodded.

"What's happening?" she demanded softly.

"Full brief materials will be on the ship, waiting for you. You need to leave now, Your Majesty," William urged her.

"Very well then." She looked over the Marines, settling on the centurion in charge. "I am in your care."

Apollon shifted uncomfortably. "This way, Your Majesty."

Lydia started to follow them, only to notice that William wasn't falling in step with her. "William? Are you not coming?"

"I'll be on a later skimmer," he promised. "Someone has to coordinate the evacuation; otherwise we'll be lucky if anyone escapes the city."

She sniffed, unhappy with that, but finally nodded and followed the Marines as they headed for the hangar on the roof of the palace.

William watched her go until she was out of sight, then turned and headed back to the operations room.

*

Lydia found herself hustled on board a rough-looking Marine transport along with her guards, who were giving dark looks to the centurion in command of the squad as he passed by the Imperial ships in the hangar without a glance.

When challenged, Apollon gave a firm rebuke. "We don't know those ships, and we may have to fight. We're taking our transport."

Simple as that, he turned to a small woman who was walking in step with him. "It is ready to fly, right, Jan?"

She nodded. "I prechecked her myself when I woke earlier. I do it every day; you know that, centurion."

"Load up," Apollon ordered simply.

The evacuation was proceeding apace, even on the palace roof, Lydia could see. Men and skimmers were moving around in a chaotic scene that somehow managed to not wind up with anyone tripping over anyone else. She supposed that meant they were doing their jobs correctly.

She was hustled onto the dirty ship and forcibly strapped in by one of the Marines who, while looking a little nervous about his actions, cinched her in so tightly she winced.

"Sorry, ma'am," he told her. "Orders."

"I understand, marine," she said.

Clearly relieved, the Marine checked her straps one last time and then retreated as quickly as he could. Her eyes followed him to where he ran, very nearly as far from her as he possibly could, and strapped himself into an identical seat.

She was near the front of the ship, near the pilot's compartment, and she could hear the chatter as the pilot got them cleared on a priority queue.

Lydia dearly wanted to know more about what Brennan had found, but there wasn't time. She would get more information once they reached the cruiser they were destined for, she was determined of that. If neither Brennan nor William had arranged for that much, there *would* be words between the three of them in the very near future.

"Palace Control, Marines' *Wind* requesting priority clearance," the pilot, Jan, said quietly as she settled into the cockpit.

Lydia didn't hear the response back-and-forth, but clearance was almost instantaneous. She wasn't surprised. The call identifier told the control tower just who was on board this flight.

The transport shuddered into motion a few moments later, being towed out onto the platform outside. Lydia felt more than heard when the sail projectors launched, and she braced herself. She was surprised by the smooth liftoff, having expected something more in line with her brother's preferred high-acceleration pulls into the air.

The Marine pilot, however, smoothly put them into motion such that only a very slight forward lean of the deck really told Lydia they were moving at first.

Unable to look outside to watch the palace recede, Lydia had to content herself with trying to figure out just how badly wrong things had gone this time.

Frankly, she would have preferred the view.

Free Corsair *Excalibur*

"We've got a scanner hit!"

Brennan and Gaston both rushed forward, eyes on the projection display that dominated the center of the *Excalibur*'s command deck. Red lights were indeed showing on the screen now, well above their altitude relative to the empire, but accelerating down.

"Bring us around. New course on your board, Paul!" Gaston called. Having already prepared for the moment, he turned to look at Brennan. "Our blaster cannons won't do a thing against blocks of imperanium the size we're detecting, Bren."

Brennan closed his eyes. "Can we do anything?"

"We have imperanium kinetic warheads of our own," Gaston said. "That's what allowed Corian to assault the palace in the first place, if you'll remember."

Brennan scowled, but nodded. He did indeed remember that day, all too well.

"Our best chance will be to fire on them as they come toward us," Gaston said. "Use their own velocity against them."

He was looking intently at the display as he spoke, his head shaking slightly.

"But we have more problems than I'd hoped for," he continued finally.

"As if we didn't have enough already." Brennan forced a smile. "Give it to me, Gas."

"Well, first, we don't have that many kinetic warheads," Gaston said, gesturing to the screen. "And second? Their course is diverging. They're not all going to the same place."

Brennan swore under his breath. "So we need to pick and choose."

"I can figure out which ones are going to hit the palace," Gaston offered.

"Damn the palace," Brennan told him. "The palace will be evacuated. What about the capital?"

"We can prioritize those," Gaston said.

"Do it . . . and try to determine where the others are going to hit as well," Brennan said. "Any warning is better than nothing."

"You got it, Bren," Gaston said. "We'll get it done."

"Thank you, Gas."

Alliance Cruiser *Grand Muria*, Alliance Airspace

Corian stood on the flying deck of the command cruiser, looking out over the skies around him with a proprietary air. Alliance colors filled the air, with more sails than he could count now gathered for their push on the empire.

With the havoc raining down on them, the Imperial forces should be thrown into chaos and demoralized. Their command structure would be effectively decapitated by the strike, and this would combine with the disruption of communications due to atmospheric interference from the charged dust each hit would throw up.

This war had gone on too long, every passing moment actually *weakening* the very forces he had intended to strengthen with his coup.

Damn the Scourwind blood, he thought with grim amusement.

Weak though their policies may be, a pathetic mewling drain on the very empire they had forged with their own hands, the bloodline itself was well known for taking anything the universe could throw at it and just grinning while asking for more. If they were half as strong as rulers as they were as warriors, the empire would control the entire world they inhabited and none of this would have been necessary.

Today.

Today he would correct an ancient mistake, and *his* empire would be set on the path to their destiny.

Today.

CHAPTER 22

Free Corsair *Excalibur*

The black ship turned back toward the Imperial habitat well before reaching the onrushing torpedoes, adjusting her course to maximize the possible engagement time against the already much-faster targets they were tracking.

Brennan had mostly been left sitting in the large throne that occupied the center of the command deck of the big ship, feeling relatively useless while everyone else worked around him. He had tried to get Gaston to take the throne—as far as he was concerned the ship was now Gaston's to command—but the engineer was more at home playing the consoles like fine-tuned musical instruments.

"Targets isolated," Gas announced. "I've got the ones aimed at the capital as well as the outer rim of the palace."

"Forget the palace, Gas."

"Can't. The city is built around it, remember?" Gaston said. "Maybe the palace will contain a couple of hits, but it certainly won't contain the ones striking the rim."

"They're going to hit *that* hard?" Brennan asked, having a difficult time believing it.

"Bren," Gaston said quietly, "some of these are likely to strike bedmetal."

"Oh."

Brennan felt sick, and he was pretty sure it wasn't due to the odd shifts in gravity they'd been experiencing since leaving the atmosphere.

That kind of power would do more than destroy a few sections of the city, and Gaston was right, the palace wouldn't do much to contain the explosion.

"I understand," he said finally. "Do we have track targets for the rest?"

"Some. Still working on others," Gaston said.

"All right. Prioritize large populations," Brennan decided. There didn't seem to be anything else he could do, really. "Let me know if anything seems aimed at something vital?"

Gaston nodded. "I will."

"In the meantime, let's get started."

"As you command, Bren."

Brennan shot him a mild glare but didn't say anything.

"Stand by for kinetic warhead launch!" Gaston announced. "Sound the call."

"You got it, Gas," Haeve said from the tactical station. "Targets loaded into the system. Alarm sounded."

The alarm, though muted slightly in the command deck, could be clearly heard in the distance. Gaston signaled him with a wave.

"Fire salvo one."

"Salvo away."

Even as big as the *Excalibur* was, the intense force of the kinetic launch was felt in a deep shudder that ran right through the ship's metal and into the crew's bones. Everyone on the deck watched the track as the warheads lanced away from the ship and out into the face of the onrushing doom.

"Contact in five," Haeve said from here he was stationed, counting down to one.

The display was anticlimactic. Just two sets of lights intersecting, then nothing. Brennan leaned in, trying to discern what had just happened.

"We're scanning debris . . . ," Paul said from the scanner station. "I . . . Contacts still coming . . . no longer accelerating!"

Gaston nodded fiercely. "That's about the best we could hope for."

"What? They're still coming . . ."

"We don't have the power to take out blocks of imperanium that size," Gaston explained again. "I'm sorry, we just don't."

"So what's the point?" Brennan asked.

"We killed their tractor drives. They're no longer guided, nor are they accelerating," Gaston said. "Some will still get through and hit the ground, but the destruction will be a lot less, and hopefully not anywhere important. Best we can do."

Brennan grimaced, but nodded and slumped back.

"Prepare salvo two!" Gaston ordered.

"Salvo ready."

"Fire!"

*

Salvo after salvo lanced out from the black ship as it fell back toward the atmosphere, racing ahead of the swarm of torpedoes coming from behind.

It was a race the *Excalibur* could not win.

With longer time accelerating and less mass to push, the torpedoes were already moving faster than the *Excalibur* could hope to match, and they were still pushing with every passing moment. Still the ship tried, firing her kinetic launchers dry before the swarm caught up and passed her.

*

"Did we do it? Did we get enough of them?" Brennan asked, his expression sickly.

"Hard to tell," Gaston admitted tiredly. "Three-quarters of them were damaged enough to stop accelerating, but they're still going to enter the atmosphere. We're calculating those vectors as fast as we can. Without having to fight the tractor drives, we might be able to shift them if they're going anywhere dangerous."

"And the rest?" Brennan asked.

"Those are going to strike," Gaston said firmly, "and there is not a damn thing we can do about it."

The two looked to the display as the first of the swarm entered the atmosphere ahead of them.

Marine Transport, Imperial Airspace

"Sky fire," Irons announced, leaning forward and looking up through the armored glass of the transport cockpit.

Apollon frowned, craning in from the passenger compartment. "I didn't hear of any warnings this far south."

"That's because there weren't any, boss," Irons told him, and he had to concede she would know. Pilots weren't the sorts who liked sharing airspace with unguided objects, as a general rule.

She was scowling rather deeply as she looked up again, then checked her instruments.

"What is it?"

"Angle of attack is way too deep and fast," she said. "Nothing enters atmo like that. I'm trying to work the impact point . . . What the hell?"

Apollon followed her gaze and his jaw dropped as he saw what she was cursing about.

There were now dozens of streaks of flame in the skies above them, and they seemed to be coming down from every angle.

"It's an attack," Irons said simply, now ignoring the sight above her in favor of her instruments. "Has to be."

"Are we under one of those?" Apollon demanded. "We have the empress on board, Jan."

"I'm checking; I'm checking," the pilot said, sounding harassed. "So far we're clear, I think."

"Don't think," the centurion ordered, *"know."*

"I'm working on it. Go bug someone else!" Irons growled, reaching behind her to shove Apollon physically out of the cockpit and back into the transport.

Apollon stumbled back from the shove, regaining his balance just in time to see the door separating the cockpit from the transport section slamming shut.

"Centurion." A soft voice caught his attention.

He turned to see the empress looking at him from where she was strapped in. "Your Majesty?"

"What is happening?"

Apollon thought about that for a moment before he answered, partly because he really wasn't sure, but partly because he had a bad feeling that he actually didn't need to be.

"I think," he said carefully, "we now know the reason for the evacuation order, Your Majesty."

Lydia Scourwind set her expression, then immediately proceeded to begin unstrapping from the combat bolster.

"Your Majesty!"

"I am going to see what is happening," she told the objecting guard, her eyes daring him to continue. He settled back, leaving her to turn her glare on Apollon. "Unless you want to object?"

As a centurion, Apollon had never been accused of being particularly intelligent. That wasn't generally part of his job, as such things went, but there was a world of difference between intelligent and *smart*. Faced with the empress's glare daring him to object, Apollon just stepped back and knocked on the door to the cockpit.

"What do you want now?" Irons's irritated voice was clearly heard through the closed door.

"Her Majesty would like a word," Apollon said simply.

There was a long silence, and then the door popped open.

"She can come in." Irons glowered, twisting around to look at Apollon. "You stay the hell out."

"Yes, ma'am," the centurion told his subordinate.

Imperial Palace

"Sky-fire trace!"

William turned to look, eyes on the display that monitored objects in the upper atmosphere. There were multiple tracks across the entire display, vectoring down across the empire.

"How many are coming here?" he asked.

"Three."

William was surprised. Given the news of how many missiles had launched, he'd expected more. More tracks in the sky and more targeted at the city and palace. He nodded slowly.

"Good job, Brennan."

"Sir?"

"Never mind." William waved off the question. "It's time for you all to leave."

The staff, still at their posts, looked at him, uncertain.

"What about you, sir?" one of them asked.

"Don't worry about me. There's a fast transport waiting for you on the roof. Go," he ordered as he walked around to the tactical station.

When no one moved, he glared at them all.

"I said go!"

They finally left, leaving William alone as he took control of the palace defense systems and analyzed the incoming tracks for a second.

He targeted the one heading for the city with everything he had and set the controls to automatic, every gun in the palace and city air-defense systems suddenly opening up in unison. William didn't know if they would do much good, but it was what he could do.

It didn't seem like there would be much use saving munitions now.

With a final look around, William stood and then he too retreated from the operations room.

*

The rooftop of the palace was a hive of activity, all sense of orderly dispatch now forgotten. Despite that, the remaining pilots and controllers were among the most skilled, so as they launched in seemingly chaotic motion and with risk they would never take under normal circumstances, somehow no one died.

The last skimmer out was a small one-man courier that had been waiting through the entire emergency.

It left minutes ahead of the roaring freight train of fire that slammed into the palace and drove down deep through armor, floors, subfloors, and dirt right to the bed of metal below.

Marine Transport, Imperial Airspace

Lydia sank into the copilot's seat, taking a moment to look around before saying anything. She'd been in her fair share of flyers in her life, of course, but rarely did she sit up front, not after some of the stunts her brother had pulled when they were both younger.

"I'm going to turn us around for a moment," Irons said softly. "You may want to brace yourself."

Lydia looked over sharply but just nodded. She would find out what was happening faster by keeping her mouth shut, so she did just that.

Irons pivoted the craft in place, flying it backward for a moment so that they could look back the way they had come. Lydia found herself staring in confusion more than anything until she realized the magnitude of what she was seeing.

A cloud of smoke and dust erupted on a scale she had never *imagined*, reaching up to the very heights of the sky before billowing out in all directions.

"What is that?" she whispered, shock seeping into her voice.

"That is sky-fire impact, the likes of which the gods have never seen."

Free Corsair *Excalibur*

The *Excalibur* was reentering the atmosphere as the first strikes landed, visible even through the mist hundreds of miles away. The crew on the command deck watched in stunned silence, not knowing if they'd done enough and whether their efforts had saved any lives.

Immense rolling smoke and dust clouds rose from the capital, obscuring the devastation below. Occasionally an opening in the cloud would reveal a section of the city. Fires burning. Smaller incidental explosions going off. People dying.

"I am not a man of prayer," Gaston said, looking at the horrendous destruction from above, "but if there is a creator watching over us . . . damn Corian to whatever eternal punishment exists."

Brennan watched, his face a rictus of pain and failure.

"A creator can worry about Corian's punishment in death," he said. "I am going to focus on arranging that meeting, Gas."

Gaston nodded slowly but said nothing in response.

"Did we get warnings out to the other strike points?" Brennan asked. "In the moment, I . . . I honestly forgot."

"We did," Gaston replied. "No idea how many were able to get out in that time, though."

"I understand. At least some have a chance."

Imperial Army Mobile Base, ICV *Sunken Muria*, Perrin District

"Move! Move! Move!"

The deck commander walked between skimmers as they lifted off, ignoring the very real chance of one of them taking his head off.

"I want every skimmer off this deck in five or I *WILL* know the reason why!" he snarled, his voice carrying despite the screech of metal on metal and the regular thumping of projection launchers from all around.

Men and women ran in every direction, some boarding skimmers and some clearing the deck for the next one in the queue. They all knew what was coming, in vague terms at least, but no one had time to worry about it.

Possibly there were some, down belowdecks, too paralyzed to move. The deck commander figured it was a big world, anything was possible, but no one in sight was wasting their time like that. He turned as a skimmer pulled hard skyward behind him and noticed the general in command approaching.

He almost saluted and dropped to attention, but that would have slowed him down, so instead he just nodded.

"General, sir."

"Commander," the general said with an oddly peaceful look on his face. "Are we going to get them all off?"

"They'll be flying, sir. My crews know what they're doing."

"Good. Get as many of them off as you can with the last wave of transports, commander."

"I will see to it, sir," the commander said, before hesitantly broaching the subject on his mind. "I have a seat waiting for you on a transport that's ready to go now."

"Give it to someone else."

"General . . ."

"I'm an old man, and this is my last command, commander," the general said fiercely. "There is nothing else after the *Muria* for me. Give the seat to someone else."

"Yes, sir."

The two men walked side by side as they saw the last few skimmers off, getting them clear just as the sky-fire trace above them grew too bright to ignore any longer.

"General," the commander said, "it has been an honor."

"Likewise, commander."

No more words were spoken as the first of many strikes rained down along the line, the third of which struck just a few hundred yards west of the *Muria*. The blast wave tore across the deck, scouring it clean of the two men just before the great land carrier slowly upended under the massive force, crashing to the ground on its flight deck and breaking into pieces that were blown away by subsequent strikes.

Alliance Cruiser *Grand Muria*, Alliance Airspace

Plumes of smoke and dust were packed so tightly in the distance that the entire line looked like a massive example of destruction on par with mythical devastation straight from legend.

Corian smiled at the thought.

With much of the Imperial fleet located in a known sector, the strikes should have disabled or outright destroyed a significant portion of the empire's current active combat units while hopefully not irreversibly crippling the forces he hoped to soon have under his command.

Some would, of course, hold anger over this action and would be a problem.

Well, he had more of this waiting for those fools if they pushed him too far.

He walked down from the admiralty section of the flying deck to where the captain and the others were staring, openmouthed, at the scene before them.

"Captain, signal the advance. I want to mop up any survivors while they're still stunned," Corian ordered.

The captain nodded slowly, swallowing.

"Yes, sir."

The signal went out shortly after, and the Alliance fleet began to move slowly on the Imperial line.

CHAPTER 23

Alliance Cruiser *Grand Muria*, Alliance Airspace, Approaching the Imperial Line

The Alliance fleet moved slowly, approaching the destruction zone along the Imperial line with caution as they scanned for hints of turbulence, radiation, or anything that might threaten the crews.

"Hold positions," Captain Gonn ordered, calling the fleet operations to a full stop. "Full scans, all frequencies. I want to know everything there is to know. Can our smaller ships survive in that mess?"

"As you command, captain. Scans running."

Calling a fleet to a hold wasn't an easy thing, but they'd prepared for just that. The ships that could, such as the *Muria*, slid to a smooth stop while the rest hovered or just orbited a close area.

The fleet scanned and continued to scan for several minutes until the general came down from the admiral's deck.

"What's the holdup?" Corian demanded.

"Just ensuring that the smaller ships can survive the turbulence in there," Lister Gonn said.

"Can they?"

"Yes, sir, but they'll be blind going through. We will risk collisions."

Corian nodded curtly. "I'll take those risks. Order us forward."

"Yes, sir . . . All ships, move—"

"Captain!"

The voice startled them both, and they turned to see the scanner watch officer looking up and at the display. Gonn and Corian turned to look themselves, both stunned by what they were seeing.

Gleaming light sail after light sail emerged from the cloud, sailing under full power, and coming right into the teeth of their formation.

"Impossible!" Corian swore. "They can't have so many left! They didn't have that many there in the first place!"

Gonn couldn't blame him for his shock. There were . . . hundreds, not dozens, of sails pouring out of the smoke and dust of the attack.

"Battle stations!" he called on reflex, setting alarms blaring across the ship and, shortly thereafter, across the fleet.

Thorin's Blade

"We're breaking through the static interference, and the dust is falling off, admiral."

Deava Orin nodded at the captain's statement. "Get me fleet contact as quickly as possible. I want to know how many made it through."

"Building the list now, ma'am. To your console."

She glanced down, noting that the list was indeed there and growing quickly. Most of their ships were small fighters, the survivors of the land carrier. Their pilots were in no mood to play anything safe right now and had been the first through unto the breach, with her navy ships following hot on their tails.

The dust was receding, and Corian's fleet was now visible, right where Deava had been told to expect it.

"Deploy to prearranged formations," she ordered, "and someone remind those army pilots that this isn't a ground support mission. They need to watch their sky or we'll lose more people to accidental collision and friendly fire than in the fight."

"We're trying," the *Blade*'s captain said, sounding more amused than frustrated, "but they're really not happy about the loss of the carrier."

"I don't blame them. Lock in the closest targets. All ships engage at will," Deava said with finality.

Alliance Cruiser *Grand Muria*

The Imperial line of ships exploded in blaster fire, causing everyone to flinch back as the wall of flames tore into the lead elements of the Alliance fleet, sending most of the advance scouts spiraling toward the ground in seconds.

The fleet returned fire, but it wasn't organized or planned. Plasma trace crossed paths between the two lines of vessels, sending dozens of ships plummeting out of the sky in the first few moments of the battle.

"Where did they get so many ships?" Corian raged.

Lister looked up from his displays. "Most of their force are small skimmers, Imperial Army fighters. I think we're looking at an entire carrier's complement and maybe a bit more."

Corian stared blankly for a moment. "They must have launched everything right ahead of the strike . . ." He closed his eyes. "That damned Scourwind actually got his message out in time."

He hadn't believed it was possible, frankly. He had thought perhaps the brat might have been able to save his sister, but to get that many skimmers in the air meant that not only did he get a warning out, but he had been able to calculate precise strike points as well.

"What is our comparative strength?" Corian demanded, trying to make sense of the mass of information on the displays in front of him. He wasn't a fleet man. Most of it meant little to nothing to him at all.

"They have more ships, but they're mostly strike fighters and lighter craft," Gonn answered. "That gave them an initial surprise advantage, and we lost a lot of our light screening elements in that opening salvo. However, we have more heavy elements than they do."

"Final word?"

"Final word, we win but they make us bleed for it," Gonn answered simply.

Corian grimaced. "How badly? We need enough of a force to secure the key bases in several sectors of Imperial territory."

Gonn managed to hide his frustration as more ships tumbled from the sky, on both sides, wanting nothing more than the order to move in and end this farce.

"Badly," he had to admit. "We'll need to call up reinforcements."

"Call them now," Corian said. "We can't lose any time after this. Call them now, and bring our cruisers into this fight."

Finally. Gonn said nothing aloud, however, just nodding to his officers, who went to work.

The *Muria* was first to move, but in short order the rest of the Alliance cruiser fleet began to lumber forward under tractor drive and into the teeth of the enemy.

Thorin's Blade

"Keep hammering the screening units. I want a clear run into his cruisers," Deava ordered, practically snarling as she leaned over her operation table, fists planted on the projection of the battler.

"The army units are getting chewed up, ma'am," her aide said. "They're not going to last."

"Call them back," Deava said. "Bring in light frigates to shore up their losses."

"We already did. They're not listening anymore."

Deava looked over, unbelieving for an instant but, frankly, she didn't have time to untangle the mess she was currently flying through.

"Fine. Back them up with our frigates. If they want to run into the jaws of Corian's fleet, give them all the support we have available," she said.

She wasn't in favor of suicide runs as a personal principle, but she wasn't above using anything available to win a fight.

Especially not one that had become this personal.

No one in her fleet was quite certain just how badly Corian had hit them, but they knew it was bad. They all knew that the strikes had hit more than just the line. Word had filtered back through the communications relays before the dust had brought them down. Smoke and dust reaching to the upper atmosphere had been seen to the south, right in line with where the capital was.

That meant civilian deaths, which ultimately meant the friends and families of everyone under her command.

There was no hesitation in any of their actions this time, for better or for worse. As soon as they got the oversight feed from Scourwind, there hadn't even been much discussion.

Maybe this whole attack is a suicide run, Deava thought. She didn't know, and she honestly didn't care at that point.

"Admiral," her aide called, "Corian's made his move."

Deava looked at the threat board and, sure enough, Corian's main element was coming forward into the fight. He had a strong reserve of Bar-class cruisers, similar in design to the *Blade*, but his outnumbered hers by four to one at least.

Unsurprising, as he had known this fight was going to happen.

"Well, we knew his surprise couldn't last forever," she admitted, taking a deep breath. "Move our remaining frigates in to support our cruisers as we hammer Corian's forces."

"Our cruisers, admiral?"

She didn't even need to look up. "Yes, I'm including the *Blade*. Tell the captain he's off the leash. I want at least *two* of Corian's cruiser silhouettes painted on our sides after this fight is over. You tell him I said that."

"Yes, ma'am."

It didn't take long for that message to be sent, Deava noted with amusement. They were under power within seconds of the aide leaving the room.

Around the *Blade*, the slaughterhouse skies over the disputed line were only getting bloodier.

Free Corsair *Excalibur*

"This is not good," Gaston mumbled to himself. "I need my numbers checked."

"You?" Dusk laughed nervously. "Gas, you're the only person on this ship who doesn't need the computer to confirm your math."

"This isn't math," he said, "or, rather, it's not math I'm familiar with."

"What's the problem?" Brennan asked as he walked over.

Gas looked up. "I don't think the empire can win this. Corian's forces are much stronger on the heavy elements, and while the initial strike decimated their light screening elements, which will cost him in this fight . . . he just has too many Bar-class cruisers."

Brennan looked over the display, not sure about those numbers, but frankly, it was far from his specialty. He was a stunt pilot at heart and a commando by his rather limited training.

"I'll take your word for it," he said, not doing more than glancing at the numbers. Trusting Gaston was by far the least risky option available to him. "The question becomes, what do we do about it?"

Gaston looked at him helplessly, shaking his head.

"I don't know," he admitted.

Brennan twisted his lips around, considering what he knew about the *Excalibur* and the battle in general.

"If, if, if . . . ," he mumbled. "Every tactic I can think of, we can't pull off. If we had kinetic warheads in our magazines, we could hammer those ships from above. We don't. If we knew where Corian was, we could try to take the head off the snake . . . but we don't."

He threw up his hands, frustrated. "I know what we can't do, but I don't know what we can."

"That is why I wanted someone to check my numbers," Gas admitted wearily. "I was hoping I was wrong, because I don't see a way out of this now."

Brennan glared at the threat board, shaking his head faster and faster as he got more and more frustrated.

"No. No," he said firmly, his voice growing. "I don't accept that."

"Bren," Gaston said softly, "if we tell them to withdraw, we may save much of the force."

"No, we won't," Brennan said. "Corian will pursue, and we'll lose so many in the withdrawal that the rest will be defenseless. No, if there's no way out . . . then we *make* a way out."

He stood up, eyes drifting over to the throne that served as the commander's station.

"Gas, I think I have an idea but . . . it's a gamble," Brennan said, looking back, "I can't ask you for this, you've already done so much . . . but . . ."

He trailed off, leaving Gaston to turn and look at the others on the command deck.

"Anyone objecting," he said, "speak up now. I know there are others not here, but we don't have time for a vote."

"Gas," Paul said after looking around the room. "We all signed on with the skipper, and not because she would make us rich. We signed on because, while we may not be the finest and most upstanding examples of the empire, we're still loyalists. Corian started this war; now he's escalated it. Maybe we can't end him now, but we can remain loyal."

Gaston nodded. "All right."

He looked over to Bren. "The *Excalibur* is yours . . . sire."

"Save that for my sister," Brennan said, taking a seat with a look of distaste that no one, not even he himself, could tell if it was aimed at Gaston for the remark or at the throne itself. "Gas, I'm going to need you to do some fast work with the projectors. Can you reconfigure them from here?"

Gaston nodded, clearly confused. "Certainly, but why?"

"We're going to give them what they expect to see," Brennan said. "I'll send you a quick file."

Gaston nodded, heading to the station where he could work.

"Helm," Brennan said, "take us in. Guns, stand by to clear on my command."

The two stations acknowledged him as the *Excalibur* started moving.

"Comms," Brennan added, "tell our side that we're coming in. Let's not get shot by the good guys."

*

The black silhouette of the *Excalibur* was almost lost in the smoke and dust as she cut in from her high orbit over the fight and dropped altitude at near free-fall rates. Her approach took the Alliance fleet almost entirely by surprise, as they were focused on the fight ahead of them and few noted the nearly invisible contact coming from above and behind them.

She dropped right in between a pair of cruisers, clearing her gun ports at the last moment, and opened two full broadsides right in their faces.

The two cruisers broke away from the *Excalibur*, reflexively, and both managed to collide with their frigate escorts as a result. The entire maneuver took only a few seconds from matching course to devastation, and it left three Alliance ships crippled and falling while another was limping away with smoke pouring from the multiple blaster strikes she'd taken.

The Alliance forces realized their presence quickly, of course, but Brennan and the crew of the *Excalibur* largely ignored the return engagement. It was mostly light blaster fire, barely enough to warm their plates, and the heavier strikes were coming from targets they already had in their sights.

The presence of the black ship renewed the Imperial morale, which hadn't really dropped much, since anger wasn't something you got over by taking a beating. The renewed fighting didn't favor the alliance by any means, but Brennan knew that spirit wasn't the element the Imperial forces were missing just then.

"Comm?" He spoke softly, but the *Excalibur*'s communications station was currently being manned by Gaston, who was waiting for the question.

"Ready, Bren."

"Open a channel," Brennan ordered, "and do your magic."

"We've got the smoke; let me see if I can't supply a few mirrors. Give a good performance," Gaston said seriously.

"The best."

Gaston nodded. "Comm channel open. Go for it."

"Been a while since you got your ass handed to you in the capital, Corian," Brennan said darkly. "Want another beating so soon?"

While he spoke, Gaston went to work, this time using the sail projectors.

Alliance Cruiser *Grand Muria*

Corian snarled, rising to his feet. He recognized the ship even if he didn't know the voice.

The *Excalibur*.

A laugh. It was his *Caleb Bar*. That the damned woman had had the nerve to rename it . . .

He clenched his fist.

"Open a channel," he ordered.

The channel opened quickly and without question. No one wanted any part of the general when he had that look on his face.

"Brazen words from someone commanding a ship that belonged to someone else that I ended for being an obstacle to my plans," he said, forcing a smile to his face.

"Really? I have a recording here that says you killed her because she beat you, three times," the voice shot back. "Couldn't take the humiliation, Corian? It's all right, you've lost a step . . . and a leg, it's understandable."

Corian's lips twisted up, but he resisted the urge to snap back.

"I don't think I need to worry about accusations coming from someone too cowardly to show his face over a communication channel."

There was a very brief silence before the image snapped into clarity, and Corian found himself staring at a rather familiar face.

"Edvard . . ." he whispered, briefly shocked.

"No, that would be my father." Brennan Scourwind glared at him. "But I suppose you should know him, given that you ran him through with your blade."

"It was easy," Corian said as he recovered from his surprise, managing to sound bored. "I don't suppose I might convince you to try your hand at taking me with the weapon I see at your side."

He nodded to where he could see the edge of an Armati showing from Brennan's clothing.

"Another time," Brennan told him.

"Oh, I don't believe that there will be any more times," Corian told him. "You failed, boy. Yes, you and Delsol have cost me more than I wanted to spend . . . something that your names will be *reviled* for, I promise you. However, in the end I will win this battle, and even that ship—that *Excalibur* will not save you."

Corian was surprised when the Scourwind had the gall to *laugh* at him.

"General—not that you deserve the rank—I promise you that there will be another time," Brennan said, leaning forward as his face became as if carved of stone. "You murdered my father, my brother, my first mentor in the Cadre. You will die, and I will be there. Whether I have an army at my back when it happens or we face one another alone . . . that doesn't matter to me. You are dead now. Your body and mind just haven't realized it yet."

Corian sneered. "Child, you aren't going to live out this day. That ship of yours is not enough to swing the winds in your favor here."

Brennan laughed at him, again.

"I know that," he admitted freely. "That's why I'm stalling you."

Corian stared blankly, then looked sharply aside to where his scanner officer was waving excitedly for his and the captain's attention. Corian flicked his gaze down to the repeater display that was showing the scanner information, and he paled as the silhouettes of several more cruisers became just barely visible in the dust.

He killed the channel. "How many are there?"

The scanner officer shook his head. "I don't know. They're being occluded by the dust. It's still thick and roiling in there, but I think

I've got at least four, maybe a lot more . . . and I think they're still coming in."

Corian swore.

More cruisers would indeed tilt the scale of the fight, not enough perhaps for him to lose, but he *needed* no small force to be left when it was over.

I should have brought more ships. Corian cursed as he glared at the scanner data. *The Imperials must have been calling up every ship for sectors in order to gather this many. Damn that Scourwind brat, and damn Delsol.* He'd have had to strip Alliance defenses to call in the reinforcements, but it would have been worth it. This might have been his last real chance at the empire. Victory had been so close, and now he could taste the burning ashes.

Still he wavered; so much had been put into this operation.

Corian seethed, thinking about all the things that had led them all to this point. *Edvard, your stubbornness has bred true, and it will be all our ends.*

"Eight more signals approaching through the dust cloud, general."

Corian's hands were clenched into fists. His eyes saw the future, and in it was nothing but death, destruction, slavery, and dishonor. He had spent so much, sacrificed so many, in order to hold off that future, and it was all being flushed away by a woman and a whelp not yet fit to shave.

In the end, however, Corian was a soldier. Sacrifice was what he did, so long as there was cause for it. He would pursue victory unto the end of *time* itself, so long as he felt it could be achieved. If not, then he'd walk away. No regrets, no looking back.

As he watched the numbers climb on the other side of the battle lines, Corian found himself faced with the hardest decision any military leader could find himself faced with. Knowing that victory was still possible, how much would you . . . *could* you . . . afford to pay?

He had to weigh the future against the present, the effort and costs sunk into the current project, and the likely losses if he pursued the fight to its inevitable conclusion. Not merely his own losses, but Imperial military losses as well.

Corian closed his eyes, swearing vile oaths in the back of his mind. *So close, so much waste, and so many useless deaths.*

Now it was over, however. Time to pull back.

His eyes snapped open, decision made.

"Captain," he ordered, "signal the fleet. We're withdrawing."

Free Corsair *Excalibur*

Brennan slumped in the throne when the channel went dead.

He'd done everything he could, and now it was up to Gaston and Corian himself. He hated depending on someone like Corian, but the man had seen too many battles to want to throw all his money after a bad deal.

Just do what you're trained to. It's time to save what you can to fight another day. Brennan prayed internally. Corian was used to working with limited forces, often against much stronger ones. It was stamped into his psyche not to waste resources unless you had a real shot at winning.

"The cruisers are pulling back!"

Brennan's fists went up, along with everyone else's on the deck. Gaston was sitting by the engineering station, grinning more widely than seemed healthy.

"Give me a fleet-wide channel," Brennan ordered, getting control of himself.

"Channel open."

"To all Imperial ships, this is Brennan Scourwind. Do *not* pursue. Let them go," he ordered, knowing that the command would be highly unpopular, but right now, while Corian was convinced he was the one with the weak hand . . . Brennan knew that it was the empire who needed to fight another day. "Just . . . let them go. We'll get our justice for today. You all have my word on that."

The channel was closed with a flick of his hand, leaving Brennan to collapse back in the throne, relief flooding him as he closed his eyes and offered up a prayer to whatever hand was guiding the fates.

"That was too close," Gaston said quietly from beside him.

Brennan nodded, opening his eyes and taking in the engineer's appearance. Sweat had plastered Gaston's hair to his forehead, his face looked clammy, and Brennan could see the shakes shuddering through his hands.

"Yeah," Bren agreed. "If he'd decided to fight."

"No"—Gaston shook his head—"not what I meant. Another few seconds and they'd have spotted the scanner ghosts I was projecting for sure."

Brennan winced. "That close?"

Gaston nodded. "That close."

The two just stared silently at the tactical display as the lines of ships broke apart, signifying the end of the fight.

It was a victory, Brennan supposed, but thinking about the devastation behind him, he couldn't really make himself believe it.

Another victory like this, and we may as well just shoot ourselves and save Corian the trouble.

*

The two lines of ships broke raggedly apart, some refusing to stop fighting despite their orders, but most willing to listen to the chain of command.

Below where they'd fought their skirmish, the ground was littered with burning ships and dying bodies, all being slowly covered in gently descending dust and ash.

The only thing that those still flying knew for sure was that, after this, nothing would be the same again.

Imperial skymen stood their watch, a retreating fleet ahead of them, devastation and horror waiting behind them. It was, they supposed, a victory. The thoughts of the Imperials almost entirely mirrored those of Brennan Scourwind on that, however, so no one was celebrating.

Victory wasn't supposed to taste like blood and ash.

EPILOGUE

Imperial Cruiser *Empress's Own*

Lydia Scourwind stood in the center of the command deck of the *Empress's Own*, one of the few Imperial Bar-class ships they'd managed to complete since the coup. The feelings around her were mixed. Some of the younger officers were cheering as they watched the Alliance line falter and break. They saw the triumph, but had forgotten the cost.

She hadn't. She couldn't allow herself to do that.

Not with casualty numbers from the capital still filtering in, the devastation still being tallied.

It would be days, weeks really, before they had final numbers on just how many had died in the attack, but that would just be a punctuation at this point.

Corian had gone too far.

"Your Majesty?"

Lydia glanced sharply to one side, noting the admiral standing a respectful distance off while under the stern gaze of the Marine guard she'd been escorted to the ship by. Lydia gestured and the Marine stepped back, allowing the admiral to approach.

"What is it, admiral?" she asked softly.

"We are going to need orders," he told her. "Not just for the immediate situation . . . We can handle that, but our people need to know what we're going to do, going forward."

"Do?" Lydia just barely kept her lips from tightening into a snarl that would bare her teeth.

She straightened slightly, her voice rising unconsciously.

"Admiral, that *man* went too far with this . . . this massacre!" she said. "This was no mere attack on my family. I cannot . . . I *will not* leave this to twist in the wind. For now, we see to our wounded. Later . . ." She paused, eyes alight with fires that the admiral had not seen in the Imperial line for many years. "We will take this fight to the alliance and *end* this farce," Lydia Scourwind growled. "Like I should have done from the start. No more giving that *insane bastard* breathing room."

She took a deep breath before speaking again.

"No quarter, admiral," Lydia said finally. "*Those* are my orders."

ABOUT THE AUTHOR

Evan Currie is the bestselling author of the Odyssey One series, the Warrior's Wings series, and the first two volumes of the Scourwind Legacy series. Although his postsecondary education was in computer science, and he has worked in the lobster industry steadily during the last decade, writing has always been his true passion. Currie himself says it best: "It's what I do for fun and to relax. There's not much I can imagine that's better than being a storyteller." For more information on the author and his work, visit www.evancurrie.ca.